WHO KNEW THE RIDPATH GIRL

STACY JOHNS

This one is for Bumpa, who told me not to use so many I's, and Nana, who loved a mystery and always said our family had books in our blood.

Published by Poisoned Pen Press, an imprint of Sourcebooks
1935 Brookdale RD, Naperville, IL 60563-2773
(630) 961-3900
sourcebooks.com

Cataloging-in-Publication Data is on file with the Library of Congress.

Printed and bound in Canada.
MBP 10 9 8 7 6 5 4 3 2 1

PRAISE FOR *WHO KNEW THE RIDPATH GIRL*

"Stacy Johns delivers an atmospheric, chilling mystery, populated with complex, guilt-ridden characters, that explores how easily false perception can morph into a deadly reality."

—Daniel G. Miller, bestselling author of *The Orphanage by the Lake*

"*Who Knew the Ridpath Girl* is as tender as it is tense and finishes with a twist Johns wields like a weapon. My obsession grew with every page. I couldn't finish fast enough!"

—Marlee Bush, author of *Whispers of Dead Girls*

"Engrossing and original with a twist I did not see coming! Clear your schedule before you crack this one open."

—Mia Sheridan, *New York Times* bestselling author

PRAISE FOR *WHAT REMAINS OF TEAGUE HOUSE*

"Prepare to be captivated by *What Remains of Teague House*, the kind of slow-burn suspense that hooks you with every twist while drawing you deep into its aching exploration of family bonds and secrets. With gorgeous writing and characters so vividly drawn that you'll feel like you've known them your whole life, this mystery is impossible to put down."

—Jess Lourey, Edgar-nominated author

"An impressive first novel from Stacy Johns, *What Remains of Teague House* is a sinister mystery wrapped within layers of secrets harbored by the members of the dysfunctional Rawlins family. Effectively told from multiple points of view, the story follows a somber gathering of three siblings for their mother's funeral at their gloomy childhood home. The home has enough sordid history—including the father's suicide—but nothing that compares to the chance unearthing of multiple corpses in the woods located on residence grounds. Every character is delightfully gray, each with their own secrets, and it's up to private detective Maddie Reed to solve a dark mystery decades in the making. A powerful debut, and one that will keep you guessing."

—Carter Wilson, *USA Today* bestselling author of *The Father She Went to Find*

"A thrilling story of murder, betrayal, and a family home that hides dark secrets. I couldn't put it down!"

—Stacie Grey, author of *She Left*

"Who doesn't love a dark and twisty family saga with literal bodies buried in the backyard? In *What Remains of Teague House*, Johns give us the ominous mystery of the Rawlins family, where shocking sibling secrets are revealed in the wake of their matriarch's death. Set against the foreboding Teague House, Johns slowly builds a delicious tapestry of murder, betrayal, and a twist ending that had me guessing until the final pages. A compulsively readable debut."

—Kali White, author of *The Monsters We Make*

"Part murder mystery, part family saga, a dash of Gothic horror—and totally gripping! *What Remains of Teague House* had me hooked from the first atmospheric page to the last chilling twist. Don't miss it!"

—Andrew DeYoung, author of *The Day He Never Came Home*

PROLOGUE

GRACEN

Meander, Oregon—2006

Douggy pouts in Gracen's doorway while he stuffs his backpack with everything he'll need for overnight. He ignores her. He's about to poison both their lives, but he doesn't know that yet. He only knows it's his best friend's birthday, and there will be a trip to the wave pool and a sleepover party after school. Waterslides, pizza, and *Super Mario Bros.* dance through Gracen's mind, and he skips the stupid-looking pajamas Mom told him to bring. Bathing suit—check. Sweatpants—check. Clean underwear and toothbrushes are for babies.

Douggy, nicknamed for the Doug firs that grow around their house because she wants to be a tree when she grows up, is only in kindergarten. With her arms crossed over her chest, she sighs loudly in his doorway. The two of them usually play "Highest Tower" before school, a made-up game that combines their old wooden blocks and a knock-knock joke book Mom bought at a yard sale. Yesterday his tower was almost waist-high before Douggy giggled so hard she knocked it over. Today, he needs to pack, though, and he's explained that twice.

After more sighs and recrossing of the arms, Douggy says in her best trying-to-sound-grown-up voice, "Fine. We can play tomorrow morning."

He shoots her a frustrated look as he struggles with his backpack zipper. "No, dummy. It's a sleepover. I'll be at Blake's, and you have ballet on Saturdays."

Douggy's chin juts, and her lip trembles. He opens his mouth to take it back, but it's too late. She runs to tell Mom, who's in the bathroom getting ready for work. Gracen follows to defend himself. Mom emerges with tight lips, her hair half-curled, and shakes her head. "You guys are going to miss the bus. Gracen, hold Douggy's hand. Get out of here, quick!"

"Can't Dad drive us? I'm not ready!" Douggy's whining now.

Gracen checks the clock. He's dressed and the backpack zipper is almost entirely closed, but Douggy doesn't have socks on yet. Snot shines between her nose and mouth.

Mom swipes a tissue at Douggy's face. "He went to work early today because he's helping with the Mushroom Festival this afternoon, and I don't have time to drive you. Now, go!"

She shoves Douggy's bare feet into rainbow sneakers and kisses the top of her head. "You're going to have fun today, you'll see. Got your lucky rock?"

Douggy nods, but her face screws up. "My feet feel weird without socks," she complains but shrugs her fuzzy panda backpack onto her shoulders.

"It's no big deal. I do it all the time," Gracen tells her. Mom blows him a kiss before returning to the bathroom, and Gracen leads the way outside. The sunny day has a crisp bite to the air, and his heart lifts. At school all his friends will compare waterslide stories and make plans for tonight. It's going to be awesome. His steps quicken.

"Mom said you have to hold my hand," Douggy calls, trotting after him.

"You're not a baby." Why can't she act her age for once? He's got big-kid things to do. And she better not count on sitting with him on the bus. He's sitting with Blake today.

A low chain link fence encloses their yard, and Gracen waits at the gate for Douggy. The grass is brown from a dry summer, dotted with fallen leaves. Douggy's nose is running again. She wipes a slug trail across her face with the back of her hand and glares at him. "Why are you so mean today?"

He teeters on the brink of apologizing and making her laugh with a stupid joke. Someday, he'll distill the trajectory of his life down to this moment, the choice that ruins everything—but it doesn't feel like a choice, just an inconsequential prickle of spite. He's usually a good big brother, but it's work. Today is for fun.

"Not my fault you're a loser." He starts down the street, hands around his backpack straps. Their house, at the end of a gravel road, is two blocks from the bus stop. No sidewalk, but people drive slow because of all the ruts and potholes. It's safe except for what Gracen calls the "danger zone."

The challenges face each other on either side of the street. On the right, a scary bearded man lives in a trailer with weird stains along the sides like veins. Every day, rain or shine, he's smoking on his sagging porch when Gracen walks by. Sometimes he mutters softly, and other times he talks loud enough to make out the words: stuff about the president and the FBI and the whole neighborhood being under surveillance. His eyes bore into Gracen long after he walks past. Mom and Dad say he's a good guy—a war hero who got hurt and can't be a soldier anymore, but when he's staring bullets at Gracen, it's hard to believe.

The other side of the street has the mean dog behind a leaning wooden fence. Gracen can see through gaps and missing slats to a mossy, swaybacked house. Weeds straggle around a dirt yard with one tall Doug fir that casts everything into shadow.

The chained-up dog looks like a German shepherd, one of Mom's favorite breeds. Whenever the family goes for a walk, Mom shakes her head sadly. The poor thing is always chained.

He goes nuts, barking and lunging whenever anyone passes, the chain jerking him to a stop just short of the fence.

Gracen used to speed past the danger zone in the middle of the street. Now that Douggy's with him, he has to be a good example, or she'll tell. He usually takes her the dog way. Dad says even if the wood rots away, that heavy chain is forever.

Douggy's stuck in her mood, scuffing her feet far behind him.

"Hurry up," he calls. "You'll ruin your shoes."

She pouts. "There's dirt on my toes. It's gross."

He rolls his eyes. "You're making it worse. If we miss the bus, Mom will kill us." Worse, she might change her mind about the sleepover.

Douggy halts, brow coming down and lower lip sticking out—the signs of an oncoming tantrum. He forces a lilt into his voice. "If you hurry, I'll bring you some birthday cake tomorrow!"

"I don't care."

The bus stop is a block and a half away. Cleo, the fourth grader who shows up at the last minute, is already there.

"Fine. I'll go without you. When you miss the bus, run home and tell Mom by yourself."

Douggy narrows her eyes. "Mom said you have to stay with me."

"Not if you're this slow. Kids get in big trouble if they don't go to school when they're not sick, you know."

He turns his back and walks away. Only five steps, and she yells for him.

"Wait!" she cries. "It's the danger zone!"

He smiles to himself. He'd known that would do the trick. He can already hear the dog's chain clinking through the fence. Across the street, the scraggly guy mumbles to himself and taps his cigarettes against the table.

Gracen walks backward, keeping an eye on Douggy, who runs to catch up. She's halfway to him when she trips, falling to her hands and knees. The brakes of a bus screech as it pulls around the corner, but it doesn't stop. It must be the high school bus. Theirs won't be far behind. Douggy climbs to her feet, red-faced, and pats her pockets with a panicky look.

The dog pants rapidly, chain jingling as he runs back and forth.

"You're okay. Come on!" Gracen calls. The dog barks as if in response.

"My rock is gone!"

Under his breath, Gracen says, "For shit's sake," which is what Dad mutters when Mom nags at him to pick up after himself. The lucky rock is just a random rock that's sort of heart-shaped. Louder, he says, "We'll find another one at the bus stop. Let's go!"

The dog yelps when it hits the end of the chain. Probably no one's stood next to his fence for this long since…ever. Through a gap, the dog's shape blocks the light as it lunges again. Gracen channels Mom's stern voice. "Now. Or turn around and go home."

Douggy takes a few uncertain steps, then stops. "I'm scared."

Gracen darts a glance across the street. The scary guy/war hero blows a plume of smoke from his mouth like a dragon in a jean jacket, gazing toward the sky as if the kids weren't there.

Gracen sighs. "Okay, 'fraidy-cat. See you tomorrow, after ballet. No cake for you." He picks up a stick, turns his back on Douggy, and drags it along the fence in a show of fearlessness. Douggy ruins everything. They should have been at the bus stop five minutes ago, and he's the one who'll get in trouble if they don't make it.

"Stop!" she yells. He glances back to see her eyes squeezed shut and her hands over her ears. "I'm telling Mom!"

"Good!" He keeps going, thwacking marks into the soft dark wood of each fence slat. Will he be called to the principal's office if he arrives at school without his sister?

No way. Douggy's the one being a pill. She'll go home in tears, and Mom won't have time to do anything but drop her off at school. After the party tomorrow he'll get a talking-to, and that will be that.

Another thud and a strangled yelp end in a clanky jangle. Gracen looks through a crack. The dog hesitates over a tangle of chain topped by a broken leather collar. Free.

Faster than thought, the dog hurls itself against the rotting planks near Gracen. The fence shudders and creaks. The paws and the huge head loom at the top as it scrabbles for purchase, whining and growling. Gracen's frozen, staring at its grizzled muzzle.

"Gracen!" Douggy runs toward him. The last glimpse of his sister before he falls is carved deep: her sweet brown eyes and stubborn chin, her pumping elbows. Her determination to save him.

Then—pain. His skull lights up, and he crumples. There's a weird crunch—his neck?—and sparkly stars fill his vision. The ground slams him, forces the air from his lungs, and he gasps with a sound like a drain. He gropes for understanding—why is he down on the road?—when a snarl snaps him back to alertness.

Douggy shrieks. Gracen squirms to get free, but he's stuck. He can't breathe. He can't move. A man yells: "Down! Stop! No!" Douggy's shrieks fade to whimpers. Gracen tries to yell, "Run!" but only wheezes.

A gunshot cleaves the world.

The ringing silence goes on and on until Gracen whimpers and pushes out from the fallen boards. He gasps like a drowning man. His shirt and the skin of his back are shredded, but he barely notices. Something warm and sticky drips in his eye, and he wipes it away, blinking at Douggy.

The scary guy is kneeling beside her, the German shepherd behind him as still as if it were a stuffed animal. There's red on his sister's face and shirt. Red on the man's hands where they press, trying to keep it in.

This can't be real. It's like a movie, the kind he's not allowed to watch. Pretend blood, like a video game.

His stomach twists. When he asks, "Is it bad?" his voice is small and far away.

Clear gray eyes meet Gracen's. Same old scraggly beard and hollow cheeks, but this close, the deep lines of his face make him look sad and scared instead of crazy. His voice is calm, but he doesn't answer Gracen's question.

"Nine-one-one, boy," he says. "Phone's inside the door. Haul ass."

Gracen hauls ass and answers his own question. Over and over he'll answer it, through the coming decades. It's bad now, and it only gets worse.

"Gracen Ridpath of *Gracen's Hot Mess* here. Yeah, that funny guy who does stupid food tricks and dropped sixty-five pounds on Oreos and orange juice alone. (Remember, kids—don't try this at home, especially if there's no one else to clean up the vomit.) If you've ever wondered what caused the mental dumpster fire behind my quirky exterior, check out my new limited series vod-cast where I open up about a family tragedy. Maybe it'll help someone to hear it, and maybe I need to share. *The Ridpath Girl*... on your favorite podcast platforms."

—trailer for *The Ridpath Girl*, present day

1

QUINN

In the predawn darkness, Quinn sits cross-legged on the bare twin-sized mattress that serves as their bed, sleeping bag draped around narrow shoulders. Quinn's eyes are closed as they replay the last lines of the podcast episode yet again, despite knowing them by heart: "Douggy wasn't the happy child we wanted to think she was, and her death was no accident."

For Quinn, it's like picking a scab. An infected scab.

With a twitch, Quinn taps to stop Gracen Ridpath's rumination on his dysfunctional parents, his scarred little sister, and the dual tragedies that reduced his once-happy family to a husk. Gracen's little sister had been Quinn's best friend. The podcast takes the only time in Quinn's life when they experienced unconditional acceptance and poisons it. Douggy was a joyful, fierce, loyal friend, and she didn't kill herself. No fucking way.

They take a deep breath and reach for the clean clothes piled next to the mattress. It's been ten days since they moved in, but they haven't bothered with furnishings or decor. This is a temporary home—just another couple of weeks, and they'll go back to their real life in Portland, or whatever's left of it.

In the past ten days, Quinn's located Mom's address, done several walk-bys, rehearsed their pitch, and changed the words a hundred times. They even approached the door once and retreated, shaking. Procrastinating has been easy to rationalize because they've been working so much. Family emergency or not, they have to eat.

Today, they only have an evening shift—nearly twelve hours from now. It's time to act.

The cloudy January sky lightens through the bare window, and Quinn pulls on black cargo pants and a burgundy wool sweater, wool socks, and their lace-up Doc Marten boots. One thigh pocket holds their phone, the other a Ziploc bag with a woven bracelet in it, all Quinn has left of Douggy. Too frayed and old to wear safely, but here in Meander, Quinn's been carrying it for luck.

Douggy's death had been their mother's excuse for sending Quinn and their brother away, nearly fifteen years ago, and Quinn hasn't been back until now. An untimely end of childhood, at age eleven. Maybe that's why they feel so old.

As Quinn emerges from the bedroom, the scent of coffee greets them, along with the sounds of humming and chopping.

Viveca, Quinn's landlord and roommate, must be up and getting ready to leave for work. Since moving in, Quinn's seen Viveca mostly in passing, which is as it should be. Nothing against Vee, as she likes to be called, but Quinn usually avoids small talk. Today's not a day for retreat, though, and Quinn enters the kitchen with a polite, nervous nod.

"Good morning!" Viveca says with a broad smile as she dumps a handful of celery sticks into a container. With her curvaceous figure, understated makeup, and close-cropped natural hair, she has more presence in purple scrubs than Quinn would have in a tux with tails.

Quinn offers a reserved smile back. "Morning." They start the water for tea, then rummage in the cupboard where they keep their small stash of food.

Vee says, "Morning shift today?"

"Just errands."

"You look tired! There's coffee and muffins if you want."

"No, thanks." Guilt pinches at Quinn for turning down the hospitality, but caffeine is worse than small talk for making their anxiety go haywire. It's the last thing they need before facing their mother. They carry crackers, peanut butter, a banana, and a butter knife to the table, then return for their mug of tea.

Viveca doesn't seem offended. She sips from her steaming dolphin mug, one among many ocean-themed collectibles that colonize the house. "I've been meaning to ask you. What year did you move away, again?"

Quinn suppresses a sigh. When Vee first asked why Quinn wanted to rent a room in Meander, Quinn was less than truthful, leading her to believe they were moving here because they had happy memories of living here as a child. They didn't want Viveca to know they planned to leave as soon as they connected with their mother. The hotel is too expensive, but Viveca would probably prefer a renter who'd stay for months, not weeks.

Unfortunately, the story caused its own problems. Viveca, a Meanderite from birth, is perplexed about why she can't remember Quinn. Quinn hasn't felt like explaining that back then, they had a different name, a different hair color, a different gender, and a different body type. But now, looking at Viveca's open, friendly face, they realize their instinct toward privacy may be hobbling them. Douggy and Quinn were too young to be Viveca's friends, but Gracen was older, closer to her age. Maybe the two of them were in touch. While in Meander, Quinn means to confront Gracen, but he's proven a hard man to reach.

Quinn says, "It was the year Douggy Ridpath died. She was my best friend."

Viveca's eyes widen with dawning recognition. "Oh. I didn't realize. You—you're Kathy?"

Quinn's ears grow hot. "Not anymore."

Viveca nods slowly. "Got it. I remember you now. You were so shy!" She snaps her lunch box shut and shakes her head. "My god, Douggy's death—it was awful. You must have been devastated."

Quinn hides their discomfort by carefully applying peanut butter to several more crackers. They regret it immediately as they chew through dry, sticky crumbs. With a hand shielding their mouth, they ask, "Did you keep in touch with Gracen?"

Viveca raises elegant eyebrows. "He's a little high and mighty for the likes of me. And I doubt he's shown his face here since sticking his mom in the nursing home."

"You don't sound like you like him much."

"Are you kidding? Have you been following him online? His food channel was hilarious, and I even think his new podcast is cute, the stay-at-home dad thing. But this limited series where he's trash-talking Meander—" She frowns at Quinn. "You've heard it, right? About Douggy?"

Quinn nods. Episode two *is* harsh. Gracen ruthlessly describes the treatment his sister suffered at the hands of townspeople who responded to a little girl's scars with cruel words and stares. He doesn't name Meander, calling it "a small town in Oregon," and he hasn't named anyone but himself and Douggy. All the same, a quick look at Wikipedia identifies Meander as Gracen's birthplace, and some of the citizens in Gracen's episodes would be easy to identify with a little detective work. Quinn isn't surprised some Meanderites feel defensive.

Quinn remembers everything differently. The town hadn't seemed so bad, and Douggy wasn't scarred on the inside, where it counted. But it's not just the podcast that concerns them. The last time Quinn spoke with Douggy, days before she died, was a late-night phone call. Douggy begged Quinn to sneak over so she could tell them something important, but Quinn wimped out. If Douggy died by accident, like everyone always said, that's bad enough. But if Douggy killed herself, it's Quinn's fault, for failing to come when they were needed.

Vee presses her lips together, then shrugs. "It probably wouldn't bother me so much, except the Parents and Teachers Association invited him to speak to the middle schoolers this year. A friend at work is one of the moms. They're celebrating his success to inspire the kids because he grew up here, and meanwhile he's claiming we bullied Douggy into killing herself. It's ridiculous. This town was good to her, no matter what Gracen seems to think."

"You really think so?"

"Yes!" Viveca smacks the counter. "Because guess what. I'm the evil babysitter Gracen talks about. Only I wasn't." Her dark skin turns rosy. "Yes, maybe I said something thoughtless, trying to impress some stupid boy. But Douggy knew I loved her. And she was self-conscious about her scars, but once she relaxed, she was a ray of sunshine! Maybe some people stared, but, hey, I got looks too, as one of the only Black kids in town. There was no bullying, no 'pattern of abuse.'"

Douggy was eight when Quinn met her, and ten-year-old Gracen was in charge when their parents were out. Gracen and Douggy's dad was usually home anyway, unemployed or working short hours at one garage or another. Viveca must have babysat for them before the Fontaines moved to the neighborhood.

Quinn says, "I agree. I didn't think she was—"

"You know what I think? Gracen's trying to wring a few extra dollars out of the tragedy now that their parents are both gone. Such a pathetic thing to do! He'd sell his soul for another hundred K, let alone the memory of his sister."

She pulls her quilted jacket off the back of the chair and heaves her stuffed bag to her shoulder. "Anyway. If I can't get the school to cancel his visit, I'll tell him to his face when he comes to town." She turns to go.

"Wait!"

Viveca turns, jingling her keys impatiently. "What?"

"Your friend in the PTA. Do you think they'd have his contact info?"

"I'll ask." She throws Quinn a quick smile. "He'd probably be happy to hear from you, since you were Douggy's friend. Maybe you can get him to stop bad-mouthing us." She twinkles her fingers in Quinn's general direction. "See you later! Lock up if I'm not home. I've got plans tonight." She winks.

When the door closes, Quinn stares at the crumbs on their plate, heart pounding. Gracen had been ignoring Quinn's emails for months now—or maybe it was his assistant, or his agent, whoever acts as a filter—and Quinn had almost given up. Suddenly, the possibility of talking to him seems very real. But today is Sheila day, for Kade's sake. They need to stay focused.

Rising, they clear Vee's mess, then duck into the bathroom to check their look in the mirror, trying to see through Sheila's eyes. The difference between the woman their mother thought their child would grow into and the Quinn who actually exists might startle her—Gran had certainly had a problem—and for a split second, they fantasize about jumping in the shower, then borrowing clothes and makeup from Viveca. A disguise. Quinn shakes it off. They're not looking for acceptance. Today, the focus is on Kade and what Kade needs.

Mom's going to step up, for once in her life.

They zip their worn black hoodie over their sweater, add the bulky black jacket, then step outside. The sky is low over the thick trees that surround the town, but the rain, which has been nearly constant for weeks, is holding off. Meander feels like it used to, a two-stoplight town nestled in the folds of a deep, dark forest. Downtown is only two blocks long, and, across the street from a single-truck fire station, the library and town hall share space in an old Victorian. Quinn had researched their mother's current address there, under her husband's name, in the county clerk's office.

Quinn walks briskly. Where Main Street crosses the swollen river, they lean against the balustrade and look into the rushing waters, icy fingers curled into their cuffs. They have a right to ask for Sheila's help. Quinn is a confident adult, an artist—they rub the tattoo on their left hand—*not* a kid begging for crumbs of attention. They're demanding a pittance of what is owed to Kade—some small token of care.

An SUV passes too close, shushing through the puddles and dashing their clean black pants with mud. Quinn moves on, only to slow again as they come to an empty lot where a For Sale sign sprouts optimistically from a bed of weeds and broken concrete.

Here, the Fontaine kids once lived with Sheila in a one-bedroom duplex where water stains marred the ceiling, mold freckled the drywall, and grime mapped the linoleum floor. Quinn pauses for a moment, watching the ghost of a house that isn't there.

They haven't had the courage to walk by Douggy's old house yet.

Mom and her replacement family live in the antithesis of the old duplex: an imposing two-story new build with a double garage and a landscaped yard. Until Kade needed it, you couldn't have paid Quinn enough to visit. Why waste time on someone who'd abandoned them?

A cowardly part of them hopes the husband's car will be in the driveway—any excuse to put off the door knock for another day. This visit requires privacy. Quinn can't imagine what she's told him. Do her new kids know she abandoned her last set? Her husband must, unless they never socialize or shop in town. Someone would have asked after Kathy and Kade, at least once. Or maybe not. It all feels like a very long time ago.

Too soon, the house is in front of them. They clamp their teeth together. If they blow this, Kade could end up with a life sentence. They force their feet along a concrete path lined with potted yucca in beds of lava rock. Mouth dry, they mount the slate steps and hesitate in front of the holly wreath on the shiny red door.

On a previous walk, they watched Sheila shepherd two brown-haired girls in white karate uniforms into the back seat of an SUV. She was chatting away on Bluetooth as she slammed the car door and paused with her hand on top of the vehicle. Confidence exuded from her highlighted hair to her high-heeled leather boots. She looked good for forty-five. If Quinn hadn't caught a distracted expression that echoed the exhausted, tearful, resentful woman they lived with for their first decade, Quinn would have concluded they had the wrong address.

When Quinn was younger, they fantasized about confronting that old version of their mother. Puffy and straggle-haired, in worn leggings and pilly sweatshirts, smelling of cigarettes. Defensive and short-tempered, and no match for Quinn's spiky, righteous anger. The present version looks well-armored, like she could step over a discarded child and keep right on going. Which she had, all the way to her nice house and her beautiful children.

With a deep breath, Quinn jabs their finger at the doorbell. A moment later, the door swings open.

Sheila DeCelles Fontaine Ehler looks Quinn up and down with distaste. "No soliciting." The door starts to close.

Despite the time Quinn's put into rehearsing this moment, despite the anger and fear burning inside, a weak and pathetic "Mom?" escapes their lips.

Sheila's still-familiar hazel eyes widen. Her lips open, maybe to speak, maybe for an indrawn breath.

Then she slams the door.

"Thank you for sharing, it helps so many broken people even if they don't know it. You are an enlightened soul in a cruel world, and you've inspired me so much."

—*The Ridpath Girl*, Episode 1: "A Family in Pain," Comments section, 3 months ago

2

KIRSTEN

The throbbing behind my forehead may fade if I sit here at the dining room table massaging my temples instead of following Trav to the kitchen. One minute of peace. With my eyes closed, I hear the fridge door bang open, then the freezer, then more drawers and cupboards than seem reasonable for a simple before-school breakfast. He's going for noise, a passive-aggressive move, since he knows I have a headache.

When I was a child, my parents' bedtime stories all began with the words *Once upon a time, there was a beautiful young princess.* The princess's name was Kirsten, and she lived in a land of splendor and kindness, and the challenges she faced were always surmountable. Friendly, misunderstood dragons. Lima beans. Marauding wolves.

The world of law enforcement is not full of splendor and kindness. I've worked well with entitled assholes, eaten my vegetables, and taken out a lot of wolves. That's what I live for, and just because I work in a flawed system that sometimes prosecutes the innocent—

I swallow. Trav's angry words still echo through my mind: *You're not fine. Look at you.*

Stifling a groan, I rub my temples.

The Sanchez case went wrong. I did my best. We all did. A little insomnia and a few headaches are a small price to pay. It will pass, and I'll make up this rough patch to Trav and the kids.

A double drumbeat of feet announces the twins are awake. Their voices harmonize in an unintelligible give-and-take that soothes me. The bathroom door slams, and water starts running. One of them—probably Henry—shuffles down the stairs with a pause between each step, as if he were playing on his game console while he walks. Someday, he'll fall and break his crown. I massage my eye sockets, rehearsing the cheerful Mom greeting that will signal to Trav that our daily truce has been called.

Henry appears in the doorway. No game after all. His eyes are bleary, his cheeks splotched red. A blanket is clutched around his shoulders. "Mommy, I don't feel good," he says and rushes to me. I pull him close, inhaling the warm, sour scent of sleep.

Trav appears in the doorway, a spatula in hand. "You okay, bud?" He's transformed from the self-righteous ogre of our argument into affable Daddy, the sweet, bearded teddy bear of a man with endless patience.

Henry shakes his head against my shoulder. "My tummy hurts."

The words are muffled, but we both understand. Trav meets my eyes. He lifts his eyebrows. This winter has been one illness after another, with one or both twins sick or recovering at any given moment. Technically it's Trav's turn to use a sick day, but I went in Saturday to catch up on paperwork so was considering flexing today off. And—the migraine. I nod that I'll stay home. Trav pats Henry's shoulder. "Don't worry, big guy. Mom will see what she can do about that."

"First, let's take your temperature." I nudge Henry forward and push to my feet. My heartbeat drums inside my skull, and I lean on the table until it eases. Migraines and coffee and sleeplessness, oh my. I'm not sure where one ends and the next begins, but it's time for meds. And once Trav and Fern leave, Henry and I can doze on the couch with *Kung Fu Panda* on low for the next few hours. Bliss.

When we reach the upstairs hallway, Fern rushes past with a "Hi, Mommy!" Her fine brown hair has a rat's nest on one side, but three zebra-patterned clips hold her bangs out of her eyes. Good enough.

"Have a great day, sweetheart!" I call. In a moment, her high, clear voice floats up from the kitchen. Something about endangered lemurs and a field trip to the zoo.

In the bathroom, Henry plops on the toilet lid, and I check the medicine cabinet. No thermometer. "Shoot. Wait here. It's in Mom and Dad's bathroom."

Mentally, I correct that to "Dad's bathroom." It's been weeks since I spent the night in our bedroom, which has become a foreign country. Trav's iPad is on my nightstand, his pillows are in the center of the headboard, his dirty clothes block my closet door. The room smells stuffy and sweaty, an offense to my aching head. Through half-closed drapes, the backyard is a mud pit under layers of gray clouds that have been hovering for weeks.

In the bathroom, ignoring my haggard face in the mirror, I retrieve the thermometer and pop a pain pill. My phone buzzes from the back pocket of my sweats as I return to Henry.

The number is Eb's. My heart starts racing.

He wastes no time. "Docker, head to Meander. Dunwoody Park, south entrance. There's a body, and you're on deck."

Fantasies of *Kung Fu Panda*, of sleep, of peaceful one-on-one time with Henry all evaporate. My stomach contracts with dread, and for one second, I'm certain I'm going to vomit. *Get help*, Trav says, but it's not Trav's face I see. It's the nineteen-year-old kid who didn't make it to legal drinking age because I thought—no, *knew*—he was a killer. Because I saw the wolf in his eyes.

I tamp it down.

"On my way," I tell Eb and hang up.

I force a smile and slip the thermometer into Henry's mouth. "Dad will be up in a minute, okay? Mom has to work after all." I kiss the top of his head, inhale one last breath of his damp, salty hair, then go break the news to Trav.

3

QUINN

Early Thursday, Quinn stumbles into the dark kitchen, then stops, startled to be the first one up. They squint down the hall to check the coatrack by the front door. No lavender coat or purse. Whatever Vee did last night must have turned into a sleepover. She'd waved to Quinn at the diner around eight, picking up takeout, but Quinn had been busy with a table of teenagers and only nodded in return.

Hopefully Vee won't start bringing dates home before Quinn's business in Meander is finished. This house is too small for a third wheel, especially one uncomfortable with public displays of affection. Or private ones, at that. They shudder, thinking of Paz. Paz is a fellow student in Quinn's tattoo program in Portland, but the relationship had been creeping incrementally toward something more when Quinn heard about Kade and took off for Meander. Paz probably thinks they left because of the kiss. Unless Micah, the owner, explained the family emergency thing.

It *had* been convenient timing. The kiss—Paz's eyes shining with hope, her brave lean-in sending Quinn's stomach cartwheeling—had seemed like the end of the world or, in a scary-wonderful way, the beginning of everything. Then the private detective located them. One second, Quinn's biggest problem was figuring out if it was time to have an awkward talk about sexual expectations. The next, Gramps's hireling broke the news that Kade was in prison and Gran dead, and Quinn's priorities changed completely.

Quinn ignores a pang of regret and puts together a hurried breakfast. They slide a folded paper out of their back pocket and set it on the table, then ingest toast and a banana while gazing at the blank side as if they have X-ray vision. The message was composed around midnight last night, after hours of reliving Sheila's door slam.

They push their empty plate aside and gnaw the inside of their cheek.

The message is a quid pro quo. If Sheila meets with Quinn, Quinn will stay away from the replacement family. Quinn's heart beats hard at the thought of forcing their way into the middle of a family dinner, but the only other option seems to be repeating yesterday's visit. Quinn doesn't have time to fuck around. Kade's sentencing hearing is mid-February. To have any effect at all, Sheila needs to write to the judge as soon as possible.

Quinn's eyes fill as they picture their baby brother in a jail cell and imagine the pain he must have been in to do what he did. They suck in a sharp breath through their nose. They should never have left him with Gran. And Sheila should never have left either of them with her in the first place.

When their phone vibrates, they're relieved at the distraction, although they guess it must be the diner before even looking at the screen. They're right. Bella, one of the morning shift servers, has car trouble, and Sunny needs Quinn to cover. "I'll head right over," Quinn assures her. More hours, more money to help fund this interlude from Quinn's real life.

Even so, they unfold the letter and read it one last time before they leave.

Sunny's is a glass-fronted diner on Main Street, popular with everyone from the oldsters who belly up to the counter for morning coffee, to the mayor at lunch, to teens getting snacks after school. Quinn, in all their years of hardscrabble menial jobs, avoided food service like the plague, but in Meander there was no other choice. So far, they suck at it. Last night a tray of tuna melts slid from their shoulder to the floor, splattering enough to leave them reeking for the rest of the shift. Today has to be better.

The regulars seem to be warming to them, getting accustomed to their reserved attitude, not to mention their tattoos and piercing. In Portland, Quinn's look is tame and understated—dark, chin-length hair, a single nose ring, and their left hand and arm inked sparingly in monochrome—but in Meander, they sometimes feel like a zoo exhibit.

Mid-afternoon, they scribble Mom's address on the envelope and jog to the post office despite a downpour. After they hand the letter to the clerk, they push back outside and find the rain has eased, leaving the whole world brighter. Maybe it's an omen.

If things are really looking up, Viveca might come through with Gracen's contact info too.

Around four, a woman Quinn recognizes settles in their section. Despite Meander's size, this has happened less than they dreaded, so when it does, it puts Quinn on alert. Alicia Finch had been the school secretary—middle-aged then, elderly now. She sat behind the office counter, an enforcer of inside voices and walking feet and signing in. As a child, Quinn had feared her, but then, they'd feared everything. A frisson of shame goes through them as they flash again to that shameful nighttime retreat from Douggy's house. It's been a lifetime pattern. Even now, Quinn keeps a wide boundary between themself and the world.

I'm here, Quinn reminds themself. In their own estimation, they've done two brave things in their life: escaping Gran and coming back to Oregon to face the woman formerly known as Mom.

The escaping-Gran part backfired badly for Kade. Facing Sheila has to make up for it.

Ms. Finch must be seventy, or possibly eighty. She cups a hand to her ear when Quinn recites the soups of the day, so Quinn leans to repeat them, smelling talcum powder and mint. Her hair is a faded orange bob bisected by a wide part, instead of the brassy blond updo of Kathy's childhood, but her fashion sense hasn't changed a bit, from her chunky heels to her flowered cardigan.

For the few months Douggy went to regular school at the start of fourth grade, she'd bonded with Ms. Finch. Two or three times a week, she'd end up behind Ms. Finch's counter, doing worksheets under her watchful eye after a stomachache or headache got her out of class. The secretary kept a jar of root beer candies in a drawer, and Douggy would suck on one after another until she'd reluctantly admit to feeling better and return to her teacher's care.

Quinn begged her to stay in school, but considering how much time Douggy spent at the office, it was no surprise when her parents switched her back to homeschooling. Quinn treasures the memory of those happy months—having a best friend to eat lunch with, giggling over cardboard-crusted pizza and canned pears. Having Douggy watch their back.

As Quinn finishes taking her order, the old woman grasps their hand in one fragile claw. "Thank you, Kathy."

Quinn's eyes dart around to see if anyone noticed—the last thing they need is for the whole town to start deadnaming them and gossiping about why they've returned. Quinn's always known there was a chance of being recognized in Meander, but the reality is unsettling. They don't want to drag Kathy around behind them like an ill-fitting shadow. It's unsettling enough that when Sunny offers the opportunity to leave early during a lull, Quinn jumps at the chance. They pull on their hoodie and hurriedly exit.

Outside, it's drizzling again, but not badly, as they walk to grab some food before returning home. Earbuds in, they open Spotify. The third episode of *The Ridpath Girl* downloaded overnight. Quinn's eyes widen as they see the episode title: "A School of Bullies."

It's surreal to walk with Gracen's expressive voice coming through their headphones as intimately as if he walked beside them, nuanced with irony, anger, sorrow—even, at times, his self-deprecating humor. "Our elementary school was a typical small-town school, limping along in need of funds for repairs and updates. It should have been a safe space, and, you know, let's give credit where credit is due. I have deep respect for teachers and administrators and those who devote their time and energy to raising children well. But as a dad—and as a brother recognizing his sister's death was self-inflicted—there's got to be more of a spotlight on how kids interact with one another and the messages that adults' actions and attitudes transmit. My sister was *not* safe there."

Quinn is carried back to life at Meander Elementary like there's been a stitch in time. Except this is a warped Meander, crueler than the one Kathy knew. Meander Elementary had been lonely for a kid like Quinn, but full of bullies? No. At least, they wouldn't have said so, but Gracen makes a compelling argument.

As in the other episodes, no names are named, but even fifteen years later, Quinn can identify some of the kids and teachers Gracen mentioned. The "staff person in the office" has to be Ms. Finch. Instead of seeing her as a sanctuary, Gracen blames her for isolating Douggy and making her a target. She'd undermined Douggy's return to school, sowing the seeds of exile, loneliness, and depression. Quinn had never thought of it like that, and now, they wonder who's right.

The episode ends as Quinn draws close to home, their backpack weighted with cans of soup and some fruit. They're preoccupied with the sense of looking at the past in a funhouse mirror. As they slide their key into the lock, they're wondering if Ms. Finch will ever hear this episode, and if Gracen spoke with her before publishing his story.

When the door swings open, Quinn finally grasps that something is wrong. The square of carpet their gaze should land on is blocked by legs in charcoal slacks, and they snap their eyes up and let out a yelp.

A tough-looking, fortyish blond with a badge in one gloved hand cocks her head, staring Quinn up and down with a frown.

4

KIRSTEN

Dunwoody Park's main entrance is on a barren stretch of rural highway surrounded by trees. By the time I pull into the nearly empty lot, my headache has receded to a bearable throb.

The deputy stationed at the park entrance holds an umbrella against the drizzle and retrieves the crime scene log from under his slicker for me to sign. He points past a playground to a trail leading into the forest, and I slip shoe covers on to keep my tracks from confusing the scene.

Through dripping gloom, the trail winds under a canopy of evergreens, and a light fungal scent plants itself in the back of my throat. Melakwa County is small and rural but home to its share of violence. As I make my way past bare tangles of briar and drooping fern fronds, I attempt the "Mission Now, Emotion Later" mind-set that usually serves me well. But this is my first suspicious death since the Sanchez boy died. My teeth grind, no matter how many deep breaths I force past them.

Eb agreed about Sanchez. We were certain he'd killed his wife. Nineteen-year-old newlyweds, with Thomas known for his hot temper. The district attorney agreed. We all did our best, and while I wish we hadn't gone down the wrong path… it happens. People make mistakes.

Trav expects me to be more torn up about it. He keeps bringing it up. "You seem like you're struggling." But I'm not. I saw a wolf where there was only a teenage boy reeling from loss. Law enforcement has to be able to move past that. Eb did. The DA did. I did. I am.

A fluffy gray squirrel races across the path and darts up a tree, where it chitters angrily from a branch. A dozen feet ahead, the shape of a woman emerges from the greens and browns, a bright petal against the forest floor. She's crumpled at the foot of a huge Douglas fir, in a quilted lavender jacket and multicolored pants that cling wetly to the shape of her legs. Mud is clotted around her bare feet, and her hands clasp a bouquet of fir fronds on the ground before her. Rain drips in pink rivulets down her face from an ugly wound at her temple.

Peripherally, I register the presence of others working the scene as I crouch to peer more closely. The lower half of the woman's face is overlaid with mottled discoloration, either bruising or dirt.

Fury rises like a drug, counteracting the fog of my pain pill. Someone abandoned her like this. The fir fronds and the arrangement of the body suggest someone—most likely the boyfriend or husband—regrets what they've done.

I embrace the clarity but try to shake off the assumption. The evidence will speak for itself.

Of course, that was the plan last time too.

I wonder if Eb, my sometime-partner, should be primary on this. I know what Trav would say. But Sarge senses weakness like a lioness on the savanna.

When a throat clears nearby, I turn to see Eb a few feet behind me, snug in his navy police-issue rain jacket. Mine is in the trunk, and as the breeze cuts through my fleece, I suppress a shiver.

"Do we have ID?" I ask.

He takes in my bedraggled state with a lifted eyebrow. "We do. Viveca Crandall, local veterinary assistant. The runner who found her breeds cats, so he's a frequent flier at their office. He recognized her right away."

"Did you talk to him?"

"Nah. Riley's got him in his unit, wrapped in a foil blanket with the heat blasting. Guy was jogging in the rain for an hour before he stumbled across her and called us in. Looked like he was going to faint, but I knew you'd want to talk to him yourself."

Want is not the right word, but I nod. How likely is it that a runner would come down this path on a miserable January morning? A runner who knows Viveca, no less.

"How old is she?" I ask.

"Thirty-three. Single, no kids. No record."

I study the planes and curves of the body, the flashes of gold on one forefinger and at the neck of that lavender jacket. There will be plenty of photos, but I want to burn her reality into my mind. Her nails are short and manicured, but one is torn past the quick. With luck, she clawed off some of her attacker's DNA. The rain may not have scoured under her nails the way it washed the rest of her.

I turn back to Eb. "Any weapons?"

He points over to the left. "See those ferns next to the fallen log? Underneath is a hefty rock. Looks like blood on it."

There's already a plastic evidence marker there, and I brush ferns aside to see the rock. Not only blood but hair is visible to the naked eye, and I imagine the killer letting it thud into the underbrush rather than tossing it. A stroke of luck it landed semiprotected from the rain. "How about her shoes?"

He gestures. "Other side of the clearing. Tan heels with a torn strap. She might have ripped them off to run."

They rest in the shadow of the evergreen salal growing knee-high around the clearing. Not shoes intended for hiking. There's no sign of a chase or struggle, but with the rain and wind, footprints and other signs may have been obscured. "I wonder what's under her."

"Carrie plans to put up a pop-up shelter before Gene arrives, but she's getting some pics first."

"Good." I snort, imagining our rain-averse ME kneeling on the sodden ground. Gene moved his family from Utah two years ago and hasn't stopped threatening to leave since his first Oregon storm. I hope he'll toughen up. Melakwa County has trouble hanging on to qualified professionals and can't afford to lose him.

From nowhere, the thought flashes—they can't afford to lose me, either. Gotta hold it together.

Over Eb's shoulder, I notice Melakwa County's lone civilian crime scene tech, Carrie Torres, stalking the clearing with camera in hand. Deceptively quiet, she has an eagle eye and cutting wit. We exchange nods.

Cold drops of rain run down my collar. "Did you check the other trails?" An overgrown path seems to head farther into the woods, and a wider trail goes off to one side.

Eb nods. "No sign our vic or attacker went that way."

If there's anything here pointing to our killer, we'll have to wait for further processing to find it. "Let's leave Carrie to it, then. I've got coffee in the car. We can regroup before I talk to—what's his name, the witness?"

Eb pulls his phone from a raincoat pocket and checks his notes. "Jeffrey Kitzner. The cats are a retirement side hustle, he says. Hairless. Can't imagine who buys those things."

"They'd never make it in my house." It's hard enough

wrangling the twins into sweaters. I spare a thought for Henry and make a mental note to text Trav later.

In the parking lot, I click the ignition on my SUV and settle gratefully into the heated seat as Eb seizes the travel mug in the console.

"For me? I think I love you."

I'm not in the mood for banter, but I reply automatically. "Your girlfriend won't like that."

"I was talking to the coffee." He closes his eyes to sip.

I follow suit. After a moment, Eb asks, "Hey, Docker—you okay? You seem a little off."

Docker is a play on "Boondock," my nickname among the team. Eb (short for Ebenezer Scrooge, thanks to his habit of squeezing pennies) and I have worked dozens of cases together, and I trust him. But he, like Trav, keeps prying at my feelings. If anyone needs counseling, it's Eb, whose cop armor has empathic fissures a mile wide, but he's not the one Thomas Sanchez's mother has been emailing in her grief.

A pulse pounds in my temple, and I rub it through rain-damp hair. Eb's habitual smirk has fallen into lines of concern.

"Migraine." I flick my hand dismissively. "Meds will kick in soon." Fuck. I should have brought the bottle.

I pull out my notebook, and he brings me up to speed. Viveca Crandall owns the gray Nissan Altima, the only civilian vehicle in this parking lot. A rudimentary search has been done, and there's no purse or phone in the car. I'm crossing my fingers they'll turn up back in the clearing.

We put warrant requests in motion for Viveca's home and financial records, then Eb accompanies Gene and his assistant back to the scene while I question Kitzner. He's older than I expected, mid-seventies, with the sinewy build of a lifelong runner. He says he jogs through the park in every kind of weather, although now he's getting up there it's "only" three or four times a week.

When I push against his claim that he's never seen Viveca outside the veterinary office, not even in the grocery store, he blushes, but it's from embarrassment at getting his groceries delivered. "The only places I go anymore are the doctor and the vet," he confesses. "It's not good for me, I'm sure, but everything I can order online, I do."

"You're getting out and running, that's more than people half your age," I tell him. "There's a running group in Polallie. You should check it out." I'd tried, but between the twins and work I'd never made it. My fitness gets tucked into odd nooks and crannies of time. After giving him my card in case he remembers anything else, I ask one of the deputies to drive him home.

When I'm alone in my car again, I can feel the skitter of the pulse in my throat, the heavy sky pressing down on me. I need to get this one right. I need to keep moving.

My phone buzzes, and the warrant to search Viveca Crandall's home comes through before I spiral into anxiety.

Her landlord emails me a copy of the lease. Viveca shared her two-bedroom house with Samantha O'Brien, a thirty-four-year-old red-haired Caucasian who also has no criminal record.

I pick up a key at the landlord's office before meeting Eb at a small house on a block of close-set 1960s bungalows. The front yard is mow-free, just gravel and juniper bushes.

We knock. I flip open the mailbox next to the door while we wait. The post office's "occupancy" card inside only shows Viveca's name, and I wonder if O'Brien is no longer in the picture.

No one comes. I shrug at Eb and use the key. The front door leads into a small living room, drapes closed. The electric wakefulness that pierced me at the first sight of Viveca's body has withered away. I'm fighting a current of fatigue, and the dim interior looks and sounds subtly warped, as if I were under water.

We call out just in case someone missed the knock, then walk through together, looking for hints to Viveca's character, as well as anything out of place. She enjoyed bright colors, and she'd invested in a nice leather couch and what appear to be original artworks. There's an ocean motif, with splashes of aquamarine blue, and little collectibles here and there: a wall hanging with a giant silk-screened wave, a leaping dolphin in blown glass, orca salt and pepper shakers. The primary bedroom's king bed has a cloud-like duvet of dark teal, topped by an assortment of throw pillows, and the walk-in closet is organized by color and season and could stock a boutique. The bureau has three empty drawers, and the nightstand to the left of the bed is bare, as if saved for someone. A long-distance boyfriend, maybe, or a breakup so recent she hasn't reclaimed the space.

I flash to Travis's iPad on my nightstand.

At the door of a second, nearly bare bedroom, we pause. No one's gotten around to decorating in here. A mummy-style sleeping bag curls like a caterpillar across the bare twin-sized mattress on the floor, and a zippered duffel is surrounded by little piles of folded clothing. Is this O'Brien's stuff?

"Look at the carpet." Eb motions to the far side of the room, where multiple lines are worn into the pile. Furniture stood there recently, and darker rectangles on the green walls indicate posters or photos have been removed.

Nowhere in the house is there any sign of struggle. There are no dishes in the sink, and the bed in Viveca's bedroom is neatly made. A cold load of towels sits in the dryer.

Carrie arrives, and I point her to the desk. The laptop is password protected, and she boxes it to bring back to the office before moving on to the drawers.

Eb starts a more thorough search of the bedroom, and I'm opening kitchen cupboards when Carrie calls, "Someone's coming up the walk. White, late teens or early twenties, baggy clothes."

I go out to peer through a window. On the stoop, a slight person with dark hair and pale skin is pulling out a key.

Samantha? From the DMV photo, I expected a robust, red-headed woman, but weight and hair color can change. I pull out my badge and stand in front of the door as it swings open. The incomer freezes in the act of removing a set of earbuds.

"Samantha O'Brien?" I ask crisply. "I'm Detective Kirsten Boon with the Melakwa County Sheriff's Bureau."

5

GRACEN

Gracen rises from his desk and stretches, spine crackling after hours over the laptop. The office is small, dominated by a massive desk holding his computer, microphones, and mixing equipment. He turns to the single window on the outer wall, triple-paned with heavy drapes to reduce noise pollution while recording.

He's not recording today, and winter light glows from a pale sky ripe with precipitation.

Down on the lawn, he catches movement; Aurie gallops into sight, arms out like airplane wings, even the one with the cast. Gracen cringes, dreading a fall in the slick grass. Her foot will slip, the weight of the cast will twist her shoulder and hit the fragile pencil-width of her jawbone. Her hair will fly out as she collapses to the ground—

He fumbles with the window, heart pounding. It won't

open. Mac must be distracted, in the house, on the phone. The sash jumps upward with a screech, and damp, chilly January air billows in with Aurie's laughter.

Mac comes into view, jeans-clad legs eating up the ground behind their daughter. She cries, "Gotcha!" and grabs Aurie up, swinging her in a circle before pulling her close. They collapse breathless and giggling on grass mucky from weeks of seemingly constant drizzle.

Gracen slumps, but tension still gnarls his forehead. Aurie shouldn't run with her broken wrist. He's nearly positive the doctor said exactly that. If he brings it up, Mac will shoot him a withering look over the top of her thick glasses, meaning he's suffocating Aurie with his neuroses again.

She's probably right. He'd love to be more like Mac. Brave. Spontaneous. Not haunted by doom. He massages his left bicep, where a calligraphic "F~H" scrolls across the forehead of a stylized, flowery skull. The letters were meant to signify "Forever in my Heart" as a tribute to Douggy, with her initials and dates down below, but as soon as the ink was set, it shifted in his mind to a label for himself. "Forever in Hell."

Mac tickles Aurie, and delighted giggles float up to his ears, ending the spiral into negativity. He forces a smile and shakes himself. All that doom and karma shit is prepandemic Gracen. Presuccess. Pre-Mac and Aurie. Present-day Gracen is—usually—in a much better place. Aurie's fall from the monkey bars last week is triggering a little relapse.

He bites his lip, calling his own bullshit. In truth, he'd been struggling since Mom's death a few months back. After he scattered her ashes, he'd discovered an old photo album hidden among the family pictures on the bookshelf downstairs. It tugs at him even now from its hiding spot in his desk, under a stack of miscellaneous equipment manuals.

Straightening, he knocks on the window. "Hello, down there!"

Down in the grass, Mac notices him and beams, nudging Aurie. "Look, honey! Daddy's up in the window!"

"Hi, Daddy! Zee-ba says hi too!" Aurie waves the stuffed gray horse that goes everywhere with her.

Her munchkin voice brings real warmth to his smile. "Hiya, pumpkin! Hi, Zee-ba! I'll come play in a few minutes!" He watches as they walk toward the play structure, then slides the window shut. What's all the money for if he can't enjoy time with his family? But social media is more art than science. The public can turn in a nanosecond, or worse, ignore you. Gracen's been in the game long enough to see some of the old guard flounder and sink, forced to find real jobs. Or to hide in their parents' basements, too embarrassed to show their faces as they wonder where the money went.

Gracen has no safety net, no parents to shelter him from bad decisions. He leans over the back of his cushy leather chair to close the browser where he'd been researching potential interviewees. Later, he'll continue, or tomorrow. He needs some family time.

But the photo album still tugs at him.

He'd never seen it before the fire that took Mom's life. Mac says it must have been there all along, tucked unnoticed among old textbooks and fantasy novels. Of course she's right. It must have been stuck in a closet in his last bachelor pad, in a box he never got around to opening. In the aftermath of Mom's death, it seemed to appear one day on their living room bookshelf in response to his grief. After the initial shock at its existence, he's found that looking at this curated slice of the past brings him some kind of peace.

Mac thinks his compulsion is not about peace but masochism, which is why he keeps the album out of sight. She claims Gracen is replacing his mom's hostility with the photos. That he's so fucked up, he needs to flagellate himself, to fill the hole Mom left in his life.

It's not that. He's just a guy who had zero record of his early family years until he found the album. Mom hoarded everything from before Douggy's death, and when Gracen moved out of the family home, he'd rebelled by taking nothing. When she moved into assisted living, he'd trashed the left-behind hoard out of sheer overwhelm. The photos are artifacts from a past he thought was lost.

When he'd first conceived of *The Ridpath Girl* as a limited series vodcast, he'd hoped organizing his thoughts about what happened to his sister would help him move on—and he needs to move on. Last spring, there had been an incident at the playground. Aurie yanked a toy away from another preschooler, and it wasn't dismay or embarrassment that Gracen felt, but deep-seated terror, as if she'd run into a busy street. He lost his cool and blew up at her, then bundled her back to the car as she kicked and screamed. If anyone had posted a video of that online, he would have been canceled. His overreaction equated normal little-kid egocentrism with death and doom, and even he could see that has to do with him and Douggy and the terrible things that happened to his family. It was time to pull the monster under the bed into the light, which turned into *The Ridpath Girl*.

Then Mom's death, so soon after he released the first episode, put the project on pause. He hadn't pulled it together until the New Year, but he'd been releasing the prerecorded content weekly since then. As of midnight last night, three episodes were in the world. His family, his town, his school—his and Douggy's. The fourth, "Tempted to Death," will tie them all together and bring the story to the brink of his sister's terrible choice. He's going to reveal everything he remembers, everything he knows.

So far, his attempt at closure hasn't freed him, but surely, that one will, though not everyone will appreciate it.

With a guilty look toward the window, he settles in his chair.

The photo album is in a style they don't make anymore, with a puffy vinyl cover and waxed white cardstock sheathed in plastic to hold the photos in place. The stickiness had long since dried out, and the photos stay put through force of habit.

He flips it open. Infant Douggy appears, swaddled in a white blanket with a white cotton cap on her head and a dark curl clinging to her forehead. "Melissa Rose Ridpath" is printed in gold cursive above her date of birth, years before Dad would coin Douggy's nickname. In the next, baby Douggy, maybe six months old, smiles toothlessly with a rakish purple clip in her silky topknot, gazing up at her big brother. Gracen's childhood self seems a stranger: his own gray eyes in a freckled face, under a crown of golden curls. The freckles have faded, the hair has darkened; only the eyes are the same. Maybe. The innocent boy looking out, before all the family troubles, might as well be a ghost. Just like Douggy.

He turns the pages slowly, drinking in each frozen moment. Lots of shots of Douggy on her own, at playgrounds and fairs and at home. Incremental growth through her first five years: haircuts, Band-Aids, tan lines, and T-shirts, as her features become more defined. Mixed in are pictures of the two of them. Aged five and two, at a Halloween party, he a cowboy and she a ladybug. Maybe two years later, holding puppets at a children's museum. And here, cross-legged in front of the Christmas tree the year before the dog bite, wearing matching Grinch pajamas in a nest of torn wrapping paper.

He spends the longest on the only photo with the whole family, the very last one in the album. They stand behind freshly carved jack-o'-lanterns in the kitchen of the house where he grew up. "Marjorie, Warren, Douggy, Gracen, October of 2006," according to Mom's neat cursive handwriting. Mom smiles wickedly, pointing a carving knife at the same jack-o'-lantern she made every year, with triangle eyes and a three-toothed grin. Dad, eyes red in the camera flash, has one arm over Mom's shoulder and his lips against her cheek. The pumpkin on the table in front of him has cartoon eyes and a wide smile. Douggy, next to Dad, beams as broadly as her pumpkin. Dad helped her make a cat face, triangle ears stuck on with toothpicks. Gracen, allowed to do his own cutting for the first time, holds the most disturbing pumpkin, with jagged holes for eyes and a mean, down-turned mouth. In the photo, Gracen's mouth is downturned too, his face flushed. The picture was taken about three minutes after he'd been coaxed back into the kitchen post-tantrum, enraged by his failure to make it come out the way he wanted.

Gracen stares at himself, wishing he could see into his long-ago heart. Wishing Mom had saved a family picture that didn't present him as a sullen brat. He'd been a happy kid, before everything.

He swallows. Then he flips through the remaining empty pages as if trying to find the rest of the story.

When he lets the back cover fall into place, it closes with a smack. Gracen looks up. The world has shifted darker while he's been absorbed, and there's a constant, steady hush against the roof. The rain has started again. He's lost his chance to play outside.

Later, in the night, he faces Mac in bed. A thin line of moonlight sneaks around the blackout curtain above their bed to stripe her nose and cheek. He strokes hair back from her temple, and she closes her warm hand around his. Her eyes gleam. "I'm serious," she says. "How many times did you weigh yourself today?"

Gracen's history of disordered eating means there are danger signs he needs to watch for, especially when he's anxious or stressed out. Mac thinks he's been both since his mom's death, but it's been years since there was a real problem. Mac and Aurie are the world's best motivation to stay healthy, so he does. Mostly.

He's not sure how she knows some of the things she knows though. She couldn't rig the scale to spy on him, could she? She's a law student, not a… He can't even imagine who would hack a bathroom scale.

He shrugs under the blanket. "I guess a couple." Less than he used to mid-pandemic, when he'd check and recheck after eating, after exercise, after sleep, because before and during Hot Mess, he was a mess.

Mac squeezes his hand. "You seem…tense. You still stuck on Aurie's accident?"

He hears "Douggy" instead of "Aurie" at first, and his mind jumps to her intact face in the photos upstairs. The Halloween photo was the last before the dog attack. Then his ears catch up. Mac's talking about Aurie's fall from the monkey bars, which sent him into a spiral. Embarrassing, in retrospect. "Aurie's great," he says. "I'm great."

Mac nods against the pillow, eyelids drooping. She doesn't usually stay up this late—she'd been working on a paper until eleven, and then they'd made love. "I love you," she murmurs.

"Love you too."

He watches as her breathing evens and she relaxes into sleep, then tugs his hand free to turn over and wait for his own descent. It doesn't come, and he's beginning to wonder about edging out of bed to get a snack—maybe a bunch of simple carbs to knock him out.

He's picturing himself opening the cupboards, the fridge, getting a glass of oat milk…and it segues into dream. The cupboards are deep and shadowed, full of everything he needs to hide. He's in the kitchen on Honey Street where jack-o'-lanterns flicker on the table. The door to the backyard is open, and the forest has overtaken the yard, full of vines and fungi and night-blooming flowers under the moon. He spies the tree house, a rudimentary lean-to Dad nailed together on a warped piece of plywood, and inside is Douggy. She's not like the photos but mushroom pale, huddled with bony arms wrapped around bony legs. A hole in her cheek reveals yellowed teeth.

Someone calls her name from below, and she turns to Gracen as if—

The hoarse scream tearing from his own throat awakens him. A high-pitched cry follows—Aurie! Aurie is in danger! He's up on his elbows, shaking, ready to fight—but a hand closes gently on his shoulder.

Mac comes into focus, cuddling their sobbing child. Gracen sucks in air, drinking in the mundane dimensions of the room around them. The roughness of his scream lingers in the back of his throat, and when he speaks, his voice is uneven. "Sorry. Nightmare."

"I figured." Mac releases him and strokes Aurie's back.

"When did Aurie come in?" He must have terrified her. He can't even remember her crawling into their bed.

"A while ago. Her cast was itchy."

Gracen fumbles to check the time on his phone. He'd swear he just fell asleep, but the glowing screen says two-thirty. "Sorry, honey," he says, laying his hand on the back of Aurie's head. Her sobs ease into the occasional hiccup, muffled by the stuffed horse she holds against her face. Mac shifts her gently to the mattress, then lies down with a sigh.

"Go back to sleep," she says.

Gracen relaxes onto the bed. He'd do anything to be able to delete the dream from memory, but the image of skeletal

Douggy hovers in his mind. Eyes wide in the darkness, he silently admits to his sleeping wife she was right. He has been anxious since the fire, since the photo album, and it's worse since Aurie fell. Binge eating and then fasting. Ruminating on all the ways Aurie could be hurt. Thinking more and more about Douggy's last days.

Mac wants him to talk with a therapist, but Gracen has a better idea. He transformed himself the first time, from stagnating loner to viral success, by sharing his crazy diet plans with the world when all he'd really wanted was to curl up and die.

Maybe *The Ridpath Girl* hasn't purged him of his obsession with his childhood yet, but if he pushes against his default urges, he could still transform again, from a man haunted by demons to one who's mastered his own past.

The only way out is through.

Mom's assisted living home in Meander has a few of her belongings in storage, but he's resisted every suggestion to pick them up, saying he'll do it when he drives over for his speaking engagement in the spring. But he has no intention of picking up her things or speaking at the school; he just hasn't figured out a graceful excuse yet. His instinct is to avoid Meander altogether—and that's exactly why he needs to go there.

Tomorrow.

Due to a death in the family, *Gracen Stays Home* and *The Ridpath Girl* are on temporary hiatus. Thanks for respecting my privacy—I'll get back to it soon. —Gracen

—Various platforms, 10 weeks ago

Sorry you lost your mother, but at least you know she deserved it.

—Comments section on Gracen Ridpath's Instagram

6

KIRSTEN

What? No!" The kid in the door speaks with nasal roughness and a touch of the East Coast edging the panic in their voice. Boston?

"You're not Samantha O'Brien?"

"No!" Adamantly. "What are you doing here? Where's Viveca?"

"There's been a problem." Euphemistic, but accurate. "I'm with the sheriff's department. Are you a friend of hers?"

"I live here," the kid says.

Behind me, Carrie's footsteps recede as she fades out of the living room. Eb's probably hovering out of sight too, waiting to see how I play this.

"Come on in. What's your name?"

"Quinn." They step in like a deer alert to the slightest danger. Their eyes are a warm light brown, darting through the room and landing on the banker's box with Viveca's laptop sticking out.

"Quinn. Sorry to spring this on you, but I need to ask some questions. Let's go into the kitchen."

Without a word, Quinn leads the way to the table, shrugging off their coat. The faded black hoodie underneath is mottled with splotches where the rain soaked through. Their fingers, barely protruding from the cuffs, are pale and bluish.

I sit opposite and pull out a notebook, then gesture to the body cam on my jacket. "I need to tape this, okay? Could I get your full name?"

"Quinn DeCelles."

"Thanks. Does Ms. O'Brien live here?"

"Not anymore. They broke up. That's why Viveca needed a roommate."

"They were a couple?" I kick myself. What is this, the dark ages? Eb and I hadn't considered Viveca might be gay. We got thrown off by the two-name, two-bedroom situation.

Quinn blinks. "Sam is—I mean was—Viveca's girlfriend. But when she left, she screwed her on the rent."

"She 'was' her girlfriend?" The past tense raises a prickle of suspicion. Quinn doesn't look strong enough to lift a rock, never mind overpowering Viveca, who'd appeared to be 160 or 170 pounds and in good shape. Quinn must be fifty pounds lighter, but rage or drugs or surprise can make up for a lot.

"They broke up," Quinn repeats, then startles when Eb's unintelligible voice intrudes from another room. Quinn crosses their arms low and tight, trying to hug warmth into themself or hold themself together.

Their vulnerability gives me an opening. "This must be upsetting, to find us here. Can I get you some coffee or tea to warm you up?"

"No." Their voice comes out in a near whisper. "What's going on?"

"May I see your identification?"

With a shaking hand, Quinn pulls a cell phone from a pants pocket and an ID card from the phone case. I snap a picture. On the card, their sex is marked with an X, the non-binary gender-code standard in Oregon as of 2017. The birth year is 2001, making them twenty-six. Shows what I know. I would have put money on nineteen.

I slide the ID back. Quinn stows it and sets the phone on the table. They meet my eyes, and I notice striations of gold in the brown. After a hesitation, they ask, "Where's Viveca?"

"A couple questions first. Do the sleeping bag and duffel in the small bedroom belong to you?"

Quinn nods.

"Do you have a vehicle?"

They shake their head.

"Where was your previous residence?"

"Portland."

"Oregon? Not Maine?"

A nod. I need to get them to relax. "You sound like you're from the East Coast. When did you move out west?"

"I lived back east for a while as a kid, but I moved to Portland over a decade ago." Quinn chews their lip.

I tease out that Quinn hitchhiked into Meander two weeks ago and saw the room advertised on Facebook Marketplace. Viveca put in a good word for them at Sunny's Diner, and they've worked there ever since.

Time to get to the hard part. "I need to ask what you did last night."

Quinn stiffens. "I worked the dinner shift. Got home around ten."

I study their face. Innocent people are often flustered by police questioning, but I'd love to know if Quinn's always this anxious. "Were you alone at the diner?"

"Aside from customers? I was on shift with Denise. I walked home by myself."

"And when you arrived, was Ms. Crandall here?"

"No. She told me she might be out late and I should lock up. She wasn't home by the time I left for work today."

With luck, Viveca's plans are in a calendar or planner. "Did she call or text?"

A flash of impatience crosses Quinn's pinched face. "We're just roommates. She doesn't update me on what she's doing."

Eb appears in the doorway and beckons me. "Excuse me," I tell Quinn.

In the living room, he speaks softly. "I tracked down Samantha O'Brien. She's moved in with her brother in Coos Bay. I found his place of work. They gave me his cell, but"—he shrugs—"no answer, no voicemail. I left a message. What's the story on this one?"

"Very...wary."

"You like her?" He means for the murder, not as a person.

"Not a her. And not sure. They seem too frail to be the killer, but they're kind of jumpy. Hard to imagine a motive, but we don't know enough yet."

"Murder for the bigger bedroom?"

I roll my eyes and return to the kitchen. Quinn is slumped at the table. When I pull my chair out, they startle as if awakening from a trance.

"Sorry about that. Just a few more questions. What can you tell me about Samantha?"

"Did Sam hurt Viveca?"

"Would you be surprised?"

"I don't know. I never met her. Viveca mentioned 'anger issues.' When I moved in, I noticed a dent in the drywall and offered to patch it. She said something like, 'Goddamn Sam.' I didn't ask more."

"Did you get the idea Sam was abusive?"

Quinn shrugs. "Vee doesn't seem like someone who'd put

up with that. But she mentioned they were together for a couple years. Like I said, we've barely talked. We work different shifts."

"You seem to know a lot about her."

"Most of that is from the day we met, when I looked at the room."

I set my pen down. "Viveca Crandall was found dead this morning in Dunwoody Park. I'm very sorry."

My announcement catches Quinn off guard. Their eyes widen and they look away, frowning hard before rubbing their face. A tattoo becomes visible as the cuff slides back on their left wrist. It's black and gray, winged: a butterfly or moth. I only glimpse it before they tug the cuff down.

Quinn asks, "Are you sure? It's definitely her?"

People always ask that. "She's been identified, yes."

"Oh," Quinn says in a small voice. They shrink even farther.

So far, their reactions seem sincere enough, but since the initial spate of anger at the door, they've been corkscrewing down like a leaky balloon. Homicide is almost always committed by the nearest and dearest, and as roommate Quinn was at least near. I change tack. "Were you sleeping with her?"

Quinn looks horrified. "No! No way." Their face flushes an uneven dark red.

"Was there interest on her part? Did you get the feeling that's why she asked you to stay?"

"No! That's not—She didn't 'ask me'—she advertised!"

Quinn's petite frame is upright again, their voice heated.

I nod calmly. "I have to ask these questions. No offense intended." Standing, I say, "Come on. Let's get you packed."

"What?"

I look back when they fail to follow. "You can't stay here. My team needs to finish up, and I imagine the family will be arranging to pack Ms. Crandall's things."

"But I paid for the month! You can't kick me out."

I push away pity and remind myself Quinn is not a kid, despite their appearance. They need some perspective. "You can't crash here anymore. Find another place to stay, and let me know where you end up. We may need to speak with you again." I hand Quinn my card, then continue to the spare bedroom. They trail after me and resentfully bundle their sleeping bag into a stuff sack and their clothes into the duffel, then retrieve a toiletry bag from the small bathroom.

I walk them to the front door, and Quinn turns to me there, thin skin blotched with emotion. "What am I supposed to do? I can't afford another place."

I dig in my pocket for a Victims' Services card. "If you have family or friends in the area, try them first. If that doesn't work out, call this number. Tell them I referred you. Victims' Services can find you a bed, but it will probably be in Polallie." At Quinn's blank look I clarify, "The county seat. Where the sheriff's office is. If that's what happens, text me and I'll send a deputy to drive you over."

Quinn's fingers feel icy when I push the card into their hand. "I can't stay in Polallie. I have to work tomorrow!"

I herd them out, then lean against the closed door, eyes shut.

"Docker," Eb says, and I have the sense it's not the first time. "Is she gone?"

I force my eyes open. "They're nonbinary, it's on their ID."

Eb lifts an eyebrow. "Fine. Are *they* gone?"

"Yes. Why?"

"O'Brien's brother called. She moved in with him a couple weeks ago and is looking for work in Coos Bay."

"Can he confirm she was there yesterday and last night?"

"Nope. She took off camping a couple days ago and isn't due back until the weekend. She wanted to go off-grid and get her head straight."

"Did you get her number?"

He shrugs. "Straight to voicemail."

I try to dredge energy with a deep breath. The inside of my skull pulses with an echo of this morning's pain. "Let's see if we can find anyone to corroborate a history of fighting, then get a ping request on O'Brien's phone. I've got a dent in the drywall with her name on it." I relax my hands, which have closed tight. Significant other is looking like a good fit.

Don't jump to conclusions, Sanchez reminds me. I flinch, annoyed. I can't keep taunting myself like this.

It's a good point though. I've seen a ninety-pound woman beat the shit out of her three-hundred-pound husband when she was pushed too far. It's too soon to rule out anyone, especially before we start checking alibis and hear back from Carrie and Gene. So far, the Persons of Interest board in the back of my mind has two names, Samantha O'Brien and Quinn DeCelles.

My sister had one friend at school—one little girl, as socially ostracized as she was. You'd think it would be sad to see them together—surrounded by all the so-called normal kids who didn't know what to do with them—but it was actually pretty great. I was jealous.

Unfortunately, it turns out, one wasn't enough.

—*The Ridpath Girl*, Episode 3: "A School of Bullies"

7
QUINN

Quinn stands with clenched fists on Viveca's front stoop, rain wending into their collar, duffel at their feet. That cop bulldozed them out of the house. If Quinn had a lawyer on speed dial, it wouldn't have gone down that way.

Of course, if they had money for a lawyer, they wouldn't have been staying here in the first place.

Quinn squeezes their eyes shut, then opens them again, an ache in their throat. Where they're going to sleep means nothing in the face of what's happened. Viveca is dead. Yesterday, chopping carrots, and today...gone.

Another thread of cold rain crawls down Quinn's neck, and they shiver. They can't process this standing in the drizzle. Quinn needs shelter, but if they call Victims' Services, it will be a struggle to find rides back and forth to Meander. More trips, more expense. If they spend a couple nights in a motel, they can make it to work easily and call around about room rentals, but they'll need money from Gramps.

Quinn squeezes their eyes shut as a cold knot binds their stomach. It crosses their mind—should they ask their mother for a loan instead? It's an emergency, after all. Quinn wouldn't expect her to offer a place to stay, but a hundred bucks isn't much to ask after years of neglect. But Quinn doesn't have a cell number for Sheila. They'd have to knock on her door and ask face-to-face.

Quinn can't do it. If by some miracle Sheila says yes, it puts Quinn in a worse bargaining position. Now, Sheila owes them the total value of all the parenting she didn't do, from the day she shlepped Quinn and Kade off to Gran and Gramps—emotionally, practically, financially. If she helps Quinn out, it lessens the debt. If she says no, Quinn will have humiliated themself for nothing.

Gramps won't say no. He never does. And this *is* an emergency.

They gnaw the inside of their cheek as they walk to the library, head down and lugging their bag, and request a private study room to talk out of the rain. Talking to Gramps is always tricky. When Gran was alive, she forbade communication with Quinn as soon as they moved out and embraced their identity. Gramps facilitated an underground relationship between Quinn and Kade, and Quinn loves him for that—but he never, throughout their childhood, defied Gran to her face with more than the mildest of protests. Quinn still can't decide whether he was a victim, an enabler, or a collaborator.

"Quinn! It's great to hear from you," Gramps says warmly when he answers. Quinn's heart melts before they force a mental step back. They can imagine forgiving him. But they can't depend on him.

"I need to access some funds."

"Of course." Quinn imagines the barest hint of an "I told you so" in his tone. He'd warned them a trip to Meander was a mistake. Sheila is his daughter, but he has no expectations that she'll help Kade when she never has before. But Quinn, who fled at eighteen, left Kade to deal with Gran on his own. Quinn owes it to him to help in any way they can, even if success is unlikely.

"My roommate was murdered. I have to find a new place to stay."

He's silent for a second. "Are you safe?" he asks.

"I'm fine. I paid for the month up front, that's all. I don't have enough to do that again."

"You have plenty," he says mildly. "Your grandmother left everything to me, and I'll be passing it on to you and Kade. Shall I mail you a debit card?"

Gran's money was conditional while she was alive, and Quinn suspects it will always carry that taint, even with the strings cut by death.

"No debit card. Can you please just wire me the cash?"

"Kath—Quinn. If that's what you need, then that's what I'll do. A thousand?"

"No! Just—" They calculate quickly, then bite their lip. What if they need a deposit on top of rent?

"Five hundred. Please."

Gramps is typing in the background, online already. After a moment, he gives them the address of the Meander 7-Eleven, where they can pick up the money.

"Thanks, Gramps. I'll let you know what happens with Sheila."

"Thank you, sweetheart," he says. "I talked to Kade yesterday."

Quinn braces themself. It hurts to hear about their brother secondhand, and they hate it. But it's all they have. When he graduated from high school, Kade wanted to move in with them, and they refused. Kade's never forgiven them. Quinn had good reasons—they couldn't support him financially through college, and they thought Kade was safe with Gran. He'd been her golden boy when Quinn left—athletic, smart, and handsome, he could do no wrong. If Quinn had known the truth of the pressure he faced from the woman who'd made Quinn's tween and teen years a living hell—well, they'd do it differently. They would do everything differently.

It seems unfair that Gramps is still in Kade's good graces, despite failing to stop Gram's increasing demands or Kade's gradual unraveling. But Gramps had been there and done what he could, and Quinn hadn't.

Quinn swallows. "How is he?"

"He's healthy. He says he's eating." There's silence.

"He won't respond to my emails." Quinn can't keep a plaintive note from their voice.

Gramps sighs. "Keep trying. He asked if you'd talked to Sheila yet, so he must be reading your messages."

The jail has an email portal where Quinn had registered for an account. They'd received a message back that Kade approved it, but that's the only sign he hasn't rejected them completely.

"I've got to go," Quinn says abruptly. "Thanks." They hang up in the middle of Gramps's "I love you," but they know he said it, and they know it's true. Quinn wishes it made more of a difference.

The Best Bet Motel's sheets have an inherent dampness, and the air reeks of mildew and roach spray. Quinn makes the best of it, standing under the hot water until it runs out, then watching cartoons until bedtime. Their exhaustion is so deep, they fall asleep during the new *Ridpath Girl* episode.

In the morning, they wake from uneasy dreams of Viveca and Douggy together. Douggy's insistent voice, carved in memory: *Sneak out tonight! I need you to come over.* The last thing she'd said to Quinn, ever. In dream logic, Viveca had been on the line too, whispering urgently that she needed help. Douggy's retort: "Don't bother. They never come."

Quinn clenches their teeth and gets out of bed. They throw on their uniform before walking out into the drizzle.

When they arrive at the diner, unsure how they'll make it through this shift, Denise is busy with a long-winded old couple. She gives a grateful smile. Quinn assesses the situation. Their shoulders go up defensively as they notice Alicia Finch, dressed in pale lavender, eyeballing them. Ms. Finch's menu is squared away on the table in front of her, and as Quinn looks, she pushes it farther away and raises her penciled-on eyebrows.

Reluctantly, Quinn approaches. "What can I get you today?"

"About time. Having a day, are you?" She shoots Quinn a look over her reading glasses, then sighs and picks up the large cell phone lying face down on the table. "Just get me a bowl of oatmeal and a cup of fruit salad. Make sure there's cantaloupe. And no grapes. Last time it was all grapes."

Quinn takes the order, then gazes down at the pink scalp. The fizz of nerves in their stomach remains, but the old woman's rudeness awakens an answering contrariness in them. Like Ms. Finch, Quinn doesn't really care what people think of them. And Ms. Finch, who spent so much time with Douggy in the school office, must remember her well. In *The*

Ridpath Girl, Gracen alleges that the secretary told his mother taking Douggy out of school would be better for everyone. Maybe Ms. Finch remembers it differently.

Quinn clears their throat. "Ms. Finch, do you think we could talk sometime, about when I used to live here?" Still hoping for privacy, they speak quietly, then remember Finch's deafness. "When I was a kid," they repeat louder. "When Douggy died." The diner seems to pause, but that's likely Quinn's paranoia.

Ms. Finch looks up shrewdly. "I imagine we could." Her hand rises to thoughtfully twist one oversize pearl earring. "I'll give you my phone number. Perhaps we can arrange a visit."

"Quinn, come on back when you get a sec." It's Sunny, poking her head through the swinging door.

Quinn nods to Ms. Finch. "Thank you. I'll get your order in."

In the back, they peek around the door to Sunny's tiny office, a closet with a desk and two chairs shoehorned in. Sunny, a big, brusque woman with coarse hair dyed blond and heavy makeup, looks up with brows knitted. Trapped behind the desk, she gives off the vibe of a large bird about to take flight. "Come on in. Close the door."

Quinn does so with a sinking feeling. The cops must have contacted Sunny to confirm Quinn's employment.

Sunny leans forward, hands flat on the desk in front of her. "I heard about Viveca's murder. Are you all right?"

The unexpected kindness fills Quinn's eyes with tears. They blink them quickly away. "I'm fine," they croak. What else can they say? Viveca is dead. Anything Quinn goes through by comparison is nothing.

"I doubt that," Sunny says firmly. "I doubt that very much." She sits back and looks at Quinn with lips pressed together. "You know, maybe one of the other servers told you. My son. He's twenty-one. He's autistic."

Quinn nods slowly.

"He's so smart and independent, but he struggles. Sometimes he doesn't know he's struggling because...you don't know what you don't know." Sunny shrugs. "He's on his own this year, for the first time. He tossed aside all his school plans and decided to travel."

Quinn's not sure what this is leading to. "I'm not autistic." The words come out blunt, startling Quinn, and they glue their lips back together.

"No, that's not what I'm saying," Sunny says. She's silent, looking at her hands. "I was just—you know. I recognize when someone is struggling and doing their best. What happened—Viveca's death—has got to be traumatic for you. Hell, it's traumatic for half the town. But you were living with her. I want you to take a couple days off."

Quinn's chest tightens. "I can't." Not without calling Gramps to ask for more money.

Sunny looks startled. "Why not?"

"I can't afford it. The cops kicked me out of Viveca's house. I can't afford a new place unless I'm working."

Sunny nods slowly. "Of course. How stupid of me. Do you have a place to stay tonight?"

"I'm at the Best Bet for now, but it's expensive." Cheap, for a motel—but higher than Quinn can afford.

Sunny taps a pen against the desktop thoughtfully. "I might know someone. Let me check. You go back to the motel. Watch TV, take a walk, whatever you like to do. Give me a few hours to see if it might work. And here—" She digs in the satchel hanging from the back of her chair, then holds out a couple fifties. "I owe you overtime, anyway. I don't want to see you again until Monday."

Quinn slowly takes the cash. "Thank you." They're not sure if they should protest more. If they should trust Sunny to solve their problem. But the specter of the online hunt for a rental, the difficult phone calls, the interviews—if Sunny takes that off their plate, maybe Quinn can rest for an hour or two. Maybe they can find a laundromat. Or sit and get used to the fact that Viveca's murder really happened.

Maybe they can glue their mind together so they'll be ready when Mom calls in response to the letter.

"Thank you," they say again and slide the money into a pocket.

Sunny waves them away. "Don't mention it. I'll text you later."

Quinn starts to leave but turns back when Sunny continues. "Quinn? It's going to be okay. This terrible thing—it will leave scars. But life goes on. I promise."

Quinn nods, feeling their throat close up again, and flees the office. They've already shrugged into their bulky black jacket when they remember—Ms. Finch's number. Out front, the old woman is digging into her fruit salad, but Denise beckons to Quinn before they interrupt her. "Ms. Finch gave me this for you. Are you heading home?"

Home. Their tiny apartment in Portland comes to mind, with tattoo designs covering an entire wall. But that's gone. They couldn't afford the rent and this trip too. An ache of homesickness runs through them.

Quinn nods, pocketing the napkin dotted with shaky blue numerals that Denise hands them.

Denise digs into the tip jar. "Half of this is yours. Take it. Take care of yourself."

It's not true. Quinn helped only one customer before Sunny called them away, while Denise has been running off her feet all morning. They accept anyway with a shaky "thank you" and flee before they melt into a heap of messy emotions.

Out in the rain, they hesitate, fingering the bills in their pants pocket. It's tempting, in the light of all the stress, to indulge in a treat. Something they normally wouldn't allow themself. A candy bar? Then inspiration strikes. Best Bet Motel isn't big on luxuries, but it does have one thing Quinn likes. Only it will need to be scrubbed like hell before they can use it. In the corner drug store, they buy a bleach-infused sponge for the tub, a packet of lavender-scented bath salts, and a single votive candle. All the motel needs to provide is hot water, and Quinn knows from their shower last night that there's plenty of that.

They're on their second tub refill, the smell of roach spray subsumed by lavender, when their phone rings. Hoping it's Sunny calling about a place to stay, Quinn fishes their phone from the pile of discarded clothes and sees the number is Sheila's. Quinn's heart leaps.

Sheila speaks before they can say hello. "Come tomorrow morning. Nine a.m., not before. I have half an hour, but that's it."

"Okay." Before they figure out what else to say, Sheila hangs up.

8

KIRSTEN

When the alarm goes off, my limbs feel heavy and flaccid, melted into the too-soft cushions of the couch. In the tiny downstairs bathroom, a frigid shower shocks me awake, and I dress before forcing a look in the mirror. My roots are coming in, but I can't seem to give a shit, and I brush my hair angrily before weaving a tight French braid.

In the cold kitchen I shovel leftover chili into my mouth while staring out at another miserable stormy day. Trav was in bed at nine-thirty last night when I got home. I kissed the sleeping kids before having a beer and stale corn chips in front of Netflix with the sound down low, turned to stone by exhaustion. I'd been too tired to turn off the lights and lie down.

Eventually, I must have.

Trav normally drops both kids at school on Fridays, but I wonder if I should make sure everyone's healthy before I leave.

Instead, I scrawl a quick note—X's and O's, and a promise to see them all at dinner. Then, without another look at the dark and quiet house, I slip out the door.

The wind dashes bullets of sleet against my cheeks until I'm safely ensconced in the car. I peer into the storm, preoccupied with the possibility of Fern having Henry's bug today, and Trav being furious that I've left him to deal again. I could have stayed home longer if I delegated the autopsy, and maybe I should have, but obsessing over details pays off. Anything Gene discovers, I'll know right away. Trav will be fine.

At the county hospital, I slam the car door and make my way through the shockingly bright lobby to the elevator, forcing control of my thoughts. No self-pity, no wallowing, no second-guessing what Trav is thinking and feeling and expecting me to do. For the rest of the day, I belong to Viveca.

By the time I'm buzzed into the small basement morgue by his assistant, Gene's already suited up. He flashes an apologetic smile. "I wasn't going to start without you. One of the kids has a school thing this morning. I'm hoping to make it."

I hurry into protective clothing, grateful he's the kind of guy who came in early to get this done. The previous ME would have delayed until Monday if he had so much as a game of golf planned.

"Let's get this done," I tell him, balancing to pull the elasticized bootie over my shoe. Gene has four kids, all adopted. If he doesn't flee back to Utah before spring, we've got to get him to bring the family to a get-together so I can finally learn their names.

I stand back while Gene and Jeff, his assistant, get down to business. Gene starts recording, stating Viveca's full name and describing her condition. When I was a baby cop in California, my first autopsy was the victim of a motorcycle crash. I white-knuckled it without vomiting out of stubbornness. I still use the same strategy, narrowing my focus to a tiny square.

Usually, it works.

I'm fine through the initial examination. When Gene and Jeff turn Viveca over, I concentrate on three stab wounds across her back. Two look deep. The third is a long, shallow slice. Based on the crime scene and my victim's height, I try to visualize how they were inflicted. I'm wondering if she was already on the ground, and I'm about to ask Gene about the angle of entry when déjà vu hits. Another body on the table before me, another woman's life wrenched away by violence.

Faith Sanchez, the nineteen-year-old newlywed, with her long dark hair ropy with mud. She'd been found half-submerged in a ditch under the wreckage of her bicycle. Perhaps we were meant to think it was a hit-and-run, but on the table, free of dirt and clothing, her body told a different tale.

Cold anger had driven me through the steps to her husband's arrest. Now, as I try to focus on Viveca, acid burns my throat, and my mouth floods with saliva. I turn my back on

Gene without a word because if I open up, bile will pour out. After backing out of the room, I rush down the hall to the ladies' room, where I sacrifice my breakfast.

If you have to vomit in a toilet, an industrially sanitized restroom is not the worst choice. I squeeze my eyes shut as if to wipe away the residue of the Sanchez case, then put myself back together and rustle up an old cough drop, sticky inside a waxed paper wrapping. After I rinse my mouth, I pop it in, hoping to overwrite the taste of bile. Then I eye myself in the mirror. "Keep your shit together."

The second stall over, reflected behind me, is closed although no feet show on the floor. I have a horror movie moment, imagining Faith or Thomas Sanchez in there, gloating over my discomfort—and flick the door open on the empty stall. It bounces closed again.

They were so in love, his mother's letter said. *We told them to finish college, but they couldn't wait to marry…*

I return and change into new protective gear, stomach still churning. I suck harder on my cough drop, feeling the menthol cool my throat.

Gene is still masked, but I read the concern in his eyes. "Guess I shouldn't have had that vending machine sandwich," I joke lamely. "Did I miss anything?"

His eyes crinkle. "I found fibers in her mouth and nose. In conjunction with the bruising"—he indicates the discoloration on the lower half of Viveca's face—"we're looking at suffocation as the cause of death, although the head wound would have been sufficient."

I narrow my focus again. "Three attacks: knife, rock, and suffocation?"

"The victim's back was to the attacker, who stabbed from above a couple times in succession, with a small-bladed weapon—maybe a folding knife, a switchblade, something like that. My assumption is she tried to get away. See that shallow slice? She evaded most of the force there. But she fell again and our attacker gives up on the knife, or drops it in the struggle, and whaps her with a rock. It was a single hard blow that would have stopped all resistance instantly. But her respiration continued, so the attacker pressed her scarf over her face."

He gestures to a cart where Viveca's clothes await processing. A fuzzy black scarf shot through with silvery thread is visible.

Gene asks, "Have you spoken with Carrie?"

I nod, staring at the scarf. Someone had wanted to make certain Viveca was dead—out of a need for certainty, or a sense of mercy?

He holds up a tweezer. I can't see what he's got, so I step closer and squint. "I found five of these on the cuffs of Viveca's jacket, and a couple on the knees and thighs of her outfit. Did she own a dog or cat?"

The hair is wavy, about three inches long, and coarse, of a beige or dun color.

"No, but she worked for a veterinarian."

"I'd tend to think the dog was at the crime scene, considering the crispness of the paw prints beneath the body. They had to be recent. Jeff's sent some enlarged photos of these hairs to Carrie to match up."

"Maybe Viveca knelt to pet the dog, and the attacker stabbed her from behind."

He drops the tweezed hair into a bag. "As far as I can tell, that fits the facts."

"Are you able to extrapolate anything about the killer from that? Dominant hand, strength, height?"

"I'd say right-handed based on location and angle of the wounds. Height might be in the same range as the victim, but don't quote me. Too many other factors." He glances at his watch.

According to the DMV, Samantha O'Brien is only a few inches shorter and a few pounds lighter than Viveca was—unlike Quinn. My hackles raise. I'll ask the brother later today if Samantha's right- or left-handed, if we haven't heard from her. So far, she's ticking all the boxes. Unless the field opens up or I learn something to the contrary pretty quickly, I'm going to be hunting in the wilderness.

9

GRACEN

In the early-morning gloom, Gracen and Mac bundle Aurie into her winter jacket, with Zee-ba tucked into the panda-shaped backpack. Mac is pale and irritable, but insistent; no way is he going to Meander alone. They drop Aurie at the home of their friend and frequent sitter, Jane, and Mac falls back to sleep as Gracen navigates through wind and freezing rain.

Mac hadn't asked what changed his mind about visiting Meander. Maybe she guessed it was the nightmare.

The wipers lull him into a near trance, then a gust of wind sends him hydroplaning into the other lane. He corrects with a jerk and steals a glance at Mac, who's undisturbed. He focuses on the road, the small farms and stretches of firs, but it's not long before his mind starts wandering again. Douggy and her "accident." Mom and her accident. In a disturbing parallel, each death had possibly been intentional. Mom resisted every action intended to prolong or improve her life. She would have smoked herself to death slowly, in the filthy, falling-down house on Honey Street, if he'd let her. For her to manage an escalated version in assisted living is a testament to her determination.

Even so, he can't bring himself to believe she meant to burn alive.

Two hours later, the rain has softened to a steady mist as they roll into Meander. Instead of heading straight to Wild Lilac Living Center, Gracen parks outside Sunny's Diner for a dose of caffeine.

Mac cracks open her eyes. "Are we there yet?"

"Almost. We're in Meander, but I need coffee first."

Mac rubs her face, then fishes her glasses from where she'd tucked them over the collar of her sweater. She puts them on and blinks into alertness. He slides his hand under her ponytail and rubs her neck. "Do you want anything?"

"I packed muffins and a flask of matcha, but I could use a restroom."

She breaks for the Ladies' while Gracen keeps his head down on the way to the counter. He's seldom been to town since moving away, but he can imagine what public opinion of him must be. They probably think he abandoned his mother, never realizing it was the other way around. And now, the horror of her death…

It's probably not fair to paint the whole town based on a few stray whispers, and he knows from the PTA invite that some people don't care about the past, but walking through the diner, he feels eyes on him. He can read their thoughts: *That's the loser with the dead sister. Did you hear he lucked into money?*

When so much misfortune rains down on a family, it means something, doesn't it?

When he raises his gaze to look around, the only familiar face is Sunny, who's owned the diner since he was a kid. She normally bestows perfunctory smiles to blood relatives and complete strangers alike. Now, however, she frowns at him.

"Did you say something to Bella?"

The question is nonsensical. He looks behind himself to see if she's addressing somebody else, but there's no one there. "Bella who?"

"My waitress."

Gracen shakes his head. "I didn't say anything to anybody. Could I just get a house coffee?"

"You like to shake things up when you're here, huh? Your little podcast isn't enough?" She crosses her arms, frowning at the swinging door to the kitchen, then grabs the pot and fills up his travel mug. "Three bucks. Have a nice day."

He bites down a retort and pays. It's his day to face things. The care home, his mother's belongings. Why not the opinions of Meander? He shouldn't be surprised to get blowback.

In the car, Mac digs out muffins for each of them. "Where to first?" she asks through a mouthful of whole wheat.

Gracen looks sideways at her. There is no "first." It's a one and only stop. "Wild Lilac. Where else?"

She shrugs, picking at her muffin. "Since we're finally here, maybe we could do some drive-bys?"

"Like what?" He has a bad feeling. His brilliant wife sometimes fancies herself his psychoanalyst.

"You told me you used to hang out at the library all the time," she says innocently. "I'd love to see it."

The library is the most innocuous location of his childhood—an easy yes, from a master negotiator. He looks at her suspiciously and starts the car. "It might not be open. Or it could have moved by now." Back then it was a haven a kid on a bike could reach on days when he couldn't stand the dreary loneliness of home.

"It's close to where you guys lived, right?"

Aha. There it is. "You want to see the house."

"I do."

"It might be gone. It was in shitty shape when I sold it."

"You can tell me how it used to be." She pins him with her vivid, dark eyes. "Unless you don't want to. It's up to you."

He blinks, exhales through his nose, then nods. "No. It's a good idea. After we're done today, I'm never coming back here again, so it's now or never."

In gracious recognition of victory, she smiles and squeezes

his arm. He appreciates her not gloating, but she ruins it by saying, "You're coming back for the school thing though. Isn't that in a couple months?"

Mac does not approve of flaking on things, but after Sunny's welcome, Gracen feels even more strongly about skipping the speech. He gives a noncommittal "Mmm," as he pulls into traffic.

The library is still in the same historic Victorian left to the city over a hundred years ago by a former mayor. Unsurprisingly, considering it's 8:30 in the morning, it's not open yet. When Gracen was a kid, it was run by Mr. Sheffly, a kindly man who allowed Gracen extra computer time and saved him first go at all the Rick Riordan books. Gracen wonders if he could possibly still be there. When they pull into the lot shared by the town hall and look through the rain-spattered windshield at the tall yellow structure, Gracen's surprised to find his throat closing up.

Mac grabs his hand. "Does it look the same?"

"Almost exactly." He thought seeing the place where he'd spent so many hours would bring back that mix of loneliness, self-disgust, and desperate hope that characterized the years after Douggy's death. What comes up instead is a memory of being here with Dad and Douggy when she was maybe three years old. Gracen picked out a stack of picture books a foot high, and when they brought them home, he read them to her haltingly, sounding things out. Summer Reading Program, he remembers suddenly. She squealed with excitement when she got a T-shirt from the library to match his.

After the dog bite, he'd come in alone to pick out books for her. She hadn't wanted to go anywhere for a while.

Mac squeezes his hand. "Is it okay though?"

He squeezes back. "Picture me sitting in there all by myself to avoid having to hang out with my unemployed drunk dad." It sounds way more bitter than he intended, so he adds, "No, it's fine. It was a good place."

She must read something darker in his expression. "Let's skip your house. One of these things is enough for today."

"No, we're doing this. Now or never. And seriously—it's just more of the same." More family memories, but they're already in his head. He lived in that house with his mother for years after Douggy died and Dad took off. He's got as many memories of driving home from his high school job at the movie theater and eating microwave pizza in his room as he does of the once-upon-a-time Ridpath family. They just don't have the same gravity.

When he swings into the familiar turn, the road is still rutted and potholed. Vic Dillard, the veteran who saved Douggy's life after the dog bite, passed away before the pandemic, his trailer replaced by a cutesy tiny home. The owner of the German shepherd across the street left after the attack, and the house sat vacant for years. Now, the lot holds a brand-new two-story house, complete with For Sale sign.

"Interested?" Mac nudges him, trying to lighten the mood.

"Be a bit of a commute, don't you think?" He doesn't tell her that's where the dog lived, the actual spot where he destroyed Douggy's life and much of his own. Mac's never heard the nitty-gritty details, and now is not the time. Holding it back feels dirty, but it's far from the worst of his sins.

He lets the car roll down the street. After Dad left, neither Gracen nor Mom did any upkeep. Mom seemed to want it to rot around her, to reflect her hatred of the present. When Gracen got a job where he could afford to rent a crappy apartment for himself and (barely) a crappy care home for her, he sold the house as quickly as possible and never looked back. Until now.

Someone has fixed it up. It's dark green instead of putty tan, with azaleas planted along the front. A low wooden fence has replaced the rusty, knee-high chain-link, and dog toys are strewn across the lawn. Lamplight glows through sheer curtains in the picture window.

"Which was your bedroom?" Mac asks.

He looks around, but there are no cars in this driveway and neither the house across the street nor the one next door show signs of life.

"Over there." Gracen points to the left corner of the house. He and Douggy had matching small bedrooms on either side of the bathroom, hers facing the backyard and his the front. He'd been jealous. At night when they were watching TV in the living room, his parents could tell if Gracen's light was on, but Douggy's was hidden because of the angle. He would get yelled at to turn off his light, but hers stayed on and they never bothered to check.

"I didn't realize you were living in the forest," Mac says.

Where did you think the mushrooms came from? he almost snaps and then checks himself. Mac knew about his family's tragedies before their first date, because she'd looked him up online—he'd found that most women did, these days, and he'd wondered a time or two if he should change his name. But Mac hadn't been one of the misfortune-groupies who picked over his sad story like vultures, and he takes a breath before he responds.

"Dad used to trim back the trees and blackberries when I was a kid. We had a swing set in the backyard, but we played in the woods too. There's a creek back there. A tree house."

Silence spreads through the car. Then Mac asks, "Do you want to knock on the door?"

He laughs. "For what?"

"Sometimes people will let you in." She shrugs. "I've done it. The owners were really nice."

"What am I supposed to say? 'Have you heard about the tragic Ridpath family who owned this house before you? I'm the only living member! Sure hope you do better here than we did!'"

Mac elbows him. "I saw that photo album. You've got happy memories here too."

"Right." A jagged retort begs to fly from his tongue. How can she not see they make it worse? The happy memories were lies, promising a happy future. A cruel mirage that dissolved into nothing.

He bites the inside of his cheeks. Sometimes, he can appreciate the better moments of his childhood as self-sufficient bubbles, beautiful and transient, unshadowed by befores and afters. With Mac and Aurie, he tries to grasp each moment, hoping to value them forever. Even after whatever sorrows the world has in store for them extract their pound of flesh.

His lungs feel shallow, tight, as if his chest is being squeezed by a fist. He starts the car.

"I'm sorry," Mac says.

"It's fine. Let's go."

The guy said, "Where are you?" and the babysitter said, "It's that girl's house who had her face chewed off."

—*The Ridpath Girl*, Episode 2: "A Town of Cruelty," 2 weeks ago

Not acceptable. People need to be taught a lesson.

—Comments section

10

KIRSTEN

Melakwa County funded a new building for the sheriff's department a few years back with a large space allotted to the detectives. Prior to that, we were cramped into the bullpen with everyone else. Being able to spread out still feels almost too good to be true.

The team—me, Eb, and Deputies Riley and Akina—gathers for a brief update. Thanks to losing my breakfast at the morgue, my stomach growls, and low blood sugar is making me growl too.

Riley sketches a timeline of Viveca's last weeks on the whiteboard. There are still too many unknowns, and we haven't identified a great candidate for whomever she was supposed to meet that night, or where. Riley and Akina will continue door knocking around Dunwoody Park and Viveca's neighborhood, but we're still waiting on information from her laptop and phone.

According to Carrie, there were no usable fingerprints from the park—unsurprising, considering the rain. But she shares an image of a pawprint that had been protected by Viveca's body.

"Between this and the hairs, can we identify the breed of the dog?" I cross my fingers, but even to me, it sounds a little Cinderella. Imagine if all we need to do to solve the case is check with local vets to see who owns what breed.

Carrie smiles wryly. "They're just not that distinctive—visually, we're not going to be able to give you more than a likely match. If you find the right dog, we can match DNA, if you're willing to spring for the testing…"

She also found frayed purple fibers on the trunk of the tree Viveca was under, which proved to be 100 percent nylon. Identical broken threads from the ground led her to believe the rope was sliced with a blade. Who knows how long they were there—anyone using the clearing could have tied a hammock or hung a tarp—but in tandem with the paw prints they support the idea of a dog tied to the tree. As a lure? If it were me, I'd leave my pup home, unless it was part of the plan.

Carrie moves on to close-ups of the fir fronds in the victim's hands. Their broken ends were dry, not freshly cut or torn; they were likely scavenged from the ground. They're the same species as most of the trees in the park, Douglas fir. The fronds are an over-the-top flourish on the bizarre arrangement of the body. I'm guessing regret—like, say, an ex-girlfriend might experience.

Together, we review the pattern of stab wounds, the scraped hands and knees. I chew my lower lip, imagining the killing as Gene and I discussed earlier. A blitz attack with the knife, stabbing wildly. Dropping the knife by accident, maybe when it skidded over bone. Did Viveca make it to her feet, or was she incapacitated enough to be crawling? In any case, the killer caught up to her and whaled a rock into the side of her skull—and Viveca fell, dazed or unconscious.

I swallow hard, imagining the sickening thwack, the sudden give.

I am not fucking going to throw up again.

"Kirsten?" Carrie nudges me. "You there?"

"Yeah. Sorry."

"It's a bad one, right?" she says sympathetically.

"Yeah." I shake it off. "This killer was desperate." I imagine a pause, while the killer caught their breath and felt whatever they felt—relief? Triumph? Or horror?

I recall my first view of Viveca with her colorful coat and the smooth drape of the fabric, like a woodland flower. Even with the weight of the rain, her clothes should have been rucked up as she was dragged into place. The killer must have smoothed the coat and the voluminous panels of the wide-legged slacks to hide dirt and blood and the tears around the knees.

I sigh. There's no way to be one hundred percent sure of any of this, but it helps to contextualize. Without locking myself in, I like to get a sense of who our unknown killer is and what they're capable of.

"Still nothing from the computer or phone? Or the car?" I ask.

"Nothing in the car from anyone other than Viveca, except a couple stray hairs. The killer either took extraordinary precautions or arrived separately. Our software couldn't get into her devices. I'll have someone deliver them to the FBI lab in Portland on Monday."

"Damn." Not that I'm convinced the answer is hiding on the computer, but it could be. Viveca could be a member of a dozen dating sites. Her email, her search history...we have no idea yet what she was into. In the Sanchez case, Faith had done multiple searches for "what to do when a customer won't leave you alone," and it was a former customer at the salon where she worked who eventually confessed.

I stand abruptly to break the familiar litany of thoughts. "Keep me posted." Eb follows me out for our scheduled interview with Viveca's bosses.

In the car, we unpack the facts again.

"Samantha's camping trip is still the most suspicious piece, in my mind," I say and pull up the veterinary practice on GPS. It's on the outskirts of Polallie, meaning Viveca had a twenty-minute commute each day.

Eb shrugs. "A big breakup makes you do funny things. I'm still interested in our little roommate. No record, but they're living under the radar for a reason. Hang on—Deputy Akina found something." He scrolls his phone. "Okay. DeCelles is enrolled at a tattoo school in Portland. Akina talked to the guy who runs the place. He said Quinn had a 'family emergency' and took off, even though he couldn't promise to hold their place. Sounded kind of peeved."

"Quinn said they had no family. How can you have a 'family emergency' with no family?"

"Right. They lied. Either to him or to us."

"To your previous point—the school means Quinn wasn't 'under the radar' though. They had some kind of life up there. Until they rushed off to Meander to live in Viveca's house."

"Maybe they came specifically for Viveca. To kill her?" Eb shakes his head. "We need to talk to Quinn again."

"Hard to believe they would have walked in on us at Viveca's home like that if they left her body in the park," I point out.

"Let's say they got Viveca to meet them at the park, then the two of them got into an argument. Quinn stabs her with a pocketknife and finishes her off in a fury. When Quinn stumbles on us at the house, they brazen their way through."

Nothing quite fits, but that's what this stage is for—brainstorming and poking holes in each other's theories. "If it was a chance argument, why would Quinn have lured her into the park? Viveca wasn't expecting to walk on muddy trails, not in those heels. And whoever she dressed up for couldn't have been Quinn, who was working. Plus, Viveca wouldn't have picked up the takeout. She would have waited for Quinn to bring it home."

Eb suggests, "Maybe they were making excuses to see each other. The excitement of a new romance."

"Quinn seemed shocked, even offended, when I suggested that." They also seemed too transparent to dissemble well. I try to imagine their slight frame stabbing frantically at Viveca's back and shoulder, and it won't come into focus. Anyway, if it is Quinn, where's the dog? I suppose they could have killed it. After killing a human, why not? I make a mental note to confirm we've checked dumpsters and trash cans near the park.

"Let's hope the vets will have some answers," I say as I pull into Viveca's workplace.

Over the phone, I'd learned Fridays are reserved for surgeries, and they only had one on the schedule. The place looks deserted, and the door is locked, but a woman dressed in scrubs lets us in and flips the light on in the lobby before excusing herself. A moment later, Doctors Celia and David Pope emerge from a hallway, both dressed casually in jeans and sweaters.

They're a sturdy blond couple in their thirties, him crewcut and blue-eyed, her with a bob and wire-rimmed glasses. They must have vacationed somewhere warm over the holidays to get that tan. We introduce ourselves and settle on the vinyl benches in the waiting area. Eb starts recording.

After offering condolences, I ask, "How long had Ms. Crandall worked here?"

David looks to Celia. "Five years, almost exactly," she says, straightening. "We'd just bought the business, and one of the original techs resigned. When Viveca interviewed, we knew she was a good fit. So warm and funny, but with a spine of steel. People get very upset at the loss of a pet or the cost of a medication or procedure. You need to be able to handle that."

"Did Viveca share much about her personal life? Do you know anything about her friends or a significant other?"

"Her best friend was Carlie," David says. "Every other story Viveca told was about the two of them as kids, but Carlie moved to Seattle last fall for a job. Viveca missed her."

"Do you know her last name?"

They look at each other and shake their heads. "Someone will," Celia promises. "They both grew up here, so just ask around."

"Anyone else? We don't know who she met up with Wednesday evening. Who else would she hang out with?"

David says, "Our crew socializes outside of work quite a bit, but it wasn't us."

Celia adds, "Just a few weeks ago, she spent all her free time with her girlfriend, Sam, but you must have heard they broke up? Viveca told us Sam and Rocky moved to Coos Bay."

I sit up straight. "Rocky?"

"Sam's husky. Poor Viveca, she loved that dog."

"What does he look like?"

She's taken aback by my interest. "Gray and white, with some tan. His most distinct feature is heterochromia—one blue eye, one brown."

"If we bring in a fur sample, would you be able to identify whether it's his?"

"I could confirm similarity, but that's it." Celia sounds apologetic.

Better than nothing. I arrange to have one of the deputies drop off a sample later today. Then I circle back. "What can you tell us about Sam?"

Celia smiles. "We all liked her. She was so good for Viveca."

"Until recently," David amends. Celia makes a face but nods agreement.

"What happened?"

"They were arguing the past couple of months."

Celia sighs. "Sam wanted to get married and have kids. And Vee didn't, not yet. She liked her independence. She wanted to travel."

"Did Viveca mention anything about the arguments escalating?"

"No. A time or two, we saw Sam snap at her. I doubt Viveca would have said anything, no matter what. She was loyal. When they broke up, all she said was they wanted different things."

"Do you think Sam has something to do with…what happened?" Celia asks, getting teary. "I can't believe it."

"We're still putting pieces together," I say. "Did Viveca mention anything about a new roommate?"

David nods. "She put an ad up on craigslist, I think. Or Facebook."

"Did she talk about this person at work?"

"No. She mentioned she'd found someone, but if she gave us a name, I can't remember."

"Does Quinn DeCelles ring a bell?"

They look at each other, frown, then shake their heads in unison.

I move on. "You mentioned there are customers who've gotten upset with the staff. Can you think of anyone in particular who seemed angry with Viveca?"

David grimaces. "No, no. I meant upset, not homicidal."

"When Mr. Kim's corgi died?" Celia prompts him. "I wasn't there," she tells me and Eb, "but he threw a dog bowl at Viveca. One of the ceramic ones with the heavy base. He was cursing up a storm. She had to threaten to call the police before he would leave."

"He came back two days later, with an apology and a gift certificate to Red Lobster," David reminds her. "Our clients are wonderful 95 percent of the time. The few issues we've had were someone having a really bad day. Nothing to hold a grudge over."

Celia grabs a tissue and dabs her eyes and nose. "This is so awful. I keep thinking there must be some mistake."

"Forgive me for asking, but you must handle pharmaceuticals. Have you had issues with missing drugs? Any thefts?"

David says, "No. Nothing like that. Everything's secured out of the public eye, and we have a trustworthy staff."

I nod sympathetically, then raise my eyebrows at Eb, asking if I've missed anything. He shakes his head. We both stand. "We'll let you get back to your day, but we need to speak to the rest of the staff." I pass them my card. "Have them give us a call on Monday."

"Thank you so much for your time. We're very sorry for your loss," Eb says. We shake hands and exit. Through the window, I see the Popes embrace.

Back in the car, Eb says, "Sounds like Sam could be temperamental."

"Yup." I reverse out of my spot. The rain is still coming down.

"But only Quinn DeCelles got the impression there was violence involved."

I'd noticed that too. "Viveca may have been more likely to let it slip with a near stranger than work friends. Let's find the bestie, Carlie."

"I'll put Akina on that. Maybe she can get the last name through school records." He taps his phone.

"We need to get the timeline filled in. And get the phone records ASAP. Maybe take Riley off—"

My cell trills with Travis's ringtone. I've been waiting all morning for him to reach out, and I hold a finger up to Eb. "Got to take this," I say and hit answer. "Hi, Trav, sorry I missed you last night. Everything okay?" My voice is conciliatory. "Henry feeling better?"

"Hang on," he says, then calls, "Wait a second! I'll be right there." I make out Fern in the background over the sound of tinkling music, probably a kids' show. Trav comes back, his voice cool. "Henry's fine. He puked once yesterday morning, took a nap in the afternoon, and woke up with a good appetite. Today, completely normal."

"Great. And you and Fern didn't pick it up?"

"We're fine."

"You get my note?"

"Yeah. Don't need to rush home for my sake though."

I pause. That sounded hostile, but I push forward. "I want to eat with you guys at least once this week. Should I bring pizza?"

"No. We won't be here."

My hackles go up. As lightly as I can manage, I ask, "Oh? Where will you be?"

"Dad's birthday is this week, remember? I'm going to bring the kids up for the weekend."

His parents live outside of Seattle. And he knows I remember, because we talked about this. It's been on the calendar for weeks. "We're going up next weekend. Together. That was the plan."

"Their old friends from California are coming up then. It makes more sense for me to take the kids now. I assume you can't go."

I bite my tongue. "Okay. I'll call the kids later this evening. You coming back tomorrow?"

"No. Sunday afternoon or maybe evening. My brother's family is coming too. I want the kids to have a chance to play with their cousins."

A family reunion with everyone but me. Great. Out loud, I say, "Drive safe."

He hangs up.

Eb shifts in the passenger seat. I say, "Looks like I have the house to myself this weekend. Can't remember last time that happened!" My tone is too perky.

Eb says, "Trade you. I'll be neck-deep in people. It's Cole's wedding."

"Oh, right." He's been sweating over a best man toast for over a month. "At least I can cover for you if anything comes up on the case. Wouldn't want you to miss your big moment."

"I'll give you a hundred bucks to fake an emergency right before the reception. Two hundred."

I elbow him. "You'll do fine." And I will too. I'll at least sleep in my own bed. Maybe a little extra peace and solitude will break my run of insomnia. When Trav comes home, I'll be well rested and caught up on the case, and we'll talk like adults. I can start untangling the mess I've made with him.

The queasy dread in my stomach warns me it won't be that easy.

11

GRACEN

Gracen pulls up in front of the Wild Lilac Living Center and parks next to the custom van used to transport residents on field trips. He keeps his eyes on the building, not wanting to glimpse where the shed used to be in the garden off to the left. He nudges Mac as she fishes for her purse. "Did I tell you I used to work here as a busboy?"

"Here?"

"This building used to be the nicest restaurant in town when I was in high school. People drove over from Polallie, especially on weekends. Sunday brunch was big. The job only lasted a couple months though."

She's found the purse and sits upright, ready to go out. "Didn't like food service?"

Gracen snorts. "I liked it fine. There were good tips. No, I humiliated myself so bad I had to quit." Talia Parrish was a cute sophomore, far out of his league as a freshman. They worked the buffet table together, setting up and refilling everything from ten to two every Sunday, then breaking it down again. Week after week, he made her double over laughing by making fun of the customers, until one day, while she was still stuttering with uncontrollable giggles from his last joke, he asked her out. It was like hitting mute, and her eyes went round as buttons. He said, "Just kidding! I wasn't serious. I have a girlfriend, sorry."

Gracen quit the next day. He cringes, telling Mac. Poor, idiotic him. It took years before he allowed himself to get seriously interested in a girl again. Not until Celeste, that first semester at university, before he dropped out. She'd been out of his league too—but she'd returned his feelings. For a while.

Mac kisses his cheek. "You've come a long way. Usually you only embarrass me."

He rests his head against hers. Why spare a thought for the Talias and Celestes of the past when he had Mac? She must have forgiven him for his snappishness, despite the silence that's prevailed since Honey Street. "I'm not sure I want to go in," he confesses.

She pulls back and studies him with concern. "Do you want me to do it?"

Now he looks around, if only to avoid her eyes. Even in the winter gloom, the place looks good: the huge lilac-painted house with purple-and-gray trim, the grounds with wide accessible paths, landscaped with shrubs and grasses that withstand the winter cold. A lot of that prettiness is thanks to Gracen. After the restaurant closed, the building had briefly been a bed & breakfast and lost money fast. After that, as an assisted-living center, it had limped along. It was an understaffed dump when he moved Mom in here, but all he could afford. Even after the house on Honey Street sold, he'd needed a second job to finagle the payments.

When *Hot Mess* started making serious money, he proposed moving her somewhere nicer, but she'd recovered enough spine to refuse. To salve his conscience, he poured money into Wild Lilac so it could become what it is today: a boutique sanctuary for those who need close access to a nurse but still value independence.

If he'd gotten better advice, maybe he would have bought the place and hired a manager—but he hadn't wanted to. His conditional donations had allowed him to rationalize leaving Mom alone, which they both preferred.

Mac elbows him.

"I'm going. Just...give me a sec." One last breath, and he climbs from the car. The fresh air feels good on his face, but under the clean green scent, he imagines he can smell smoke.

Mac joins him and leads the way. "Come on. It'll be fine, I promise." She opens one of the double doors and gestures for him to precede her.

Gracen's mouth is dry. He takes a shaky breath and follows Mac into a small parlor, furnished with dark wood pieces that may or may not be antique. A set of French doors leads into the game room, and the manager's office is through a door to the right. A framed sign reads "Visitors, please ring bell!" Before they can, Laurel, the manager, steps in from her office.

Gracen hadn't warned her he'd be coming today, and dismay flashes across her austere features. She hides it quickly behind a professional smile with a hint of sorrowful sympathy. "Mr. Ridpath, how nice to see you."

He winces. "It's just Gracen, Laurel. Please." When he'd been in the habit of calling to ask how Mom was doing, she always called him Gracen, but in the aftermath of the fire, she's become much more formal.

Mac shakes Laurel's hand and says, "So nice to meet you again. I doubt you remember me. I'm Mac, Gracen's wife. Sorry it's taken so long to come for Marjorie's things. We haven't been this way in a while."

"Oh, yes!" Laurel cheers up. "You said you weren't interested in her clothes or furnishings, so we donated those as you asked, but there were some items I thought you might want."

Gracen pictures the dumpster he'd rented to clean out the Honey Street house. Douggy's toys, clothes, artwork, and schoolwork from birth to eleven, plus Gracen's own crap, and the detritus Dad left behind when he slunk away.

"Very kind of you," Mac says, when Gracen fails to respond.

Laurel lifts a banker's box off the radiator behind her desk and sets it down in front of them. "Well, it's not a lot. But someone was digging in the art closet for colored pencils last week and discovered Marjorie's sketchbook. I'm sure you'll want that. She was getting quite good."

Gracen peers inside the box. Knickknacks and jewelry are jumbled together with a few old books and something knitted. A stack of framed pictures and photos, 8x10s and 5x7s, leans along the inside edge.

Mac says, "Pictures?" and peers over his shoulder. Gracen flips through and spots some decorative prints from the old house, like a stenciled pineapple and a watercolor of a seaside scene. He recalls hurrying a tearful Mom through the house to pick out a few things to bring to her new home and feels a rush of shame. He could have shown a little more patience, but he'd been hurt and angry. Frustrated that he had to build his life around her inability to get past her grief. No wonder she'd ended up with random decorations in her belongings.

He knows without touching it that the knitted thing is Douggy's baby blanket. That's going straight in the trash.

He feels sick, but this is good, this is why he's here. It's the pain of drawing out a splinter. "No photo albums?"

Laurel seems disconcerted. "Oh dear, I didn't find any in her room. But now that you mention it, your mother did have some photo albums she liked to page through. I'm not sure where they could be. Unless... Oh dear."

He reads the rest on her face. Unless Mom had them with her in the fire. It was possible, since his mother dragged her wheeled oxygen trolley with her into the garden shed that became her crematorium. The trolley had a carryall for her purse and other belongings. "Was there more than one album?"

"I assume so, but I don't know for certain. Marjorie liked to sit by the patio window in the game room and flip through the pages on her own. If you interrupted her, you were liable to get barked at!" Laurel laughs nervously.

Gracen exchanges a look with Mac, who asks, "Can we check the game room? Make sure nothing got overlooked?"

Laurel glances at a slim, bracelet-style watch. "There may be a couple of residents in there now, but that shouldn't be a problem."

In the game room, a twentysomething man with Down syndrome is working on a puzzle at one of two round tables, and beyond, near a large-screen television, an elderly man naps in an armchair.

"That's where your mother liked to sit," Laurel says. "We need to check that bookshelf, but I don't want to wake Tim."

"We'll wait." Mac smiles reassuringly.

Gracen wanders over to look at the puzzle, which is circular. The outer rim of white has been completed, but so far, nothing but tiny patches of color show within. The young man lifts the top of the box off a nearby chair to show Gracen. "It's all kinds of dogs," he says.

"Cool. Looks like a tough one." Gracen respects people who have the patience for puzzles, but he never has.

"It's only five hundred fifty pieces. I did one that was a thousand pieces, even though they were small. And my friends helped. I like this one because it has dogs."

"What's your name? I'm Gracen."

The man puts the box top down and holds out his hand with a wide smile. "I'm Davy. My name is David, and my friends call me Davy."

Gracen shakes his hand. "Good to meet you."

Laurel and Mac head toward them, empty-handed. "I see you've met Davy," Laurel says. "He was good friends with your mother."

"Really?" Gracen hadn't considered his mother capable of friendship.

"Davy's a charmer," Laurel says warmly. "Davy, Marjorie was Gracen's mother. He stopped by to pick up some of her things."

Davy's face turns serious. "Marjorie burned in the fire. I miss her."

That's the most sincere statement of loss anyone's uttered for Mom. Gracen hasn't been able to be that unambivalent, himself. "She was lucky to have you for a friend," he says.

The young man nods seriously. "Marjorie had lots of friends. Everyone here is my friend, and Marjorie's friend, and she had more friends too."

Gracen looks quizzically at Laurel, who says, "Do you mean her visitors, Davy?"

Davy nods, but he picks up a puzzle piece and tries to fit it along one edge. "Hang on. Hang on. Hang on," he mutters. When the piece slides in, he says, "Yes, got it!" and pumps his fist.

Laurel says, "Great! We'll say goodbye now. Enjoy your puzzle."

Gracen echoes, "Goodbye, nice to meet you," as Laurel leads them away.

"Bye!" Davy calls without looking up.

"What visitors?" Gracen asks Laurel. He can't begin to imagine. Maybe someone from one of the jobs she'd had when he was a kid?

Laurel closes the French doors behind them and says, "Davy's been so upset about Marjorie's death. All of us felt her loss, of course, but the fire still gives Davy nightmares. The puzzles help him manage his emotions. If you'd like, I can find the visitors' names for you. There were a couple in the months before she died. She'd been so adamant she didn't want to see anyone, but when it came down to it, she was rather grateful."

Gracen's not sure if that's a jab at him, but if it is, Laurel must have blocked out all the breakable items Marjorie threw the last time he tried to visit. He supposes he's glad his mother wasn't completely friendless. He's not sure why a level of hurt is sneaking through, but it must show on his face because Mac takes his hand.

Laurel opens a guest book on her desk and points to the current page. "Here, I should have had you two sign in, do you mind? Then we'll look back to find those names for you."

Gracen and Mac comply, then Laurel flips back through previous pages. "Let's see. It must have been around the Fourth of July that the gentleman came, because your mother was arguing with Fawn about fireworks."

She flips more slowly. Gracen sees she's almost reached the end of June 2026. He asks, "Do you remember what he looked like? Or how he knew her?"

"He was a hippy-looking fellow. Weathered, with a ponytail and beard and such. Nice-looking though. Good head of hair for his age!"

"How old?" Mac asks.

"Your mother's age, roundabouts? I'm only guessing. Oh, here we go. This must be him." She titters, then puts her hand over her mouth. "I'm surprised I didn't catch this at the time. Not that I'm checking IDs, but I would certainly have commented."

"What is it?"

"He put down Willie Nelson, like the musician. Not an uncommon name, I suppose. It's just the combination. I never noticed!"

"He wasn't the famous Willie Nelson, then?" Mac asks with a smile.

Laurel laughs. "I wish! I'm not a huge fan, but it would be fun to have a celebrity visitor. No, this man was tall and stout. The thought crossed my mind that he'd played football when he was younger, or boxed."

There's no field for phone number or address in the book. Gracen shrugs. "I was just curious. Surprised she had visitors I didn't know."

"Yes, of course. It's only natural."

"You said there was another one?"

Laurel flips forward again. "That started more recently. The gentleman—Willie!—he only came once. But the young woman came several times. She sat with your mother in her room. I think her name was Melissa?" Laurel flips pages, running her finger down the "Guest of" column for Marjorie's name.

Gracen's heart stutters. Melissa was Douggy's real name. Of course, he's met other Melissas, but it's odd to hear in this context. "Did she say how she knew my mother?"

"Here it is. Melissa Smith. She was a nice-looking girl. Big-boned, you know, and with those piercings they like these days. But pretty." Laurel points down at a line in the guest book where a loopy scrawl overflows the line top and bottom. "She said she was a friend of yours. Or a friend of the family. Something like that."

"Do you remember how old she was?" Mac breaks in.

"Young," Laurel says definitively. "Mid-twenties. And very nice."

Gracen shudders as if someone's walked over Douggy's grave.

Mac drives on the way home. She tries to start a conversation but soon gives up and puts in an earbud to listen to something. Gracen stares out the window.

He doesn't know what to feel. The catharsis he hoped for hadn't come. Going to the house and then the care home blew his emotional sensors.

When Mac stops the car, he's startled to see they're in Corvallis already, but the house in front of them isn't theirs. Heart lifting, he realizes they're picking Aurie up. She's exactly what he needs right now. "I'll get her!" he says, unlatching the seat belt. "Be right back."

Mac calls out behind him, but he doesn't catch the words over the door slam.

When Gracen knocks, Jane opens the door immediately. She must have heard them drive up, because Aurie's on the little bench near the front door, working on her shoes.

"Gracen," Jane begins, but he's got eyes only for his little girl.

"Hi, pumpkin!"

"Hi, Daddy! Look at my pants, I ripped-ed them on the nail."

Gracen's glance falls to Aurie's knee, where gauze shows through a gaping hole in the fabric of Aurie's leggings. Gracen's stomach flip-flops, and he turns on Jane.

She throws her hands in the air defensively. "Didn't Mac tell you?"

"Tell me what?" he growls.

"Aurie hid under the back porch during hide-and-seek and got caught on a nail. She was so brave! She got three stitches, and she watched the doctor the whole time, didn't you, Aurie?"

"I did, Daddy, an' I wanna be a doctor—" Aurie continues, but Gracen's fixated on Jane.

"You let them play under the porch?" He can only imagine what else might be under there. Black widow spiders? Snakes? Rat poison?

"I'm so sorry," Jane says. "I came running as soon as I heard her yell. I never thought any of the kids would go under there. Willow freaks at the sight of spiderwebs!"

Gracen grabs Aurie's backpack and her uncasted arm, hard enough for her to protest. "Ow, Daddy!"

"We're leaving," he tells her without another word to Jane and marches through the front door. He nearly runs into Mac, who's on the walk, reaching for the knob.

Gracen pushes past, dimly aware of Aurie's protests and Mac's conciliatory voice behind him. He straps Aurie into her car seat, almost blind with rage, then jerks the driver's door open and reaches for the keys in his pocket. They're not there, and he pats himself down before remembering he's a passenger on this ride. He clenches his teeth, staring down at the seat. Mac's still inside Jane's, the door closed behind her.

Face hot, he walks to the passenger door and lets himself in. Aurie says nothing but sniffles theatrically.

After a minute, he asks, "You okay, honey?"

Another sniffle. Then, "You pulled my arm! My sneaker's not closed, even!"

"I'm sorry, Aurie. Daddy's mad but not at *you*."

"Well, I'm mad at *you*."

When he glances in the rearview, her lips are pouted, eyes narrowed. Gracen leans his head back, closes his eyes. His heart is still beating too fast.

Mac's footsteps approach. Gracen keeps his eyes shut. Her weight settles in the car, and the door shuts with a calm thunk. The engine starts. As she pulls into the street, Mac says, "Willow and Jack and Jane said bye-bye, honey, and they'll see you soon."

"Okay," Aurie replies. "Daddy's mad."

"I noticed. Everyone gets mad sometimes, and sometimes it's hard to know what to do when you feel upset."

"Yeah," Aurie agrees. After a minute, she says, "I was mad at Daddy, but I think I'm not now."

Gracen opens his eyes. His heart rate has slowed somewhat. "Thank you, Aurie," he says. "Daddy's sorry." They're already at the walnut tree marking the turn for their driveway.

Mac glares at him. "Daddy might want to go for a walk when we get home," she says. "So he can calm down."

Of course she's taking Jane's side. He'd known she would. What's a few stitches, after all? Or lockjaw? Why not add in a concussion? Maybe Jane should take Aurie deep-sea fishing without a life jacket next time.

He bites back the words. A walk might be good. As a matter of fact, a run sounds great. He hasn't been getting enough exercise, and if he pounds his thoughts into order, Mac won't be able to steamroll him when the time comes to talk this through.

"But it's raining, Mommy!" Aurie says.

The car stops. Gracen steps out into the driveway. It's just a light mist, cooling his overheated face, and he pauses, breathing the fresh, cool air. Mac wordlessly unbuckles Aurie from the car seat, and the two walk past him, Aurie looking back with brows knotted in concern. Gracen smiles, and she smiles back.

He follows them in, noticing a piece of lattice along the side of the porch is askew. The shrub in front of it, some kind of squat evergreen thing with prickly branches, is also looking sad. It rings an alarm bell in his mind. The wood shouldn't be rotting yet—the house is only ten years old, and everything checked out when they bought it a few years ago.

Home maintenance hasn't made it to the top of his and Mac's priorities. Could they have termites? How do you get rid of termites?

He makes a mental note to look it up online later.

Mac and Aurie are in the kitchen, Aurie chattering away about her adventure in the "me-mergency" room. Gracen trots upstairs to change into shorts and a long-sleeved tech shirt. He can't find his running shoes and remembers he left them on the porch to dry last time he ran in the rain. Chances are, they're wetter now than when he left them out.

In stocking feet, he heads back outside. The mist has intensified into fat, cold drops, falling steadily, but he's committed. He lowers himself gingerly onto the wet bench and reaches for the shoes.

As he picks up the first one with a finger hooked under the tongue, something unexpected rolls within. A rock? Or maybe Aurie stuck something in there as a joke.

He dumps the object into his palm. It's gift wrapped far too neatly for Aurie to have done it. A gift? Here he is, getting ready to run off his temper—and here's Mac, undermining him with a present. Strange place to put it though. He hasn't been running much with all this rain. It could have been weeks until he found it. Or maybe that was the point, a hiding place until she retrieved it at a suitable time.

He cradles the small package in his hands. It fills his palm, round and heavy, wrapped in silver. Red ribbon cascades from the top in tiny scissor curls. He checks for an attached card, then looks in the other shoe. Nothing. He tugs at the wrapping, at first delicately, and then with a swift rip.

In his hand is an exquisitely shaped dolphin of blue glass, leaping out of the waves.

He looks at it, perplexed as to why Mac would give him such a thing, but shrugs. He'll find out later. He sets it on the bench and takes off into the everlasting rain.

12

QUINN

Quinn had been sure the slovenliness they remembered from childhood would show up in some way in Sheila's house, but the interior feels spacious and clean. Maybe Sheila pays a maid. Sunflowers are everywhere—on throw pillows and refrigerator magnets and even the wall clock. Sheila reminds Quinn of a dried sunflower herself, leggy and overly tanned, with crow's feet around her blue eyes and blond hair with expensive-looking highlights and lowlights. The substantial diamond on her ring finger pokes out like a weapon.

Quinn shifts on the cushion tied to their kitchen chair while Sheila makes coffee. The time limit, reiterated as soon as Quinn entered at nine, ticks closer.

"Thanks for agreeing to talk," Quinn says. Sheila's back is to them, her movements agitated as she sets cream and sugar on a tray.

"I didn't have a choice, did I?" Sheila says, turning. Her lips are tight as she approaches, clutching her tray as if it were about to escape. "I'm not even certain you are who you say you are, although I don't know why you'd lie." She studies Quinn like a potentially cancerous mole.

Despite the adrenaline zinging through Quinn's limbs as if they were about to take flight, Quinn looks back calmly. They have no doubt that Sheila recognizes them, despite the changes time has wrought in Quinn's bonier, grimmer face. "If you don't feel safe around me, I'm happy to talk in a public place. Maybe you haven't heard, but my roommate was murdered yesterday, so I get it if you want to be careful."

Color drains from under Sheila's tan. "You were staying with Viveca Crandall? I heard—but I—"

Quinn speaks over her. "And don't worry. I don't consider you to be my mother anymore. I'm sorry you felt forced into this meeting, but I need you to listen." Their heart beats so hard against their ribs, Sheila must hear it.

Abruptly, Quinn remembers being nine. Mom, pale and frightened, sat on the mangy, torn sofa in the old house. Douggy and Quinn had played in the woods all day. A long cold snap froze the creek after a wet autumn flooded parts of the forest into a marshland. The kids had skated in their sneakers through a magical landscape, trees and brush encased in glittering ice under a shining blue sky—until Quinn broke through into shallow but frigid water and foundered in the mud and broken ice. Douggy had been heroic, grasping their hands and yanking hard, yelling, "Get out, get out!" as if the two were stranded in Antarctica with no supplies instead of fifteen minutes from hot baths and cocoa. Sheila's face, when Quinn stumbled home filthy and shivering, was as pasty as if she were looking at a future where her child never returned.

Sheila sits heavily, taking one mug for herself and pushing the rest of the tray halfway across the table. Coffee sloshes from the mug intended for Quinn.

Quinn ignores it, swallowing, their eyes on Sheila.

Sheila says, "Kathy—"

"Quinn."

"Fine. I relinquished parental rights to your grandparents. And you're an adult. I can't imagine what you want."

"I'm sure you can. Gramps said he told you about Kade. Before you hung up on him. And blocked his number."

Sheila flushes. "He passed along that Kaden has a request. I didn't care to hear any more."

The distaste in her voice brings Quinn's temperature up. They swallow the angry words poised to launch from their mouth. Kade needs Sheila, or at least his lawyer thinks it might help, and he deserves her attention this one goddamn time. Quinn will be as strategic and diplomatic as necessary to get Sheila to make one tiny fucking effort.

They'd known it wouldn't be easy, but they'd braced for tears and deflection. Not this seething woman with a gold-star chore chart on the fridge and a blown-up portrait of two replacement children hanging over the fireplace. She seems as enraged with Quinn as Quinn is with her.

When Quinn speaks, their voice is so small, so soft, it could emanate from their childhood self. "Why did you send us to *her*? How could you?"

Sheila stares at them, nostrils flaring. Her eyes dart to the sunflower clock, and she sighs, this time loudly. "Look. You were too little to remember—maybe you've painted some nostalgic picture. But you weren't happy here. It wasn't just being poor, although that was bad enough in a town like this. People were awful to us. You were miserable and lonely at school, and Douggy was your only friend. You needed a new start."

Sheila's avoiding the "*her*" piece that's been a burr in Quinn's mind for the past dozen years. Sheila knew Gran was abusive and Gramps enabling. She grew up with them and experienced it for herself—she'd fled from them! How could she consign her own children to their care? And Meander hadn't been that bad. It had been home.

Quinn bites their lip, staring at Sheila. Sheila stares back, chin raised—but as the silence stretches, she looks away.

Another flash from the past—Sheila passed out on the couch, Quinn and Kade pretending she was a sleeping dragon while they built blanket forts around her. Quinn remembers keeping the front door chained shut, talking through the crack, claiming Mommy was sick when the carpool lady came to pick her up for work. Making frozen peas in the microwave for Kade's dinner three days in a row because that's all that was left, while Mom smoked on the couch in front of the muted television.

Maybe it was no surprise that when Douggy died, when the Ridpaths were suddenly no longer a haven of support for the kids but another quagmire of grief, Sheila had been overwhelmed. But she'd sent them to *Gran*. And then (Exhibit A, one sunflower-themed house) she'd pulled herself together. She'd had weeks, months, years, to reunite with her children. And she never had.

Last night, Quinn rehearsed their lines over and over, and they yank themself back on point. "This is the first time Kade ever needed anything from you. The least you can do is write a letter of support for the court. It could make a difference of literal *decades* in his sentencing. You sent us to Gran, knowing how she was. This situation is your fault." *And mine.*

"Your brother killed her! He's violent, like your father was. I cannot, I just cannot—" Sheila's chest heaves. She looks startled by her own outburst.

Quinn stares at her. It's been so long since they thought of their father, but Sheila's words conjure up the gritty floor on their cheek as they lay in darkness under their childhood bed, pulse echoing through their body. Watching the line of yellow light under the bedroom door for Daddy's boots to pass safely by. That had been long, long ago, in the time before Sheila fled to Meander without him.

Quinn's throat tightens. "Kade is nothing like that. Which you'd know if you were any kind of parent."

Sheila clamps her mouth shut, lips bloodless. She looks at the clock again and swallows. "Do you know Gracen Ridpath? Are you in touch?"

Quinn looks at her sideways, startled. "Why?"

"The podcast about what happened to Douggy. My husband can't know I was— He can't have bad publicity. If you can get Gracen to swear that nothing about me, nothing even remotely recognizable, gets shared—I'll consider helping you." Quinn sees her throat work as she swallows.

Quinn blinks, confused by the shift. "Gracen hasn't been naming—"

"Yet. But there's going to be a book, maybe a movie. I heard it on some morning show. He's going to do whatever pays, just like everyone else."

Quinn swallows down bile. There's nothing on any reputable site about a *Ridpath Girl* book or movie deal. But even if the rumors are true, why would Gracen listen to Quinn? "I—"

Sheila shakes her head and stands. "I need to get ready. It's time for you to leave."

The sky is still a woolly gray, but the rain has stopped. Quinn squeezes their hands into fists as they walk, reliving the conversation, but gradually, their mood starts to lift. Sheila's ask is not so terrible. So far on the podcast, there's been a brief mention of "Douggy's only friend," but no reference to Sheila or Kade. Quinn hates Gracen's reinterpretation of the past, but he claims he's sharing Douggy's story to help people, and Quinn can't see how naming their mother would help anyone.

Quinn takes a breath, eyes on the treetops against the silvery sky, and dares to hope. Sheila may not feel a responsibility toward Kade—although Quinn would swear they glimpsed real pain, real guilt, somewhere in there—but she needs, or thinks she needs, something Quinn may be able to get.

And Quinn has a lead on Gracen.

Viveca and her PTA connection are now out of reach, but there's another link to childhood—Ms. Finch. She'd been the school secretary. Maybe she knows PTA members connected to Gracen's upcoming event. Quinn slides their hand into the pocket of their parka and finds the crumpled napkin with Finch's phone number.

Ms. Finch might also remember incidents Douggy hadn't shared with Quinn or have an adult perspective on something Quinn hadn't grasped as a kid—something to support or disprove Gracen's suicide theory.

Again, they hear Douggy's voice. "You have to come. You'll be mad, but I need to tell you something. It's important."

Quinn crept past Sheila, snoring on the couch, and ever-so-quietly undid the chain on the door and eased it shut. Jumping at each tiny noise and movement in the dark, they forced themself to the end of the block before a ripple in the threatening shadows—a man, hiding, with yellow eyes and rotten teeth!—sent them fleeing back home.

A long history of cowardice. Starting with letting Douggy down.

Quinn makes the call. "Ms. Finch, this is Quinn from the diner. Uh, yeah, I used to go by Kathy, but not anymore. Is today a good time to ask you a few questions?"

Ms. Finch gives Quinn detailed and precise directions to her house. On the way, Gran's expectations of proper guest etiquette pop into their mind, and Quinn stops at Main Street Market to purchase a tin of sugar cookies. Belatedly, they wonder if they should have done the same for their mother, but no. There's a line between diplomacy and hypocrisy.

Ms. Finch's neighborhood is older than Sheila's, the houses modest and some in disrepair. Ms. Finch has a neat but tiny one-story duplex with a narrow doorless side facing the street, a house number at each corner. A driveway runs parallel to a concrete walkway covered by an overhang. Midway down, a stoop holds a plastic lawn chair and a can for cigarette butts as well as a few dead plants in terra cotta pots. Quinn rings the doorbell wondering if this is really the right place.

Ms. Finch opens the door, tilting a welcoming grin of worn teeth up at Quinn. Gravity has rounded her shoulders and curled her spine. Quinn, looking down at this woman who once seemed tall and intimidating, is suddenly self-conscious of their youth and ease of movement.

"Well, come in," Ms. Finch orders with authority, like Quinn is still one of her charges. Quinn obeys, and the door quickly shuts behind them.

The cramped living room is almost tropical in temperature, and a jungle of plants supports this impression. The chill in Quinn's bones melts away, and their fingers uncurl. The house smells of onions and beef, and their stomach turns.

"You want soup?" Ms. Finch asks, eyeing them up and down. "My helper puts together a bit pot on Fridays, and it gets me through the weekend."

"Uh, no, thank you," Quinn says. "I brought you some cookies." They hand over the tin, and the old woman's face lights up.

"Wonderful! I'll make some tea. Cinnamon spice okay? I think there's plain black too. I'm going to have the cinnamon."

"Cinnamon's good, if it's no trouble."

Ms. Finch shoos Quinn toward a pale-blue overstuffed chair as she cane-steps through an archway into the kitchen. The chair is kitty-corner to a love seat where an amorphous knitting project takes up a whole cushion. A remote control sits on the coffee table in front of the other cushion, along with a stack of craft magazines and large-print romances.

Quinn sinks into the armchair and takes a breath. Ms. Finch's home is comfortable, if small, and Quinn imagines her sitting here, knitting and talking to the television. An open door reveals the edge of a bed in a dim room, and a second door, slightly ajar, must lead to the bathroom. School photos of half a dozen children decorate the walls, and Quinn, who'd believed for no reason in particular that Ms. Finch was childless, wonders if they're hers or perhaps grandchildren or foster children.

The kettle whistles, and a moment later Ms. Finch returns with two steaming mugs. She sets one down near Quinn, the other in front of the love seat, then stumps back to the kitchen for the cookies, which she sets precariously on a stack of magazines.

"Help yourself." Ms. Finch settles into her spot, grabs a cookie, and dunks it into her mug. "Mmm. I love these. Such a nice gesture."

Obligingly, Quinn takes one and nibbles it. "Ms. Finch, I'm hoping you can talk to me about Gracen and Douggy Ridpath."

Ms. Finch sets down her mug. "Can I ask first? I heard from Sunny. She said you were staying with Viveca. It's so awful, what happened. Shocking. I knew that girl when she was in kindergarten."

Quinn bites the inside of their lip. If gossip about who's dating whom makes the rounds in hours, news of a murder must fly through in seconds. "I was renting her extra bedroom," they confirm.

"That Sam seemed like a nice girl. Not from around here." Ms. Finch breaks a cookie in half, and crumbs fall to her lap. She dips one side into the tea and eats it.

"I never met her."

"Well, when you're young, these things don't last." Ms. Finch nods to herself, then, with a coy look, says, "I heard you were Viveca's new girlfriend. Moved in fast, didn't you."

"That's not true!"

The old woman chuckles. "Oh, well. People will talk. If I hear it again, I'll set them straight. You were staying in the spare room, then?"

"Yes. We barely knew each other."

"Why'd you come back to town?" Ms. Finch chews avidly, her birdlike gaze fixed on Quinn's face.

Quinn's already lost control of the conversation and probably shouldn't have expected otherwise. It comes back to them: Ms. Finch at her counter in the school office chatting away, a relentless collector of information. Which means Quinn is in exactly the right place.

"I have some family issues," they say, certain that Ms. Finch knows all about Sheila and her new family. "I'm not planning to stay long. But since I've been here, I've been thinking a lot about the old days, about me and Douggy. I thought you might know more than I do. Have you heard of her brother's podcast?"

Ms. Finch pins them with those bright little eyes. "You're not here as a reporter? Or writing some kind of book?"

"No. Just as a friend. Did you hear something about a book?"

"My helper told me she heard something." Ms. Finch's face falls.

Quinn realizes she'd hoped for a juicier story and hurries on. "Gracen's podcast makes me wonder if there was something I missed. Something Douggy hid from me. I was sent away right after she died, so—"

"Sent away." Ms. Finch bites thoughtfully into another cookie. "That's right. Taken clean out of school, after you'd started fifth grade and all. And your little brother—Kaden, was it? In third. A bright kid. Must have been hard for you both. A tough decision for your mother, I'm sure."

"Maybe."

"You don't think so?"

"I'm sure she did what she thought was best," Quinn says, hoping to curtail exploration of this topic.

Ms. Finch nods. "Well. I guess I might be able to fill in some things for you. You're all grown up now, after all. Old enough to deal with any details your mom wanted to protect you from. What about your mom, by the way? How is she doing? I haven't seen her in years. She married a lawyer, didn't she?"

"I thought he was a realtor," Quinn says, then realizes they've given away how little they know. They can imagine the gossip spreading around town: "That Kathy Fontaine girl? Calls herself Quinn now and doesn't even know who her stepfather is!"

Their face warms. It's fine. They don't need anyone here to understand them or their life choices. "My mother's doing well," they add with finality. Inside the cuffs of their hoodie, their hands curl, fingernails seeking palms.

"Did you ask her about what happened? About Douggy?"

"We have a lot to catch up on. But I will."

"Well. Good. That poor little thing. Such a short, tragic life, one disaster after another."

Quinn forces their fingers to relax and wrap around their tea mug. "Gracen, Douggy's brother, has been saying Douggy"—the word suicide doesn't want to emerge—"didn't die by accident," they finish lamely.

A long, drawn-out "Yes..." from Ms. Finch. She frowns. "Such a terrible thing to think. But it does happen. You hear about it more these days, with the online bullying. Out-of-control, no adults to step in. Not that adults are better! I hear about the trolls and the catfish and all." She nods sagely.

"Gracen seems to think it was people in Meander, not online."

"Well." Ms. Finch's pale-orange hair brushes the shoulders of her flowered cardigan as she shakes her head. "People can be awful. Especially with a disfigurement. I told her mother back then, putting her back in the public school system was a mistake."

"You did?" So Gracen was right. Another crack in Quinn's rosier view of the past.

"Oh, yes. Children are predators. They'll circle the wounded and attack when they're down. I knew it would go badly. But the mother, Marjorie, hoped it would increase Douggy's confidence. Help her grow a thicker skin." She shakes her head again. "I'm sure if Douggy lived, she would have eventually returned to a normal life. There was no need to rush it. Plastic surgery is amazing nowadays. That actress with the curly hair? Did you know she's seventy-nine? She doesn't look a day over forty-five! They're all on crazy hormone cocktails, I suppose."

Quinn barely notices Ms. Finch's veer into social commentary. Back then, Douggy said she'd begged to go back to school against her parents' wishes, not that Marjorie was behind it. "Douggy spent a lot of time with you at the office."

"Oh yes. I told her she could come whenever she was having a tough time. Her teacher didn't like that much, but what could she say?" Ms. Finch shrugs. "I had my doubts she'd be able to cope with a special needs kid like Douggy."

"Douggy didn't have special needs." Douggy was quick, funny, and precocious—not slow. Quinn turns red at the thought, realizing they're putting kids into limiting boxes—the very thing they always wished wasn't done to them. They struggle for the right words. "What I mean is—"

"It's a terrible label, isn't it? Almost snide in its vagueness. I certainly don't mean her intelligence. She had *emotional* special needs, and that can disrupt a classroom as much as anything else." Ms. Finch nods to herself.

Quinn swallows. "So you agree with Gracen? You think Douggy was bullied and killed herself?"

"It's possible, isn't it? A horrible way to die, mushroom poisoning. But that family, they ate wild mushrooms as a matter of course. Not sure why anyone would take the chance. Something was bound to happen."

"What do you mean?"

"Oh, that father. What was his name? Gordon? Walter? No, Warren! That's right. They were poor, but they must have had food stamps, so it wasn't like they couldn't get real food. He fancied himself a forager. Liked to harvest wild plants and things from the woods. He gave a talk to Gracen's class, once, if I remember right. The Ridpath children knew all about poisonous things in the woods. Douggy would have known exactly what she was doing."

Quinn gets a flash of Warren pointing out a salmonberry bush behind the Ridpath house, and the seediness of the tart orange berry. "If that's true, why call it an accident? Even if they didn't want to call it suicide, wouldn't it be negligence? Allowing your kids access to dangerous substances?"

"Simple human decency, dear. Even the cops could see the parents had been punished enough. If they took Douggy to the hospital sooner, she might have been saved. Imagine living with that." Ms. Finch shudders. "No, the police didn't push too hard to find out exactly what happened. Called it an accident and let everyone get on with grieving. Now the parents are both gone, so if it helps that young man to acknowledge the truth, so be it. He has a daughter of his own, you know."

Quinn weighed that a moment before pushing on. "Viveca used to babysit Douggy. She was pissed—I mean, angry about the idea there was bullying. She said everyone was kind to Douggy and her family, especially after the dog bite. She said it was a small town and everyone was supportive."

"Pfft," Ms. Finch says. "Not to speak ill of the dead! But back then, Viveca was a child herself. Pretty enough but spoiled rotten. No emotional maturity. How would she recognize that kind of pain? Leaving casseroles at a family's door can keep them eating well during a hard time, but it won't heal the spirit of a little girl whose friends won't look her in the face."

Quinn pauses. Ms. Finch has a point. They remember how Douggy would shy away from people's reactions. That kind of pain would be hard to blame on anyone in particular. "Do you know if anything major happened? Was there some kind of incident that Douggy might have been too embarrassed to talk about?"

Ms. Finch shakes her head slowly. "I don't remember anything like that. Not with Douggy. I remember when the Rice boys were suspended for what they did to Irene Fedler, but that was years later..."

Quinn brings her back on track. "So there was no one specific who was picking on Douggy?" Someone who might have escalated things, especially that final week, when Douggy insisted Kathy sneak over in the middle of the night.

Ms. Finch's penciled-in brows draw together. "Why? Are you going to report them?"

"No. But I might talk to them." Heat rises into their cheeks. Anyone Ms. Finch names will be someone Kathy knew too. The thought of confronting a bully is terrifying but also attractive.

If Quinn had confronted Gran years ago about her draconian rules and expectations and programs, instead of running away, would Kade have suffered less?

Their throat closes up, and they flinch from an imaginary flash of Kade's mind in chaos, his foot hitting the accelerator. They pinch the web of their thumb to bring themself back to the moment.

Ms. Finch has the trick of lifting one eyebrow. She gives Quinn a wry look. "I don't think it will be a shock to you if I say Drew and Jessica, will it? Drew had a gift of drawing other kids into her name-calling and teasing, but she and Jessica were the masterminds, no mistake."

Quinn remembers them. One girl with a constellation of freckles across a turned-up nose, big blue eyes and all the cutest outfits, smuggling a cell phone into school long before anyone else had one. That was Drew. Everything Quinn was not—skinny, rich. Mean.

Drew's best friend, Jessica, comes back to them too. Athletic, with dusky skin and long dark hair, thick eyelashes around wide brown eyes. Kind when grown-ups were around and wicked when they weren't.

"I remember them," Quinn says. They remember teasing and spitballs on the school bus and avoiding Drew and Jessica at recess. Nothing devastating. Just constant, low-key social signaling to keep Quinn in their place, and Douggy too, for the short time she was at school.

Jessica had lived in the neighborhood. The two of them could have harassed Douggy outside of school when Quinn wasn't around. Douggy, feisty and fierce, tended to push back. Maybe that had escalated into something she couldn't live with.

Ms. Finch says, "Jessica's family moved away years ago, but the Armstrongs had some financial difficulties. Drew ended up at Polallie High and then the community college. Had a bad marriage too, poor thing. Her ex had a porn addiction, and now she's living at her parents' with three kids. Her mother goes to my church," Ms. Finch adds quickly in response to Quinn's shocked look. "We both do soup kitchen every other Friday, so..." She shrugs. "We chat."

Quinn puts Drew's name in their notes app and asks, "I don't remember Jessica's last name, do you?"

"Cheng, with an e."

They add that to the note. The heat in here is making them feel wrung out, but they still need info on Gracen.

"I heard the PTA arranged for Gracen to speak to the middle schoolers in the spring," they begin.

"I'm an honorary member, you know. I have more decades of experience setting up events for kids than anyone else in town."

"Would you have a direct number for Gracen? It would really help." Quinn holds their breath.

"Oh, my. Let me see. I didn't speak with him. We went back and forth with his agent, you know, but I think the agent stuck Gracen's number in one of the emails, for emergencies."

"Really? Could I get that from you?"

It takes a good five minutes, with Ms. Finch mumbling as she scrolls and swears. Quinn carries the mugs back to a neat little kitchen and hand-washes them as they wait. At last, Ms. Finch finds the number, and Quinn copies it to their contact list.

"Thank you so much."

Ms. Finch flaps a hand at her. "Thank you for the visit and the cookies, my dear," she says. "You know, I still have files of old photos from my days at the school. I couldn't bring myself to throw them away. Maybe my helper can dig up the year when you and Douggy were both there. Come back Tuesday, will you?"

"I'd love to," Quinn says. They exit hastily, dying to leave the humid little space. Photos will be excellent. Right now, however, Gracen's direct phone number sings a siren song from the cell phone in their pocket.

13

KIRSTEN

Saturday morning I wake with a hangover, my brain a collection of jagged pieces that grind at one another with every move. I drink a tub of coffee to wash down a handful of painkillers, bow my head under a scalding shower, and leave the house.

I'm glad Trav and the kids are gone. I don't have to feel guilty for my compulsion to get back to the office. Three days in and Viveca's case has generated a massive amount of data, but no one admits knowing who she was meeting Wednesday evening or seeing her after she stopped at Sunny's. The ex's cabin reservation has been confirmed, but that alone doesn't rule her out.

Eb's at the office ahead of me, glumly sipping what's most likely a quadruple shot Americano. He'd probably hoped to be hanging out with his buddies and practicing his toast today, but I'm grateful he's here.

I punch him in the shoulder. "Samantha O'Brien call yet?" I ask.

"Nope."

"Shit."

"Her brother said Sunday."

"Yeah. I hoped she'd check her phone and call in early though. Who doesn't check their phone?" I know the answer—people who are out of service. But my patience is short.

Eb slurps, then sighs. "We'll get there."

We stare at the timeline on the whiteboard, updated with new entries by the deputies. The weekend before she died, Viveca met up with a couple of friends on the coast. I skim Akina's notes in our shared case folder. The women said Viveca seemed okay aside from disappointment things hadn't worked out with Sam and had expressed no worries or fears about anyone bothering her. The trio walked on the beach, shopped, and shared a late seafood dinner before spending the night at an Airbnb. When Akina asked about Quinn, they said Viveca told them Quinn was quiet, used they/them pronouns, and kept to themself.

Monday through Wednesday, Viveca worked her normal schedule, early morning to mid-afternoon. Monday night, she attended her book club, the members of which had been interviewed by Riley. The eight women had discussed *How Far the Light Reaches* by Sabrina Imbler for two hours over wine and snacks. Only a couple were aware of Viveca's breakup, and no one shed light on anything more personal. Tuesday night, Viveca seems to have stayed home, and Wednesday she delivered community meals to people in need after work. She told Quinn she'd be home late, and multiple people saw her pick up an order at Sunny's around eight p.m.

This reminds me—no one from the community meals program has returned my call. I try the phone number again.

"Community Meals. Fred Marcowicz speaking," an elderly voice says wearily.

I identify myself and ask, "Did you see Ms. Crandall Wednesday evening?"

"I did." Fred tells me Viveca picked up meals for a few homebound people in Meander every Wednesday around quarter to five at the charity's headquarters in Polallie. He'd liked her. She gave him free advice about his two cats and said she'd arrange for his granddaughter to volunteer at the vet clinic over the summer. A series of muffled coughs follows, and I recognize he's sobbing with the phone covered up.

"Everyone I've spoken to has mentioned how kind Viveca was," I tell him.

"It's so hard to understand why—"

"We'll do our best to learn what happened," I say firmly, trying to avoid more tears. "Do you remember what you talked about Wednesday? Or what Viveca was wearing?" She'd changed out of her scrubs at some point, but we don't know if she wore one thing for meal delivery and then went home and got dressed up.

"My wife says I wouldn't notice if she wore a grocery sack."

"Do you remember what Viveca said? Her mood?"

"She told me a funny story about a dog that escaped from an exam room and piddled in someone's purse. She seemed happy. Relaxed."

"How about her plans for the evening?"

"Just—the community meal was turkey again. It's all leftover from the holidays. I asked what she was going to make for her own dinner because she liked to cook, and she often makes something fancy. But she said, 'Not tonight! I'm taking a break, Fred!'"

Another spate of coughing—or perhaps muffled sobs. I feel like I'm torturing the man. "Did Viveca ever mention Samantha O'Brien or Quinn DeCelles?"

"No."

"Last question—I'm trying to identify Viveca's best friend, Carlie, who also grew up in Meander. We don't have a surname. Would you know her?"

"That one, yes." He sounds relieved to be able to help. "Carlie volunteered for us as well. The two of them signed on together, but she moved away last year."

Fred looks up Carlie's cell number for me and then hesitates before giving me contact info for the delivery clients along with a reminder that they're unwell and should be treated gently.

"We'll do our best to be sensitive," I say and thank him.

Eb watches me add details to the timeline for Wednesday evening. "Not a whole lot, huh?"

"I got a number for the best friend and the community meals clients. Ready to play call center?"

I reach Carlie's voicemail box and request a return call as soon as possible. Then I dial Edie, first on Fred's list, who turns out to be an elderly woman caregiving for a forty-five-year-old daughter who'd suffered a stroke.

When I bring up Viveca's death, Edie collapses into a puddle of sobs and the daughter, Claire, takes over. "Viveca brought me a kitten. She was going to help—" Now she's sniffling.

"I understand," I say. "That was Wednesday, when she brought the kitten over?"

"Sorry, no." Edie reclaims the phone. "Claire's sense of time isn't the best. Viveca brought Tumbleweed over weeks ago, at Christmas. Claire's worried about how we'll get him to the vet without her help, but we'll figure it out."

"Can you remember anything else about Viveca's visit Wednesday?"

"Oh, let's see. She seemed happy, I think. She played with Tumbleweed, and I told her she looked nice and to watch out for his claws on her fancy clothes. She said she had a date."

I catch my breath. "Did she say who with, by any chance? Or where they were going?"

"Oh, no. She told us she broke up with that Sam girl, which was sad, but she didn't name names this time. It must have been someone from out of town though."

"What makes you say that?"

"Well, we don't have many lesbians here. Franny and Dani are the only ones I know of, and they're almost as old as me." She titters.

In the background, Claire says, "Mom! Sorry, Detective. She thinks there's still only a few hundred people living here."

"I do not!"

The women tell me that Viveca arrived a little later than usual and recommend I check with Mr. Griswold, who must have talked her ear off.

"We're working on it," I tell them.

By the time I hang up, Eb's spoken to both Allen Griswold and Patti Hannaford, which fills our timeline through 6:15 p.m., when Viveca left Patti's house with one stop to go. She'd been in a rush, Patti told Eb, but Viveca's clients were used to her falling behind and didn't mind because they enjoyed talking to her.

The last of the four recipients doesn't answer. I leave a message and end the call, only for my phone to ring immediately. Carlie Windliss is in the parking lot.

Eb and I sit with Carlie in an interview room. She'd been on her way to a marketing conference in Bend, Oregon, when she heard the news about Viveca and changed her itinerary. She's staying with an aunt in Polallie to help Viveca's brothers with local arrangements.

Carlie's hair is a short, artificially scarlet pixie, and her swollen eyes are nearly red enough to match.

After introductions, I get right to the meat of it. "How often did you and Viveca speak?"

"Speak? Maybe a couple times a week. Text? Much more. Most days, at least once. I knew something was wrong Thursday morning because she hadn't weighed in on the new episode of the podcast we've been listening to." She shakes her head, tearing up again. "I *knew* something was wrong. I should've done something, called someone."

"It was too late by then, I'm afraid," Eb says gently.

"We think it was late Wednesday night when Viveca was attacked," I add. "Did she tell you who she was going out with?"

Carlie's eyes widen. "She wasn't ready to date yet. No way. Some of her stupidest romantic decisions were on the rebound."

My hopes plummet. "She didn't tell you she had a date on Wednesday?"

"No! She didn't mention it. I assumed she'd head home after her meal deliveries. I had drinks with some friends from work and didn't get back until almost ten, and I thought about texting but figured she might be in bed already. She was an early bird. Her brothers didn't tell me—"

Disappointed, I look at Eb. He holds out the tissue box and lets her collect herself, then touches base on what she knows about the breakup with Sam and the new roommate situation. Carlie liked Sam a lot but says she knew all along it wasn't going to work out. "Sam's too much of a homebody," she says. And as far as she knew, all was fine with Quinn. "Viveca had a strict budget. She was saving for a big trip. When Sam refused to pay her share of the last round of bills, Vee was pissed. It was a huge relief when she found a roommate so quickly."

Eb's shoulders sag. No sign of motive there, either.

I ask, "Can you think of anything else we should know? Did Viveca mention being stressed out about anything lately? Had she been nervous or upset?"

Carlie shakes her head. "She was upset about being mentioned on the podcast in a bad light. I told her no one would know it was her. There were no names. She said if someone wanted to, they could figure out who the babysitter was, and next thing you know, it would be all over social media. She was wondering if she'd have to hire a lawyer."

I settle back in my chair. "Now, what podcast is this?"

She looks from Eb to me. "Did you guys grow up in the area? Were you around when the Ridpath girl died?"

In the late afternoon, I start episode one of *The Ridpath Girl* in the car on the way to the gym. Eb and I did some homework after Carlie left, and when I hear the narrator's expressive tenor, I know I'm listening to Gracen Ridpath, the YouTube celeb who made bank on funny food and diet videos during the pandemic. His voice is grim as he says, "When I was thirteen years old, my little sister Douggy died from eating a mushroom known as the Death Cap. It was considered an accidental death. My mother, my father, and me—we all shattered, each torturing ourselves in our own way with what we should have seen, what we could have done.

"Now that I'm an adult, I'm able to look back with a more critical eye. Douggy *knew* what Death Caps were. Our dad, an accomplished forager, warned us, and Douggy was smart and comfortable in the woods. She wouldn't roll in poison oak, and she wouldn't eat a poisonous mushroom.

"She *knew*, and she ate it anyway. The more I think about it and look at the circumstances of her life, the more I believe my sister killed herself. And when an eleven-year-old commits suicide, you have to look hard at the reasons to prevent it from happening again.

"This podcast is that look."

I hit pause right there and take a deep breath. Carlie's take on it had been cynical and offended on behalf of her friend. She'd stressed the "YouTuber expanding his audience with his childhood tragedy" angle. I'm not naive, and that's undeniably part of what's happening, but it's not the whole story. Gracen sounds raw. I can't help thinking of cases I've seen where a child was pushed to self-harm, and then, inevitably, of Henry and Fern. I drive the next few blocks in silence, considering. By tomorrow, I'll have the case file from the girl's death, and we can dig a little deeper.

My gym is in a strip mall, the parking lot nearly deserted on a Saturday evening. In the locker room, I change into running clothes and start lacing up my sneakers. *The Ridpath Girl*, continuing in my earbuds, is interrupted by the buzz of a phone call. "Detective Boon speaking."

"This is Samantha O'Brien." A woman's voice, hesitant. "You left a message?"

My interest sharpens. The ex, finally checking in. "Thanks for returning our calls." She sounds like she's in a wind tunnel, and I'm guessing she's on the road. I'm alone in the locker room, but I can't count on it staying that way, so I push through the emergency exit into the cold of the parking lot. Goose bumps cover my arms and legs as I huddle in my car in my T-shirt and running shorts. "Have you spoken to your brother?" I ask.

"I got a message." Her voice catches. "He told me about Vee."

Not surprising, but considering Samantha's a person of interest, disappointing—it would have been nice to catch that first reaction. "We're gathering information from people who knew her. Are you driving? Can you pull over for a few minutes?"

She hesitates. "Ah, is it okay if we talk when I get home? Or tomorrow? I'm filthy, starving, and exhausted, and I don't want to sit on the side of the road in the dark."

I look out at the rainy night, irritated. "Time is critical," I tell her. Then I do a quick calculation. It'll take me about four hours to reach Coos Bay, and Trav won't be around tomorrow anyway. "I can come to you, first thing in the morning."

She hesitates. "I'm staying at my brother's place."

"The local police may be able to set us up with a place to talk if you're uncomfortable in his house."

"Uh. No, that's okay. Sure." She gives me the address.

"I'll be there around nine." I end the connection and stare at my phone, torn. Eb will give me shit if I tell him. Then he'll insist on coming with me, even though he couldn't make it back in time for the wedding, so he'll complain the whole time—or, worse, he'll insist I take one of the deputies.

No thanks. I slide the phone into the pocket on the side of my running tights and dash through the rain to the gym entrance, where I have to ring endlessly to get buzzed in because I left my key card in the locker room.

14

GRACEN

Kneeling on cold slate in front of the toilet bowl, Gracen grips the seat and spits drool and bile into the water.

There's a knock on the door. "Hon? You okay?"

He closes his eyes, waits a second in case of another spasm, then reaches to flush away breakfast. As the sound fades, he calls a rough and insincere, "Yeah," and sits back against the side of the tub, straightening his knees with a grimace of relief.

"Is Daddy coming to play?" Aurie asks on the other side of the door.

"Daddy's tummy was oogy. Let's give him a minute," Mac says. Her footsteps retreat, and Aurie's follow double-time.

Gracen breathes through his nose, eyes still closed. This hasn't happened in a long time. In high school, he was bulimic, but no one noticed because no one noticed *him*. Just another geek whose sister died. So what if he skulked to the market to buy half gallons of ice cream, which he downed and puked up in one sitting?

After high school, the binge and purge faded away in the brief, doomed glory of college, when he fell in love with Celeste, the all-too-temporary love of his life, but nose-dived again when he moved back to Meander for Mom.

Unfounded bursts of nausea—and the urge to binge—still hit him occasionally, despite generally healthy habits. Stress, the therapist had said, before he stopped going. Self-sabotage because he doesn't believe he deserves what he's got, Mac says.

Today, it was none of the above, just looking at Aurie's stitches. He's not squeamish, but a piece of scab broke away when he was changing the gauze, and fresh, bright blood bubbled up. Next thing he knew, saliva filled his mouth, and he had to run for it.

He wipes his face with the back of his hand, wipes his hand on a washcloth hanging over the side of the tub, then stretches out on the cool tile. It reminds him of the cool weight of the glass dolphin in his hand, which had *not* been left by Mac or Aurie. Mac thinks one of the nuttier fans found their address. She wants to call the police, but he's talked her into holding off. If any more anonymous gifts show up, they'll report it, but he doesn't want police in his house. The thought makes him feel trapped, as if he were being sucked back into the aftermath of Douggy's death.

Maybe the puking *is* from stress. And insomnia. Yesterday's visit to Meander didn't magically solve his sleep issues. He woke with images from the photo album swirling in his mind like the echoes of a dream. His skull is a dollhouse, populated by young Mom and Dad and Douggy, and when he sleeps, they come to life, replaying their greatest hits. It's not the curated world of the photo album. Slavering dogs pace outside the door, and his family's expressions shift to slyness or cruelty with every flicker of shadow.

He yanks his T-shirt down, sucks a deep breath, and gathers himself. He and Mac are tag-teaming today: she, studying through the morning, while he hangs out with the kid, then switching off in the afternoon so Gracen can do some editing on *Gracen Stays Home*. The precipitous run to the bathroom threw off the plan.

He's on his knees when his gut cramps again. In a semi-salaam, he pauses, waiting to see if it will subside. Cautiously, he opens his eyes again, getting an upside-down view of his tattoo. *Forever in Hell.* Nausea turns his stomach, and he collapses to the slate floor. As he stares at the line of caulk along the tub's lower edge, a childhood memory pops into his mind. His sister, maybe five years old, face still unscarred.

She'd won the coin toss for first bath time on Christmas night. They each had new bubble bath from Santa. Douggy's was pink, capped with a plastic strawberry, scented with too-sweet perfume. They both preferred his: dark purple with a

UFO-shaped cap, filled with lavender goop that smelled like grapes. Gracen remembers Mom getting up from the couch to check on Douggy in the bath and letting out a little laugh before starting to scold. Gracen raced in to see what his sister had done. She sat in the tub, damp brown hair clinging to her head, cheeks pink. Her long-lashed brown eyes danced with mischief. The grape scent filled the air, bubbles so high they overflowed into a foamy puddle on the floor.

He'd grabbed his empty bottle and pitched it at Douggy with a wail of fury. In full tantrum mode, he'd collapsed to the bath mat, giving him a view like the one he has right now. He doesn't remember much more—breathless sobs, the scratchy, mildew-smelling rug pressing into the side of his face and his belly. His father hauling him off to scream out his frustration behind the closed door of his bedroom.

He would have been seven. Too old for temper tantrums, but Douggy could always set him off. Testing him, pushing him, even as she puppy-dogged after him, trying to keep up.

"Hon, you feeling okay?" Mac's voice again, soft. He hadn't heard her approach.

He swallows and stands, leaning on the wall for support when his vision darkens. Just a little light-headed from standing too fast, which quickly clears. "Yep. Didn't feel good for a minute. Better now. I'll be right out."

"Guess who called. Or—never mind, I'll tell you when you're done." Her footsteps retreat again.

He splashes water on his face after scrubbing his teeth, then rinses with mouthwash and adds fresh deodorant to his pits. When he hurries into the kitchen, Mac and Aurie are playing Go Fish at the table.

Mac sets her cards down and lays a smooch on Aurie's forehead. "Daddy's tapping in!" she declares. As she passes Gracen, she says in a much lower voice, "Simone called. She's got something going on. I might need to head over there tomorrow and stay for a couple days, okay?"

"Um, what?" Simone is Mac's best friend from college. Both women are so busy, they seldom visit, even though Simone's only three hours away. He winces. He's not sure he's up to Mac taking off right now.

She brushes the frown from his forehead with a gentle finger. "Don't worry. I'll tell you all about it later." She kisses his cheek, then draws back quizzically. "You do feel better? You're okay?"

"Yeah! Yeah, I'm fine. Got queasy. Too much coffee or something."

Her eyebrows go up, but she lets it pass. "See you at one o'clock?"

"You bet."

"Bye, Mommy!" Aurie says as Mac exits. "Daddy, you have those cards. And you have to tell the troof. No cheating. It's your turn."

"Okay, honey." Gracen looks down at the hand he inherited

from Mac. A pizza-making pufferfish, a dancing dolphin, and a guppy in football gear. It's Aurie's new favorite game, which means her appetite for it is endless. Literally. "How about we finish this round, then go to the playground?"

She shakes her head. "I think eight."

"Eight what?"

"Eight rounds, and then playground."

Gracen sighs. "Do you have a guppy, Aurie?"

She looks down at her cards and happily cries, "Go Fish!" The way she's holding them, tilted down and sideways, he can see not one, but two helmeted guppies hanging out among the other fish.

He sighs again and picks a card.

Gracen's lost count of how many rounds they've played before she can be talked into English muffin pizzas for lunch. She asks to eat in front of the TV, and he gives in easily, setting her up in the living room before returning to the kitchen to put the pizzas together.

As he slices an English muffin, his phone buzzes. He picks up.

"Hi, uh, Gracen?" The voice is nasal, unfamiliar. Tentative.

"Yes?"

"This is, um, it's Quinn DeCelles."

He doesn't recognize the name and frowns. "How did you get my number?"

"A friend gave it to me. I know you. I mean, I used to know

you. Sorry, I'm saying this wrong. Douggy was my best friend. My family moved to Meander when I was eight, and from then on we were inseparable."

He blinks. This is Kathy Fontaine? He dredges from memory a chubby dark-haired girl, painfully shy, who spoke to him in a whisper if she spoke at all. She and Douggy might roar with laughter in the living room, but as soon as Gracen entered, Kathy would hunch over and turn her face away, making Douggy glare at Gracen. "Go away, we're playing in here!" If he stuck around, Mom would shake her head at him and he'd retreat, wishing he could have a friend over too. But Kathy lived nearby, and her mother had been unthreatening to his parents. Equally fucked up.

He raises his eyebrows. "Okay. Kathy. Wow."

"No—well. Listen. Sorry to bother you, but I heard your podcast—"

His stomach sinks. Now that he remembers her, where she came from, he knows it's got to be one of those asking-for-money calls. People think earning millions on YouTube is like a lottery windfall, so much undeserved cash he must be dying to give some away.

"—and I've been thinking about Douggy a lot lately. I'm in town, in Meander, and I know you don't live here anymore, but you still live nearby, right? Is there any way you and I could get together and talk? It's important."

His bullshit alert is on high. She wants to make him feel a

connection, then pitch him in person. "Wait, what did you say your name was? You don't go by Kathy anymore?"

There's a pause. "It's Quinn. I'm nonbinary."

"Listen, Quinn, I don't think I can help you. Thanks for your call, but I'll be blocking your number."

"Wait! No! It is me!" The voice goes high and breathy in panic, and for an instant, they almost sound like the little girl he remembers. "Please! Test me! Ask me anything. I was at your house *all the time* for nearly four years!"

Gracen hesitates. That gets him because it's true, and he's not sure who else would know that.

He's been pacing around the kitchen, and now he peeks around the living room doorway at Aurie. She looks drowsy in a nest of blankets in front of the television. It won't be the end of the world if she naps before lunch instead of after. Pizza can wait.

He leans against the wall and thinks hard. The Ridpath tragedy merited a paragraph or two in local papers, and their family had been remarkably insular. There are a million things he could ask that there's no record of anywhere except his own mind, and maybe, this person's. "Do you remember Douggy's favorite stuffed animal?"

There's a long pause. Gracen thinks he's outed the impostor, but then the voice comes softly, sad. "Crinkle the Lion. She brought him everywhere—even to school. You warned her she'd get teased, but she brought him anyway.

Your mom sewed on a shirt button when one of his eyes fell off."

He'd forgotten the button, and he laughs a little. "Right. Douggy was worried he wouldn't be able to see." He can't imagine who else would know this. His parents. Douggy's doctor or therapist.

Douggy's only friend.

There's a little snort. "I remember."

Gracen moves to look at his daughter again. She's fast asleep, mouth open, and he turns off the TV, then returns to the hallway.

"Will you talk to me?" Quinn asks hopefully. "I heard you were coming to Meander for an event in a couple months, but I won't be around. We can meet—"

"Yes. Okay. Can you come to Corvallis? We can get coffee." His heart beats faster. Maybe talking to someone who was there and spent time, not only with Douggy but around his whole family, will ground him.

"I don't drive. But I can look into a bus..." They sound unsure.

"How about Polallie, would that be easier?"

"Yeah, definitely. I know it's short notice, but I have tomorrow off if you're available?"

Gracen thinks quickly. He'll get out of the house and talk to a real person for something other than work. Facing the demons of his past, part two. Not that part one helped much, but what the hell. "Tomorrow works," he says. "But I need to coordinate with my wife. Can I text you later?"

Gracen doesn't finish editing until after seven. He finds Aurie sucking her thumb on the couch as Mac reads from *Where the Wild Things Are*. He snuggles next to them for two more books, then carries Aurie to bed, where she demands a fourth. With his back against her headboard, he reads about marsupials, stealing glances as her eyelids droop: her translucent skin, the fragile perfection of her ear, tendrils of hair curling against her cheek. She's so close to the age Douggy was when the dog bite happened, and the thought seizes all his muscles like an electric charge.

He breathes through it, hearing Mac in his head. *Ease up.* Aurie isn't Douggy, and she isn't doomed. Mac always adds, "And you aren't, either," which makes him shiver. Or knock on wood.

Downstairs, Mac's head has fallen against the back of the couch, her eyes closed. He collapses next to her, and she blinks sleepily at him.

"Early bedtime?" He squeezes her hand.

She pushes upright. "Maybe. But not yet. Listen." Her face turns serious.

"Right. What's up with Simone?" He'd almost forgotten.

"She's hoping I can go to an oncology appointment with her Monday. They found an issue on her mammogram, and she assumed it was going to be benign, but it's not. Everything's happening quickly. I want to give her some support. A couple nights, anyway."

"Why you? I mean, don't her parents—"

Mac pokes him. "I'm her best friend. And she knows I've been through this with my aunt, so I'll know what to ask. Her parents will be watching Tyler, anyway."

Gracen nods slowly. Simone's a single mom, and Tyler's only two. Gracen doesn't feel like being alone overnight, but what can he say? That he's creeped out by nightmares and gifts left in his shoe, and what if Aurie gets hurt on his watch? He's superdad. He's *Gracen Stays Home*. And he can call Jane for backup.

"You should go," he says. "I hope she's okay."

15

QUINN

Quinn watches *Bob's Burgers*, cross-legged on the motel bed and forking beans out of a can—no continental breakfast at the Best Bet, but at least they get Cartoon Network. When the phone buzzes on the nightstand, they lean to check the screen. Phone call from an unknown number, and they answer even as bean juice drips on the pillowcase and they realize it's probably a scam. "What?"

"Quinn? It's Bella." Her tone is apologetic rather than bitchy, and Quinn guesses they're about to be asked to cover a shift, even though Sunny ordered them to take the day off. They don't mind as long as they can still meet Gracen later. But Quinn won't make it easy for her.

"Hi."

"Um, this probably sounds weird, but Sunny told me that you were living with that poor woman who got killed and you don't have a place to stay. I have an extra room I was thinking of subletting. Just for some extra cash. And more security, you know? Especially since the murder."

"Oh." Quinn's taken off guard. Bella can't stand them, and they assumed it was at least partly a homophobe thing. Although Bella's rudeness *has* eased up in the past couple days.

"It might not be what you have in mind," Bella says. "It's close to town though, so you could still walk to work. I could even drive you if our shifts worked out."

"I can't afford much," Quinn says dubiously.

"What were you paying before?"

"Viveca let me stay for three hundred a month, plus utilities." Quinn holds their breath. They're rounding down but considering how little money they make…

Bella must be desperate. "I can do that."

"I can't pay a deposit or anything," Quinn warns her. "I'm broke until payday."

"Same!" Bella laughs, sounding relieved. "It's fine. I know you're good for it. And Sunny likes you. She won't fire you anytime soon."

"Are you sure?"

"Absolutely! I'll feel much safer with another human in the house. Where are you staying? Should I come pick you up? I'm not working until this afternoon."

Quinn's silent, thinking.

Bella quickly adds, "Just to look. If you hate it, that's okay, I'll drive you back."

Quinn's eyes dart around the motel room. It will take them two minutes to pack, and it sounds like Bella doesn't expect any money until Friday. But Bella can be a real passive-aggressive bitch, and Quinn doesn't love drama. On the other hand, time is ticking. They have a couple more weeks to convince Sheila to write the letter, and then they'll leave this crappy town behind. They can put up with two or three weeks of anything. Almost anything.

"I don't want to decide until I look," they temporize. *Or until I find out why you're suddenly being so nice.* "I'm at the Best Bet Motel. I'll wait out front."

"I'll be right over!"

Bella's late, unless by "right over," she meant an hour. Quinn waits in the lobby, wondering if the invitation was a prank. "You didn't think I was serious?" Bella will say with a trill of laughter when Quinn shows up for their next shift.

But no. Bella's car eventually pulls up. It's a shit-box minivan Quinn recognizes from the alley behind the diner, with duct tape holding one of the headlights together and a passenger door of a different color. The microfiber seats and plastic console are spotless though, and everything smells of banana air freshener with a tiny hint of trash. Quinn wonders if Bella cleaned just for them.

As soon as Quinn's in the passenger seat, Bella starts

chatting away. "I don't know if I told you? I have this crazy living situation. It's great, but I wanted to explain before we got there so you don't think I'm a drug dealer or something."

"Okay…?"

"I'm like, a pet sitter? And house sitter. I've lived in Meander for about a year now, and I get lots of little jobs where you feed the cat when people are on vacation? But right now, I have the sweetest gig."

Quinn's not sure how this ties into drug dealing.

"The Tarbells are away for six months for some old-people-volunteer thing. In Guatemala, right? So I'm taking care of their animals and their house and their mail and everything. They have the nicest place, way nicer than my last crappy apartment. Huge yard. You're going to die when you see it."

"Are you sure they wouldn't mind if someone else stays?"

"Absolutely! I checked with them over the phone, and they know about the murder. They want me to feel safe."

"That makes sense." If only it was anyone but Bella offering… "What kind of animals?"

Bella grins. "Two gorgeous, old, lazy greyhounds, Dewey and Truman. Plus a black cat named Boris who hates me. He knows I'm a dog person. There are also six chickens in a pen out back."

"It sounds amazing." Quinn has lived in the city their entire adult life, and back east, Gran and Gramps had tennis courts and an outdoor pool, but never pets.

Bella glances over. For the first time, Quinn notices what an interesting shade of green her eyes are. Then, where the loose cuff of Bella's sweater has slipped downward, a shiny pink scar running down the inside of Bella's forearm catches their eye. Quinn jerks their gaze up, and Bella doesn't seem to notice. She says, "I'm glad you think so. We'll see in a couple minutes."

Quinn looks out the window. The day is gray, but at least it's not raining.

Bella says, "I was telling Sunny, I haven't been feeling safe since the murder. The Tarbells' house is very secure, and the dogs will bark if someone tried to break in, but still." She glances over. "How about you? Are you okay? I bet you feel terrible. I didn't even know the girl."

Quinn's lips quirk, imagining Viveca's sharp response to being called a "girl."

"I'm okay. I doubt there's a crazy person running around killing random people." They pause, thinking of Bella's mention of Sunny. "So, when you said before that Sunny told you I needed a place to stay—how much pressure did she lay on you? Did she threaten your job or something?"

Bella shoots Quinn an amused look. "Of course not!"

Quinn raises their eyebrows. "I'm sure you could find a roommate you don't despise."

"I don't despise you! I mean, okay, maybe I was kind of a jerk to you before, but that was because you sucked at your job, and it's not fair to expect everyone else to work harder because you don't know what you're doing." She offers an uncertain smile. "I've been told I come on too strong sometimes. Like, I'm annoyed, and people think I hate them forever."

"Imagine that," Quinn says.

Bella checks out Quinn's expression and seems to detect the dry humor. She grins, then turns on to a street where the lots are a little larger, the landscaping a little nicer, and slows in front of a ranch-style house with brick-and-wood siding. "This is it!" she says. Rhododendrons and barren rosebushes accent the front yard. Tall cedar fencing protects the side and backyards from view.

"Nice," Quinn says.

"So...are you still up for checking it out? Am I forgiven for being kind of an asshole?"

Quinn takes a second to consider. It's only two or three weeks, and Bella seems sincere. "You're sure you're not secretly a raging homophobe? Because that's kind what I suspected."

Color floods from the loose V-neck of Bella's purple sweater to the dark roots of her hair, but she doesn't hesitate before crossing her heart. "I swear. Screw anything or anyone you want—or don't. Just don't screw up your orders and expect me to split tips with you."

Quinn nods and holds out a hand.

Bella shakes it, her hand soft and cool in Quinn's, then jumps out and starts talking at top speed again. "Wait 'til you see the inside. Hey, did you eat? I guess we can talk about the food situation if you decide you want to stay. At Viveca's, did you split the grocery bill?"

Quinn follows to the front door. "We each did our own thing."

"Oh. Good. I eat a ton of frozen pizza. I worried you were going to want me to cook real food or something. I mean, honestly, I mostly take extras from the diner."

Quinn laughs. "I promise I won't ask you to cook."

"There's a code here instead of a key: 4-4-7-2-1. You can put it in your phone. If you forget, I've been leaving the sliding door in the back unlocked."

Quinn makes a face. "Maybe you should lock that. I don't *think* there's a serial killer on the loose, but still…it might be smart."

Bella turns the handle. "Oh god, you're right. I've been paranoid at night alone, but I didn't even think of that. Like a killer can't climb over the fence." She ushers Quinn into the spacious living room ahead of her.

The place is nicer than it looked from the outside. Cozy and colorful, with dark wood floors and a red Persian rug. The big-screen TV on the wall is huge, as is the distressed leather sectional across from the brick fireplace.

"Do you ever build a fire?" Quinn asks. They assume wherever their bedroom is, they'll spend their time in there, but curling up in front of the fire sounds decadent on a gray January day.

"It's gas. I'll show you how to get it going after the tour. Let's look at the bedroom first, so you'll know right away if you like it. I took the one with the en suite, but your bedroom has a bathroom right across the hall."

Bella points out her bedroom, the linen closet, the guest bath, and Quinn's bedroom. It's nicer than either the motel or their room at Viveca's place, however disloyal that seems. A wave of fatigue rolls over Quinn, tempting them to cross the fluffy expanse of the cream-colored rug to curl up on the oversize bed. Their last reservation slips away.

"You like it?"

"I love it. If you're sure you're up for a roommate, I'll take it. One hundred percent."

Bella sags in exaggerated relief. "Awesome. It'll be super nice to have another human around. I've been spooked for days. If it weren't for the animals, I would have moved into the Best Bet myself!"

"Should we make sure the dogs like me?"

"They like everyone, trust me. One chin scratch and you're friends for life. Back to the living room. You walked right past them."

Bella leads them down the hall and points to a pair of elegantly long-legged dogs sleeping on a cushion. "The darker one is Dewey, the silver one is Truman. I'm not sure where Boris the cat is. He sneaks out to eat once in a while, but don't be offended if he avoids you."

Dewey opens an eye and closes it again. Quinn must not seem like much of a threat.

Quinn says, "Okay. I guess I'm officially in."

"Just…don't embarrass yourself at work, okay? I'm not responsible if I suddenly turn into a bitch again."

Quinn can't help smiling. "I really did suck, didn't I?"

"You're not that great now. Did you know you gave Mrs. Daye the crab salad that was supposed to go to table two the other night? She's allergic to shellfish, but thank god, she was paying attention."

"Oh, shit."

"I told her it was the new cook's fault for putting the dishes up wrong," Bella says. "Don't worry. I fuck up too. Once in a while."

16

KIRSTEN

I hit the road Sunday at 5:30 a.m. hoping to return before Trav and the kids get home, despite the eight-hour round trip to Coos Bay. Trav hasn't returned my calls, but I'm guessing they'll arrive around dinnertime so the kids can unpack and settle into a normal school-night groove before bed.

I avoided the booze and went to bed early but tossed and turned, my brain jumping back and forth between Trav's prickliness and the case. I doubt I got more than five hours, but at this point I'm almost used to it.

Following a twisting rural highway toward the southern coast, I shock myself awake with gulps of coffee. My brain whirs jerkily into action. Yesterday, between my time on the treadmill and all those chores, I finished all three episodes of *The Ridpath Girl*. I winced at Gracen's memory of the babysitter's words—"the girl with her face chewed off"—and I agree Viveca wouldn't have wanted people to guess it was her. At the same time, it was so long ago, and she'd only been a teenager...would people really hold it against her?

Maybe not people close to her. Social media though—trolls with various agendas would have plastered her accounts with hateful attacks.

What if someone tried to blackmail her, to keep her name from becoming public? We didn't find anything unusual in her finances—no unexplained large withdrawals—but what if someone attacked *because* she refused to pay?

I'm not sure where that fits into a "date gone bad" scenario. Maybe it fits better with the "possibly lured into the woods by a dog" idea. The Ridpath case file is priority one tomorrow, unless I get a confession out of Samantha O'Brien today.

Today's hypothesis is that Samantha convinced Viveca to give her another chance and took her on a nighttime picnic in the woods with Rocky the dog. Viveca's dressy clothes and high heels don't make sense, but I'm not expecting to have all the answers at this stage. If I can discover something incriminating, like big holes in the camping trip story, I can return home in time to make something delicious for dinner and greet my family with a smile.

Still. I'm not going to fixate on Samantha O'Brien the way I fixated on Thomas Sanchez. I'll carry out my due diligence on any lead we turn up. The big bad wolf is not going to elude me, and if Samantha's truly an innocent, she won't have to pay.

Coos Bay is five times the size of Meander, but still a small town, centered on fishing and tourism. Otis O'Brien, Samantha's brother, lives on the outskirts in an old farmhouse whose large dirt yard is surrounded by chicken wire. It's a couple miles from the ocean, but the cool air carries a hint of salty rot. Several vehicles in various states of repair line one side of the driveway, including the green Ford Focus registered to Samantha.

Two dogs run up to the fence as I pull up. One has a short brown pelt, but the other is a husky with a thick coat of mixed cream and gray. A woman emerges onto the covered front porch. "Rocky! Minnie! Come!"

The dogs obey, and she shoos them into the house.

"Are you Samantha O'Brien?" I call.

"Yes, I'm Sam. You're Detective Boon?"

I get out and show her my badge. She glances at it in a perfunctory way and unlatches the gate so I can enter the yard. She's shorter than me, about five foot six, with broad shoulders and narrow hips like a swimmer. Short auburn curls poke from the folded edge of a brown knit hat. Her blue-eyed gaze is frank and assessing over a freckled button nose, and she nods for me to follow her inside.

The mudroom has chipped paint on paneled walls, rain gear and other jackets hanging from an array of hooks, and a scatter of dirty boots and shoes across the tiled floor. With narrow doorways and low ceilings, the house must date from when people were shorter and skinnier. "Let's sit in the kitchen," Sam says. "It's the only warm room in the house. My brother's a cheapskate."

"Is he around?"

"Is that a problem?"

"No, unless you'd be more comfortable talking about your relationship with Viveca privately."

She shrugs and turns her back. "Nah. It's fine."

A bachelor vibe makes me think Otis normally lives alone. The living room has a dusty TV on a stand, a couch, and a coffee table dotted with empty pop cans and an open pizza box. The closest thing to decor is a blanket draped over the back of the sofa.

We pass through a curtained doorway into a warm kitchen smelling of coffee, bacon, and dogs. The wood floor is scarred and dull with age and the white paint on the cabinets is chipped, but the countertops are clean. Shelving displays baking supplies in glass jars. Giant bags of dog food, beans, and rice are piled next to the shelves.

"This is Detective Boon," Sam says to the man at the round oak table. The dogs, sprawled on a pile of ratty blankets next to the back door, ignore us, but I eyeball Rocky again. His fur looks the right length to match my crime scene hairs, and my interest sharpens.

Otis, whose reddish curls surround a bald, freckled pate, is playing a game on his phone, judging by the beeps and trills. He nods at me and pokes sheepishly at his screen until the sound mutes. Grease outlines his fingernails, and I remember he's a mechanic. "I'm Otis, Sam's brother. Can I get you some coffee?"

I shake my head and help myself to a seat, adrenaline zinging through me. I lean back, trying to appear calm and relaxed, when all I want is to shake Sam until the answers come out.

Sam pours a mug before sitting next to her brother. "I would have been happy to talk to you on the phone, you know."

"Oh, it's easier this way. Less room for misunderstanding." The body cam clipped to my shirt is already going, and I let her know, but I pull my notebook from my pocket for more easily accessible notes. I'm casual today, in jeans with a button-down oxford under a quilted puffer jacket. It feels too warm in this room but downplays the holster on my hip.

"I'm still in shock," Sam says. "I can't help wondering if this would've happened if we stayed together, you know?"

I nod sympathetically. "We're putting together a picture of Viveca's life. You may be the best resource we have. I'll need details about your camping trip, as well, to rule you out."

Sam's eyes open wide. "Oh, sure." She darts a look at Otis, who seems to be tuning us out. "I was at a Forest Service cabin near Oakridge. A friend and I reserved it thinking it would be good to get off-grid for a few days."

"What's the name of the friend?"

"The guy I was supposed to go camping with?"

Odd phrasing, and her brother must think so too. He shoots her a frown. Color rises in Sam's face. She clears her throat. "He ended up getting sick."

"He didn't go?"

She shakes her head. "COVID. I called on my way to pick him up Monday morning, and his throat was sore. He did an at-home test."

Otis breaks in. "Ethan had COVID?"

Sam doesn't look at him. "That's what he told me."

Otis presses his lips together and goes back to his game.

"I'll still need to talk to him. Can you give me his full name and number?" I slide her a business card, and she scribbles it down on the back. I tuck it into my pocket. "Thanks. So, you went anyway? Can you describe your itinerary?"

She shrugs. "Left Monday. Stayed until Saturday. Thought about coming home early—I was pretty bored on my own, and there was no Wi-Fi or anything. But I had a few books, and enough alcohol for two, so I huddled over the propane heater, living off ramen and boxed wine..."

"The vehicle you took was the green Ford Focus out there with the roof rack?"

"Yup."

"Did you stop for gas?"

"Yup. I didn't get paper receipts though, if that's your next question."

"Did you bring your dog?"

"I did. You need to talk to him too?"

Her brother gives her a warning look, but I'm fine with her being snappish.

"Which one is yours?" I ask.

"Rocky." The gray-and-white dog lifts his head. I get a good look at his mismatched eyes before he sighs and drops his chin between his paws. Carrie confirmed it's not as easy as you'd think to match animal hair to the extent it will stand up in court, but if it lines up in the microscope, maybe the budget will stretch to DNA testing.

"What kind of dog is he?"

"He's a rescue, so no pedigree. There's lots of husky."

"He's a good-looking dog. So, how did you and Viveca meet?"

"Does it matter?" Her voice is sharp.

"I know this is upsetting for you. I'll try to get through it as quickly as I can."

Sam fidgets. "It was shortly after I adopted Rocky. I'd landed an IT gig with county government in Polallie but didn't like the vet I tried there. I asked around and got a recommendation for the Popes in Meander. That's where I met Viveca, and the rest is history."

"You hadn't known her before that?"

"No."

I take her through the rest of their relationship, listening to her tone of voice and watching her body language. Her brother focuses on his game, listening with half an ear. Sam's attitude is defiant, but she blinks back tears several times as she talks about Viveca.

She doesn't have Thomas Sanchez's easy charm, which raised my hackles and primed my suspicion, but there's something performative about her. Sarge once told me to listen to my gut but never dance to it. Words to live by, but I'm still waiting for that click of rightness when the pieces fall together and the lies are unmasked.

I'm not there yet. And I may not be able to trust it when I feel it.

Maybe Sam took off "camping" and killed Viveca, with Rocky along for company, but then again...maybe not. It must feel strange to have an ex die so soon after a breakup. That could be the source of her discomfort.

"So why did you two break up, anyway?"

"We started disagreeing about everything. Where to live, whether to have kids, that kind of thing. We used to say it didn't matter as long as we were together, but it started to seem like it did."

"So, it was an amicable separation?"

She hesitates. "I wouldn't go that far. She pulled the plug, but I thought we could work things out."

She seems more comfortable now than when we were talking about Ethan. I throw her a curveball. "Did you punch a hole in the wall during an argument?"

"What? No!" Her eyes narrow. "Who told you that? Was it the landlord?"

"I'm afraid I can't say."

"It wasn't my fault. We were carrying a heavy bookcase down the hall, and Viveca's hand got caught in the doorframe. She yelled like her fingers had been chopped off, so I dropped my end to help. The corner ripped into the drywall. I didn't *punch* it."

It sounds plausible. Aside from the squirreliness around the friend not actually camping with her, I'm not getting a lot of red flags. "Do you know of anyone Viveca was having issues with? Maybe a friend, a neighbor, a family member? Any threats, anyone bothering her?"

She barks a laugh. "Vee was beautiful, and she could be charming, but she was tough too. Not many people would mess with her."

Someone had though, very much. "Did Viveca talk to you about *The Ridpath Girl* podcast?"

She starts shaking her head, then tilts it. "Oh, yeah. Last fall, right? I remember. Viveca likes—liked—that Gracen Ridpath guy. She was really into *Gracen's Hot Mess* during the pandemic. She tried that newer show, about the sister, but I guess Gracen's mother died in a nursing home fire after only one episode, and he put it on hold. Vee was disappointed."

I remember the fire in Meander because it had caused a huge stir, but I'd had no idea it was Gracen's mother who perished. Any kind of assisted-living facility is required to have their sprinkler systems strictly up to code. This fire had been in a locked outbuilding not intended for anything but storage, and the victim so desperate to smoke in privacy that she'd broken in.

I ask, "Did Viveca say anything about babysitting for the Ridpaths?"

"Not that I remember."

"Thank you for meeting with me. I'll likely be in touch again. Give me a call if you think of anything." I pass over another card and rise to my feet. "Do you mind if I pet Rocky?"

On the porch, I bag my little sample of fur and breathe in the salt air. Despite our civil conversation, I'm shaky with adrenaline. Feeling eyes on me through the mudroom window, I descend the steps carefully and walk toward my car, wondering if I'd failed to ask the right questions. A hard pit forms in my stomach. The nice thing about working with a partner is they make up for the blind spots.

Maybe I should have waited for Monday, for Eb. And I need food before I head home.

I stop for gas and peanuts, then start the long drive and review our conversation, slowly convincing myself I haven't fucked up. There are solid leads. Calling this Ethan person. Checking gas station security videos from here to Oakridge and back. The Forest Service might have cameras rigged near the cabin.

When I arrive home, out of sorts from spending so much time behind the wheel, the house feels glum and abandoned. My cleaning efforts left it overly neat, as if the kids and Trav have been gone for weeks. The silence is oppressive. My head buzzes from too much caffeine, and a throbbing vein above my right eye reverberates through my skull. I toss back three ibuprofen, two acetaminophen, and a huge glass of ice water, then text Trav: will you be around for dinner?

He doesn't answer. I interpret that as him being on the road and put together a family favorite, enchiladas. When they go in the oven, I sit at the table and tap my pen on the tabletop before dialing Ethan.

He picks up quickly, and after introducing myself, I say, "Tell me about your relationship with Samantha O'Brien."

"Ah, there's no *relationship* per se," he hedges. "Hang on." A door slams on his end, and the quality of sound changes as if he were in a closet. "Sorry, what's this about?"

"I'm hoping you'll speak with me about Samantha in relation to an investigation. I've been told the two of you are friends."

"Did Sam tell you that? Because that's rich."

"You're not friends?"

"We went out, but it didn't end well."

I cross the fingers of my left hand, the pen in my right

poised for action. "So you didn't plan to go camping with her last week?"

He hesitates. "I—listen. It's complicated. I considered going. What did she tell you? Because I didn't go, so I can't help."

"But you said you would?"

"Me and her brother are still friends. He didn't like her going off alone and depressed. I said I'd go if she promised it wouldn't be weird."

"What happened?"

There's a shrug in his voice. "I remembered how difficult it had been to break it off with her and decided I didn't want to get entangled again. Even for Otis's sake. I told her I was sick."

"What do you mean by difficult?"

There's a pause. "What is this about?"

"Could you answer the question, please? How was it difficult to break it off with her?"

He gives an uncomfortable laugh. "She kept calling me, demanding to know what she did wrong. Insisting she could fix it. Saying she was going to tell her brother I betrayed her. Mostly when she was drunk. Rejection brought out the worst in her."

"During the course of your relationship, did you ever see her become violent?"

"Our 'relationship' was about two-and-a-half weeks of meeting up for sex. There was no violence involved."

"Even when you broke it off?"

"We broke up over the phone. She hung up on me. And then commenced the drunk dials that same night. But no. No actual violence."

"Why did you break it off?"

"We were better as friends. There was this little spark of sexual curiosity between us that felt like it might be something, but on my side, anyway, it didn't take."

"Okay, thank you." I still don't know whether or not Sam left her campsite to kill Viveca in Meander, but at least I know she'd planned to spend the time with someone else, even if it fell through. The fact that she'd gotten drunk and obsessive after a past breakup is interesting though, and she admitted she'd had liquor for two at the cabin...

I need to drill down on Sam's location during the murder—and find Viveca's date.

Trav pulls up with the kids long after I've eaten my share of the enchiladas. Henry's asleep, and Trav extracts him from the car seat and carries him upstairs, legs dangling. Fern's face is flushed with tiredness, but she hauls her own overnight bag into the house, chatting to me about Nan and Poppa and the eggs in the old chicken coop and how Nan made soup from deer meat. She reports that Dad said she couldn't have dessert because she wouldn't taste the deer soup, but can she please have some macaroni and cheese?

I hug her and give her enchiladas instead, then unpack both kids' bags into the washing machine. The pipes start running before I add the detergent, and I realize Trav is in the shower. When Fern finishes her meal, I get her pajamas and tuck her in.

"I missed you," I tell her when I kiss her goodnight.

"I missed you too, Mommy," she says. "Next time you should choose us instead of work."

I grind my teeth. Did Trav tell her that, or did she hear him complaining to his parents? She watches me from under her eyelashes, testing whether this is a hot button, something to worry about. I say lightly, "I always choose you, honey. But Mom and Dad have to do the jobs that take care of our family too."

She snuggles down into her pillow, seemingly satisfied. "I love you."

"I love you too." I turn off the light and cross the hall to kiss Henry's forehead, noticing silence; the shower has stopped. When I creep to my bedroom door, I hear drawers slide open and shut.

Trav's stepping into his boxers as I enter the room. His face looks soft and tired in the glow of a single bedside lamp, but his jaw tenses as he turns to me. I perch on my side of the bed, and after a moment he slides under the covers on his side, facing away.

"Going to bed already?" I ask.

"I'm tired."

"Are you angry with me?"

"No. I couldn't sleep at my parents' house. I'm exhausted."

"You took off without telling me, you ghosted me all weekend, and now you're going to bed without even a hello."

"Hello, Kirsten. Is that better?" He hits the light.

I sit in the dark for a moment, heart thumping. Then I collect my pillow, which I'd optimistically left in place this morning, hoping for a happy reunion.

I pause at the door, listening to him breathe, before going downstairs.

17

QUINN

The top two drawers of the dresser in Quinn's new bedroom are empty, and the others full of spare blankets. Quinn unpacks, enjoying not having most of their belongings crumpled on the floor. They'd misjudged Bella. Moving to a small town made them paranoid in a way they aren't back in Portland, and it's uplifting to remember—most people are basically good.

After Bella leaves for the diner, Quinn signs on to the prison website and pauses with fingers hovering over the keys, but so far, nothing's really changed with Sheila. An antsy energy fills them, a need to act. The meeting with Gracen isn't until late afternoon.

Douggy's last phone call means something had happened she was desperate to share. Maybe it's time to confront the people most likely to have been harassing her: the mean girls of Meander Elementary.

With a rush of daring, they decide to track down Drew Armstrong. On the podcast, she'd been glossed over as part of "some girls in Douggy's grade at school," but Quinn remembers, and Ms. Finch had validated, that Drew was a ringleader. Maybe she's grown up enough to admit it. Maybe whatever Douggy wanted to tell Quinn happened in the neighborhood.

Online, Quinn discovers Drew's abandoned Facebook page, where she'd posted a picture of herself with an infant and two preschoolers in front of a Christmas tree thirteen months ago. Since then, nothing.

Quinn's determination wavers. They left childhood behind years ago, growing out of many—okay, some—of their early hang-ups. Drew's probably a different person now too, who no longer feels connected to things she did and said in elementary school.

But she hasn't lived Quinn's life. Quinn can't assume anything.

Sighing, they check other social media and discover Drew has no further online presence. Ms. Finch didn't have a phone number for her but knew the Armstrong house is still on the corner of Aspen and Fourth: "the big blue one with the chain link fence and the tacky deer sculpture." Quinn identifies it on Google maps.

A phone notification alerts them Gramps called. They swipe it away and decide there's plenty of time to walk over to Drew's before heading to the bus stop to meet Gracen.

The chain link fence is draped with abandoned beach towels, faded and soaked with rain, and the backyard, visible through the fence, is a weedy field. In the front, three ceramic deer have fallen as if downed by a hunter. Paint peels from the porch, and plastic ride-on toys mildew on the lawn.

Quinn knocks, battling the urge to turn tail. A woman who's the right build and similar in hairstyle to the photo on the Facebook page opens the door, but Quinn is thrown off by her apparent age. "Drew Armstrong?" Quinn asks dubiously.

The woman grins. "Nope. Hang on." She yells back into the house. "You have a visitor!" She turns to Quinn. "I was just leaving when you knocked. I live next door." Frowning, she looks Quinn up and down. "Are you selling something? I don't want any, and Drew won't, either."

"One sec! Changing a diaper!" comes a voice.

"I'm not," Quinn assures the woman. "I want to talk to Drew about her old school." A lie comes to their lips. "I'm writing an article."

The woman's eyebrows go up. "My son goes to Polallie Community College. He's studying graphic design. He loves it."

"It's Meander Elementary I'm interested in."

"Oh my, way back when. Well, I'm sure Drew will tell me all about it later. Bye, honey!" she calls into the house and hustles past Quinn and down the steps.

A warm miasma of mac and cheese and hotdogs escapes through the open front door. Quinn fleshes out their lie by the time a rapid pattering of feet alerts them small people are approaching. Two kids, maybe four and five, race in, followed by a woman who is definitely the same Drew as seen on Facebook, only not as well styled. Blond hair falls limply around her face from dark roots, and her face is pasty and drooping. She sets a toddler down on the floor—no gender clues, just baby curls and a dirty green T-shirt hanging to their knees—and they grab her calf and stare at Quinn. The older ones take off through another doorway.

Quinn says with deliberate cheer, "Drew Armstrong, right? I'm doing a biography piece about YouTuber Gracen Ridpath, and I'm trying to talk to a few of his sister's classmates. Would you be willing to chat? Completely off the record, if you want."

Quinn smiles nervously, wondering if Drew will spot the ghost of their childhood self in their features, but a sudden tantrum distracts her. After a cursory glance, during which Quinn regrets their black hoodie, cargo pants, and nail polish—she yells, "Quiet, or you're taking a nap!" toward the other room. Someone says "Shhhh!" and the crying slows to sobs, then fades away.

"Um, sure," Drew says when she turns back to Quinn. She even offers a smile. "I could use some adult company. My neighbor stops by for coffee, but she mostly talks about her cats."

"Great!" Quinn's shoulders drop in relief. They hadn't expected the ruse to work.

Drew leads them toward a spacious kitchen at the back of the house. "What was your name again?"

Quinn flounders for a fake name but realizes just in time that Drew might show up at Sunny's Diner. Being both a server and a journalist might look weird, but not as bad as being caught in a lie. "Quinn DeCelles," they say firmly. "Nice to meet you. I love your house." What they can see of it is worn country chic, overlaid with kid clutter and too much grime for Quinn's taste, but it's comfortable and homey.

"Oh, thanks! It's my parents' place. They're at work. Me and the kids are staying temporarily."

"I got your name from Ms. Finch," Quinn says. Another truth. "Your baby's pretty cute."

"Thanks. She's eighteen months and an absolute terror." Drew lowers the toddler into a wheeled device, and she pushes off across the tiled floor with both feet. Drew catches up and dumps a handful of cereal on the tray, then sits at the oak table with a thud. A thread of the older children's conversation intrudes from the other room. "I didn't say you could use the fire truck!"

Drew says, "Ms. Finch. Yeesh. I'm surprised she's still around."

"She's getting up there," Quinn says. "But she remembered both Ridpath children, and she remembered you and Jessica Cheng being in Douggy's class at school."

"Do you want some coffee or water or something? I have Diet Coke in the fridge."

"That's okay."

"I remember the Ridpath kids. Gracen was a few years older but on my bus. Douggy was my age, but she didn't attend school for long. You know about the dog bite?"

Eagerness in Drew's voice triggers Quinn's distaste, but they keep their face expressionless. "I've heard about it. There's some talk Douggy didn't cope well. That her death was the result of suicide. Have you heard that?"

Drew's mouth turns down. "I heard about Gracen's podcast, but I haven't listened to it." She shudders. "Douggy was only eleven."

"Do you think she had reason to kill herself?"

"No one has a good reason, do they? Especially a fifth grader. They shouldn't even know what suicide is!"

Quinn feels as if they're about to jump off a diving board. Under the table, they fidget with Douggy's bracelet, safely in its baggie in Quinn's pocket. "Gracen seems to think she was bullied into it."

"That's ridiculous." Drew's answer is immediate and flat. "What kind of monster would tell a little girl to commit suicide? I mean, maybe she felt bad about herself, maybe she thought being ugly would ruin her whole life…that's possible. But no one made her do it."

Quinn looks for evasive movements, darting eyes, but sees no obvious signs of guilt. At the same time, something comes back to them they hadn't thought about in years. A teacher pulling something off the back of Quinn's shirt after recess. Fourth grade—Mr. Bloom. He'd frowned down at it, crumpled it in his hand, then glared at the class and whipped it into his wastebasket. Heat filled Quinn's face, sweat prickled under their arms, and snickers came from all around. In the lunchroom later, a girl named Mona with hair down to her hips handed Quinn the crumpled piece of paper. "I thought you should know what Drew put on your back. I would want to, if it was me." She fled back to her friends, breaking out in giggles.

Quinn knew they shouldn't look, but they had anyway. It said WIDE LOAD in neon-pink highlighter, with an arrow pointing down. Hot tears flooded their eyes. They fled and locked themself in a bathroom stall.

Quinn asks, "Were you aware of teasing at the school?"

"Well, sure. But nothing out of the ordinary. And Douggy barely went to our school, like I said. It was only for a little while in fourth grade. She was homeschooled, because of her face."

"What was the teasing like while she was there?"

Drew shrugs. "Everyone is mean at that age, right? Before I got braces, my teeth stuck out in front, and Keanu Fischer called me a guinea pig. It's a lack of filters. You have to give as good as you get, right? It's part of growing up."

Quinn bites their lip, recognizing Drew's not going to confess she tortured Douggy. She may genuinely not remember the pointing and laughing, the name-calling. In her mind, it was normal.

Quinn asks, "Do you remember a kid called Kathy Fontaine? Ms. Finch mentioned her. A friend of Douggy's?"

The toddler wails, having wedged herself into a corner where two cupboards meet. Drew jumps up to point her into the room, and the wailing stops like magic.

"I do remember," Drew answers finally. "Really shy. Like, way too shy. And chubby. She wore this one pair of pants with a butterfly on the back pocket almost every day. Her family was seriously poor." She shrugs. "I didn't know her though. I guess she moved away."

The pants take vivid shape in Quinn's memory. The synthetic fabric that whispered with every step, Pepto Bismol pink with an elasticized waist like something a teacher would wear. They were the only thing Quinn owned besides plain gray sweatpants. Heat rises into Quinn's ears, as if residual shame has been lying in wait since childhood. They straighten their spine to shake it off. "How about Jessica Cheng?"

"Jessie, right!" Drew becomes animated. "She was one of my best friends. She dated my big brother for a while. She wasn't friends with Douggy though. She never came back after college." She sounds wistful.

"You don't remember her with Douggy or Gracen?"

Drew shrugs uncomfortably. "Her family lived pretty close to the Ridpaths. I'd see Gracen riding his bike around when

I went over there. Douggy, not so much. And kids played in the woods behind the neighborhood too. We ran into Gracen and Douggy back there once or twice." Drew looks down at the tabletop.

Quinn and Douggy made up elaborate pretend games in the woods, but they were supposed to stay close enough to the Ridpath's back gate to hear the grown-ups calling for them—not that they did. Still, Quinn can't remember seeing other kids back there. It would have ruined things, to think the mean girls could have been spying on them.

Something else clicks. Douggy, watching Drew's big brother Brett through the front window as he pedaled his trick bike to the dead end and back, turning at the Ridpath house with a jump or a wheelie, over and over, week after week. Quinn had asked if he was as mean as his sister, and Douggy shrugged and said, "It depends."

What if Brett was harassing her? He'd been a big, raw-boned kid who had a reputation for getting in trouble. He could have scared Douggy into keeping her mouth shut. Quinn asks, "How about your brother? Would he remember anything?"

She twists her lips dubiously. "He probably knew Gracen. They were close in age."

Quinn studies Drew's face. "Is there anything else you can remember that might help me put more of the story together?"

The toddler flings handfuls of cereal to the floor and laughs, then does it again. Drew sighs and shifts in her seat.

"Sorry. It's been too long. It's a blur. But good luck! Is this for a magazine or something?"

Quinn can't remember what they said at the beginning. "Background for a video interview. Thank you so much, you were really helpful. I'll definitely list your name in the credits. Would you mind sharing contact information for Jessica and your brother?"

"Jessica won't know anything interesting. And she won't talk to you anyway—she left Meander behind. But I'll give Brett your number next time I talk to him. Do you have a card?"

Drew looks forlorn, as if she were unwilling to be alone with her kids again.

Feeling caught out, Quinn reaches into a pocket, pretending to look. "Darn, I'm out. But you have my number."

They make their way to the front door, Drew yelling at the kids behind them, "Get out of there! That's mine!" Quinn emerges into the light of day feeling as if they've made a narrow escape. The sky is still gray, the wind chilly and damp. The visit had summoned not only flashes of long-ago Quinn and Douggy, but an echo of Sheila's old house, albeit in a minor key—trying to entertain Kade in the midst of squalor.

They slap down a sliver of pity for Drew's apparent unhappiness. Mommy and Daddy are still lending her a helping hand. If she had to deal with the kind of issues Quinn or even Sheila had, and without a safety net, she would probably shatter.

Their mouth quirks, just a little. That may have been the closest thing to a positive thought they've ever had about Sheila.

18

GRACEN

Gracen sits in Starbucks frowning at his sugary drink in a plastic cup. Mac packed and left this morning, and an hour ago, he'd gathered his courage to drop Aurie at Jane's again. Cookies baked and gifted, apologies made, bridges mended—but it was awkward. He had to bite his tongue to keep from offering to hunt for more overlooked dangers.

Quinn isn't late yet, but the impending meeting is making his stomach roil and his palms itch. If Mac hadn't encouraged him to follow through, he'd have backed out. For now, he's reserving judgment on whose impulse was better.

When a slight, dark-haired figure pushes through the glass door, wearing black lace-up boots, black cargo pants, and a fraying black hoodie, Gracen has no doubt it's Quinn. The voice from the phone call—nasal, mid-range, with a bit of a burr—fits this figure far more than the little girl he remembers. Despite knowing about Crinkle on the phone, he wonders again if it *is* the same person—and then stops himself. He'll be able to tell. And impostor or not, if they're here to scam money, they're out of luck.

He lifts a forefinger, and Quinn nods, face pale and serious. Within the chin-length parentheses of smooth dark hair, they have fine, bony features, a pointed chin, and straight brows. The face doesn't ring any bells, but fifteen years on, it's hard to remember exactly what they'd looked like: dark-haired with a whispery voice—but had their eyes been hazel or brown? Had their nose been narrow or rounded? He couldn't say.

Moments later Quinn sits across from him with tea in a travel mug. "Gracen, right?"

"That's me!" A jolly and slightly madcap persona snaps into place. It first appeared at the start of *Gracen's Hot Mess*; a confident social veneer to plaster over his damaged psyche. "So, I should call you Quinn?"

"Yes, it's Quinn DeCelles."

He nods. "I don't remember you very well, and I'm not sure why you want to talk, but I'm intrigued!" Gracen's forced breeziness seems to make Quinn uncomfortable, and his grin sharpens until their eyes connect. Gracen loses the smile, realizing his sham personality has been recognized as a shield.

"I brought this to show you." With one black-tipped, bony finger, Quinn pulls back the frayed hoodie cuff that swallows half of the opposite hand. At first Gracen thinks they're pointing to the moth tattooed on the web of their thumb, but he quickly refocuses as his heart leaps, recognizing the bracelet before his mind catches up.

It's ragged and faded, nearly an inch wide, woven in rainbow stripes. In truth, he doesn't recognize the bracelet but the type—a friendship bracelet, like the dozens Douggy spent hours weaving long after the fad was over, walking around with bunches of embroidery floss safety-pinned to the leg of her jeans so whenever she sat, she could keep going. She'd given him several by the time of her death. He'd worn the one on his wrist until it fell off—and burned the others in a cereal bowl in front of the open window of his room one stoned and lonely night during high school, watching black streamers of smoke drift upward in a kind of memorial.

He says, "Anyone can make those."

Quinn half shrugs. "Yeah. But this is the one Douggy made for my eleventh birthday. My favorite colors. I don't normally wear it, or it would've fallen apart long ago." They carefully pick at the knot, then lay it on the table.

Gracen reaches out as if to touch it, but Quinn pulls it back, then slides it into a baggie they produce from a pocket. Gracen grabs his cup instead. "Why are you here?" he asks, resigned.

Quinn watches his face and seems satisfied. They interlace their fingers in front of them on the table. "First, I need to know. Is it true that there's going to be a book or a movie? Are you going to name names?"

Gracen squeezes the bridge of his nose between thumb and forefinger. "No. There's nothing like that planned, and there won't be. I'm not interested in pointing fingers." He wonders why the rumors are so persistent. Mac counseled ignoring them, but maybe he should release a statement. His agent won't like that though—better to keep the potential in his back pocket as a play against unauthorized versions.

Quinn's studying him. "You're positive? You swear?"

"Yes! I don't need the money, and I'm not entirely sure this whole thing has been good for my mental health."

Quinn nods slowly. "Thank you. I believe you."

"Great. That's all you wanted to talk about?" A wave of relief passes over him, as if he's been let off the hook. He's about to push away from the table, but Quinn's shaking their head.

"No, please. We need to talk about Douggy. About your theory." Their head dips, hair swinging forward like a veil as they look down at their hands and ask, "Did Douggy leave a note?"

Something hurt and raw comes through the words. Gracen deflates. Quinn is the only other person alive who'd loved his sister. "No," he says. "There was no note." He says it with complete, comforting conviction, although he's wondered the same thing—what if Mom and Dad found a note? Maybe it mentioned him. What if that's why Dad left? What if that's why Mom hated him? Trying to pretend for his sake that it had been an accident, but all the while…

If there ever had been a note, it must have been destroyed. It's pointless to wonder, although he'd give a lot to know the truth.

Quinn doesn't seem convinced. They fiddle with their mug and inhale steam. The milk frother behind the counter rises in pitch like a leaf blower, then mercifully stops. Quinn asks, "What about your parents? Did they think she killed herself? Did they…hate me?" Quinn swallows.

Gracen blinks. "Hate you? No, why would they? I…" He stops and restarts. "You've been listening to *The Ridpath Girl*. Obviously."

Quinn nods. "If she did really do what you think—on purpose—I was her closest friend. I should have known."

"No! That's not the point at all. As far as I know, my parents believed it was an accident—although I think they held themselves responsible. I don't blame any one person, least of all you. It was the rest of us. The way we treated her, after the dog bite, making her feel damaged. Less than. All the little slights and implications that built up into a heavy burden." Impatiently, he blinks tears away.

Quinn remains silent, not meeting his eyes. He prods them. "Why would you think anyone would blame *you*? Douggy loved you."

Quinn's narrow shoulders raise and lower. "We…argued. Maybe a week before she died." Quinn chews their lip. Gracen remembers the kids fighting sometimes, huffing melodramatic sighs, sitting at opposite ends of the couch to watch TV. Throwing notes at each other instead of speaking but still hanging out because the grown-ups were talking. Quinn's mom swims into focus, a tired-looking lady who sometimes ate dinner with them or smoked with his dad out back at the picnic table, the little brother—Kaden—in tow.

Quinn continues. "Then Douggy called me late one night—my mom was already asleep on the couch. Douggy had been sick, not allowed to invite me over, but she begged me to sneak out. She said she had to talk to me, that it couldn't wait, and I'd be mad, but it was important." A frown knots Quinn's smooth brow. "We'd joked about sneaking out at night before because her window was on the ground floor. But I was afraid of the dark. Afraid of everything, really. I only made it past a few houses before I freaked out and ran back home.

"The next day, I called to explain, but no one answered. And the day after that, my mom said Douggy was dead."

Gracen had never spared a thought for the way the Fontaines disappeared from their lives. Douggy was gone, so of course they were too. But they must have been gutted. Gracen shakes his head. "Her being sick—that was already the mushroom poisoning. You not making it to our house had nothing to do it."

"Our fight could have though. Maybe that's what she wanted to tell me. That she'd been so upset with me, she'd eaten Death Caps. If she admitted it, I could have told someone. I could have saved her."

"No," Gracen says. "No." He reaches out, enfolds Quinn's cold pale hands in both of his. Quinn remains perfectly still, staring down at the table. "Don't torture yourself. There's no way to know exactly what happened. I started the podcast hoping it might help another kid, another family. Hoping people might think twice about how they treat each other. I didn't mean for anyone to think—"

Quinn yanks their hands away and grabs a paper napkin, swiping angrily at their face. "I'm fine. I just don't think we can know, and I'm not going to lie to myself." They swallow. "Mom told me Douggy was sick and then that she was 'gone.' Then Mom sent me away. It wasn't until I was older that I looked online for what really happened—at least, what the papers said. That it was an accident. That she found the mushrooms behind your house and thought they were good ones.

"The closest friendship of my life ended with us not speaking to each other and me too much of a coward to sneak out when she asked—but until I heard your podcast, I didn't put it together. I didn't realize I must have been the reason she died."

Gracen forces himself to straighten. As always, he spreads doom and despair wherever he goes. "It's not your fault," he says. "You were the best friend she ever had. She loved you. You guys playing and giggling together was one of the best parts of her short life. If there was a 'last straw,' it wasn't you."

He can't tell whether the words sink in. He says, "Listen, did she ever talk to you about people bothering her?"

Quinn swipes at their face again, then blows their nose and clears their throat. "I think she would have told me if anything really bad happened. But since I first heard your podcast, I've been obsessed. I still hope you're wrong—that it was an accident. But if you're right, I need to know if it *was* me or if I missed something big. I keep trying to figure out what she wanted to tell me." Quinn exhales a humorless chuckle. "I talked to one of the mean girls from fourth grade earlier today, hoping she'd tell me something that would let me off the hook." Quinn shrugs. "She didn't admit to anything, but she suggested a couple other people to talk to. I didn't tell her my old name. I said I was doing background for an interview with you."

Quinn's cuff falls as they push the hair out of their eyes, and Gracen gets a better look at the delicate black-and-gray moth with feathery antennae inked on their hand. It had an illusion of depth, as if it were a real insect at rest. He pulls his eyes away and says, "My mom worked. You were at school, I was at school. My dad was doing short-term gigs or sleeping off benders. Douggy spent a lot of time by herself. It's possible something happened when she was home alone. But it's far more likely that she just got overwhelmed."

Quinn dips their chin minutely, clearly acknowledgment rather than agreement. They look down at the table, chewing their lip.

Suddenly, Gracen's sick of talking about all this. He'd agreed to the meeting, but he'd also decided to end this fascination with Douggy and move forward.

There was only one more episode of *The Ridpath Girl*, dropping this coming Wednesday. After that, it would be over, in his mind and in the world. And this conversation was over too.

He glances at his watch.

Quinn notices. "Do you have to go?"

"I should. My daughter's with a babysitter." Jane won't care what time he picks up Aurie, but Quinn doesn't know that. Having no intention of following through, he says, "Maybe we can talk again." He pushes away from the table and grabs the jacket off the back of his chair. "It was good seeing you though. Really. Douggy loved you. Hold on to that, let go of the rest."

Quinn stands when he does, looking flustered. "Sorry, I didn't mean to make you—"

Gracen pretends not to hear and tosses his cup in the trash as he leaves.

19

KIRSTEN

With a grin, I get off the phone with Forest Service Ranger Dylan Tan and do a little dance in my chair. "She's the one!"

Eb, hunched over his computer with the posture of a question mark, looks at me sourly. "Dare I ask?"

"I fucking knew it! There was something dead in her eyes."

Eb raises his eyebrows. "Does this have something to do with you hotdogging around like the Lone Ranger yesterday?"

He's not happy with my field trip to Coos Bay, but it worked out fine, and based on the slideshow of snazzy wedding shots he's already foisted on me, he had a blast.

I tell him, "This has to do with a message I left with the Forest Service Saturday. I was hoping one of the rangers checked up on Sam while she was there, but they don't normally do that. However—da, da, da, DA!—someone always checks the propane tank between rentals."

Eb leans back, a half smile playing on his face. "I think I see where this is going."

"Sam, who spent the whole weekend huddled next to the propane heater, eating ramen—which must have been cooked on the propane stove—used zero propane."

He thunks upright. "Are we sure she didn't bring her own?"

"I asked the ranger. All the creature comforts in the cabin—lamps, stove, minifridge, heater—are hardwired to a propane tank out back. You can't switch in your own tank, and why would you? And guess what else."

"What?"

"This guy Tan was there the day after she supposedly left. There were half dozen branches across the road, which must have been from the ice storm two nights before. She would have had to move them to get her vehicle out. *If* she'd actually been there."

"Sounds damning. What do you want to do?"

"Did Akina finish reviewing gas station footage?" Sam said she'd paid cash for gas on the way there and the way back but claimed not to be positive which gas station she'd stopped at. There were two at likely intervals.

Eb grimaces. "She didn't spot Sam, but the cameras were poor quality and don't cover everything."

"Not helpful. Carrie told me the hairs I dropped off this morning are a little longer and coarser than the originals, but they could be from different parts of the same dog. We need to chip away at the rest of Sam's story. Let's confront her. Maybe we can wrap this up."

"Yeah, right." He doesn't sound thrilled, but he unfolds from his chair and stretches. "I don't suppose you want to delegate? Riley and Akina could use a field trip."

I'm shaking my head before he finishes his sentence. "She's mine. You can come if you want, but she's mine." I'm picturing Sam's freckled face, the looks she shot me to measure the impact of what she was saying, and I get a rush of adrenaline.

After all my driving yesterday, I'm happy to let Eb take the wheel. I gaze out the window and replay yesterday's interview in my head. She knew she'd be found out if she lied about Ethan, but she got away with as much as she thought she could.

I can't wait to see the look in her eye when I call her on her shit.

No dogs greet us, and there's no green Ford Focus in the drive. I cross my fingers in my coat pocket—Eb won't let me hear the end of it if we came all this way and no one's around. We ring the bell, and the dogs start barking inside. I peer into the mudroom through a window in the top of the door, and a flurry of canine energy appears, followed by Sam in holey jeans and a fisherman's sweater. She stops short when she glimpses us through the window, then opens the door. The scent of baking bread washes around us, but the air in the mudroom is only marginally warmer than outside. "What can I do for you, Detective?"

"Sam, this is my partner, Detective Simonson. May we come in? I have a couple more questions about your camping trip."

Her face goes blank, but she leads the way, holding the curtain to one side to let us enter the toasty kitchen.

The dogs settle onto the spread of blankets by the stove, but no one else is in sight. "Otis not around today?"

"He's at work."

"Did he take your car?"

She shrugs. "It started making a funny noise on my trip. He wants to check it out."

Sam doesn't ask if we'd like anything, just gestures for us to take a seat. There's a laptop next to her chair, and she lowers the lid and waits.

"Did you think of anything further you wanted to share?" I ask. "Maybe something you forgot to mention last time?"

"If I had, I would've called you."

"So, your camping trip... You holed up in a Forest Service cabin all week, in the middle of winter, huddled in front of the propane heater and drinking too much. Surviving on ramen cooked on the propane stove."

"Yes."

"But you lied. No propane was used."

She blinks rapidly. "No, I—Maybe the gauge stopped—" she tries, but I'm shaking my head.

"Also, the road was blocked."

Her face flushes a patchy dark red, and the pulse flutters on the side of her throat above the crewneck of her sweater. For a second, I think she might run or come at us across the table.

Instead, she says hoarsely, "I would never hurt Viveca. I'd never hurt anyone. But I get hurt. All the time."

Eb leans forward and says in his gentlest voice, "What do you mean by that, Sam?"

She looks down at her hands. "I know Otis will yell at me and say I should get a lawyer, but I didn't do anything wrong. I really didn't. You need to leave me alone."

"Can't do that until we know where you were and what you were doing when your ex got herself killed," I point out, trying to keep my voice even.

"Tell us what happened," Eb suggests.

For god's sake, she's sniffling now. Eb slides the napkin holder toward her. She blows her nose, and he nods encouragingly.

Sam sighs. "When Vee dumped me, I couldn't believe it. I thought we were working things through like grown-ups. I loved her, and it made me feel like shit, because this is not the first time this happened. I dated this one woman, Nadya, for three years; we were shopping for a house, we were looking into sperm donors. She didn't leave me at the altar, but it was close. I...well, I couldn't leave it alone. I didn't get how Nadya could love me one day and never want to see me again the next. All I wanted was an answer. What did I do wrong?"

"It probably had nothing to do with you," Eb says, as if he cares. I try to hide my eye roll.

"That's what Nadya said, but I didn't believe her. I kept asking. She claimed I was scaring her and told me she was getting a restraining order."

I narrow my eyes.

Eb says, "Huh. We didn't see anything like that."

"She didn't go through with it. When she threatened me, I gave up. Nadya and I hadn't talked in about five years. But when Viveca dumped me, it felt like the same shit all over again. I swore to myself, I was going to get an answer. The breakup was too fresh to talk postgame with Vee, so…I went back to Nadya. Last week."

My heart leaps into high gear. I sit forward, my face instantly hot. "Are you saying you have a freaking alibi? All this time, you had an alibi and didn't tell us?"

Eb holds an arm out in front of me as if I were a child in need of a seat belt. "Back up a minute. You invited your friend Ethan to go camping with you, and he confirmed that. Did he lie?"

She looks flustered and removes her beanie to run her fingers through her curls before slapping it back on. "No! But he's always been flaky. I had this idea in the back of my mind. Afterward, well…I didn't want to admit to my brother I went to see Nadya again, and then I didn't want to tell you guys I was stalking my previous ex while my recent ex was getting killed...so the cabin reservation seemed like the simplest alibi. I didn't know you'd make such a big deal of checking it out!"

She flinches from the look on my face and turns to Eb. "I swear, I had nothing to do with Viveca's death. I figured the simpler the story, the quicker I got off your radar, the better for all of us."

I slam my hand down on the table and rise to lean over her. Rocky starts barking, but I speak loudly, right in her face. "If this is another lie, I am going to fucking take you down. And if you're telling the truth? Expect the cops to stop by soon. You can't fuck with a murder investigation."

I pivot and storm out, not stopping until I'm at the car, one hand on the cold roof, head down as I wait for my heart to slow.

She's lying. She could still be lying.

Or I took us down the wrong path and fucked us over, just like with Sanchez.

The front door and then the gate bang shut behind me, and I turn to see Eb, face grim, bearing down on the car. "I'm driving," he says gruffly.

My stomach shrivels. Eb hates drama. I move out of his way. He climbs in and slams the door without acknowledging me.

When I'm in, he turns the radio on—some soft-rock station I can't stand. When I start to say, "I know I overreacted, but—" he blasts the volume. The little muscles at the corner of his jaw look like walnuts.

Hours later, as we pull into the sheriff's department lot, he says, "I didn't think I had to put up with temper tantrum bullshit from you, of all people. Just so you know, I'll be the one to follow up with Nadya. Sam said they went through the checkout at a Whole Foods together, so there might be camera footage. You go get your head on straight."

I bite back the answer I'd give anyone else—*Fuck off, it's my case*—and watch him stride to the building. When my pulse slows, I slink to my personal vehicle and drive to a sports bar, where the clientele does not tend to be cops.

Later, Eb texts to say Nadya Clement confirmed Sam's story. There's no way Sam could have made it up to Meander to kill Viveca late Wednesday night.

My phone buzzes with another text, this one from Trav.

Guess you're not making it for dinner. Nice of you to let us know.

20

QUINN

Monday morning, Quinn trudges through the rain toward Sheila's house, huddled in their big jacket and clutching a funereal umbrella borrowed from the Tarbells' mudroom. Yesterday evening, they'd called to tell Sheila about their success with Gracen and demanded another chance to talk. Sheila hadn't sounded happy, but she'd agreed Quinn could come after she dropped the girls at school.

Thinking about their last meeting, Quinn revisits the pain in Sheila's voice when she talked about Kade and about their father. Quinn doesn't recall much of the man—the echo of a tickly moustache, the blur of movement before a smack. Joshua Fontaine left when they were too young to retain a solid imprint of him, at least consciously.

He left much more of an imprint on their mother. Quinn had only ever noticed Sheila's flaws, without seeing the blows behind them. The background is clearer now. Sheila fled her parents' cold, strict household for the passionate arms of a violent man. She escaped to find herself in poverty with two young children and no skills for independent living.

Maybe it's time to forgive, or at least approach her with a little more understanding.

Dread lodges in Quinn's gut. They don't want to empathize with Sheila. The whole idea has been to shame Sheila into giving what is owed, so Quinn can save Kade and deserve his love again. But Sheila can't be forced to feel the way Quinn wants her to feel.

Quinn shakes it off. One way or another, Sheila is going to write the letter Kade needs. If worse comes to worst, Quinn can pretend to have more influence over Gracen than they do and threaten to out Sheila's friendship with the Ridpaths to his entire audience.

Sheila is on a different page. A greeting-card-sized envelope saying "KATHY" in messy hen scratch is taped in the center of the holly wreath on the front door. It hits Quinn like a punch—deadnamed and stood up at the same time.

They tug the envelope free and knock halfheartedly just in case. No one comes. Above the steps, there's an awning, and they collapse the umbrella and lean it against the doorframe, then pull out the card.

There's a generic print of a bouquet on the front, a dense tangle of handwriting within. Quinn skims the first few lines.

Dear Kathy—I know you don't want to be called that anymore but I'm talking to the little girl I knew and loved who is still in there somewhere and who maybe still has some love for me. Thank you for talking to Gracen, it means a lot, but I need to think. The kids and I are going away for a few days. Don't call me, I've blocked your number, and if you use another one I'll hang up. I'll let you know when I'm ready to talk.

Quinn's breath whooshes out with the force of betrayal. Quinn was brave, but Sheila ran away. Quinn came on too strong, too fast. They should have toned themself down. They should have been more skeptical about Sheila's easy agreement, or found compassion earlier, or blackmailed her already.

You'd catch more flies with honey, Gran would comment with narrow eyes and pressed-together lips, when Quinn's outbursts came. What were they supposed to do with that?

It doesn't matter. The sentencing hearing is in just a couple weeks. Kade's attorney needs the parental statement for leniency in sentencing as soon as possible, preferably yesterday. Kade could spend extra decades in an inhumane institution surrounded by violent, twisted people, because Quinn can't deal with their mother.

Standing forlornly in the rain, Quinn wonders if they should bother to go to work. Then they remember the umbrella and return to grab it off Sheila's stoop. They're tempted to pound on the door, make a scene, as if Sheila's cowering inside. It would be satisfyingly melodramatic in an un-Quinn-like way, but Sheila's not there, and the gesture would be as empty as the house.

Quinn pulls their phone out of their back pocket, thinking to update Kade right away. Tear the Band-Aid off. He never replies to their attempts at communication, but according to Gramps, he sees them.

Instead, Quinn scrolls through contacts to find Sheila's number. They tap out a text, acid in their throat.

If you think too long, it will be too late.

They wait for a full minute, hoping for reassurance or acknowledgment. Nothing comes. Quinn moves on.

They report to Sunny's in time for their long shift. It's their first workday with Bella as a sort-of-friend. They're startled when she lays a hand on their arm and asks, "You okay? You look peaky."

"All good," Quinn says and hurries onward.

The shadows under their eyes must be especially dark, or maybe their expression is extragrim, because later, after Bella leaves, Sunny corners Quinn as they load a tray with dinner specials in the kitchen. "Are you sure you're ready to come back? I may be able to find someone to cover the rest of your shift tonight."

Quinn mechanically turns up the corners of their lips. "I'm fine. Maybe my blood sugar's a little low. I'll grab a cookie."

Sunny narrows her eyes at them. "No. I'm going to get you one of those fruit salads with the fresh pineapple, and you're going to sit down and eat it!"

"Yes, ma'am," Quinn says, surprised into a real smile.

"Is Bella coming back later to pick you up?"

There had been no talk of rides when she left at four-thirty. Quinn says, "It's not much farther to walk than Viveca's was."

Sunny snorts. "Like I'm going to let you walk home in the dark with Viveca's killer still out there."

Quinn's smile fades. Sunny may be right. Quinn has a canister of pepper spray in their backpack and resolves to move it to their jacket pocket for easier access from now on.

Sunny drops them off around eight-thirty. Bella's in the TV room in yoga pants and a red hoodie, her hair in a loose bun on top of her head. The two dogs sprawl at her feet, limbs protruding from under the large coffee table.

"Hey," Bella says and yawns, putting her phone down. "I just got back from a walk a little bit ago."

"Did you go alone?"

"The dogs were with me. No one's going to bother me with these two by my side. Not that they'd hurt anyone." Bella scratches one of them along his neck, and the dog twists to look up at her adoringly.

"If you want, when I'm around, I'll go with you."

"Cool, I might take you up on that."

Quinn heads toward their bedroom, but Bella's voice stops them.

"Oh, hey, do you want to watch some Netflix in a bit? What do you like?"

Quinn hesitates. "I don't watch much TV." And they have a lot to think about. They never even read the rest of Sheila's card. It's the thought of all that tangled handwriting that clinches it. Fuck Sheila. "But a little vegging out sounds good right now. Maybe something funny? I need to jump in the shower and grab a snack first."

"Okay. I'll pick out some options."

When Quinn returns, wearing flannel pajama pants and an old Henley, Bella is curled under a fleece blanket and scrolling through comedy movies on the menu screen. The gas fire flickers, and Quinn feels a little bud of happiness at the sight of the blaze. The tension that's wired through their skeleton these days, even in sleep and under the heat of the shower, ratchets down a notch.

Bella speaks through a full mouth. "Did you see the cookies I made? I keep getting up for more, can you grab the plate for us?"

"I—sure," Quinn says, not wanting to go into their various

food sensitivities. One cookie won't kill them. And they should make an effort with Bella.

The kitchen is spacious and warm-looking, the tile floor softened by handmade rag rugs and the dark countertops alleviated by a profusion of plants clustered in corners and hanging from the ceiling. The cookies smell mouthwatering, peanut butter and chocolate. Quinn grabs a plate and paper towels.

"I hope you like them," Bella calls from the other room. "They're not that sweet, just a little maple syrup, and they have flaxseed instead of egg. Gluten-free flour. I'm experimenting with healthier snacks."

"Great!" Quinn calls, slightly more enthusiastically. They stick a mug in the microwave and return to the living room to set the plate and paper towels on the coffee table. Dewey and Truman start sniffing, and Bella diverts them with a treat, which they gnaw with gusto. The microwave beeps, and Quinn runs into the kitchen to grab their herbal tea.

"Did you find a good show? I'm not picky." Quinn settles on the free end of the sofa with a cookie, which they nibble and then finish off. Bella's right, they're not too sweet.

"How do you feel about *The Great British Bake Off*?"

"Is it a movie?"

Bella laughs. "No, it's a TV show. A cooking contest. Super light, super fun."

Quinn yawns. "Sounds good." They'll excuse themself and go to bed in an hour. They grab a second cookie and a third as their stomach rumbles, reminding them it's been a while since that fruit salad.

Bella starts the episode, and Quinn zones out quickly, saying "Mm" in response to Bella's comments about the contestants and their assigned bakes. When Bella says, "Quinn, can I ask you something?" they realize she's paused the program. Quinn blinks, feeling as if they'd been on the edge of sleep.

"Sure."

"Someone said you used to live here, as a kid. Is that true?"

Quinn's stomach plummets. Their face must show something. Bella says hurriedly, "You don't have to tell me. Sorry. I know you're a private person."

Quinn swallows and nods. "I don't like to talk about the past much, I guess. But yeah. I used to live here. A long time ago."

"You must have been happy here. To move back." Bella's voice is tentative.

"I guess I was, in some ways."

Bella looks expectant, waiting for more. Quinn flounders. It's the type of thing they've talked about with Paz, maybe, but no one else. "I was just a kid. You don't need much at that age."

Bella nods. "I've been thinking about it a lot—how to be happy. I don't want to be a waitress forever, you know?"

"Oh, um, right." They're relieved that it's Bella's turn to share. This is how you get to know people. "You don't like waitressing?"

Bella shrugs. "It pays the bills, but it's not fulfilling or anything. Don't you want more?"

On easier ground, Quinn points to the hawk moth tattooed on the web of their left thumb. "This," they say. "This is what I've been doing. Being an artist. Learning to ink. It's on hold for a minute, but I'll go back to it soon. If you have something, some kind of dream, you should work on it."

Bella scooches to look more closely at the moth. She reaches out a forefinger as if to trace it, but Quinn pulls back and tugs their cuff down.

Bella says, "C'mon, let me see! I never paid attention before, but it's really good, isn't it? Are there more?"

Reluctant and proud at the same time, Quinn eases the sleeve up to their bicep, revealing the graceful vine wrapping from midway below the elbow up toward the shoulder, and the oversized moths clinging to it, some not yet filled in. The design came out well, and they've done a lot of the inkwork themself.

"I love it." Bella's voice is soft, her eyes wide. "Is that all?"

Quinn rolls their sleeve down. "Mostly. I practice on myself, but not too much. I want to save the real estate for when I'm better. I do a lot on fake skin. There's still six months before I get to work alone."

"So, maybe this is rude, but how old are you?"

"Twenty-six."

"Ha. You don't look it. I'm already thirty. And when did you start learning?"

"The tattoo part, last year. I always loved to draw, but my life's been one thing after another, and I never settled down to anything. Until I realized if I didn't pick a direction, I might not like where I ended up." They shrug, uncomfortable with Bella's attention.

She nods. "Amazing. I mean, I've been sort of the same way, too much drama and not settling down. I'm not sure I could handle school." She looks down. "It would feel weird, being there with, like, eighteen-year-olds."

Quinn laughs. "That's not what community college is, at least. There's all types, all ages. You'd be surprised."

Bella settles back into her corner of the couch. "Yeah, maybe…" She picks up the remote control and a couple more cookies. Quinn sips their tea and takes another one too. The heart-to-heart seems to be over, and they didn't do too badly. They hope. Quinn eyes Bella.

She's holding the remote balanced in her hand with a thoughtful expression on her face. Instead of turning the show back on, Bella says, "I'm superstressed these days. My aunt died not too long ago. She's the one who brought me up."

"Oh, sorry," Quinn says. "Was she—was it expected?"

"No, she was young. I mean, middle-aged. Too young to die. She suffered for a long time though."

Quinn doesn't want to press. Maybe cancer? "That's awful. Were you close?"

Bella laughs bitterly. "Close enough. I mean, it was a

mother-and-daughter thing, even though she was my aunt. So, I miss her a ton. But it wasn't all great."

"Yeah," Quinn says. "My family's like that too. Not all great."

Bella looks up, wide-eyed. "Oh, right. Sorry, I didn't mean to make things all about me. I always do that. What's your family like? Do you have brothers and sisters?"

Quinn usually deflects questions like this, but they're tired of trying to figure out what's okay to say and what's not. They tilt their head back onto the couch cushion. "Just one brother. My gran died recently. She raised us, along with my gramps."

"So you know how I feel, kind of. Was she old though?" Bella sounds genuinely curious, not like she's trying to win the sadder-than-thou contest.

"She was an eighty-is-the-new-sixty kind of lady. Yoga and spin classes and swimming. Her mind was sharp as ever." Quinn lets out a bitter laugh, thinking sharp is the perfect word for Gran, who'd jab into any vulnerability like a splinter—or better, a fishhook, to drag you along.

For which Gran paid in spades.

"You look sad," Bella says.

"Not really. There's a little more to it." Quinn's not going to go there. They've talked to no one but Gramps—and Paz—about this. But then they do. "My brother hit her with his car. Kind of on purpose, although he wasn't totally in his right mind."

Bella sits upright in her cozy nest. Her face flushes. "He… killed her?"

Quinn wishes they could rewind the last minute. Now Bella will hate them and suspect them of being violent and twisted. Maybe she'll even reconsider renting them the room. "I don't know why I told you that. I'm sorry. It's not… I mean, it is as bad as it sounds, but Gran was manipulative. Psychologically abusive." And physically, in Quinn's case, with Gran's draconian diet and exercise program, but as far as they know, those requirements had not been applied to Kade.

"I'm not judging you. I'm not even judging him!" Bella laughs nervously. "I get it. My family was not great, either. I mean—the reason I lived with my aunt and cousins? My parents OD'd. They were addicts."

The mystery of Bella's sudden kindness is solved. Of course she's drawn to Quinn. The few people who like them almost always turn out to be damaged in some way. Broken calling to broken. Except Paz, who's likely given up on Quinn by now.

On-screen, one baker's cake layer is paused in the act of sliding from the top of the cake. Bella scooches over and squeezes Quinn's arm. Startled, Quinn looks into her eyes and is surprised to see genuine sympathy.

"It's okay!" Bella says. "It's not a big deal to me at all. I was just trying to tell you I get it. Life sucks sometimes. Not all of us get dealt a great hand."

"Right." Quinn reaches for something more to say and

can't think of anything. Weakly, they ask, "So, um, do you want to watch the rest of the show? I'm pretty tired."

"Can I ask one more question? I know, I'm nosy." Bella flashes a grin.

"What?"

"Why did you really come back here? You have your tattoo stuff. What are you doing working at a dinky little diner in the ass end of nowhere?"

"You don't give up, do you?" Quinn says, but they smile a little. "I might as well tell you, I guess I told you all the rest of my shit. My biological mother lives here. She knew her mother—me and Kade's gran—was abusive, and she sent us to live there anyway. Kade hasn't been sentenced yet, and the judge might consider input from family. I asked her to intercede on my brother's behalf. She owes him."

Bella nods. "What did she say?"

"No."

"Oh. Shit."

"Right."

"You're still trying?"

Quinn rolls their neck back and forth. They feel loose, warm, but that ache at the base of their neck never fully goes away. "Until it's too late, I guess... And I'm trying to figure out what happened to Douggy too..." Their eyes close.

Bella's hand squeezes again. "Douggy Ridpath?" Quinn doesn't even open their eyes.

"My best friend..." Quinn mumbles. They're so sleepy. After some amount of time, a minute or an hour, there's a click, and the room falls into darkness.

"[...]between the kids who stared or blatantly made fun, the secretary who told my sister she didn't belong in the classroom, and the teacher who couldn't manage the class, it was a disaster from the first."

—*The Ridpath Girl*, Episode 3: "A School of Bullies," 1 week ago

They should all pay the price, slowly and painfully. Like Douggy died.

—Comments section

21

GRACEN

When Gracen awakens, Aurie's gazing at him calmly from next to the bed, cuddling Zee-ba. She pulls her thumb from her mouth to announce, "Daddy, I'm hungry."

The phone on the nightstand says 8:34, a decadent sleep-in in the days of daddy-hood. He reaches out and tickles her, making her giggle. "Must be time for breakfast, pumpkin."

"I see your 'too," she informs him, and he glances down to see the left sleeve of his threadbare Simpsons T-shirt has ridden up to reveal the brightly colored skull. He tugs it down with barely a thought of doom. No more wallowing in the past. No more obsessing about his sister, no more dwelling on Aurie's resemblance to her, no more imagining Mom's last moments. He's practicing his best self, his *Gracen Stays Home* self—the balanced and loving parent he never had. It's working. Yesterday, he and Aurie had fun, he got caught up on work, the house stayed intact, and Mac was coming home tonight.

And he hadn't peeked at the photo album once.

"It must be breakfast time, pumpkin. What should we have?"

Aurie's one-track mind is still on the skull. "I want a 'too, too."

He hopes she hasn't inherited his tendency to obsess, but that's a worry for another day. For now, there are temporary tattoos in the kitchen junk drawer. "If you get dressed and eat all your breakfast," he says. With the cast, she's been struggling to dress herself, but he and Mac are holding fast to expectations or Aurie will have them waiting on her hand and foot. She looks glum. Gracen adds, "You have to escape the monster first!"

She shrieks as he lunges for her and pursues her in slow motion until she flees into her room and slams the door. He's halfway downstairs when she sticks her head out and yells, "I want French toast!"

"Nope, peas and carrots. With peanut butter!"

In the kitchen, he putters, making coffee, putting together French toast, making himself a smoothie and starting to think about the day. The last day without Mac, thank god.

There's more editing to do. During the salad days of *Hot Mess* he had a production team, but the vodcasts have been a one-man job, aside from a little contract work for the intro/outro music and website updates. Mac says he should hire an editing assistant at least, but the downshift in revenue still bothers him even though overall, they're fine. Overworked is better than bored, anyway. Feeling useless leaves too much time for introspection.

"Did you do my French toast?" Aurie asks sternly.

He looks up from his organizing app to see she's wearing sparkly blue leggings, a red T-shirt with a dancing hippo on the front, and her painting smock, which is one of Mac's old button-down shirts splattered with previous creative efforts. Clips hold back her staticky, unbrushed hair.

"Great job on the clothes, hon. Come sit down and I'll get your French toast. Can I pull your hair into a ponytail so it doesn't get in your syrup?"

She levers herself into a booster seat and nods. He's become a man who usually has at least one hair tie on him, and he smooths the fine dark hair into something Mac would find acceptable. "Blueberry or maple syrup, ma'am?" he inquires.

"Bofe. And two cooties."

Cooties are "Cuties," the little oranges she eats by the bagful. He obediently peels them and adds them to her plate, then asks, "Are you wearing your smock so you can paint after breakfast?"

She nods. "I want to paint my garden."

He has no idea what she's talking about but nods encouragingly. "I'll get you started. And you're going to Jane's house later, so Daddy can get some work done."

"Is Mommy coming home today?"

"That's the plan," he says. Mac's been updating him nightly. Simone's surgery is scheduled, and Mac will probably go back then too. For now, she's offering much-needed emotional support.

Aurie gives a sigh, and he looks up to see her pushing one of her oranges around her plate with a troubled look. He asks, "Do you miss Mommy?"

"I'm making her a picture." Shaking off her melancholy, Aurie pushes back from the table and slides to the floor.

"Hang on! I want that dish brought to the sink, little girl, and let's get some of that syrup off your face."

She complies, rolling her eyes. "Can I have water for my paintbrush, Daddy?"

"I'll be up in three minutes."

She hops away. He drinks the dregs of his coffee, oddly cheerful. With Aurie busy, and a planned work block later in the day, maybe he can relax. When Mac's around, he can't goof off because she's always busy, in class or studying or doing chores or spending time with Aurie. He has to stay equally busy to feel like they're a team, and when they chill, they chill together. This is a rare opportunity.

He can't remember the last time he dusted off the PlayStation.

After setting Aurie up with the easel in her bedroom—and strict instructions that any drippy pictures go faceup on her table and not facedown on the bed—he tells her he'll be downstairs if she needs him.

She ignores him, considering her blank paper with lips pooched out and a line between her eyebrows, like her mom hitting the law books. He snaps a quick photo and, in the hallway outside her door, texts Mac: Look, it's mini-Mac!

The PlayStation lives in the seldom-used family room, where their retired sectional couch watches over their previous TV and the pool table and pinball machine from Gracen's "Woohoo, I'm suddenly rich" bachelor pad.

Gracen discovers this is also where the banker's box from Wild Lilac ended up. Mac must have stuck it here Friday when he was out of sorts.

He collapses on the couch, realizing this has to take precedence over gaming. He tries to reclaim the optimism he'd woken with. Willpower! Willpower to leave the past behind. This box is too small to derail him, and he ignores a niggle of dread. When Mom first moved to Wild Lilac, it had been hell facing Douggy's stuff, Dad's stuff, even his own stuff. He'd trashed almost everything without looking at it. This box is a tiny subset of the few things he let Mom save from the purge, and most likely, it'll all go in the trash too. But because she's gone, and because the dose is small and he's older and wiser and wishes he had more photos and didn't burn all the bracelets Douggy made for him—and because Mac will ask and he doesn't want to seem like a coward—he's going to force himself to look at the contents instead of tossing the whole thing in a Hefty bag.

The knitted thing is a worn and pilly baby blanket. Hardening his heart, he tosses it. There's a handful of jewelry, nothing that looks valuable, but he hesitates, wondering if he should ask Mac about saving a memento for Aurie.

Then he tosses them. Mom had the opportunity to be a presence in Aurie's life, and she'd declined.

The knickknacks go into the wastebasket, even a carved elephant that ignites an ancient memory of zooming around at the Oregon Zoo, maybe five or six years old, while his parents lagged behind with Douggy in a stroller.

Among a series of banal home decorations, he finds a photo of Mom and Dad on their wedding day, looking impossibly young, that used to sit on the living room mantel on Honey Street.

He can't bring himself to throw that away, but he doesn't want to see it every day. He sets it facedown for now.

A few books remain. Two hardcovers missing their dust jackets: Stephen King's *The Stand* and an anthology of short mystery stories. He checks inside for inscriptions from mysterious visitors or new friends and finds nothing. Shrugging, he sets them aside. He or Mac may read them someday.

The final item is the spiral-bound sketchbook the manager mentioned, the same size as the other books but with a soft cardboard cover. Gracen suspects it found its way into his mother's belongings by chance. She never showed any interest in art or drawing when he was young, beyond heaping praise on what her children created.

When he opens it, he finds her initials. On the first page is a still life of a vase and two pears, childishly rendered but recognizable. Beyond that, the smooth corners of an envelope protrude above the rough-cut edge of the drawing paper like a bookmark.

He flips to it and finds multiple awkward attempts to sketch a squirrel darting up a tree trunk. The envelope itself is more interesting, letter-sized with "MARGIE" inscribed in blue ink, the paper thin enough to show the yellow of its contents.

He looks at the name for a long moment before flipping the envelope over. It's been torn open, and he withdraws a folded sheet from a legal pad.

Careful, tiny blue printing, all in caps, cover it like little blocks stacked on top of one another. A lot of people use block printing. It's neat and legible. But a lot of people didn't call Mom Margie. He flashes to his father at the kitchen table, inking the daily crossword in all caps, a beer in front of him.

With a sick feeling, his eyes skim the beginning.

DEAR MARGIE—

I'M SO SORRY FOR EVERYTHING AND I WANT TO MAKE AMENDS. I KNOW IT'S TOO LATE, BUT IF THERE'S ANYTHING I CAN DO, I'LL DO IT. IF YOU DON'T WANT TO HEAR IT, TEAR THIS UP AND FORGET ALL ABOUT IT.

Gracen's hands, holding the letter, drop to his lap. His heart is racing, chest heaving, as if he were sprinting for his life.

Dad is dead. At least, Gracen has assumed so for years. When Gracen sees toothless, hollow-cheeked men camping under the overpass, he flinches away, imagining that's how his father spent his last years before cirrhosis or malnutrition or exposure got him.

Shaking, he picks up the envelope. Not addressed, not stamped. Delivered by hand. Possibly by "Willie Nelson."

WE WERE TOO YOUNG I GUESS. I FELT SO LUCKY WHEN YOU CHOSE ME. GRACEN AND DOUGGY TRIPLED THAT. BUT I COULDN'T TAKE CARE OF MYSELF, AND SUDDENLY I HAD ALL OF YOU. I THOUGHT I COULD FAKE MY WAY THROUGH UNTIL I FIGURED IT OUT.

IT'S NOT AN EXCUSE. I TAKE RESPONSIBILITY FOR EVERYTHING. BUT THAT'S WHERE MY HEAD WAS AT WHEN WE WERE BROKE AND EXHAUSTED. I WAS SUPPOSED TO FIX

EVERYTHING BUT I COULDN'T MAKE ENOUGH MONEY, OUR HOUSE WAS A PIECE OF SHIT AND YOU AND THE KIDS NEEDED MORE THAN I COULD GIVE.

It sounds like Dad, and yet, not. Making amends—that's an Alcoholics Anonymous thing. It makes sense. If Dad is alive, he must have changed his ways.

Gracen runs his eyes down the laundry list of wrongs, looking for an acknowledgment that Dad wanted to make things up to Gracen too. But this letter is just about Mom.

It doesn't matter. Right now, he doesn't know what matters. The idea that Dad's maybe—no, probably—alive, feels like a battering ram to the chest. It's worse than the photo album creating nostalgia for an airbrushed past. Worse than Quinn wounded by his exploration of Douggy's death. Worse than his fears for Aurie.

Without conscious will, his eyes fall back to the page.

THE AFFAIR WAS UNFORGIV—

He stuffs the page back into its envelope like it's radioactive and tosses it to one side, then leaves the mess to trot upstairs where a four-year-old will save him from darkness and confusion.

22

QUINN

Quinn wakes on the living room couch. Gray light seeps around the edges of the blinds. They push to their elbows, noticing the duvet from their bedroom is over them, trying to remember why they're not in bed.

Bella steps from the kitchen in her work clothes, hair up into a bun. She yawns before saying, "Hi, sleepyhead. You crashed in the middle of that show. I didn't want to wake you."

"Oh," Quinn says. "Sorry." They normally struggle to fall asleep even when it's silent and dark.

"Don't be silly. I do it all the time. Not at nine-thirty though! You were wiped out. Maybe the CBD got you."

"Wait. What?"

"CBD? The superharmless part of pot? I put some in the cookies. It's like an antianxiety vitamin." Seeing Quinn's expression, she adds, "I only put a teeny bit in, I swear!"

Quinn scowls. They remember feeling more relaxed than normal, but they'd thought it was natural. "You should have told me."

"I'm so sorry. I didn't think. I swear, it was just a few drops to take the edge off. It's safe, I do it all the time. You're not allergic, are you?" Bella's face is aghast.

Despite themself, Quinn believes her. They roll their eyes, anger transmuting into amusement. "I'm fine, but if you'd told me, I wouldn't have eaten so much. The one time I tried CBD on purpose, it knocked me out." They suppress a yawn. "It's probably a good thing. I haven't been sleeping all that great."

"Well, just so you know. I promise not to actually, like, drug you."

Quinn snorts. "Any other add-ins I should know about?"

"Heroin, crack, meth… Just kidding!" Bella grins, seeming relieved to be forgiven. "I gotta go. The dogs are in their pen. They don't need anything. You on lunch and dinner today?"

"Yeah. See you later."

Silence closes around Quinn after the door closes. They lie back on the couch in the dim living room. For a second, that felt almost like bantering with Paz. A cramp of homesickness squeezes their chest. The long-haired black cat enters and stares up at them. Quinn reaches to pet it, and it runs away.

After showering and eating alone in the kitchen, they pull up New Hampshire State Prison's email app.

Hey, Kade—Managed to talk to Sheila. Even after I tried to help her out, she's too fucking self-centered to bother sending a letter and doesn't give a shit about either of us—

They slam a hand down on the table, then delete the draft. What can they say? He doesn't need to know Sheila equates Kade's act of desperation with their father's violence. He has a right to know he can't count on Sheila's help, but everything Quinn puts into words seems self-serving, as if they're blaming their mother instead of shouldering their share of responsibility. Nothing can change the fact that they abandoned him to Gran too.

For the first time it occurs to them—they could forge a letter to the judge. It would be a serious crime: mail fraud, perjury, who knows what else. But who cares? It seems unlikely the court would follow up, but if Quinn did get caught—well, maybe they deserve jail time too.

When the phone buzzes, they've been staring toward their blurred reflection in the stainless-steel refrigerator door for an unknown amount of time. They check reluctantly, wondering if they're being called into work early, but the text is from Drew Armstrong.

got Jessie Cheng's #. She agreed to talk to you😊

Drew had sounded so bitter about Jessica, it amazes Quinn she'd reached out to her. There's a fluttering in Quinn's chest, as if they're getting close to something important. Jessica dated Brett Armstrong, who may have confided in her. If whatever Douggy wanted to tell Quinn about that night happened in the neighborhood, Jessica may know, firsthand or secondhand.

Unless Quinn was right the first time, and Douggy wanted to tell someone she'd eaten the Death Caps.

Quinn swallows, wishing they could go back to believing Douggy's death was an accident. It's too late. Only the truth can free them now.

With phone in hand, Quinn looks through the glass sliding door, planning what to say to Jessica. One of the dogs is nosing around the base of a leafless tree as the endless drizzle continues.

Drew may have given Jessica a heads-up on hiding anything she'd already lied about, making the conversation pointless. But Quinn has to try. They hit dial and prepare for voicemail, but Jessica picks up on the first ring.

"Hello, Jessica Cruz speaking."

A married name? The voice is cool and professional. Quinn sits up straight in their kitchen chair and attempts to match it. "Jessica, hi. This is Quinn DeCelles. I believe Drew Armstrong spoke with you about me. I'm doing a biography piece about the popular YouTuber and podcaster Gracen Ridpath, and I'm speaking with some of his and his sister's classmates."

"Yes, I spoke with Drew. I'm curious about this project you're doing. I haven't been able to find any of your work online."

Ouch. Quinn fumbles for a response. "My work so far has been for small papers without an online presence. I'm just starting out with, you know, broadening my scope."

"Drew mentioned you got her name from the old school secretary, so I gave her a call."

Quinn's heart pounds. "You called Alicia Finch?"

"I did."

Quinn's expecting it but nevertheless freezes when Jessica pointedly adds, "Kathy."

Heat boils into Quinn's face. They never were good at lying. Half defensively, half in anger, they say, "Yes. That was my birth name. But it really is Quinn now."

"So, what are you doing, if not background research?"

Quinn clenches their jaw and then regroups. "I heard Gracen Ridpath's podcast about Douggy, that she was bullied into suicide. She was my best friend. I need to know—"

Jessica laughs harshly. "So you go to Drew and me, naturally."

Quinn remains silent.

"I get that," Jessica says. "We were awful to you. To both of you."

Quinn hears regret in her tone. "I remember."

"Believe me, I felt bad about it, even then."

"But you did it anyway."

"I thought I had to. It was the way things were. I'm hoping to teach my kids to be better, but back then, even though we knew it wasn't nice, we didn't have an alternative model."

Jessica sounds contrite, if overly academic, but Quinn's not sure they agree with the distinction she's trying to make. They wait.

Jessica says, "That's why I told Drew to give you my number. I've always felt terrible. Even though you called under false pretenses, I wanted to apologize."

"Too late for Douggy," Quinn says.

"Yes. I'm so sorry."

Quinn bites their lip. The loneliness from those years faded so much in comparison to living with Gran that it's like it happened to someone else. But offering forgiveness would imply condoning Drew and Jessica's treatment of Douggy, which they can't do. "Do you remember what you did to Douggy? Specifically?"

"Oh, jeez. Horrible stuff. Laughing at her in gym class because of her scars. We said it looked like her nose was going to fall off and nobody would ever kiss her. I hate myself for this now. If someone ever shames my daughter for how she looks…I'll kill them."

"You lived near the Ridpaths. I'm trying to figure out if something happened outside of school that I missed. That last summer after fourth grade, or in early fall?"

Jessica hesitates, then says, "Not that I know of. We didn't hang out together. You remember."

Quinn's curiosity is piqued by Jessica's caution. "I wasn't around all the time. Did you run into Douggy and Gracen outside? On the streets or in the woods?"

"Sure, in passing, but it's not like we threw rocks at them. I don't know what Drew told you, but it never went beyond name-calling. I wish we'd been nicer, that we'd tried to be friends. But at that age, it feels like you have to choose."

Quinn doesn't remember having to choose; they just remember being chosen only by Douggy. There has to be more to it. "What about Drew's brother?"

That elicits a drawn-out groan. "Brett was not a nice guy back then."

"Do you remember anything related to the Ridpaths? Maybe beyond name-calling?"

Jessica answers reluctantly. "Oh...there were snowball fights. Pushing, shoving. Brett didn't like Gracen. He took against him in a big way."

"Drew said you dated him."

Jessica laughs. "That was my bad-boy phase. But seriously, he'd matured by then. I'm sure he's sorry for how he acted in those days. You know, I bet he'd talk to you. He's on Facebook. You should reach out."

Quinn pictures big, ham-handed Brett pushing and shoving Douggy and shudders. "Sure, I'll do that. Do you remember anything else?"

"No..."

She sounds uncertain, and Quinn pushes. "But?"

"Brett used to hang out in the woods behind the neighborhood. He and his friends had a stash of stolen booze back there through most of middle school and into high school. Me and Drew would spy on them. Once in a while, the Ridpath kids would play back there too. They could have run into the older kids or stumbled across the stash."

Something to ask Brett about. Quinn scribbles a note. "Can I call you if I think of anything else?"

"Sure. Good luck with finding the truth about Douggy. I understand why you want to know, but my guess is, you're going to have to move on. We all do." Jessica hangs up, but her words echo in Quinn's ears.

There's a knot in the pit of Quinn's stomach as they head to the diner at eleven. The air is still under a low gray sky, and they walk through a landscape of yellowed lawns with leftover Christmas lights glimmering in a few windows.

Quinn tries giving themself a pep talk. No solid answers from Drew and Jessica, but maybe Ms. Finch's caregiver found the photos she mentioned, and those will ring some bells. And maybe Sheila will return as soon as tomorrow with a change of heart. Maybe everything will work out.

At work, they submerge themself in the noise and stink

and surface demands of the diner to drown their circling thoughts, and at four-thirty, take a break before the dinner rush to visit Ms. Finch. Sunny's given them a take-out box with a half dozen cinnamon muffins left over from breakfast. Quinn expects the photos to raise more difficult emotions but braces to receive them with a happy face for Ms. Finch's sake.

The little duplex looks the same as before, and Quinn knocks briskly. A loud noise emits from inside, maybe the slam of a door, and Quinn wonders if they've startled the old woman. Maybe they should have called.

Tiny pellets of hail begin to bounce off the concrete sidewalk and the road beyond, collecting like scattered gems in the grass. Quinn huddles into their big black jacket as the sound changes and the hail shifts into a downpour of freezing rain.

Still no answer. They lean close to listen, then knock again. She could be in the bathroom. Maybe the noise came from the neighbor's house. Gently, Quinn twists the knob and finds it locked. Sighing, they check the time, then perch on the chair by the door with the muffin box on their lap, warming their hands as they watch the rain drip from the gutter. After a few minutes, they dial Ms. Finch's number.

A phone rings inside. No one answers.

Okay, not home and she left her phone. Quinn unearths a pen from their backpack, scribbles on the muffin box. *These are for you! I'll stop by another time for the photos. ~Quinn.* They tug their hood up wishing they had the Tarbells' giant umbrella with them, then resign themself to the deluge.

A niggle of worry stops them. What if that noise was Ms. Finch falling? What if Quinn's knock surprised her and she fell and hit her head? "You always expect the worse," Paz often tells them.

Well, yeah. Exhibit A. Quinn's life.

They move past Ms. Finch's door toward the chain link gate, which appears to lead into a minuscule backyard. It's not locked, and Quinn follows the concrete path to the back of the house, where the kitchen window is at eye level. The curtains are open and the lights on. Quinn peeks inside.

At first they think the room is empty. Then a movement off to one side, low and quick, draws their eye. They squint and reangle themself and make out a yellow-socked foot, jerking erratically.

Quinn runs back around and shoves at Ms. Finch's front door. It flies open, and Quinn dashes through the cramped entryway and around the two-seater table. They fling the pantry door open to help Ms. Finch—

But she is beyond help. Quinn gags at the blood and the look on her face. Stumbling blindly, they retreat to vomit into the arborvitae between Ms. Finch's driveway and the neighboring property, then dial 9-1-1 with shaking fingers.

23

KIRSTEN

When Eb calls, I'm massaging my left eye socket where a headache is threatening, even as I continue to squint at the computer screen. We haven't spoken since the debacle at O'Brien's, and I keep going back and forth between feeling like I owe him an apology and being pissed that he overreacted to my overreaction. On the other hand, his bottom line is professional, all the way, and it's made me a better cop trying to live up to it.

"Boon here," I say, finally picking up.

His voice is electric with tension. "We've got another body."

No doubt it makes me a terrible person, but my first reaction is relief. Viveca's case notwithstanding, murder is rare in Melakwa County. Our interpersonal shit will go on the back burner, and by the time we get to it, it'll have expired.

"Guess who called 9-1-1." He answers himself with satisfaction. "Quinn DeCelles."

Beginning to draw my wits about me, I ask, "Who's dead and where?"

"An elderly woman named Alicia Finch, at her home in downtown Meander. Sarge wants me to be primary, and if the two cases are linked—it will be a stunning coincidence if not, but who knows—we're already collaborating."

The county's one other detective, Arlen Thomas, is on extended medical leave. If our cases aren't open-and-shut, which they won't be if they're linked, the sheriff will have to request backup from one of the city police departments. Things are about to get complicated.

My thoughts race. I was initially suspicious of DeCelles and still don't understand why they moved to Meander. Their presence at another homicide is a coincidence too far.

"Docker! I said, where you at?" Eb asks.

His raised voice stabs behind my eye. "Office."

"Get down here. Forty-nine and a half Oak Street, the unit on the left." He ends the connection.

I head over after swallowing a painkiller. The neighborhood is a row of little bungalows, some divided into duplexes or triplexes. The victim's address has a cruiser out front. A few neighbors hover anxiously on covered porches, out of the rain. I cut across the lawn, glancing at Quinn DeCelles in the back of the cruiser. The car door is open despite the weather, and they hunch over a steaming paper cup as if praying to it, unmoving as I pass.

I pull on my bunny suit and booties once I'm under the overhang that runs along the side of the house. The door is held open with a brick, and Eb and Carrie are talking within.

Crossing the threshold, I get an impression of warmth and colorful clutter. A tiny kitchen with yellow countertops is to the left, a crowded living room full of plants to the right. I smell something familiar that niggles until I place it—cream of mushroom soup mixed with the tangy scent of blood. Ugh.

Eb comes up to me shaking his head. "It's bad."

"When is it not?"

"She was a frail old lady. Who'd be in such a hurry for her to die?"

"Maybe someone should look into that. Oh wait, that's our job." I'm giving him shit because no matter our victim's age, gender, or position in life, he finds a reason to be personally offended by each death. It's one of my favorite things about him.

Eb gestures toward the kitchen. "She's in the pantry. You'll see her once you go in, but it's a tight squeeze. We'll be in the living room."

I enter with a lump in my throat. Alicia Finch is on her back on the floor of a closet lined with canned soup, cereal, and other household necessities. Her legs in yellow slacks extend into the kitchen. A shiny, apparently bloodless butcher knife is near her outflung right hand, and a wooden cane with a crook-handled top lies across her torso. A hank of hair like cotton candy is stuck to the cane. Blood saturates a slice through one shoulder of the fuzzy yellow sweater and pools shockingly bright on the laminate floor below. Her thin orange hair is matted to the side of her head.

No doubt Gene will have an opinion, but it looks like she fell straight back after being walloped in the head with that cane. When was she stabbed, and with what? If the butcher knife is the weapon that sliced her shoulder, it must have been wiped clean—or it could be a decorative flourish, akin to the fir fronds at Viveca's scene.

Like Viveca, Alicia Finch appears to have been stabbed and bludgeoned, but almost all the other factors are different: race, age, location of death. She's less artfully arranged, if at all.

I scan the rest of the scene and then retrace my steps into the living room. A worn love seat half covered by a mass of knitting and a balding blue recliner face the TV. A jigsaw puzzle on a card table takes up one corner, and an open door leads to a bedroom.

Evidence markers have been placed, and Carrie's taking photos. Eb searches through magazines and other objects piled on a glass-topped coffee table.

"Did you talk to Quinn?" I ask.

"Not much. You two already have a rapport, so I saved that

for you. And guess what. Carrie found white hairs on the body. Reminded her of your scene."

My heart picks up. "Dog hairs?" Sam O'Brien's dog, Rocky, is out of the picture, thanks to her alibi. The hairs from Dunwoody Park remain unattributed.

He shrugs. "Could be."

"What else do we know?"

"The 9-1-1 call was a little before five. Quinn came by on their dinner break from Sunny's, supposedly at Alicia's invitation. There was no answer when they knocked. They heard a noise, thought Ms. Finch may have fallen, and peeked through a window at the back of the house. Saw the body, thought she was still moving, and ran inside. Quinn swears the door was locked when they got here but open when they went to help the old lady. It doesn't look like anything has been forced."

"What was the noise?"

"If they're telling the truth? Possibly the cane hitting the floor, or maybe that pantry door slamming against the wall. Quinn may have missed the killer by inches."

"Did they touch anything?"

"Quinn? No. Saw it was too late for Alicia and went outside to call for help. They lost their cookies in the bushes."

I'd picked up a whiff of that, walking by the front door. "What do you think of their story?"

"They seem pretty shaken, but that could happen whether they killed her or just found her. Viveca Crandall's whole scene was staged. Not that her death was cleaner. But the killer took some time to make it look peaceful. Finch looks rushed."

I noticed that too. It could suggest there are two different killers—maybe Alicia's killer was inspired by Viveca's, emboldened by the reality of a murder in town. Or it could mean the killer heard Quinn's knock and rushed out before finishing.

Speaking of which—"There's only one door?"

"Yeah. If Quinn's telling the truth, the killer was inside when they knocked, waited while Quinn went around to the back, and then booked it out the front, leaving it ajar."

"Or, Quinn came in, cornered the victim in the kitchen and killed her, then went outside, puked, and called 9-1-1."

Eb plays devil's advocate. "No obvious blood spatter on them, which there should be after the stabbing. And—why call 9-1-1?"

I ask, "Any corroboration from the neighbors? Anyone seen running away?"

"Riley and Akina are taking statements now."

Someone knocks, and Gene's voice calls, "We're here!"

"I'll get out of your way," I tell Eb. "Keep in touch."

When I slide into the cruiser, Quinn looks up. I glimpse devastation before they clamp their jaw, but their eyes and nose are both red and there's no hiding the shivers that travel through their body every few seconds or so despite the big black jacket. I scan for stains, but Quinn is soaked with rain from head to toe. Everything will have to be tested.

"I figured you'd turn up," Quinn says sourly.

"Your lucky day," I answer. "Are you okay?"

There's a short silence. Then, "Not especially. I've never seen anything like that before."

I give them a moment, then ask, "Can I get your name and contact info again, for the record? You have a permanent address yet?"

"I'm staying with one of the other servers from Sunny's. I can't remember the house number, but the people who own the house are the Tarbells, and it's on Aspen Street." Quinn rattles off their name and cell number.

"How did you come to be here today? You knew Alicia Finch?"

"Oh, god." They squeeze their eyes shut. Another shiver goes through them.

"Hang on, let's get the heater going." I jump out and get the keys from the deputy, then start the engine. "Close your door. You're probably in shock."

They obey. The warm air blows, and they relax minutely, then say, "I didn't really know her, but when I was a kid here, she was the school secretary."

I gape in disbelief. There was something about Meander's school secretary… I place it in seconds—*The Ridpath Girl.*

My mind ping-pongs among newly emerging connections, like a constellation outlined in the night sky. Was Ms. Finch the one who'd undermined Douggy's attempt to go back to school? And Quinn. If Quinn lived here back then, they may have known the Ridpath girl too. Their proximity to a second homicide is that much less likely to be coincidence.

Trying not to give away my level of excitement even as the pulse in my throat jitters like a jumping bean, I ask, "You lived here as a kid? You went to Viveca's school?"

Quinn nods, color rising in their face. Busted. "I didn't know Viveca though. She was older, and I left when I was eleven."

"Did you know the Ridpath girl? Melissa 'Douggy' Ridpath?"

Quinn's brows draw down, and their pupils widen. "Douggy? You think this—this is about Douggy?"

I wait.

"I mean—yes. She was my best friend. Until she died."

I take a breath. Meander is less than two thousand people. It was likely even smaller fifteen years ago. Everyone here may have known Gracen and his family.

But not everyone seems to have been hiding that fact.

Quinn shrinks away. "Douggy has nothing to do with Ms. Finch's murder."

"How do you know?"

"I—How could it?"

I grind out, "Tell me everything. Who you are, why you're here, and all of your movements for at least the past twenty-four hours."

Quinn tells me about their years of friendship with Douggy, and their return to town to request help from their deadbeat mother. They confirm Alicia Finch was the school secretary when Douggy attended. I learn Ms. Finch was recently part of a school committee that invited Gracen Ridpath to speak in town—and she had a caregiver, which Eb may not know yet. This person likely has a key to the house and will need to be questioned.

I ask, "Do you know the helper's name?"

"No idea," Quinn says, sullen now. The car is almost too hot, and they've peeled off their jacket, releasing a peppery smell of body odor and diner food. "I just know they did shopping and cooked and brought her to doctor appointments."

"Did she mention their schedule?"

"I think they had weekends off. She said something about them leaving her with a pot of soup for the weekend."

I look at Quinn and sigh, my anger fading. Even if I'd known Quinn went to Viveca's school, I would have gone down the Sam O'Brien road. The ex had to be ruled out. Quinn will need to come in and go over this again, but they're looking rough and I cut it short for now, asking, "Did you notice the photos she promised you when you went in today?"

"I didn't look." Quinn shudders. "I could have helped her! She was moving when I got there. I saw her move!" Their shoulders shake as they hunch over and hide their face.

I hesitate. Usually, I'd offer a shoulder squeeze, but Quinn gives off a strong don't-touch-me vibe. I pull a pack of tissues out of my jacket pocket and wait for them to recover. When they straighten, sniffling, I hand it over and say, "Keep it."

"Thanks." Quinn wipes their face without meeting my eyes. "God. This is fucked up."

I can't afford to take their apparent shock and despair at face value. "We need the clothes you were wearing when you went in. I can drive you home—"

Quinn shakes their head. "I need to go back to the diner. I'm already late. I called Sunny and told her, but—"

Oh, shit. "Did you tell her who the victim was?"

"Yeah—I didn't think not to." Quinn looks at me with wide eyes.

I groan internally. The whole town must know every detail of Quinn's story by now, served up with burgers and fries. "Tell her the police asked you not to share any more, okay? Tell her we haven't notified Ms. Finch's family yet. They shouldn't have to find gory details on social media."

"I had to tell her something."

"I know. Actually, you're in no shape to go back to work. I'll call Sunny and drive you home so you can give me your jacket, hoodie, pants, and boots."

"You must be shitting me," Quinn says.

I open the cruiser door. "We'll take my car," I say. "C'mon."

In the evening, I review the interviews the deputies conducted on the Viveca Crandall case. Phone records finally came through, showing a number of calls to and from a burner phone in the last weeks of Viveca's life. Some were as long as twenty minutes. I'd love to know who owns that phone.

At ten, I pull up to my house. It's mostly dark except for a dim glow at the rear, and I can't help but feel relieved to avoid Trav. My stomach rumbles, anticipating leftovers and maybe an episode of something to relax by before I pile my blankets on the couch.

I'm two steps into the kitchen when I notice him sitting at the table in the gloom, wearing pajamas. Belatedly I register the smell of hot chocolate and notice the bottle on the counter that says the mug in front of him has been doctored.

It must be serious. "What happened?" My mind goes straight to the kids, although I can't imagine why he didn't call—

"Nothing." My husband's voice is flat. "There's a casserole in the fridge. I would've heated some up for you, but I didn't know when you'd be home."

I'm back-footed, not sure what to make of that. When I called earlier, the kids were getting ready for bed and Trav rushed off the phone after I said my goodnights. "I can talk before I eat, if it's so important you waited for me," I say and sit across from him. Trav's thicket of hair is pointing in different directions, and his beard is frazzled. There's an ache behind my eyes from staring at the computer all evening, and it increases to a throb as my heart rate picks up.

"You want some cocoa?" He's stalling. Whatever this is, he's not looking forward to it, either.

My stomach curdles. "No, thank you."

"Fine. This isn't working. I'm tired of waiting for you to pull yourself together." He studies his hands on the table, then looks at me. There are dark circles under his eyes. "I want a divorce."

It's almost funny, how long I freeze. My face is pointed toward him—he must think I'm staring in shock—but it feels like time has slowed down. I understood the words but missed something important. Did something happen at his parents' house? Did he meet someone new?

When I say nothing, he hurries on. "We'll work out something for the kids. Maybe you can visit on weekends. This isn't about taking you out of their lives. We'll work something out with the house too. I can pay you for half, maybe, so the kids won't have to move. We can negotiate."

Little drops of spittle come out as he speaks too quickly. His thick fingers pick at the cuff of his shirt. His eyes, usually so jovial, look puffy and red.

"Is this about the Sanchez case?" I manage, finally. There's a shake in my voice.

"This is about you not being the person I married. I thought time would help, I thought I could get through to you, but"—he laughs, harshly—"the you I was trying to reach is gone, isn't she? You keep trying to prove something no one cares about. You don't eat, you don't sleep, you won't get counseling… You stay out late at the bar instead of coming home. Your kids barely see you. When's the last time we even had sex?"

My stomach sinks. There's so much coming at me, I can't figure out what to contest. My mouth is dry, my mind spinning. Mostly, I just want that cruel look to soften, for him to reach for me and tell me we'll figure it out.

This is the man who held me when I learned Sanchez hanged himself and again when I learned he was innocent. I shook in our bed, night after night, until Trav's warm arms grounded me in the present. How has it gotten this bad in a matter of months?

"This is about…sex?"

"Are you not listening?"

"I am! We don't need a divorce, that's crazy. I'm busy with a murder case right now, but I'm fine. Everything's okay—" I mean to be careful. I intend to be cool and discuss things and show I can listen and we can fix this…but something gives way, and hot tears well up. I can't suppress the sobs. His retort is punctuated by my own gasps for breath.

"You keep saying that. But look at you. You won't let go."

He stands above me. It's true, I haven't been spending a lot of time with Henry and Fern. When I'm with them, I think about all the bad things that can happen to them, regardless of how desperately I love them. The ghost of that boy turns everything dark. At least when I'm working, I'm doing something to fix it.

I see myself suddenly as he sees me—sick, and not getting better.

Eb went home to his girlfriend hours ago. I could have gone too.

When I catch my breath, Trav's disappeared up the stairs. Maybe I should follow. Maybe he wants me to follow, to prove I care, but I just stand at the bottom, looking up.

24

GRACEN

Honey, you've got two and half minutes to finish getting dressed," Gracen calls from the hallway. Aurie woke up in a surly mood. Maybe she's picking up his vibe. Last night, he returned to the land of nightmares—no surprise after finding that letter—and although he's trying to mask his agitation, Aurie's sensitive. She only ate one bite of the scrambled eggs she insisted on for breakfast, and she's been demanding and argumentative ever since.

When he enters her room, she's tossing clothes out of her bureau with abandon. One of her T-shirts flies toward him, and he snags it out of the air. "Aurie, stop!"

She whirls to look at him, pink-faced and frowning. "I'm looking for sumfing! I need it!" She's one frustration away from an explosion.

"You want any help? How 'bout a hug?"

She shoots a disdainful glare. "I can't find my daisies shirt!"

He picks his way over to her. "Here, let me look. Can you bring me the shirts you threw, please?"

She hovers by his side. "Mommy knows where my flower shirt is."

"If we can't find it after we check all these, we'll send her a text and ask."

Aurie nods grudgingly.

Before he can check another shirt, the doorbell rings. Gracen glances at his watch. It's too early to be Jane, but he's not expecting anyone else.

"Daddy, keep helping me!" Aurie's face crumples.

"Hang on, hon. I'll get the door and then help you. You clean up, okay? I'll be right back."

She follows like a duckling anyway. He peers out the peephole and sees no one, then opens the door. A gift-wrapped box sits on the welcome mat.

"A present, a present!" Aurie cries.

Gracen steps out and glances around, but whoever delivered it is already gone. A video camera above the door is supposed to feed into an app on his phone, but it was inherited from the previous owners. Half the time it loses the network, and he seldom checks it.

In her bare feet on the scratchy mat, Aurie crouches to embrace the package, then pops up with it in her arms. "It's light!" The wrapping paper is eye-popping with green and pink stripes, and the white ribbon is frothed into curls on top. There's no postage or address label.

Uneasy, he scans the road and driveway again. Whoever delivered it was quick. He must have just missed seeing their car.

"Let's open it!" Aurie suggests.

He sighs. "Let's go in. We'll take a look."

He locks the door behind them.

Aurie hops from foot to foot, hugging the package. "Is it for me?"

"I don't know, honey. I didn't see a card, and we're not expecting anything. Maybe it was left at the wrong house." He takes it from her. It *is* light for its size. He wonders if it could be empty, which would be a weird joke. The thought of anthrax passes through his mind, and he winces at the grandiosity of his paranoia. He's a low-level lifestyle podcaster. No one hates him enough to kill him.

In the kitchen, Gracen sets it on the breakfast bar, hoping to open it above her sight line, but she scrambles up on a stool like a one-armed mountain climber. He yanks the wide, elaborately tied ribbon, reminded of the bow around the dolphin that showed up in his sneaker. Different colors, but the same amount of care. Too late, he wishes he hadn't untied it or touched the box at all. If it's linked to the dolphin, maybe the police will fingerprint it.

He's being silly. The people resourceful enough to track down his physical address have been superfans, sending him gushing praise and little gifts meant to acknowledge how his content touched their lives. The tiny percentage who were somehow offended have restrained themselves to nasty letters, not presents.

Or photo albums on his bookshelf.

Now he's definitely being paranoid, conflating everything together. The bows link the dolphin and this box—in a loose, coincidental way, because lots of people put bows on gifts. But Mac's right about the photo album. Mom must have mixed it into his stuff at some point when he lived on Honey Street, and he never noticed. The photo album at Wild Lilac had burned in the fire, not made its way into his living room.

"Open it, Daddy, open it!"

He rallies. "Right, honey." If there's something...unsavory inside, he'll slap the top of the box on before she sees.

"Look, there's the card!"

"What?"

She points. A tiny white envelope hangs from the ribbon. The white envelope he's been avoiding in the family room pops into his mind. But it's just a coincidence, because envelopes are everywhere. There are probably some in his mailbox right now. He tugs until the tape gives way.

"What does it say, Daddy?"

A small greeting card slips out with jelly beans printed on the front, the kind mass-produced for flower deliveries.

Gracen is scrawled in loopy cursive letters inside a wonky-looking heart.

"I guess it's for me," he tells Aurie.

"Open it, open it!"

The lid has been wrapped separately and comes away easily, revealing an interior full of green tissue paper. Aurie reaches for it, but he nudges her hand away. "Let me see first, pumpkin." The tissue paper lifts out in one large mass, crumpled in the shape of the box, leaving a plain 9x12 manila envelope below.

Aurie starts pulling at the tissue. "Daddy, can I have the pretty paper?"

"Hang on—" The manila envelope is secured with a metal clasp. He guesses by the weight and stiffness there's more than one document or card inside. He tears it open and peers in to see a stack of photos of different dimensions, some faded, some Polaroid.

Something clatters on the countertop, and he looks up. Aurie scrabbles in her crumpled paper pile. "Look, Daddy, this one is for me!" She displays a strand of lavender beads.

He holds out a hand. "Can I see?"

Reluctantly, she passes it over. The beads are elongated ovals, smooth and heavy, probably made of glass. The clasp consists of a tiny barrel that screws delicately together, not designed for little hands. The whole string can't be more than twelve inches long.

"It's beautiful! I love it, Daddy." He hands it back, not sure he wants her to have it but not wanting a tantrum. He'll reclaim it later when she's distracted.

"What did you get?" Aurie asks politely.

"Well…pictures of a bunch of strangers," he says. Then he sees they're not, as he focuses on the largest item. It's a class photo in a cardboard folder. Twenty-five kids and one teacher arranged on bleachers with a signboard in front: MRS. ARNOLD'S FOURTH GRADE.

He doesn't remember this photo, but he recognizes the backdrop of the gym. The teacher too, a woman who always wore sneakers and long skirts. And Douggy, on the far side of the front row, looking down into her lap with one hand cupped over her nose and chin.

With a gush of relief, he remembers Quinn. Kathy Fontaine. That's who must be behind this. Why they left no real note, he can't imagine, and the gift box and necklace are a bizarre touch, maybe something they had lying around. Maybe they didn't realize the necklace was hidden in the tissue paper. But the photos—Quinn must have dug them up after the two of them met Sunday. He's not sure how they got his home address, but…it's fine.

He smiles at Aurie, who's frowning at the clasp with great concentration as she tries to manipulate it. He sifts through the other photos. A few are candids that include Douggy in school-related settings, sometimes with one or two other kids in the frame. The book fair in the school library. In a classroom, reaching to touch a guinea pig. At a desk in the music room with a wooden block in front of her. Sitting at the counter of the school office, head bent over a worksheet.

He recognizes Kathy Fontaine in some as well. She's not in the class picture, and he remembers Quinn mentioned they were in the same grade but not the same class, but here she is at what looks like field day, arm around Douggy for the three-legged race. A young girl with a half-hearted smile and sweat stains showing under the pits of her pale-pink shirt.

He reaches for his phone to text Quinn, but Aurie demands, "Put this on me, Daddy!"

"Jane will be here soon. How about you save that to show Mommy, and go upstairs to pick up your mess before it's time to go?" He crosses his fingers, hoping against hope she's forgotten about the flower shirt.

"I want to show Jane!"

"What if it gets lost, and then you can't show Mommy?"

"I won't lose it. I'll be careful." She waits, wide-eyed, as if his decision were going to make or break the rest of her day.

He sighs. "Okay. Wear it then. But you still have to get ready. You have your pajamas on, silly!" As soon as he screws the clasp into place, she's off, prancing up the stairs.

Before following her, he texts Quinn: Thanks for the pix. Where did you get these? My daughter loves the necklace.

Gracen and Aurie are playing Go Fish, waiting for Jane to arrive, when Quinn texts him back. The phone is muted, and his eyes jump to it when the message flashes across the screen.

Wasn't me.

He frowns.

"Daddy, I said Go Fish!"

"Sorry, honey. Give me one second."

She huffs and looks away from him, crossing her arms across her chest.

"One second, I promise." He taps out a reply to Quinn.

You didn't send pix of Douggy 4th grade?

He picks up his cards and asks Aurie for dancing dolphins, keeping one eye on the phone as they continue to play. Nothing comes, and he realizes Quinn's moved on from the conversation. Which he should also do, but apprehension is curdling his stomach again.

Aurie's demanding his scuba-diving sharks when the phone rings with Quinn's call, and he holds up a "one second" finger to Aurie. She scowls as he snatches the phone and rises from the table.

"Is this a bad time?" Quinn asks but continues talking without pause. "It's weird though. You don't know who sent those pics? Was it digital, hard copies, what?"

"Printouts and Polaroids, along with a necklace. I was so sure it was you. You're serious, you didn't—"

"No, of course not. You heard about Ms. Finch, right?"

It takes a second to change gears. "The school secretary? What—"

"She's been murdered. As of yesterday. I'm the lucky one who found her. You don't look at the news?"

Gracen swallows. Ms. Finch. He'd thought about her a lot when he was working on *The Ridpath Girl*. He hasn't actually seen her since he was a kid, but she emailed his agent about that Meander speaking event. A vague impression comes to mind from way back: lipsticked smile, brassy hair. "She's dead? But—why?" His voice rises in disbelief. Viveca Crandall and now Ms. Finch both murdered, in little Meander?

"Well, it's a safe guess she pissed somebody off."

The edge in their voice startles him. Belatedly, he processes what they said—*they* found Ms. Finch's body. And Viveca was their roommate. Is that coincidence? A chill goes up his back. "That must have been awful."

A sigh, then Quinn answers less stridently. "It *was* really fucking awful. But also bizarre, because guess what."

"What?" He doesn't want to know.

"The reason I went to her house was to pick up some photos of when me and Douggy were kids. I'd talked to her about what she remembered from that year, and she offered to go through her stuff."

"She had pictures of my sister?"

"She kept a file of photos and art for displays in the front hall, and when she retired, she couldn't bring herself to trash it."

He's pacing the living room now. Aurie hops in front of him and puts her hands on her hips. "Daddy, I'm waiting for you!"

He holds the phone away and says, "Sorry, pumpkin. Daddy's got to finish this call. Jane will be here any second. Can you pick out one of your beautiful paintings from yesterday for her?"

Aurie's face falls, but she turns toward the stairs. By the time she reaches the landing, she's singing, and he tries to pick up the thread of the phone call. "Sorry. Did you end up getting Ms. Finch's pictures, or..." Then he puts it together. "You think these are her photos," he says flatly. "You think someone killed her and dropped the photos on my doorstep." He snorts. "No. I don't think so."

"What, then?"

"Any of my fans could have come across some old pics." And found his address. And included a necklace for Aurie. He's grasping at straws. He definitely feels sick now. Very nauseated.

"Your fans would have access to Meander Elementary School photos from over a decade ago?" To Quinn's credit, their voice stays even, with hardly any sarcasm showing.

"Someone in Meander, who dug this stuff out of their attic." It makes more sense than a delivery fresh from a murdered woman's house.

"You need to let the cops know what you have. I can give you the number of one of the detectives."

His heart skips a beat. "I don't see how that's necessary." Dragging his family into an investigation… For a moment, he feels thirteen again, his family in pieces and under scrutiny by strangers. "I'm not doing that," he repeats more strongly.

Quinn's voice cools. "What *are* you going to do?"

It's a good question. He turns, and a glimpse of movement out the front window saves him from answering. Jane's black SUV is rolling up beyond the trees that line the driveway. Relieved, he says, "I have to go. My daughter's getting picked up. Please don't say anything to the police yet. I'll figure it out, okay?"

He taps end, his finger shaking, and only then notices he's missed a call.

25

KIRSTEN

I roll in early while the office is quiet. Eb is at the Finch autopsy, and Deputies Riley and Akina are filling in holes on the neighborhood canvass before our noon meeting.

I spend time comparing our two victims and seeing where their lives line up. Meander is a small town, so there's a lot. They shopped at Safeway, ate at Sunny's, and spent years of their lives at Meander Elementary. So far, the most unique piece is both being called out on Gracen Ridpath's podcast as a significant influence on Douggy Ridpath's alleged suicide. And both knew Quinn, who also knew Douggy.

I keep coming back to Quinn. Absent for fifteen years, they suddenly rent a room from one victim and visit the other. They have no alibi for either murder, and they admit to being at Alicia's house while she was dying. And yet, there's no motive I can see, unless Quinn is seeking revenge for Douggy's suicide, inspired by the podcast.

Physically, it's hard to see Quinn as a killer, but Viveca was lured in and stabbed from behind, which would even the odds; and Alicia Finch was in her seventies and frail.

On the other hand, Viveca fought back and was then overpowered, and I can't figure out why Quinn called 9-1-1 if they killed Finch.

I'm chasing my own tail. Either way, Quinn needs a more in-depth grilling.

I click on one of the many tabs open on my desktop and skim the case file on the death of Ridpath, Melissa: how the child's liver was already failing when she was brought to the emergency room, too late to save her; how poisoning was suspected by the emergency room doctor, who sent in tox screens that would come back too late to help the girl; how foraged mushrooms were discovered in the family's refrigerator but found to be innocuous chanterelles and boletes; and how the father, on being asked about his mushroom hunting, turned pale and said he'd warned his children away from the cluster of rare and poisonous Death Caps that fruited in the woods that year.

Amatoxin poisoning was confirmed. The cluster of Death Caps was found to have been harvested, and the brother agreed that he and his sister had been warned away from them. The grief-stricken father said he'd meant to destroy the mushrooms after taking photos to share with his hiking club but hadn't gotten around to it.

He blamed himself, but the official finding was accidental death, the assumption being that the girl had forgotten the warning.

My heart aches with sympathy for the family. Listening to Gracen's podcasts, I'd felt for him but also been put off by his need to find someone to blame—even if he was spreading that blame through an entire town and, by implication, all of society. Now I wonder if he's subconsciously trying to exonerate his absent father.

Quinn or, as they would have been known, Kathy Fontaine is absent from the report despite their claim to have been Douggy's best friend.

Eb ran Quinn's record when Viveca was killed, and it was clean. Now, I put in records requests for Gracen, Marjorie, and Warren Ridpath. I know Marjorie's gone, but it's worth including her to get a broader picture of the family's issues.

A name jumps out from Douggy's case file. The deputy who'd written up the report was Shauna Greenlea, currently serving as sheriff. I pace the empty office. She may remember something incidental about the case, like someone who rubbed her the wrong way, who might have harbored the seeds of obsession about Douggy's death. I wonder what she thought of Gracen back then. Sibling rivalry can lead to very dark places.

Eb will be here soon. I'm not ready to face him alone—the warmth in his eyes and voice will loosen everything I'm struggling to keep locked down, and the d-word will come spilling out. Much safer to stay away until the team meeting, when the deputies will be around to protect me from myself.

Grabbing my bag, I call Todd, the sheriff's civilian secretary. "Does Sheriff Greenlea have a couple minutes?"

"Now?" He sounds both disbelieving and affronted, which is fair, considering she's usually scheduled up to her eyeballs with meetings.

"I'm hoping for soon. It's about a case she worked years ago that may be related to the Meander murders. What's the earliest slot?"

"Hang on."

Phone to my ear, I skip the elevator and mount the back stairs in silence, thinking if the sheriff is busy, I'll grab a cup of coffee in the lunchroom, review what we know about Gracen Ridpath, and start with him instead.

Todd comes back on the line. Bitterly, as if against his better instincts, he says, "Drop by in an hour."

The sheriff is stout, with short wavy hair wired with gray and a penchant for having at least two pairs of reading glasses tucked about her person: on top of her head, in her breast pocket, in the collar of her shirt. She squints at me from across the desk, where she was typing madly on her computer when I walked in.

"Sit down," she commands and finishes whatever she was working on before looking back at me. "You're looking a little rough, Detective Boon. The lieutenant already updated me on the Crandall case. Shouldn't you be out investigating?"

"Ah, yes, ma'am," I say. She intimidates me, I admit it. She's got a military background, and although most authority figures give me the urge to stick out my tongue, in her presence I suck in my gut and try not to salute. Normally I would have at least combed my hair before stepping into her office, but I'm not myself today. "There's a possible link to an investigation from 2012. I saw your name on the case file and wondered if you might recall any details that didn't, um, need to be in there."

She squints at me. "What case?"

I swallow. "The Ridpath girl's death, ma'am. There's a podcast out about Douggy—Melissa—Ridpath, and you were the—"

"Oh, yeah. Gracen Ridpath." She shakes her head. "I really liked that *Hot Mess* show. Never would have guessed he had it in him. I listened to the first episode of *The Ridpath Girl*, but it wasn't funny at all. Brought the case back though."

"What can you tell me about it?"

She folds her hands and eyeballs me. "Tell me real quick what your link is."

I go over Viveca Crandall, Alicia Finch, and Quinn a.k.a.-Kathy Fontaine, all tied to Douggy in some way, and doubly tied by Quinn's association with each victim. "I'm wondering if someone—maybe Quinn, maybe Gracen, maybe someone we don't know about, is pissed off about Douggy's death. Either they just learned about it through the podcast, or they knew about it all along and Gracen calling it suicide makes them want revenge."

"I don't remember Kathy," she says thoughtfully, pulling at her earlobe. "From what I remember, both the Ridpath kids had been sick for days at the time of death, so no friends had been around."

"Gracen was sick too?"

"Stomach flu."

He had mentioned that, in episode one. I'd forgotten. "Was he tested for the toxins?"

"Nah. By the time we got the results back on the girl, it was too late for anything to show up on him."

"Was anyone so angry about the girl's death that you can imagine them taking revenge now?"

"The parents were devastated. I thought the mother was going to implode. She was the silent type, but you could see she was shattered. The father was a drinker, hadn't held down a solid job for a while already, and being the one who'd showed her the mushrooms, I wondered if he was a suicide risk."

"The mother died recently in the fire at the assisted living place in Meander, I heard. Do you know what happened to the father?"

"All I know is he stayed off my radar."

"What about the brother? What did you think of him, back then?"

"He was what? Thirteen, fourteen?" She's silent. "I remember thinking, that kid looks haunted. Pale, dark circles under the eyes, really grieving. I think the siblings were close. No red flags, nothing that pointed to funny business. The coroner, the DA's office, and Sheriff Black all had to sign off on accidental death, and I told the sheriff it was an easy call. Poor kid ate something she shouldn't."

"And there was no one who might have been pressuring her or harassing her outside the family? Gracen seems to be arguing there was bullying from almost everyone in town."

She rolls her eyes. "Listen. People need a scapegoat. To me, you don't have to look far—the parents didn't watch her closely enough. The dad should have destroyed those mushrooms. Obviously. But at the time, we talked to the school, even to some of the kids. No one remembered any incidents that indicated that little girl was any more of a target than anyone else. Unless there was a conspiracy of really great liars, it was what it looked like—an unfortunate combination of an unsupervised child and access to a deadly toxin."

Afterward, in the restroom, the mirror displays under-eyes smeared with residue from yesterday's mascara and hair falling loose from an uneven braid. No wonder she told me I looked rough. I rectify the situation, then, in the empty hallway, call a number I dug up earlier this morning.

"Gracen Ridpath? This is Detective Kirsten Boon of the Melakwa County Sheriff's Office. I'd like to speak with you in regard to a case. Please call me back at your earliest convenience."

My email already holds the results of my records requests. Marjorie and Gracen are clean, give or take a couple of parking tickets. But, interestingly, Warren built up a bit of a sheet between Douggy's death in 2012, and 2017. The kind you see for someone living on the streets. In Warren's case, perhaps he was living in a vehicle, because he ended up with a DUI causing serious bodily injury in 2017 that put him in Washington State Pen for seven years.

Since his release, he's been clean, and apparently living just a few hours from here in Ashland, Oregon. The address on file with the DMV belongs to an organic farm, and although I can't find a personal number for Warren, when I call the number listed on the farm's website and ask for him, they say, "Hang on."

I pull up my big-girl pants, hang up, and instead go talk to the man I've been avoiding.

Fortunately, Eb doesn't look at me with those big brown eyes and ask how I am, and I manage not to spill the dirt on Trav. Instead, we agree to request that Ashland PD visit the farm and invite Warren for an interview.

They must be having a slow day. Within the hour, I get a call back from a Detective Judy Suarez. "We have your boy here, but he's insisting on talking to the Meander police, by which I'm guessing he means you. Wants to make a confession."

"Did he say what he wants to confess to? Does he have an attorney?" I should be excited, but instead, I feel frozen, cautious.

"No attorney. Won't give us any details." Her voice is bemused. "This is a first for me. When the officer stopped at the farm, this guy basically walked out with his wrists bared, expecting to be cuffed."

The relief of a guilty man, who killed two women and has been praying to be caught before he kills again?

God, I hope so. "Can we do a preliminary video call? We've got two homicides up here. I don't want to rush down to get him if he's yanking our chain."

"No problem. I'll get it set up and get back to you."

26

GRACEN

Through the driver's side window, Jane calls, "I'll bring her back after dinner—maybe six-ish?"

Gracen shoves his phone into his pocket and gives a thumbs-up. Aurie waves frantically as the SUV pulls away. When they're gone, Gracen drops his grin and walks back toward the porch. Quinn's phone call left him with an unpleasant buzz in his belly, but he needs to work while Aurie's out. Then he'll decide what to do about the photos.

He stops to glare at the dying bushes and loose lattice on the side of the porch, reminding him he also sucks at home maintenance. Termites. He meant to check into termites.

He's circled to the front of the porch to eyeball the condition of the wood—calling the exterminator will take five minutes—when his phone buzzes again. He has yet to listen to the voicemail from the last missed call—Quinn most likely, unsatisfied with his refusal to call the police.

He silences the phone and climbs the steps. Termites and Alicia Finch's murder—he'll allow himself ten minutes on the internet before focusing on work. Sometimes it's best to get those impulses out of the way.

He double-checks the missed call to make sure it wasn't Mac, who's supposed to text him when she leaves Bend but hasn't yet. The number isn't hers, but it's not Quinn's, either. Sighing, he drops on the bench and plays the voicemail, straightening when he realizes it's a police detective from Melakwa County asking for a call back.

Goddamn Quinn. Squeezing his eyes shut, he tries a breathing exercise. This is not a big deal. He would have preferred to wait. He would have preferred to talk with Mac. But he can talk to the cops, and obviously, they'll realize he and his family have nothing to do with whatever's going on in Meander.

He's not a helpless child anymore, either. He's a successful, wealthy content producer with a large audience. He can hire an attorney without breaking the bank if the level of police interest feels misplaced or intrusive.

He hits dial.

A crisp female voice says, "Mr. Ridpath. This is Detective Boon. Thank you so much for returning my call."

"Of course. What can I help you with?"

"I have questions I'd very much like to sit down and ask you in person, today if at all possible."

His mouth is dry. "What is this about?"

"It's mainly background for a current case. I'd prefer not to share over the phone, but it's standard, nothing to worry about."

Gracen pauses, stymied. The police can't possibly be calling everyone who knew Viveca Crandall and Ms. Finch, especially way back when. It has to be about the photos. But he'd feel so much better if it's not. "Can you at least tell me if it's about the murders?"

She pauses, then repeats, "It's just background information, sir."

If she's not going to give a little, he won't, either. "I've got an appointment this afternoon, and I need to pick my daughter up around six or six-thirty. If you come at five-thirty, I should be able to fit you in."

Detective Boon agrees to the time and takes his address, then ends the call with a curt "Thank you, sir."

Inside, he gathers the tissue paper and photos from the breakfast bar and packs them back into the box, which he carries up to the office along with his lunchtime salad.

At the computer, he sits, thinking, before pulling up the security system app. The camera is working today, not that it does any good. The gift-wrapped box was delivered by a figure in a hooded rain poncho, with the bill of a ball cap sticking out, obscuring all but pale hands and a slice of cheek. Below the poncho, jeans disappear into tall rain boots. So, great. A white guy. Or woman. It's not even suspicious. Any delivery person is going to be geared up against the rain on a day like today.

He eats his salad while learning that Alicia Finch was killed in her home Tuesday afternoon and police are investigating. Not helpful. With a sigh, he switches to interview prep. It's pretty standard fare for *Gracen Stays Home*—Jax Tiner, the lead singer and guitarist for the band Crabbie Maddie, a stay-at-home dad of two who still rocks.

Gracen can't concentrate. He checks again for a text from Mac and hovers his finger above the call button before tapping it.

"I was just about to call you," she says when she picks up.

He smiles at the sound of her voice, low and warm, but says, "Are you on the road?"

He hears background voices, static, like Mac's muffling the speaker, then she's back. "Sorry, honey. I'm still here. I'm thinking of spending another night, do you mind?"

"Is everything okay?"

"It's not that. Simone's parents will be here with Tyler soon. I'd really like to see them—they were my emergency backup parents in college."

"Oh, right." Mac's concerns seem a world away from the gift box now on his desk and his appointment to talk with a police detective. Compared to what Simone and her family are going through, his worries are nothing. "You should stay. We're having a blast here. Not right now—right now I'm prepping for that interview with the guy from Crabbie Maddie and Aurie's at Jane's—but seriously, we're fine."

"You're not too stressed out?"

Mac knows him so well. He won't get away with an outright lie. "I know I've been a little edgy. But I'm getting my mojo back."

She pauses, and he holds his breath. Apparently she decides to believe him because she says, "I'm glad. I'll call later to say goodnight to Aurie."

His smile fades as he hits end. With some effort, he puts Meander and Douggy and all things not *Gracen Stays Home* out of his head.

Postinterview, he hears a honk and finds Jane's car idling in the turnaround, hours too early. He approaches her rolled-down window with trepidation.

"Sorry, Gracen, the fun was cut short today. My older son's practice was canceled. I have to pick him up in Polallie. If you're home anyway, you may not want Aurie to spend her afternoon driving back and forth. I was going to text you, but we were in the car on the way back from the park when we found out, so..." She shrugs. "I can still take her if you're busy!" she adds quickly, seeing the look on his face.

Technically, all he has left is the editing for today, and he can do that after Aurie goes to bed. But the police interview might be weird. On the other hand, why would it? He can set Aurie up with a movie in the other room. "It's fine. I'm here, no reason Aurie should go along for the ride," he reassures Jane. "No worries."

She glances into the back seat, packed with three booster seats in a row. She lowers her voice. "They're all wiped out from the park. Looks like Miss Aurie's about to fall asleep."

"Nap time, maybe." Even better. "Well, thanks again for taking her. Is her bag—?"

"By her feet."

Gracen helps a droopy-eyed Aurie out of the car seat, balancing her on his hip and slinging her bag over his shoulder. He waves as Jane pulls away, then carries Aurie upstairs.

"Sleepy, Daddy," she murmurs.

"That's okay, honey." He slips off her shoes and tucks her in, then sneaks out of the room. Lucky—now he can pick up his train of thought and try to finish before the detective arrives.

The doorbell rings just when he's managed to regain focus. Irritated, he checks his watch again—is the detective more than an hour early? He's tempted to ignore it, but it might wake Aurie. Downstairs, he peers through the peephole. A tall, sturdy brunette stands on the mat. She's probably mid-twenties, with hair slicked back and a belted sage-green suit under a svelte raincoat. Straight dark brows and full cheeks, pink with the cold. Something about her pricks his memory, but he can't place it. She seems young for a detective though. He opens the door.

The woman smiles broadly. "Hi." The sound of her voice transports him back to his first term of college. His only in-person term, when he'd started at Oregon State here in Corvallis under the delusion he was leaving childhood behind for a normal university experience.

"Celeste?" he asks, surprise and disbelief infusing his tone. It's hard not to be dubious. Celeste had a rebel vibe, and this woman looks high-end corporate. Plus, Celeste ghosted him and broke his heart. When he went home that year for winter break to find Mom underfed, unwashed, and asleep with a smoldering cigarette, he left school to watch over her. Celeste dropped him like he'd turned into a bug.

"It's me, all right." She hugs him hard, awakening long-forgotten memories. "It's so great to see you."

"This is so...unexpected! Wow! How did you find me?" The question spills out, and he turns red.

She smiles, seeming not to take offense. "I did my homework, silly. Aren't you glad to see me?"

Still shaking his head with disbelief, he half laughs. "Of course! Come in, come in."

As he pulls the door closed behind her, he scans the yard, his brows drawing down. The outside world holds all kinds of surprises today. What were the chances of Celeste turning up the same day as the photos? But there's no connection between his ex-girlfriend and his sister. Celeste isn't even from Meander—if he remembers right, she's from somewhere in Southern California.

In the foyer, she smiles expectantly. "I'm not interrupting anything?"

"No. Not at all. Come on back to the kitchen."

He gestures her toward the archway, and she goes ahead, taking in the messy living room and the study, removing her raincoat and carrying it over her arm. She's statuesque, solid-looking, and busty, and he can still feel the echo of her body against him. "I can come back another time. Or, hell, I could call you on the phone like a normal person! I'm only in town for a bit, so I thought I'd try stopping by."

"Seriously, this is great," he says, still wondering where she got his address. Corvallis has a population of 65,000, so it's not like you can ask at the general store. On the other hand, considering the random gifts showing up at his door, maybe it's posted publicly somewhere.

It's good to see an old friend though. Celeste was outgoing and outrageous and outdoorsy, and they'd talked for hours on every possible topic. He'd been in love with her—until she dumped him.

In the kitchen he seats her at the table. "Can I get you a coffee?" Aurie usually sleeps for an hour or so. He should wake her before too long or bedtime will get messed up, and of course, the detective will be over soon after that. But there's time for a beverage.

"Married with children?" she asks, gesturing to the clutter: Aurie's crayons and ABC placemat, Mac's red cardigan over the back of a chair. The family photos on the refrigerator.

"Yeah, very happily, one little girl. How about you?"

"Not yet. Haven't met the right person."

He starts the coffeemaker, then turns back to her. She's wearing a soft-looking black sweater under the suit jacket. Her makeup is understated, her jewelry confined to little gold hoops in her ears and a chain at her collarbone. Her hair's twisted off the back of her neck. The overall effect is stunning, but he sort of misses her thrift-store grunge and cat's-eye glasses.

What about him? He'd had a matching wardrobe plus a scraggly soul patch and the beginnings of a mustache. Abruptly he feels self-conscious in his cashmere hoodie and jeans, his hair tousled with product and his beard trimmed close the way Mac likes it. His hand wants to fly up to the recession in his hairline.

She's watching with lips quirked up, and he forces himself to speak. "I don't know where to start. What have you been up to? I always guessed you'd end up on a farm somewhere with thirteen kids and a bunch of alpacas." He's not joking.

Celeste had been a year ahead of him and fed up with college. She'd wanted to leave school and save up for their own plot of land to farm.

She laughs. "Oh, wow. That seems like a million years ago. Well, I was depressed when you left and got into a crazy rebound relationship. I followed this guy—a true asshole—down to LA. That didn't last, but I stayed in the city for a long time before returning to Oregon."

He sits across from her while the coffee gurgles. "You look amazing. You look happy."

She shrugs, but her smile is dazzling. "I had some tough years, but I got through them. I'm doing well now. But tell me about you! I discovered your YouTube channel during COVID, but I was too shy to reach out. Congrats, by the way! Are you still doing that?"

In the back of his mind, the voice of paranoia speaks up—is she here to ask for money? She doesn't look like she's hurting for cash, but that means nothing. Investment dollars, charity donations, medical bills—he's been approached for all that and more. "I switched to podcasting. It's lower profile, but I'm enjoying it, and it's easier to stay sane."

The coffeemaker beeps, and he fills two mugs. "Sugar, milk?"

"No, thank you."

He brings them to the table, and Celeste rummages through her large leather purse. She says, "Sorry, I had a root canal the other day—gross, right?—but it's still healing. I should have some Tylenol or something in here..."

"We must have some in the medicine cabinet. I'll grab it for you."

"No, that's okay..." She keeps rummaging. Her purse is bottomless. A little line forms between her eyes.

"Are you working? Where are you living now?"

Distractedly, she chuckles. "You're going to laugh, but I'm in sales, and it turns out I love it, because I get to travel. I'm a pharmaceutical rep. It's great." She looks up from her bag, shamefaced. "Okay, I give up. Do you mind grabbing me something? Anything. Advil, Tylenol, whatever." She massages the edge of her jaw. "The pain comes and goes."

"I'll be right back." He jumps up and jogs upstairs, checking Aurie as he passes. She's fast asleep, hair clinging to her temples in sweaty ringlets, and he pauses, unaccountably stricken by her sweetness, before fetching the bottle of pills and returning downstairs.

Celeste has migrated to the living room. She turns guiltily with mug in hand. "Sorry. I'm always curious about what books people have."

He shrugs. "You're fine. Most of those are my wife's. The fiction, anyway. Mine are the cookbooks and the biography of Tina Fey."

Celeste laughs. "A well-rounded family. Weren't you an English major when we met?"

"Undecided. I was thinking about it."

"Oh, right."

He hands her the Tylenol. She strolls back toward the kitchen, where they resume their seats. He takes a long sip of coffee as she washes down a couple pills. A silence falls, slightly uncomfortable. She caps the bottle and pushes it across the table toward him.

"You know, I've always felt bad," he says. "About the way we left things. I'm glad you're doing well."

"I don't know why you'd feel bad," she says. "You wanted to make it work. You just thought you should put your mother first. But that was your thing, wasn't it? Feeling bad for things that weren't your fault?"

It's an intimate jab, jumping him back to the student union at OSU, where he and Celeste had a favorite out-of-the-way corner to talk.

He flicks his eyes away, laughs, not sure how personal he wants to get. "All the way home on the bus, I was trying to figure out how to tell my mom I was going to take time off from school to travel with you. Then I saw there was no way I could leave her, let alone leave the state. I was trapped." The next words feel dangerous, but he lets them come. "It broke my heart, to lose you over that."

She gives a rueful shrug. "I know. Mine too. It felt like, by tethering yourself to your mom, you were rejecting *me* and everything I needed from you. Dropping out and leaving you weren't my best decisions. But everything worked out. I learned what I needed to learn. So don't feel bad."

He tilts his head. Tethering himself to his mother? She makes it sound like he was scared to cut the apron strings, not doing his best to handle a self-destructive family member. He smooths the prickle of pride. "Funny how everything worked out," he echoes.

Abruptly weary, he opens his mouth to move the conversation along. If he wraps up this blast from the past, he can finish editing, wake up Aurie, and get her some dinner before the detective shows up. No words come. He feels a little funny. His body's made of sandbags while his head floats toward the ceiling.

Celeste's voice sounds tinny and faraway, like it's coming from a music box. "Veeerrrry fuuunnnny..." she responds. Her face is large and warped, but suddenly she recedes into a blur.

He blinks. There's a heaviness, a bleariness, a dreariness... "Celesh?" His tongue won't wrap around her name. "Slesh?" A hot flame of panic tries to ignite in his chest (Aurie!), but he can't sustain it. Mac says, *Aurie's fine, stop being so neurotic.* The flame sputters and shrinks.

Something squeezes his arm hard, pulling upward. He follows the tug, watches his feet step step step across the floor. Celeste's voice booms all around him. "LOOKS LIKE YOU'RE READY, ready ready ready." A hand is on the doorknob, and the door opens. "SHOES ON! JACKET ON!" His feet slide into his shoes, his arm slides into his sleeve. Celeste catches him when he stumbles, but when did he become so weak? Aurie shouldn't be alone, and he tries to say something, but his lips are all rubbery and he gives up. His feet move, following the tug down the steps. Careful, careful. One step at a time.

27

QUINN

Quinn hangs up and stares at their phone. "What a little shit."

"What's that, hon?" Sunny asks on her way past the break room.

"Nothing!" The pulse in Quinn's throat flutters like a moth. They put a hand up as if to manually calm it. Could Ms. Finch have changed her mind and sent the pictures directly to Gracen? Maybe she had Gracen's address from the speaking arrangements, but still—why, when Quinn was supposed to come and pick them up?

The idea that a similar set of photos popped up from nowhere at exactly the same time is too much. It can't be a coincidence.

There's one way to find out. They locate Detective Boon's card in a pocket, then dial the number. It goes straight to voicemail. "Hi, uh, Detective Boon? This is Quinn. Did the photos turn up at Ms. Finch's? It's important." They end the call, biting their lip. The detective will think Quinn is the most narcissistic person ever, to be worrying about old photos in the wake of two murders.

Denise sticks her head around the door on her way by. "Almost done? We got a rush."

"I'm coming."

The next two hours pass so quickly Quinn has no time to think. When they grab a five-minute break, they check their phone, hoping Gracen had second thoughts.

Nothing from Gracen or Detective Boon. But something from Sheila.

Her voice sounds slightly high-pitched. "Hi, Quinn. I'm back in town and hope you still want to talk. We can meet at your convenience, but I'd love for it to be this evening if possible. Call me back."

Before Quinn can reconsider, they return the call. When it goes to voicemail, they say, "This is Quinn. I'm at work and it's real busy, so I can't be checking my phone. If you want to talk, pick me up at five."

Quinn taps end and takes a deep breath. A whirlwind of hope stirs in their belly. Sunny rushes by with a pointed look, and Quinn stuffs the phone into their backpack and hurries out. "Sorry. Shit is happening."

Sunny pauses and grasps Quinn's arm, giving them a probing look. "You holding up okay?"

Sunny had told them to take a day off, horrified that once again, Quinn had a close brush with murder, but this time, Quinn put their foot down. They give Sunny a reassuring smile. "I'm fine. Staying busy is a good thing."

"Ugh. Thank god you're here. But leave early if you need to!" And she's back to the chaos.

As Quinn moves from table to table, they can't help speculating about what Sheila is in a rush to say. Gracen's photos, with their hypothetical connection to poor Ms. Finch, fade into the background.

An eternity later, Quinn's shift ends. Bella's on five-to-nine today and squeezes Quinn's arm on their way out. "You okay walking home in the dark? Maybe Sunny will let me drive you real quick."

"Thanks, but I think I have a ride. Nice hair, by the way."

Bella's hair is pulled back so tightly it looks like a swim cap. Her eyes widen. "Do you have a date?"

"Nothing like that. I'll tell you later, okay?"

Quinn freshens up in the restroom. Their face looks pale and frightened in the mirror, and they tell themself it's the poor lighting. Bracing to find out what Sheila has to say is as scary as that first door knock, but the hard part is keeping their hopes from fizzing upward. Maybe Sheila's changed her mind about Kade.

Or maybe Sheila won't show.

Quinn slips into the alley, lit by bulbs glaring from staff entrances along the block, and shivers. Dumpsters and a few vehicles throw stark shadows along the ground as they hurry around the side of the building. They glance at their phone—already 5:08—and emerge onto Main Street.

There's a moment of sour validation before Quinn recognizes the SUV. Sheila sits inside with the engine running, head tilted to the glow of a phone screen.

Quinn swallows and climbs into their mother's car.

In the dim light, Sheila's coarse blond hair looks gray, the lines of her face deeply etched. She smiles uncertainly. "Thanks for agreeing to meet."

Quinn says, "Mm," and waits for her to speak.

"You talking to Gracen for me made me realize…well, a lot, I guess. That I would never be sure my secrets were safe, no matter what anyone said. That I had to tell my husband about what happened back then and deal with the consequences."

She takes a deep breath. "And I realized how much shame I was carrying around, about everything—that I would ask you to cover for me and compound it all, instead of taking my opportunity to deal with it. So, Jeffrey knows everything now. And he's…okay about it. We're still talking. But he's home with the kids. Do you want to go to your place?"

Quinn shakes their head, discomfited, not entirely sure why Sheila's telling them this. It blows the blackmail idea out of the water, but Quinn wouldn't have really done that. Would they? It's a good sign that Sheila's trying to do the right thing. Still, they're uncomfortable with the idea of bringing her to their newfound sanctuary. "No. And we can't stay at the diner, either."

Sheila navigates past the streetlights of downtown and into the darkness of the surrounding streets. Quinn doesn't ask where she's going. The car is stuffy and humid, and Quinn warms their fingers in front of a vent blasting hot air. The smell of diner food off-gasses from their clothes: maple syrup and meatloaf and coffee.

In a few minutes, Sheila pulls into a deserted parking area, where a streetlight illuminates a metal play structure. Trees loom dark beyond a ring of grass. No other cars or houses are in sight. She keeps the car running but turns off the headlights, and they sit in the dark with rain streaming down the windshield and the vents continuing to blow. It feels isolated and too quiet, and Quinn fiddles with their phone nervously.

Sheila finally begins to speak, softly and without looking at Quinn.

"I meant to apologize to you someday. To you and Kade. But I'm not sure I would have if you hadn't shown up. It's not like apologizing can change anything. I'm a mess, and I've been a mess my whole life."

Quinn clenches their jaw. Their chest aches like the walls are caving in, but they force their gaze straight into the empty playground.

Sheila blows her nose. There's a hitch in her voice, but she continues. "I shouldn't have sent you away. Or maybe I should have let you go sooner than I did, after your father died. I realized pretty quick that even without him, I wasn't okay. I wasn't a good mom.

"I kept thinking maybe it would get better. Maybe it would get easier." She takes a breath. "And then Warren came along."

Quinn turns to stare at Sheila, who doesn't meet their gaze. Warren? A heavy feeling settles in their stomach. There was only one Warren in their childhood.

Douggy's father.

Sheila continues, quickly, as if she can't wait to get the words out. "We fell in love. We were both struggling, both suffering, and it was like—all the sudden, someone understood. We weren't alone." A strangled laugh emerges from her throat. "It doesn't sound like a great basis for a relationship, does it? But it worked. Finally, we were seen."

Quinn's mind flashes to Bella's revelation about her dysfunctional parents, her tough childhood. Like attracts like. Quinn's hands grip each other white-knuckled in their lap. But Douggy's dad—that was just wrong.

Sheila says, "Sometimes I thought you knew. You'd look at me with those dark eyes when I'd say we were going to Douggy's house or when I repeated something Warren said. He and I took chances—stealing a kiss in the hallway when I dropped you off or picked you up. Marjorie kept inviting me to stay for dinner. I think she felt bad for me because I was a single mom. We'd be there a couple times a week, and I'd spend the whole time thinking about getting a few minutes alone with Warren.

"It was the first time I felt alive since your father turned out to be—not who I thought."

When Quinn glances over, Sheila's blinking back tears, trying to get her emotions under control. "Warren and I started imagining a future together. Marjorie and Warren had nothing in common, beyond the kids. If they had money, they would have split up long ago. But there was no way out for them—hospital bills, the house falling apart. If Warren left, he'd be able to be a better man, and I'd be better too. We wanted to leave our messes behind."

Quinn sees where this is going. "You were going to run away together." Separation and divorce would be too complicated for two people already drowning.

Sheila nods, sniffles. She swipes under her eyes with her knuckles, then grabs a handful of tissues out of a box in the console and blows her nose several times, tucking the used ones into a little trash bag hanging below the dashboard. Quinn waits.

"It was that fall," Sheila says finally. "That fall that…when Douggy—"

"Fifth grade," Quinn says. The summer after fourth grade had been a good one. Quinn spent almost every day with Douggy, watching cartoons and playing MadLibs on the Ridpaths' living room floor, or swaying back and forth on the rusted swing set in the backyard, talking endlessly. Quinn was so grateful for the existence of Douggy's house and Mom's willingness to let her spend most of her time there, they never wondered why Mom hung around for hours drinking coffee when Marjorie was at work. Quinn and Douggy knew their parents were screwed up, and they'd both roll their eyes about it, secure in the knowledge they'd never drink too much or cry all day or get upset about nothing. But neither had suspected an affair.

"Fifth grade," Sheila agrees.

"So, what happened?"

"Douggy's…accident. It was about a month before we wanted to leave. We planned to go after Thanksgiving. One last family holiday, and then we'd take off so that by Christmas… Well, we wanted you all to have a good Christmas. To have a chance to move on by then."

Quinn stifles a dark laugh. Right. It shouldn't take more than a couple of weeks to recover from parental abandonment. Quinn remembers that first Christmas at Gran and Gramps's house. More gifts than they'd ever seen were stuffed under the tree, but Kade, seven at the time, got it in his head that Mom would come. He waited all day, his mood more and more fragile. Gran blamed Quinn for giving him the idea. Maybe they had.

Quinn asks, "To be clear, Douggy and Gracen would have stayed with their mom in this scenario, right? So what about me and Kade?" Quinn dares their mother to lie, to claim she meant to take them with her. Not that Quinn would believe it.

"I knew I'd have to send you to my parents." She looks at Quinn, eyes pleading. "For a short time, until Warren and I found somewhere to live and got jobs. I didn't have a choice!"

She seems to be asking for forgiveness. Quinn can't hold back. "The parents you cut out of your life? By the time I was eight, you'd told us your mother was abusive, and your father went along with whatever she said." Quinn forces themself to stop.

"I had no choice," Sheila repeats, but without conviction. "That's what I told myself. I convinced myself my parents weren't as bad as I remembered. You were good kids—they'd be different with you. Plus, you had each other."

When she speaks again, it's in a whisper. "I knew it wasn't true. I knew the right thing to do would be to pull myself together and be the kind of mother you needed. But I'd never had real love before. I thought I deserved one good thing."

She pauses, swallows hard. "Idiot that I was, I believed Warren was that good thing. He was my only chance, my broken man who loved me so well, and we'd help each other heal."

The car is silent. Raindrops sparkle on the window. A fox emerges from the trees and dashes across the playground into the high brush on the other side.

Quinn's exhausted, but there's no turning back. "And then Douggy died."

"And then Douggy died. You can't imagine how devastating it was. Marjorie had called earlier that week to let me know Gracen had the flu, then she called again to say Douggy had it too. She wanted to know if you two were sick. It was all so normal. I was irritable because you were whiny and underfoot, and of course, because it meant I couldn't see Warren, either.

"Then a couple days later he called, and his voice was strange. I could hear the loudspeaker in the background—I knew it was the hospital. I don't know if Marjorie was right there, but he sounded distant, not like himself. He told me Douggy was dead."

Quinn shudders in the darkness, watching their mother's face silhouetted against the rain-spattered window as she continues.

"The funeral was a nightmare. My heart was breaking, but Warren treated me like I was just another acquaintance offering sympathy. A few days later, the police knocked on our door and asked me about Warren and Marjorie's marriage, and whether the kids were mistreated or neglected, and of course I said everything was fine. By that time, of course, I'd already sent you kids away."

She sighs. "I was sure Warren would realize at any moment that he still needed me, that he wasn't doing Marjorie and Gracen any good. But then Warren left months later. I couldn't believe it. Every time Dad called asking if he could send you back on the plane, I told him I wasn't ready. I was still waiting." Her voice fades to nothing.

"Gramps wanted to send us home?"

"Every few months at first. I kept saying I'd take you back soon. And then I stopped answering the phone. Eventually, I got brave enough to pick up once in a while and let him tell me how you guys were doing."

"And I suppose he said we were fine." Quinn's voice is cutting. They remember Gramps having his nightly cigar on the back porch, the aroma seeping in even with the windows closed, as Gran ranted over homework and Kathy's weak character, and handed down disciplinary judgment.

"Dad said he and Mom were trying, but you needed your mother. I told myself however tough it was for you, it would be worse with me."

"You never threw things at us. You never starved me or locked me in the closet."

Sheila flinches, then looks back at Quinn. "I know. But I couldn't take care of myself, and you would have ended up taking care of me and yourself and Kade."

Quinn lets the silence sit. When it seems like Sheila's done making excuses, they say, "Thanks for the belated explanation. It's fantastic. Why are you telling me this, again?"

"When you showed up on my doorstep, I'd already lied to my husband about my mother's death. I was living in fear that Gracen's podcast was going to unmask everything I was most ashamed of. You turning up on my doorstep was like a sign that everything was about to come crashing down, and all the things I promised myself over the years, about someday apologizing, someday reaching out when I was strong enough—it went out the window. All I could see was my life falling apart. So, I screwed up when I talked to you. I know it wasn't fair."

Quinn closes their eyes, unsure what they're feeling. Impatience. Pity? A tiny bit of hope. "Will you write to the judge? Will you make a plea for Kade's sentencing?"

Sheila lifts her chin. "I will. I talked it over with Jeffrey, and we agreed. I don't know what Kade's like now. But I can describe what growing up with your grandmother was like for me. I can talk about Kade's early childhood, and the time after your father and then how—how messed up and depressed I was when I sent you and Kade back to my folks and abandoned you there."

Warm relief flows through Quinn. Without conscious thought, they find themself in an embrace, tears wetting their cheeks.

There's an instant of comfort. Sheila's hair smells like coconut, and her hug is solid and warm. She's a good mother now. Her new little girls probably get bedtime stories, goodnight kisses, cookies and birthday cakes and trips to the zoo. If she and Quinn talk on the phone every week, she'll ask about Quinn's latest tattoo designs and give advice about Paz. They can visit on holidays.

Except none of that will happen. Quinn can't even begin to process Sheila's admission that they would have been abandoned even if Douggy hadn't died. And Sheila won't want Quinn around the replacement family anyway.

Stiffening, they pull back. Sheila holds on for another instant, and then, sniffling, reaches for her tissues. She offers Quinn the box, and Quinn forcefully blows their nose and tucks the tissue away.

Sheila is Sheila, and forgetting that will lead nowhere good—but at least Kade will know Quinn got her to step up. The fantasy of family recurs—Gran removed like a toxin drained away, and Kade and Quinn and even Gramps, being there for one another.

"Kade will be so happy. The maximum sentence is twenty years. He expects the full brunt of it, but his attorney thinks letters from you and Gramps and some of his professors will help."

"I'm going to visit him," Sheila responds. "I want to tell him what I told you. I want to apologize in person."

"What about what you said before, about our father?"

"It's my greatest fear," Sheila says simply. "That I triggered Kade into becoming violent when I sent him away. My sweet little boy. But I should find out for myself."

Quinn squeezes their eyes shut, then blinks. "He's not a killer. It was self-defense. I know this was hard for you. Is going to be hard for you." They stop, losing access to words. What can they say to this woman? Too many mismatched feelings wheel through them, and all they want to do is coast on the relief—and email Kade.

They turn to Sheila. "Can you bring me home?"

When Quinn lets themself in, Bella's car isn't in the driveway, and they're grateful. They want to curl up in bed and compose the email. Or maybe that should wait. They could take a shower, eat, and go to bed early. Tomorrow they'll write with a clearer head.

Half an hour later, Quinn's under the covers with a snack and their phone, looking for something mindless to watch. Their brain keeps churning up images of Sheila and Warren, but they don't have the bandwidth to deal with it right now.

Then Quinn sits up straight. Warren Ridpath. Gracen. The near panic they felt earlier rises back up. He should have tracked down the source of the photos by now—or called the police. They double-check their phone—still no text, and his phone rings straight to voicemail.

They end the call. He's probably relaxing with his wife, the kid asleep by now.

Morning is soon enough.

28

KIRSTEN

When the video meeting starts, Detective Suarez introduces herself and says Warren will be brought in a moment. Eb and I arrange ourselves in our small conference room so the camera can pick up both of our faces. I fidget anxiously in my chair. As Douggy's father, Warren has a clear motive in Viveca's and Alicia's deaths, if he heard Gracen's podcast and bought into Gracen's theory. It could have reduced the weight of his own self-recrimination and been a way to reconnect with his son.

At the conference table on the big screen, two men join Suarez: a uniformed officer and an older, lanky man with a ruddy face, wearing an open flannel shirt over a faded T-shirt. His white hair and beard are bound by elastic bands, his mustache long on the sides. Straight brows, high cheekbones, and a long nose give him a craggy attractiveness at first glance, but there's a hungry quality to his expression I find off-putting.

"Warren Stephen Ridpath?" I ask.

He nods, then adds, "Yes. That's me."

"I'm Detective Kirsten Boon, and this is Detective Donald Simonson of the Melakwa County Sheriff's Department. You requested to speak with us." Eb cringes slightly at the use of his real name.

"You have jurisdiction in Meander?" he says.

"Yes, sir. Law enforcement is through the county."

He nods once. "I killed my daughter, Melissa 'Douggy' Ridpath, in 2012 and attempted to kill my wife and son at the same time."

Eb slumps almost imperceptibly. Considering the case file I just reviewed, I suspect he's delusional and grind my teeth at time wasted. Still, it doesn't mean he didn't commit the new Meander murders. "Where were you last Wednesday night into Thursday morning?" I ask.

"I was at a meeting from eight to nine on Wednesday evening, then I helped clean up and hung out with a buddy until about ten, and then I went back to my place and went to bed. Alone."

Alibied until ten. We'll have to nail down the drive time, but in theory, he could have raced up here in time to kill Viveca.

"Are you familiar with Viveca Crandall?"

His face, already somber, saddens further. "She babysat the kids. Smart as a whip and had a mouth on her. Course, I was half-sloshed half the time, so what do I know? Nice girl though. Nice kid."

"You've had no contact with her since?"

He straightens. "No. And although I'm aware of her murder, I had nothing to do with her death, only the death of my little girl." His voice has been strong until now, but the repetition of his confession seems to be wearing him down.

"How about yesterday? Where were you from, say, noon yesterday through the evening?"

"I was working until five. The chicken coop got busted into last night, and me and another guy were fixing it up all afternoon. Pretty miserable in the rain but had to be done. I ate dinner with my boss's family after I got cleaned up, so that takes me to seven or so."

"And do you know Alicia Finch?"

"The school secretary. I must have met her, although Margie took care of school stuff. I don't know anything about her or her death."

I measure him with my eyes. He looks tired, mustache drooping, as if that frenetic energy I'd first sensed was just enough to get his confession out. "I'll need names and contact info, for both those dates."

He nods in understanding.

"I'd love to hear what happened in 2012," I tell Warren, "but we want it to stay clean and aboveboard. We need to check in with you about your rights, okay?"

He gestures impatiently. "I'm confessing to murder. I get it. I waive my Miranda rights, and I don't want a lawyer."

"For the record, why don't we let Detective Suarez recite them for you, and you can indicate that formally for the video."

Suarez does so, and Warren repeats his understanding.

"All right. Tell us more about what happened in 2012."

He pulls himself upright and interlaces his hands on the table in front of him as if about to give a speech. I imagine he's rehearsed this moment in his mind a million times.

"I'm a drunk," he begins. "It started when Douggy got bit by a dog in our neighborhood, back when she was in kindergarten. It was bad, real bad. I couldn't even look at her. I couldn't help her."

He says up to that point, he'd been a drinker but held down a steady job. He and Margie were dreaming about saving up for a nicer house and him opening his own garage.

"After the bite, we got snowballed under hospital bills. Our health insurance was a joke, and Margie had to quit her job to stay home while Douggy was recovering. Margie got real anxious. The bottle was the only break I got from constant nagging and criticism. And the look in Douggy's eyes—I knew she was wondering how Daddy let this happen to her. I told my kids that dog was safe." Warren looks down at his hands in a moment of performative self-reflection.

Beside me, Eb is at ease, nodding as if we have all the time in the world. For my part, I'm sick of hearing what sounds like

Warren's well-practiced addiction story instead of a murder confession. I prod him along. "So, you killed Douggy because you thought her life was ruined?"

Warren looks up, startled. "I'm just telling you how it was. I'm getting there."

Eb gives me the side-eye. He's a big believer in giving people all the rope they need to hang themselves, and when he speaks, he's relaxed, inviting. "You're doing just fine. Go on."

"Well, to make a long story short, I lost my job and then another one, and Margie pretty much picked up all the slack—she was supporting us, she was homeschooling Douggy, she was always doing something. I was useless.

"And this woman, this pretty blond woman whose wrists were like bird bones, who looked like she was about to faint away the first time she dropped her kid off in my living room and I stood up from a chair—she moved into the neighborhood with a little girl even more self-conscious than Douggy. The perfect friend. And the mother, Sheila, needed rescue so bad, even I would do."

"Sheila who?" I ask sharply. But I already know—this must be Quinn's mother, the one who's remarried and still lives in town.

"Sheila Fontaine. She'd run from a bad marriage with two kids in tow, and we fell in love." He clears his throat. "I know you don't want all the nitty-gritty details, but long story short,

I knew I was messed up, and things were beyond fixing in my house. Too far gone."

Warren has been narrating clearly for the mic but keeping his gaze on the table's surface. Now he looks up, seemingly reaching for the right words.

"Please continue," I say coolly.

He clears his throat again. "I realized I could have a fresh start with Sheila, if Margie and the kids were off the board."

A little shiver goes down my back. Eb's very still beside me.

"Sheila didn't know anything about that. We wanted to be together, but she was going to send her kids to her parents, and as far as she knew, I was going to leave mine with Margie. We wanted to start a new life up in Washington State or maybe even Alaska, then deal with custody and visitation and all that after we were set.

"But I kept thinking of my kids getting up every morning knowing I'd left them, and how they would feel, all their lives, like they weren't enough. And I figured—at the time, I figured—that this was actually Margie's fault, for giving me no choice.

"Marjorie hated me, my princess was scarred and in pain, my son was disgusted with me—no respect, no money, no hope, just bills and pointing fingers.

"Sheila and I set a date to leave the weekend after Thanksgiving. I never told her my real plan. I was going to mess with the furnace and rig a carbon monoxide leak in the propane heater, so it would look like an accident. I'd tell the cops I meant to fix the furnace the next day and it was so cold, I thought one night with propane would be no big deal. Then I'd drink and pass out on the back porch while the others fell asleep upstairs, for good."

Eb nods slowly. I swallow. We all know that's not what happened, but I believe he thought about it, at least.

"I was a mechanic, but I wasn't the best handyman. I worried the cops would be able to tell what I did. Then I heard Gracen dare Douggy to drink a Death Cap smoothie, and lightning struck. Everyone knew I collected mushrooms. Everyone would assume there was some kind of mix-up—they might blame me for being an idiot, but they wouldn't blame me for murder. Hell, they'd probably be sorry for me!

"The kids never knew I heard them—I was in the laundry room because I'd pissed my sheets, still half-sloshed from the night before. Gracen was just horsing around and Douggy yelled at him, and he dumped his gunk down the sink. I picked the rest of the mushrooms he'd left in the woods, cooked them in butter, and made brownies that very night. Margie was working her second job, and she was a sucker for sweets, especially when she got home late. Douggy and Gracen each ate a couple before bed, and that was that. I meant to stay awake and watch Margie, but I accidentally passed out early, expecting to wake up to…nothing. Everybody gone. Last thing I remember, I was planning my 9-1-1 call as I finished up my whiskey.

"In the morning, everyone was alive. I hadn't done my homework. I didn't know how slow and painful it would be or that some people would be more sensitive than others.

"I was weirdly relieved. Maybe I wasn't meant to go with Sheila after all. Maybe I'd misidentified the Death Caps. I went to clean out the brownie pan—no harm, no foul!—and it was empty. I didn't know who'd finished it off. It didn't matter. Everyone was okay."

He goes silent, and none of us—not Suarez or her officer, or me or Eb—move a muscle for what seems like a full minute. Then I say, "But Douggy wasn't okay."

"Right. It took a few days. Gracen got sick, and then Douggy, and then he got better but she died."

Suarez breaks in for the first time. "Wait a second. Couldn't you still have done something? Is there an antidote?"

Warren's eyes are closed. Tears run into his white beard. "Yeah. If we got her to the hospital earlier, they might have saved her. I don't know how to explain it. All the weeks of planning how to kill everyone seemed like a bad dream, like it didn't really happen. Everyone knew Margie was the smart one, and she said it was stomach flu. I just went with that."

I stare at him, nauseated but also glad that Suarez got that on tape. A defense lawyer might argue that Warren wasn't in his right mind when he poisoned his family, but in his own words, he recognized and regretted what he'd done, and *still* let his daughter die.

Eb asks, "Did you take any further action against your son or your wife?"

"No. I'd given up. And Margie was in so much pain, for a while, I felt necessary again."

"What happened with Sheila?"

Surprisingly, he offers a shaky grin, then rubs at his cheeks. "Douggy's revenge, I guess. Even wasted, I knew I didn't deserve Sheila and would end up hurting her too. After a while, I wandered off to die, until I almost killed someone else. I've tried to find redemption through the church, through service to others, but—" He shrugs. "Nothing helps."

I can't look at him. "I think we have enough for now."

Suarez nods. "I'll book him in. You'll send someone to pick him up?"

"We'll send a deputy down. Later today."

Warren is passive as he's led out by the uniformed officer. The wolfishness I saw in him is gone, replaced by relief. All he wanted was to unload his sins.

All I want is to see if the son is anything like the father.

29

KIRSTEN

The twisting residential roads are lit by occasional streetlights, but I almost miss Gracen's turn in the early winter darkness. The long straight drive ends in a turnaround at a two-car separate garage, where motion-sensitive floodlights flick on as I park. Ridpath's two-story colonial is to the right, screened from the road and the neighbors by trees. I follow a short path from the garage toward the front porch, noting that the only light in the house shines dimly from an upstairs window. An unfamiliar security system sign is tucked into the shrubbery leading up to the door, and I wonder if it's legit or just a deterrent.

Another motion-sensitive light turns on as I come to the porch and ring the bell.

No answer. Impatient, I turn and look over the yard, where a circle of grass is illuminated. It's a damp and chilly evening, the rainfall light and steady. Eb would have liked to be here, but he's following a lead on the Finch case: a neighbor with a history of assault and a beef with Alicia over his dog's pottying rights. It's more likely that tiny Meander has one killer than two, but we need to rule the neighbor out.

I'm fine on my own. This is an exploratory interview to elucidate the connections between Gracen and the victims and ascertain where he's been during the times in question.

Still no signs of life, and my irritation starts rising. My watch says 5:38. Maybe his appointment, whatever it is, is running late, but he could text me.

I check my phone. The only notification is a missed call from Quinn, which can wait. I hit the bell a couple more times. There's no sign of life from inside.

Did my call spook him, to the point where he decided to run? Or maybe, like me, he forgot about a family obligation. Maybe he had to pick up his daughter unexpectedly and didn't realize it would take so long.

My neck prickles, and I turn in a circle. All is quiet and deserted.

I shrug and reach for my phone again, to let Eb know I've been stood up, and to text Trav, who's been hounding me to relieve him of twins-duty so he can go to his men's basketball league. At least someone will be happy. But something dark and out of place grabs my attention—a muddy patch in the circle of illuminated grass. The lawn is shaggy, soft with the endless winter rains, but the blades are compressed into a slick depression a couple feet from the edge of the path. Nearby, chaotic footprints mar the grass and intrude into the mulch in the border.

Thoughtfully, I turn toward the house—and catch a curtain fluttering in the closest window. Someone may be home after all.

I remount the porch and knock hard, then retreat to eye the window. Lower than I expect, a face appears, and then the curtain is pulled aside to reveal a tiny girl sucking her thumb, staring at me with wide eyes. I listen for an adult's approach, but no one comes.

"Hi!" I'm not sure the girl can hear through the glass, so I make it loud. "My name is Kirsten. I'm with the police. Can I talk to your mom or dad?"

The little head shakes solemnly back and forth.

"How about a babysitter?"

The thumb comes out and her mouth is moving, but I can't hear anything. She presses her palm against the window, leaving a moist handprint, then disappears.

Shit. I tap on the window and try to peer in but am foiled by the folds of sheer curtains. "Come back!" Maybe the little girl is fetching a headphoned teenager in the middle of a video game or a dramatic phone call. I lean against the railing to wait before jumping to the worst conclusion.

It's less than a minute before jingling comes from the doorway. I startle upright, and the front door swings inward, leaving only the glass of the storm door between me and the little girl. She can't be more than three or four, wearing a T-shirt and sparkly leggings, her fine dark hair tangled around her head. One forearm is encased in a dark purple cast with grimy padding near her fingers, and a beaded choker is around her neck. The broken arm clutches a small stuffed horse tight against her body, while the other thumb is in her mouth.

I peer past the girl for signs of a babysitter but see no one. Stomach curdling, I fish my badge out of my jacket pocket and crouch. "Hi, honey. My name is Kirsten and I'm with the police. I'm here to see your dad. Is anyone home with you right now?"

Tears are gathering, but the girl shakes her head solemnly. Then she pulls her thumb out and says in a voice so small I can barely make it out, "My daddy goed without me."

"Is it okay if I come in?"

The girl nods and steps back. I step into an open foyer area. A large living room with a fireplace stretches to the right, and to the left, an open door leads to a study or den. Ahead, an arched doorway next to a set of stairs reveals the kitchen. No sign of violence, but the hairs on my neck are standing up.

"What's your name?" I ask, scanning the shadows.

"Aurelia."

"That's a beautiful name! And when did your daddy leave?"

Aurelia shrugs. The thumb floats in front of her mouth, ready to dock, but she says, "I was sleepy after Jane's house, and I went to sleep."

"You took a nap, and when you woke up, your daddy was gone?"

Nod.

"How about your mommy? Where is she?"

"Mommy's gone. To her friend's house."

"Do you know when she's coming back?"

The girl's eyes get big. "Daddy said I could show her my necklace!" Her lip quivers, and I think she's about to break down.

"I bet she'll love that," I say gently. "Can you answer a couple more questions for me, Aurelia? Do you know what time you got back from Jane's house?"

She shakes her head, eyes wide, mouth stoppered once again.

I try another tack. "Is Jane a grown-up or a kid? Do you know her last name?"

Aurelia's face crumples. I'm pushing too hard. "Honey, I need to call my police friends to help find your daddy. You want a snack while we're waiting?"

She nods emphatically at the suggestion of food, and I hesitate. I can't drag her around the house while I look for clues to her parents' whereabouts or a list of friends and neighbors to call.

My mind flashes to the various foods Fern and Henry's friends can't eat or shouldn't eat or won't eat. "You got any allergies?"

"I want a bagel and cream cheese. And cooties. And apple sauce."

She sounds ravenous. How long has she been alone? I could swear Gracen told me his daughter was getting dropped off around six or six-thirty, or he was supposed to pick her up. Maybe his whole "I have a meeting and need to get my daughter" line was designed to get me over here as late as possible while seeming to cooperate, so that he could flee. And leaving the daughter behind is just another tactic to delay me?

If so, it's working.

"How about this?" I tell her. "Let's wait in my car for my police friends to arrive. I don't have any bagels, but I do have crackers shaped like ducks. Does that sound okay?"

She nods. I have her step into the rubber boots by the door and put on her jacket. Her face crumples as I tug the stuffed horse away to work her cast through the sleeve, and I hand it back hurriedly, grateful my personal vehicle comes with a kid-friendly, entertainment-rich back seat.

From the car, I radio-dispatch to explain what's going on, and they contact the Corvallis PD, which sends two officers, Parrish and Yoon, over within twenty minutes. I explain Ridpath's disappearance may be related to one or both of Meander's current homicides. Parrish, a young Black man with glasses, befriends Aurelia while Yoon and I check the house. In the kitchen, a carton of almond milk puddles on the floor in front of the fridge, next to a bag of bagels with a hole in it. Two mugs sit in the otherwise empty dish drain next to the sink. A coffeemaker on the counter is half full and cool to the touch.

No one is present anywhere, dead or alive, as Yoon and I confirm to each other in the living room when we meet back up. Dispatch has identified the mother, Pamela MacPherson, and is trying to reach her. Someone from Child Protective Services is also on their way.

It's Corvallis's scene at this point. I point out the muddy depression and footprints by the front walk on my way out.

In the driveway, Aurelia is looking lost in the back of a patrol car while Parrish paces outside, talking into his radio. I wave to him and crouch by her door. She's making hissing sounds as she pulls her beaded necklace around the seat cushion. It appears to be talking to the stuffed horse snuggled in her lap.

"That's a pretty cool snake," I tell her. "I never saw one like that before."

"It's from Daddy's present," she says. "Daddy said I could keep it." The box on Gracen's desk? I try to keep my voice soft, not wanting to scare the thumb back into her mouth.

"Was it a birthday present?"

The car bounces as Parrish climbs into the driver's seat. He meets my eyes as Aurelia gives a half-hearted giggle.

"Not Daddy's birthday!"

"But he got a present today?"

She nods. I'm not sure she has a solid grasp of time, but that gift in the office did seem out of place.

"Who was it from?" I ask her.

She shrugs. "Don't know."

"Did it come in the mail?"

She's warming up, the present a happier topic than Daddy being gone. "The doorbell ringed. It was green with a bow on it and it had this for me and it had some pictures for Daddy."

A buzz of excitement fills my chest. "Did you see the pictures?"

Aurelia shakes her head, then nods. "It was just pictures," she says.

"Where did Daddy put them?"

"Maybe…in the box?" She shrugs.

"The police will find your mommy and daddy pretty soon," I promise her, praying that I'm right.

"I know." She pets the necklace-snake instead of looking at me.

Parrish breaks in. "Actually, Aurelia, your mommy is on her way home! I just talked to her. She's got a long drive, but she'll be here tonight."

Aurelia nods as she slithers the necklace up to the horse, then back onto the seat. "Daddy too?"

"We'll see," Parrish says brightly.

I squeeze Aurelia's hand. "It was nice to meet you. You were very brave, waiting alone."

Her lip pouts. I want to hug her, but I just pat her on the shoulder again and about-face to the house to examine the box that may have the photos missing from Ms. Finch's crime scene.

I stay for another hour, letting Corvallis take possession of the box to process but taking photos of each picture that was in the manila envelope inside. It cannot be a coincidence that Gracen received all this memorabilia today. With luck, the box or envelope will yield fingerprints or DNA.

On my way out, I discover that Aurie's fallen asleep in the cruiser's back seat. I tug the necklace from her loosened grasp and turn it over to Parrish, leaving Aurie a small plastic unicorn I dug out of my car's armrest.

On the way home, I update Eb. We toss around scenarios. Gracen is the killer, frightened into fleeing by my phone call. He slips and falls in the grass as he hurries out, and, considering his vehicle is still in the garage, gets picked up and driven away, leaving his four-year-old daughter alone. Maybe Ms. Finch boxed the photos and necklace, and Gracen stole them, then forgot to bring them when he fled. Or Quinn lied about not finding the photos. They and Gracen could be in this together. Quinn killed Ms. Finch, hid the photos before they called the police, then delivered them to Gracen today.

Alternatively, Gracen could be a victim, like Viveca and Alicia. If the killer is punishing those responsible for Douggy's suicide, maybe they hold Gracen responsible for the dog attack that scarred her in the first place, and soon we'll discover his body.

I shudder as I pull into my driveway. Bidding Eb goodnight, I try to return Quinn's call from earlier. No answer. I leave a voicemail for them to call back as soon as possible. There are more questions for Quinn, and although I still have suspicions, Quinn could also be a target. What if the killer is removing everyone who knew Douggy, negative or positive?

In the kitchen, Trav's on his laptop. He raises his eyebrows when I come in but keeps typing.

I grab a cookie from the jar on the counter, then a banana, which I start peeling. "How was basketball?" I ask cautiously.

He rolls his eyes. "It was fine."

"Did you get home before the kids went to bed?"

It's not meant to be a loaded question—I just want to know how the kids were this evening—but he slams the laptop shut.

"No, Kirsten. I got home about nine, as I usually do on basketball nights, and the kids were already asleep."

I'm not sure why I continue trying for a civil conversation. "What did the sitter say?"

"She said they were fine."

I really want to make a sandwich and go sit in front of the TV before trying to get some sleep, but I force myself to sit across from him. "Okay, good. So, are you willing to talk now? We haven't really talked since you dropped the 'd' word."

He's wearing flannel pajamas, his hair damp from the shower. His response is weary. "It's almost midnight, and now you want to talk? After today?"

"Today?"

"You promised you'd be home for the kids on basketball nights, and you blew them off. Blew us all off."

I don't remember ever making a blanket promise like that. "Something came up for my case—my double homicide! You called a sitter. Everything worked out."

"Oh, everything worked out," Travis says flatly. "You think this household runs itself? And you do nothing. You can't even be here when you say you're going to be here."

His anger shakes me. I can barely breathe. I cleaned the whole house while he was gone over the weekend. We share most of the household duties, although, yes, his share goes up when my caseload goes up. He's always been fine with that. "That's not fair, and you know it. Will you just talk to me?"

He glares. His fists on the table clench, then relax, and he sighs. "Yeah. Sorry. You keep catching me when I'm exhausted."

I'm the one who hasn't slept through the night for weeks, but I let it go. "Do you want to meet for lunch tomorrow? We could go to that sushi place on Third you like." Every once in a while we steal time together during our workdays: a minidate, no babysitter required. Taking things to neutral ground might be a good idea.

He shakes his head, looking grim. "This conversation can't be done in public."

My stomach knots. I've been telling myself he'll back off on the divorce. He wanted to force me to take him seriously, and I've proven I can't be bullied but that I want to work it out. So now we'll discuss things like adults.

He skewers me with his stare. "Kirsten. You're increasingly irresponsible and erratic. You don't sleep, you barely eat, you don't see the kids. You're edgy and bad-tempered. You break promises."

I clench my jaw. That's not what's happening.

"It's time for things to change. I hate it as much as you do, but you're struggling and you won't do anything about it."

My heart starts pumping double-time. He's about to say the 'd' word again.

He continues when I don't respond. "I love you and I want what's best for you. For the family. I'm only forcing the issue because you're making me."

I'm speechless.

Trav stands, holding my eyes. "Leave the job. We'll go to counseling. Maybe we can still save our marriage, our family. Think about it."

I do. I remain at the table long after his shower stops running, rubbing my eye socket where the headache still throbs, thinking about how the father of my children is trying to rob me of the one thing I'm good at. And maybe he's right.

30

GRACEN

He dreams he hears a llama barking outside the bedroom door. Some more wakeful layer of his mind interjects with the old saw about hoofbeats and zebras. *Zee-ba,* Gracen thinks. Then, *Aurie!*

The dream dissolves into looming darkness, his bones aching with cold invading from a frigid surface beneath him. Nearby, a dog barks repeatedly, high-pitched and anxious.

He jerks forward to a hard stop. Something scratchy and unyielding constricts his throat. In a panic, he reaches for his neck, but his wrists are bound too, behind his back around a cold steel post. His legs extend in front of him, ankles held tightly together. Adrenaline overflows, and he twists and pulls against the restraints. "Help! Help me!"

The dog barks louder, but there's no other response. Gracen squeezes gritty eyes shut and opens them, praying he'll wake from this nightmare. Heart racing like hummingbird wings, he takes stock. He's on the concrete floor of a huge shelter like a warehouse or barn. High above, a line of windows reveals the overcast night sky, allowing enough light to make out the dog thirty feet away, a vague shape straining at a rope around another post.

Frantically, Gracen looks for his captor, but his eyes can't penetrate the deep shadows farthest from the windows. After several moments of stillness, he's pretty sure he and the dog are alone.

He sucks in air, shakily. His muscles twitch and jump like he's been tased. His eyes continue to adapt to the gloom; dark cracks run across the floor. The walls of metal sheeting groan and shift in the wind. A loft area hangs fifteen or twenty feet above.

His bound hands press against chilly concrete and steel, but his butt and legs rest on a foam pad and a blanket is draped over his knees. For all the good it does, someone gave a thought to his comfort. He's wearing his puffer jacket over a hoodie and jeans, which is what he was wearing before—

Before Celeste showed up.

"Hey, doggy." His throat feels scratchy and painful, and it brings back incoherent memories of desperate screaming, raw-throated, while tires vibrated underneath him. Utter darkness and absolute fear, and something hard digging into his side. His panicky gasping moistening his own face, the stink of sour breath blending with motor oil and rubber.

The dog quiets at the sound of his voice. He continues. "You don't like being tied up, huh? Me, neither." The rope scrapes his neck. There are dark shapes on the floor near the dog. "You've got food and water dishes, I think. Can't tell if they're empty. But you're too tangled up, huh? Can't reach."

The dog whines pathetically. It drops into a sitting position, throat held so near the pole, it's clear it can't lie down without choking itself.

"You want me to keep talking, huh, boy? I wish you could talk back. What are we doing here? Are you guarding me? Because you don't look too tough."

The dog whimpers.

"Try breaking your collar. It's possible, you know. Maybe you can save us both. No?"

He stops, thinking he heard something over the creaking of the building in the wind. A car engine? Maybe they're not far from a road. No headlights in the windows though. For all he knows, there are infrared cameras trained on him. Or a guy with a rifle back in the shadows. His mind spins out—what if Celeste's involved with some kind of militia group? A cult? Forcibly, he reins himself in. If he goes down that road, he'll scream.

The dog whines, and Gracen whispers, "Hush, now."

He recalls finding Celeste at his front door, the surreal understanding she'd drugged him, his awareness of Aurie asleep upstairs fighting to rise above the discombobulation in his mind and limbs.

What Celeste has in mind, why she brought him here, he can't guess. Despite the occasional fan weirdness that escapes the internet, his idea of a stalker is a deranged guy fixated on a particular woman. *Fatal Attraction* doesn't compute in the context of Gracen: the dork, the clown, the anxious, binge-eating, conflict-avoiding wimp.

But Celeste saw him differently. Until—what had she said? He'd "tethered himself" to his mother.

She must have forgiven him if she wants him back this badly. Or maybe her anger has grown.

The dog's ears prick up. It stares at a space under the line of windows, and Gracen makes out the outline of a door. His night vision has improved, or the moonlight has brightened, or...there are approaching headlights. Now he hears an engine, tires on gravel.

Hope rises, making him almost nauseated. It could be the police. What if that detective arrived in time to follow him here and has just been waiting for backup? Or Mac realized something was wrong when she couldn't reach him, or a neighbor spotted Celeste stuffing him into her trunk. They would have had to use binoculars, but it's not impossible...

Or, Celeste went back for Aurie. Maybe Gracen said something in his drugged state that tipped her off, and now she's got his daughter too. He swallows a burning slug of bile and keeps eyes on the door. Fruitlessly, he jerks against the rope around his neck, raw skin burning.

The engine stops. No red-and-blue lights. No stampede of footsteps or radio chatter. A car door slams, and footsteps approach. Gracen holds his breath. The dog whines. The drizzle continues, a constant low-grade white noise, and Gracen strains his ears. Then a voice rings out, "Totesy! I'm back! Mama's here with treats!"

The dog tries to jump but is constrained by the short rope. The door opens, and for a moment Celeste's tall figure is silhouetted against the gray of the night. Then she flips a switch, and Gracen blinks against the glare of fluorescent lights bouncing from beige metal walls and the concrete floor.

"Totes! What have you done, you bad boy?" She drops an awkward armful of brown bags to the floor and rushes to unclip the dog, crouching for a reunion of sloppy kisses and petting. When she pushes her hood back, her hair is a wavy dark brown, streaked with bleachy purple and pink. She's wearing black jeans and sneakers under a hip-length plastic raincoat. That smooth chestnut updo must have been a wig.

Her eyes meet Gracen's, and she smiles. "Thank god, you're awake! I thought I overdosed you. You seemed so out of it earlier."

Threats and pleas struggle for ascendancy in his throat. He manages, "Why am I here?"

She hesitates, tilting her head with a frown. "We have a lot to talk about. Give me a few minutes to get settled first." She gestures at her outfit. "I had to come straight from work and I probably stink, but I was picturing you drowning in your own vomit or something." She wrinkles her nose.

"You're…not a pharmaceutical rep," he says.

"No, silly!" She flaps her hand at him, as if this were all good-natured fun. "I'll explain everything." She walks to a side wall with an industrial sink, microwave, and stretch of counter and dumps a can of dog food into a bowl for the dog, a terrier with stiff, arthritic movements. It gobbles hungrily while Celeste refills its water.

She sighs and unwinds the length of rope from the post. "I didn't want him to bother you while you were sleeping, but he really twisted himself up!" She adds in a baby voice, "That's not good, Totes, not good at all!" then clips the rope to his collar again. "Do better this time!"

She looks to Gracen. "You probably have to pee. This is kind of gross, but hopefully I'll be able to untie you later. Not the most romantic encounter, but trust has to be earned."

She pauses a couple feet away. "Check this out, so you don't get any crazy ideas." In a blur, she lunges.

He freezes, not breathing, to find her on one knee with a knife point pressing into his chin.

She laughs, sheathing it back in her boot. "I'm not going to use it on you, silly. But I could."

She assists him to his knees, sliding the rope up the pole, and gets his pants down. He burns with humiliation and frustration, but even if she hadn't shown him the knife, he couldn't overpower her. If he somehow took her down, lying on his back with a double-legged kick, his hands and ankles would still be bound, his neck tied to the post. He'd be stuck here until she came to, and then she'd still have the knife *and* be pissed off.

He manages to urinate, face flaming, then looks away as she buttons his pants.

Matter-of-factly, she takes the bucket away, emptying it behind a partition in the corner, which emits a flushing sound. She emerges to wash her hands under a thin stream of water at the sink, smiling over her shoulder at him. "Better?"

This place is basic, but it has electricity and plumbing. Is it an outbuilding on a farm, an old warehouse? Where is he? How far from home?

He feels calmer now that his bladder isn't complaining and makes himself mumble, "Thanks." If he's going to get her to talk, to convince her to free him, he needs to win her trust.

She retrieves the bags by the door. "Sorry it's so cold. I meant to pick up a space heater but Bi-Mart closes so early. It might not help anyway in this huge room. I have more blankets though. And a warm hat."

She makes it sound as casual as if kidnapping happened every other Tuesday. "Great," Gracen says, trying to smile. "I am a little chilly." He suspects his periodic shivering is partly from shock, but if he really is freezing, maybe he'll become hypothermic. At least he'd feel warm again.

She brings over an armload of blankets and tucks one

around his shoulders, another over his legs, then tugs a Carhartt beanie on his head. The bliss of comparative warmth is a huge relief, but he watches warily as she fetches a plastic chair from the little table next to the sink area and sets it kitty-corner to his mat, as if they were about to have a cozy chat.

She puts an extra blanket over her own lap and rubs her hands together. "Damn, it's cold. There's a perfectly good trailer on the property with a propane heater, but I couldn't figure out how to tie you up safely in there."

He tries a grin. "What if I promise to be good?"

"I'm not that dumb. You and I have things to talk about, and once you understand everything, I'll give you a choice. If you love something, set it free, right?"

Gracen's heart quickens. "What kind of a choice?"

"Whether to stay or go. Stay with me or go back to your second-rate little life." She smiles coyly, as if she thinks she's flirting.

The tattoo pulses on his shoulder. *Forever in Hell.* He feels the tug of doom, as if his happily-ever-after with Mac and Aurie has been a delusion all along. This is a minefield. Is there a path where Celeste sets him free? Carefully he asks, "What do we need to talk about?"

She studies him. Her cheeks are pink with cold, her lips chapped. Beyond her, Totes the dog slurps loudly at the water bowl before settling onto his own blanket, watching Celeste with adoring eyes. She finally says, "Us."

It's too much. She's nuts. He shakes his head, feeling the rope scraping the raw spots on his neck. Frustration erupts, destroying his control. "What the hell, Celeste? Any 'us' is long over, thanks to you! Why did you do this?"

"Tsk, tsk." She leans toward him, eyes sincere, and speaks passionately. "We were meant to be together. I was too young and fucked up to realize, but it's not too late. I've fixed everything."

He looks at her askance. "Celeste, I'm not sure how you got the wrong idea. I love my wife. And we have a beautiful little girl."

She brushes his words away with a swipe of her hand. "It's not *real*," she insists. "You always settle for the dregs, don't you, because your mom brainwashed you. You never believe you deserve anything good. You married the first not-too-ugly chick who wanted your money and knew she could boss you around. Trust me, it can be so much better than that. We're soul mates. Deep down, you know it too."

"Mac—" he begins, filled with abject terror at the idea Celeste has been spying on her.

"Oh, she's fine." Celeste waves away his concern. "I thought about following her out of town and taking her off the board, but I don't want to win that way. Anyway, I heard the cops were coming, so this is all a little rushed. I wasn't planning to pick you up until next Monday."

"You…heard?"

She grins. "I have my ways."

He swallows. How long has Celeste been watching them? Has she been in the house? Is it bugged? He tries to squash down the spiraling sense of panic. "This—" With his chin he gestures down at himself, his awkward position, his duct-taped ankles. "Doesn't feel like a great love story. Untie me. Let's talk like equals."

She gives a little Mona Lisa smile. "Oh no, you don't. I know how loyal you can be. You're going to sit there and listen, and take some time to process what I tell you."

"Is there more?"

"There's more," she says. "There were things I hid from you before, when we first met and fell in love. Because I was ashamed. I was like you—I believed I didn't deserve anything good. I believed I didn't deserve you, so I let you slip out of my hands."

She leans toward him, face shining, as she continues. "I know better now. I'm not broken, just different, and now I've given you what you need but no one else would have dared."

He draws away, shoulders complaining as he twists against the pole. The last thing he ate was that kale salad, and he feels it inside, ready to come up. "What have you given me?" That's when it clicks. The mysterious gifts. A dolphin. A necklace.

The pictures of Douggy. All from her.

"Justice. For your sister."

He can't help it then—he laughs. Douggy has her justice, all right, and here it is. Gracen, in Hell.

"Why are you laughing?" she demands.

"No, go ahead, tell me. What did you do? What justice did you mete out, Celeste?"

"Did you know my aunt was a terrible person? She pretended to foster me out of the goodness of her heart after my mother died, but she hated me. She wanted the extra money so *her* kids could have a better life. When I started the fire, I thought it was an accident before I understood there are no accidents. It was exactly what needed to happen. But everything has a cost. May he rest in peace." She looks down, apparently observing a moment of silence.

Gracen frowns. He vaguely remembers her aunt and one of her cousins had died in a fire. "You started that fire?"

She meets his eyes earnestly. "Aunt Claudine deserved to die, and I was the only one who could make it happen. I'm only sorry it got Tim too."

"What—"

"When I heard you talking on the podcast about what really happened to Douggy, about the people who drove her to kill herself, I knew fate was drawing us back together. And I knew your mother treated Douggy like shit, the way she treated you. She had to be the first to go. The world couldn't stand for her to be alive for another minute."

"The fire?" Gracen says. "It was you? You…were Melissa. You set her up in that shed."

Celeste smiles. "Yes. Fire is my friend. We've worked well

together, many times. And then I delivered a message to you. To your house."

"The photo album. You put it on the bookshelf. How did you get in?"

"It was easy. I stayed in my little nest until you all went out, and then I went through the back. It wasn't even locked."

A lightning flash of realization. "Your nest—under the porch?"

"You figured it out?" She pouts, then shrugs. "Oh well. I never said I was perfect."

"You killed my mother," he says numbly. "And what else?" But of course, he's guessed already.

"The babysitter. It was so cruel, what she said. And Douggy loved her."

Oh, god. He'd felt terrible for making Quinn question their role in Douggy's suicide. This is so far beyond that. This is a mountain, a galaxy, a universe of guilt. He swallows. "The secretary. Ms. Finch."

"She ruined school for Douggy. Douggy ended up home again, isolated. Depressed. We know what that feels like, don't we? And what it leads to." Delicately, she turns her wrist upward, revealing a shiny pink scar.

Gracen's mouth fills with saliva. He spits onto the concrete, then gags and brings up strings of bile.

Celeste kneels down beside him. "Are you okay? Are you sick?"

He can't help it. He laughs in her face, so hard he coughs, spraying droplets of spittle.

She pulls away, looking hurt. "What?"

"I just—I can't—You got it so fucking wrong!" Half laughing, half crying. "You fucking idiot! You—I'm so sorry! I'm so, so, sorry!" His stomach contracts, and he spits again. He's contorted, pulling against the rope as his stomach seizes.

Celeste kneels on the blankets and grasps his leg gently. "Tell me. Come on. You can tell me anything." She wipes at his mouth with a corner of the blanket, and he manages to look at her, tears streaming, a rictus grin on his face.

"I killed Douggy," Gracen says. "I fucking poisoned her."

"My family was broken. My sister was dead. Like any kid, I blamed myself."

—*The Ridpath Girl*, Episode 4: "A Brother Left Behind"

There *will* be justice, asshole. For Douggy AND for Marjorie.

—Comments section

31

QUINN

Quinn's cross-legged on the bed, clean and warm in sweatpants and an old long-sleeved T-shirt, next to their open laptop. A half-eaten plate of nachos is next to Douggy's bracelet in its plastic bag on the nightstand. They're compulsively flexing their left hand, where the tattooed moth shifts restlessly as if about to take off.

Boon sounded curt and hurried in her voicemail, but Quinn decides they'll call her back in the morning. Hopefully, the detective has connected with Gracen by now. The photos landing at Gracen's house was all Quinn needed to tell her. Anything more can wait.

The recurring, disturbing thought of the night intrudes. If the photos are Ms. Finch's, Gracen must be connected to the murders. He could be the killer, playing mind games with

Quinn, pretending he just "found" the photos on his porch. Or the killer is setting him up for something…

Quinn pushes that train of thought away again. It's far above their pay grade. Detective Boon will untangle it, and Quinn will find out tomorrow.

The taste of copper alerts Quinn they're chewing their knuckle again, and they yank it out of their mouth. Impatiently, they hit a key on their keyboard to wake up the laptop.

Why is everything so fucking complicated? Happy memories of Douggy are tainted by the specter of bullying and suicide. Sheila's wickedness is compromised by frailty and some of the same fault lines Quinn sees in themself. They try to recall Warren and Sheila together. Quinn can picture them smoking and laughing at the picnic table in the Ridpaths' backyard, or at the dinner table, eating with everyone else. Nothing inappropriate, nothing obviously lovey-dovey. Kathy might have been too young to pick up on subtle clues.

The front door slams, and Quinn jumps. Their laptop screen has gone dark, so they check the time on their phone. It's past their bedtime, even though they never got around to watching Netflix. Bella must have gone out after work.

Shoes thump in the entryway, then Bella calls, "Quinn? You up?"

Quinn sighs, tempted to say they're about to turn in, but maybe it's better not to curl in on themself. Bella is starting to prove herself a friend. "Give me a sec. I'll be right out."

They pull on a hoodie and a pair of slipper socks, then snap their laptop shut and climb out of bed. Bella's in the kitchen in work clothes, smelling like old food and maybe even vomit. She pulls one ingredient after another from the Tarbells' cupboards: chocolate chips, walnuts, sugar, baking soda.

"What are you making?" Quinn asks as they rinse their nachos plate in the sink.

"Brownies! Fudgy, flour-free brownies," Bella says. When she turns, her eyes are glittery, her cheeks pink. "I need a mega-chocolate fix."

Quinn laughs and slides into a kitchen chair to watch her. It's nice to be distracted from the stew of their own issues. "Is this a celebration?"

"Nah. I'm in a good mood. A fantastic mood, because all of a sudden, I figured something out. Don't you ever have a day like that, where you remember how glad you are to be alive?" There's a manic edge to her giddiness.

Quinn plays along. "Well, sure. Maybe once in a while." In truth, it's hard to imagine a time not tainted by loneliness or anxiety or fear, or the million other negatives scrolling constantly across their consciousness. Maybe it lightened when Quinn met Paz. Or maybe the first time they got a shitty apartment of their very own. And maybe—okay, definitely—when they were accepted into the tattoo program. They weren't glowing with joy, but the vision of a real life, not just survival, started to take shape.

Quinn sacrificed all of those things to come here, and in exchange, they have a promise from Sheila to write Kade's letter. A whole mess of unwanted baggage on top of that—but the letter's the important thing.

It's been worth it. So scary, but so worth it.

"You thought of something good, didn't you?" Bella asks. She's measuring, stirring, preheating, in a dance that leaves cryptographs of sugar and cocoa powder across the counter. The microwave beeps, and she retrieves a bowl of melted peanut butter.

It's too complicated to explain. Quinn settles for "I have someone back home. Kind of my girlfriend. When I'm with her, I'm happy. Is that what you mean?"

Bella gives Quinn a sharp look before she returns to chopping walnuts on a wooden cutting board. "What does she think of you being here?"

"Uh, not great," Quinn fudges, uncomfortable. Now that Sheila's agreed to write the letter, Quinn can tell Paz they're coming home and find out if she still cares. Or, maybe, Quinn will head east first, to visit Gramps and even Kade, if Kade allows it. In either case, they'll try to rebuild the life they had two months ago, before they knew about Gran's death.

"Does your girlfriend know about me?" Bella raises her eyebrows as she gently stirs the thick batter.

Quinn goggles, and Bella elbows them. "Not that way, dummy. I meant, does she know you moved in with a new roommate?"

"Uh, no. I mean, of course. I didn't tell her much though." Quinn turns dark red. The string of lies is getting more elaborate. Quinn has no choice but to keep the story going. "Don't worry, she's not the jealous type. And she trusts me."

"Well, sure. Who wouldn't?" Bella scrapes the brownie batter into the pan, then slides it into the oven and sets the timer. "Man, I have got to get out of these stinky clothes, but I had to deal with the brownie situation first. I wanted the leftovers in the dessert case, but Mr. Cavill complained they were stale and Sunny made me throw them away."

"He's always complaining. Tell me she didn't give him free pie."

Bella laughs. "She did. But I think it was legit. Sunny bit down on a test brownie and almost broke her tooth." She hesitates in the doorway. "Are you going to bed?"

Quinn shrugs. "I was thinking of it. I had a long day."

"Aww. Stay up and eat brownies with me. I want to talk to you. I promise—I didn't even put CBD in this time!"

Quinn rolls their eyes and smiles. It's nice having someone who cares whether or not they're around. And Bella cheers them up. "Yeah, why not. I'll hang with the pups in the living room while you're in the shower."

"I'll be right out."

Quinn settles on the couch and closes their eyes. When Bella enters towel-drying her hair, they jerk upright, realizing they must have dozed off.

"Ten more minutes on the brownies," Bella says. "You're supposed to let them cool before eating. Like that's going to happen." She picks up the remote and flips to the Netflix home page before jumping up again. "Oh my god. I just realized. Hot chocolate would be perfect."

Quinn, who's arranging the plaid blanket from the back of the sofa over their legs, looks up. "Brownies aren't enough?"

"This is no time for being conservative. We need a decadent, all-out, chocolate indulgence. And you know what's going on top of my peanut butter brownie?" She disappears through the doorway again, only to reappear a second later waggling a pint of chocolate ice cream.

Quinn shakes their head, laughing. "I can't keep up with you, sorry. I'm going to have one, count 'em, one small square of your incredibly decadent brownies and then go to bed. I'm wiped out."

"Okay, okay. In the interest of being respectful of your weird food rules and wanting to be able to hang with you for a little longer, I'll make you a superfancy golden milk with turmeric and ginger and cinnamon. C'mon. To go with the brownie! Live a little!"

Quinn gives in. "I can make it though."

"I'm going to be standing at the stove anyway, I've got it."

"Well, okay. Just don't take too long." They yawn.

They randomly hit play on a documentary about an octopus, hypnotized by the undulations of undersea life. Bella returns with a tray, transferring a bowl and a mug to the coffee table near Quinn and setting the rest at her end of the sofa.

Quinn inhales the delicious chai tea–like scent of cardamom and black pepper. "This smells great. Thank you."

"Wait until you taste the brownie!" Bella sits cross-legged and digs in, closing her eyes and moaning ecstatically. "I've been dreaming about this all day."

Quinn skims off enough brownie to taste. The dark chocolate and salty peanut butter balance out the sugar. "Yum."

Bella eats slowly but steadily, and she's halfway done while Quinn's still nursing the first corner. Bella puts her bowl down and cradles her cocoa in both hands. "What are we watching?"

"It's a documentary. We don't have to watch it. I just flicked it on while you were busy."

"I don't mind. I want to ask you something though."

"Yeah, sure." The warm milk is relaxing, while the sugar transmits well-being through Quinn's body. If they weren't so cozy, they'd be buzzing right now—but it's a happy glow, instead. Relief that they can set aside the mess that is their life for at least a little while.

"Do you think you're a good person?" Bella asks.

Quinn inhales quickly and coughs. "Where did that come from?"

"You seem like the kind of person who tries to do good in the world. You see both sides of things, and you understand life is complicated. Am I right?"

"Maybe… It depends." Quinn's not sure where Bella's going with this, and they wonder what makes her feel she knows Quinn so well.

"But you don't jump to conclusions, right?" Bella persists.

"What is this about? Are you in an argument with someone?" They don't want to weigh in on Bella's drama. Historically, their solution is to cut people off, which has left them with a minuscule social circle and few skills for navigating long-term friendships. It's possibly why they're holding on to Kade so stubbornly.

"You could say that," Bella says. "Or, no. I may have made a mistake. Blinded by love." One long tress of damp purple hair falls in her face as she regards Quinn.

"We all make mistakes," Quinn offers, hoping to forestall details. Then they sigh. They were enjoying this friendship thing. Maybe part of that is getting over their allergy to other people's baggage. "What's going on?" they ask.

Bella stirs the soup of chocolate ice cream and brownie in her bowl. "Once upon a time, I fell in love. I thought he was picking his family over me," she says. "It felt like a betrayal. It took a lot of water under the bridge to realize his caregiving meant he was a good guy, a loyal person, and I never should have left him. So, I decided to make it up to him."

Quinn listens, not sure where this is going. They look at their bowl and discover the huge brownie has become a pile of crumbs. The last sip of their golden milk is bitter with turmeric. Their face feels funny, almost numb, and they wonder whimsically if Bella put CBD, maybe even THC, into the milk. But no, it's probably their extremely low tolerance to sugar and caffeine and what's that other thing in chocolate—theobromine?

Bella is looking at them expectantly, head cocked. The silence has gone on too long. "Did you—" they begin, but their tongue is thick. The words sound strange and slurred. It's weird and kind of funny, and the next sound that escapes their mouth is a giggle. Their hand tries to catch the sound—Quinn doesn't do giggling—but they smack their nose instead.

"Sorry, Quinn." Bella's voice is warm but regretful. "I put something in your drink this time. But don't worry. Everything's going to be okay. I just need to weigh in on the new podcast drop, and we're out of here."

32

KIRSTEN

Thursday morning, I flick on the bank of lights in our office with my elbow as I balance my bag, my giant travel mug of gas-station sludge, and a sleeve of disgusting, ultraprocessed powdered donuts. Last night, I popped a couple sleeping pills before bed, and a leftover layer of chemical muck stifles my thoughts.

Updates on the whiteboard for Alicia's case catch my eye. The caregiver, Dolores Pruitt, retrieved photos from a storage area for Ms. Finch on Monday but was at a dental appointment in Salem during the murder. The neighbor with the assault record also has a good alibi; he was volunteering at a food bank.

I sip the too-hot brew in my vacuum mug as I move along to the photo of Alicia, smiling in an institutional setting where she's playing cards. It appears recent, and I wonder if she was in a bridge club at the senior center or had friends in an assisted living community we should talk to.

I check messages at my desk. No word yet on whether Gracen Ridpath showed up last night, and no response from Quinn.

Something niggles at me. I return to the whiteboard, eyes drawn back to Alicia's photo. She's wearing a brightly patterned top under a fuzzy peach cardigan. At her neckline, a choker of smooth violet beads.

I lean close, my chest tightening. It's the necklace Aurelia was playing with, further confirmation that the photos are the ones Quinn expected from Finch. If Gracen is the killer and gave his four-year-old his victim's necklace, he's one sick puppy. But if that's the case, why the charade about receiving a gift?

And where does Quinn fit in? I stare at their image on the board, hoping I haven't misread everything. What if Quinn was triggered by the podcast and started killing the targets they could identify, and when they met with Gracen, he said something about Douggy that put him on the "naughty" list?

Unless...Quinn and Gracen are in it together?

Ugh. My thoughts are going around in circles. I need a break.

Warren's alibis are on the agenda for Deputies Akina and Riley today. I'd like to talk to Quinn's mother personally and learn more about Quinn. Maybe Sheila herself had feelings about Douggy's death or developed an unhealthy obsession with Gracen's podcast. But first on my list is Gracen's wife.

An hour later, I'm back in the paved turnaround in front of the Ridpaths' two-car garage when Detective Dicenzio of the Corvallis unit arrives. Over the phone, we agreed to interview Pamela MacPherson together. He proves to be a barrel-shaped man with silver threads in his black hair and a morose demeanor. I brush lingering powdered sugar off my jacket as I walk to greet him. "Donuts?" he asks, his hangdog face folding into smile lines as he points to my lapel.

I shake his hand. "Good detecting."

"Yeah, well, let's hope this Ridpath thing is that easy."

We retrace my steps of yesterday to the front door. Frank points to a video camera up in the corner. "Check this out. Noticed when I came by last night. Worse than useless unless the visitor stands in the right spot and looks up. Plus, it's not hardwired into the Wi-Fi network. But you know what trumps all that? Someone stuck a piece of tape over the lens."

I kick myself for missing that last night. "Seems to imply they knew it was there. You'd think as some kind of celebrity, Gracen Ridpath would be more careful with security."

"People don't think they need it until they do." Frank shrugs.

He reaches for the bell, but I stop him. "Did you speak with the wife about the link to the homicides yet?"

"No. Last night, she was still in shock about her husband's

disappearance. This morning, we only spoke briefly. She's worried we'll decide he took off of his own free will."

"Is that what she thinks?"

"She's adamant that he would never leave the kid. I don't have a good feeling about this, I'll tell you that much."

I flash to Aurelia's sad little face through the window last night. "Me, neither."

Frank introduces the thirty-something woman who opens the door as Ms. MacPherson, but she immediately says, "Call me Mac. Come in. A neighbor is keeping an eye on Aurie in back." She's dressed neatly in jeans and a button-down shirt, but behind the bright-red frames of her glasses, her face looks haggard. The rough bun on top of her head is skewered with a pencil.

In the light of day, the living room is much homier. Mac sits in an easy chair and picks up a yellow legal pad and pen from the coffee table. Frank and I settle across from her on the sofa.

Mac's face is tight with strain. "I told Aurie her daddy had an emergency and had to leave. She seemed to accept that."

Aurie's giggles reach us from the back room, and we all fall silent. Then I clear my throat. "I need to ask you a few questions. They'll probably cover some of what you've already told the Corvallis police, so bear with me."

Mac rubs her forehead. "You're with Melakwa County, right? Which means you must be investigating the murders in Meander. God, I can't believe Gracen's disappearance has anything to do with that."

I eyeball Frank, and he shrugs. I know from Gracen's Wikipedia page that Mac is a law student—a bright woman. She must have put it together.

"It may not," I tell her, to calm her and because we're not going to share everything. "You're right, I am investigating the murders—but I'm just doing my due diligence here. Exploring a possible link to Gracen's sister's death."

She squeezes her eyes shut for a moment, then looks at me. "That goddamned podcast."

"*The Ridpath Girl*?"

"That's when things started going bad. *Gracen Stays Home* worried me when he conceived it as a YouTube channel, so I put my foot down. Podcast only, no name, no photos, no identifying details. *The Ridpath Girl*—I thought it would be good for him, to get it off his chest. But then his mom died, and he got more paranoid and obsessed with this old photo album. Then last week, he found a "present" in his shoe, so he was right, at least partially—someone knows where we live." The words end in a rush, and she raises the back of her hand to her mouth as if to stuff the panic back in.

"What did he find in his shoe?"

Frank breaks in. "A glass dolphin, left on the front porch. We collected it this morning."

My heart's thumping, as I'm picturing the blues and

greens of Viveca's house, the sea creature art and knickknacks. "Is there a photo?"

Frank pulls one up on his phone.

Seeing it, a chill goes through me. I'll have to check, but I think there was one just like on one side of Viveca's mantel.

"I told him to report it," Mac says. "He was unnerved, but he didn't want to admit anything was wrong. He wanted to think it was all in his head, but he promised if anything else turned up, we'd call the police."

I nod, recognizing it wouldn't have made any difference. If Corvallis took a report last week, they wouldn't have shared it with the sheriff's office of a neighboring county.

"Really quick, I have to ask you if you know where Gracen was on a couple of dates."

Mac looks at me sharply, her face going pale. I can see her swallow. "He didn't hurt anyone! Is that what you're thinking? That he was the one—"

"No," I say firmly. "We're not thinking anything yet. You're a law student, right? You know everything has to be documented."

She breathes through her nose, staring at me, and after a few moments, she nods. "Okay. But if I feel like you're pushing past that, I'm calling our lawyer."

"Great." I list off the approximate times of death for Viveca and Alicia.

Mac says Gracen was in bed with her last Wednesday

night, and this Tuesday afternoon, she'd been out of town. She's not sure exactly what time he would have been online with other folks or interacting with Aurie's sitter.

"Thanks. We know a lot about Gracen's family from the podcast," I say. "But maybe he shared more with you. What's your take on the situation?"

Mac looks pale. "If you've listened to *The Ridpath Girl*, you already know what I know. He's kept so much of it inside, until now."

"Just tell me in your own words."

"Let's see... Douggy died when she was eleven and Gracen was thirteen. Everyone said it was an accident at the time. She ate Death Caps from the woods behind the house. Gracen had been sick with the stomach flu, so Marjorie and their father, Warren, thought she had the flu too. After Douggy's death, Marjorie never recovered. She kept the whole house as a shrine. Douggy's shoes and jackets by the front door, her toys and videos in the living room... I can't imagine what it was like for Gracen.

"After Warren took off, Marjorie kept food on the table and a roof over their heads, but she withdrew into herself, and she lashed out when Gracen tried to help her. In some twisted way, Marjorie blamed Gracen for Douggy's death, or maybe for being the one to survive. He internalized it, and I think that's why he's become obsessed with this idea that Douggy killed herself. It would spread the blame." Mac takes off her glasses and wipes them on the tail of her oversize shirt.

Remembering Warren's story, I wonder if Marjorie knew about Gracen's dare. Maybe Warren let something slip when he was drunk.

Mac slides her glasses back on. "Gracen tried to build bridges with Marjorie, but—you know how they tease little kids if you make a funny face, it might freeze that way? She was frozen in grief and resentment. And then, of course, the fire..."

Yesterday, I reviewed the investigation of the Wild Lilac Living Center fire. Marjorie had repeatedly smuggled cigarettes back from field trips to town. She apparently discovered where a groundskeeper stashed the spare key to the garden shed and thought she could hide in there and smoke. It went up very hot and very quickly. Not my idea of a good death.

Mac says, "Gracen considered suing the home, but he didn't have the heart. She wasn't meant to be under twenty-four-hour guard, and she was allowed, even encouraged, to walk around the grounds. Gracen's still struggling to accept it, but he did everything he could to help that woman and keep her alive."

"Do you know if he's been in contact with Warren?"

Mac says, "He wasn't. He talks about him like he's dead, but I found something this morning... Just a sec."

She leaves the room, and I hear a door open and shut and Aurie say, "Mommy!"

Frank and I look at each other. He shrugs.

The door opens again and Mac returns, holding out an envelope. I pull a pair of nitrile gloves from my pocket.

Mac says, "It looks like Gracen found this in a box of Marjorie's things we picked up last week from the assisted-living place."

"You're not sure?"

"I was away. He didn't mention it on the phone. This morning I was in the back room with Aurie and noticed the box was opened. This letter was on top. It's from Warren, asking to make amends."

I skim it, then hand it to Frank. Warren hadn't mentioned he reached out to Marjorie, but it doesn't seem to have much bearing on the current case, aside from supporting the idea that Gracen doesn't know about his father's guilt or even that his father is alive.

I ask, "What about Quinn DeCelles or Kathy Fontaine? Have you heard Gracen talk about either of them?"

Mac looks from me to Frank. "Quinn is Kathy, right? I know he met up with them over the weekend. Gracen was going to flake, but I think in the end, they had a good talk about Douggy." She pales. "Do you think Quinn has something to do with his disappearance?"

"We have no reason to think so."

We review a little more ground, then Frank and I confer outside before I excuse myself, brain churning. The Corvallis police are questioning Gracen's friends and acquaintances in the area and going through his computer, which Mac had the password for. Frank promises to keep me updated.

In the car, I call Eb and summarize the interview, and tell him the question niggling at the back of my mind. "What if Gracen hired someone to kill Viveca and Alicia Finch? And these gifts—the dolphin from Viveca's, the necklace from Alicia's—were proof?"

Eb shoots me down. "Why go through the charade of pretending he didn't know where the dolphin came from? He could have pocketed it without telling his wife. And why open that package in front of his four-year-old, if he was expecting proof of murder? You'd think he'd tuck them away, rather than let her walk around with a dead woman's necklace around her neck."

"Unless the killer he hired went haywire? Maybe they weren't supposed to send souvenirs but decided to blackmail him. What if there was a threat in yesterday's box that led Gracen to believe Aurie was endangered by being near him? That would explain him leaving so suddenly. He would have known to block the camera to confuse the issue."

I'm proud of that theory. It doesn't explain the marks in the mud—but those could have been from Gracen and Aurie playing in the yard, or something equally innocent.

I quickly add, "Let's find out if Corvallis has anyone who can go deeper on Gracen's financials. I'm going to check on our ubiquitous witness. Quinn hasn't responded to my last couple calls. They've got to be tied up in this somehow. If they're not part of the murders, if someone is targeting people in Douggy's life, they could be on the list."

"Only if someone knows who they used to be."

"Alicia Finch may have told the killer before she died," I point out. "Another person who knows is Quinn's mother, Sheila Ehler. And we don't know who's in her circle, yet."

I swing by the diner on my way to Quinn's address, but it's the peak of the lunch rush. I try to spot Quinn in the madhouse, but the only person I recognize is the owner.

"Sunny!"

She waves from where she's taking an order and holds up a finger. I wait until she comes over. "Hi, Detective. You want lunch? It might take a minute."

"I just have a quick question for Quinn. Are they around?"

An impatient eye roll. "Quinn and Bella are both out sick. I guess that's the danger of them living together. I'm run off my feet, and Denise over there is going to quit if we have another day like this one."

"Bella is Quinn's new roommate? Is that her house on Aspen Street?"

"She's house-sitting, I think. Need anything else, Detective?" Her eyes flit from table to table, assessing what fires to put out once I free her.

"What did they say when they called in sick?"

"Bella said they got bad supermarket sushi last night. She was super apologetic, but…well, life happens, right?"

"Thanks."

I hop back into the car and check my phone. Nothing from Frank or Eb. Or Quinn.

If Quinn has food poisoning, maybe they're not answering my messages because they feel like crap, but with Douggy and Gracen in the center of this case, I need to talk to them, sick or not.

The Aspen Street house is dark, drapes pulled shut in the middle of the day. I can't tell if anyone's parked inside the windowless double garage, but no cars are in the drive or on the street nearby. I don't like the house's closed-up appearance. Quinn and Bella may both be stuck in the bathroom or resting due to food poisoning, but from the looks of things, they may not be home at all. Or worse. I flash to Alicia Finch lying on her pantry floor.

I approach the door, knock loudly, and ring the bell. The doorbell cam has a flashing blue light, and I give it a little wave, holding up my badge. There's no answer or sound from within, even when I try again. Urgency rises in me, and I pace the perimeter. The wooden fence is too tall to climb easily, but I discover a padlocked gate adjacent to a window on the far side of the garage. With a quick glance around, I step up on the sill and scramble over.

It's a surprisingly large yard for a residential neighborhood, encompassing a chain link animal pen large enough to enclose an old oak tree. Outside the pen, a sprawling garden rests under a blanket of rotting leaves, and a few chickens peck around in a small coop. With each step, I sink into soft, muddy soil under anemic grass. No lights glow from the rear windows of the house against the gray day.

The first window I reach looks into a large dim kitchen, then a sliding glass door reveals a formal dining room. The next window has semidrawn curtains and inside, an empty bed with rumpled sheets. None of Quinn's stuff is visible, but they do travel light.

The final two windows have open drapes and reveal a large bedroom with a neatly set bed. The rooms have been so dim and quiet, I've become certain the house is empty, but now I catch a motion in the room and my heart jumps. I relax when a greyhound rises from the foot of the bed to stare curiously at me through the window with liquid dark eyes. "Hiya, doggy," I whisper.

An array of little bottles atop a small vanity seems antithetical to Quinn and makes me think it must be Bella's room. Amid the clutter sits a furry animal with exceptionally long, light brown hair—a cat, I think at first, but as I squint, it resolves into a discarded wig.

I'm turning to backtrack to the gate when something leaning against the inside of the window catches my eye.

A roll of wrapping paper, striped green and pink.

33

QUINN

In the near darkness, Quinn becomes aware their neck hurts. They straighten with the sense that the nerves have been screaming for ages. Relief floods in, only to be swamped by other, lesser complaints. Their mouth is parched, and their shoulders throb. Cold chews at their feet, their knees, their nose and ears. Their hands throb, swollen, with occasional hot needles of pain.

Tattooing? An image comes to them of both hands gloved in a tapestry of moths with shifting, prickling feet. A wave of goose bumps surges under their layers of clothes. The blanket over their legs fails to fight the chill, but even in the dim light, they recognize it from the Tarbells' couch with a jolt.

A confusing mélange of memories—Bella tut-tutting at Quinn's missing coat and tucking the blanket around them, saying they were going on a little trip. Bella, going on and on about Douggy and how terrible that an innocent child was killed. Bella, swearing tearfully to make it right.

Quinn's head swims, and a bubble of hysteria collects in their throat. Bella.

Where is she?

Quinn strains their eyes and ears. The building rattles and groans in the wind. They can make out shapes and tones of gray. It's a huge space, a barn or warehouse. A dog sleeps on a mat, maybe twenty feet away. On their other side is another figure—a dark-haired man. Quinn's almost certain it's Gracen, in a nest of blankets, sitting against another pole with head lolling, eyes closed.

Quinn's heart thunders, and they shudder. The rope around their neck is a tight band, itchy and irritating. Their throat and mouth are too dry to speak, and they summon up some spit. "Gracen!"

He doesn't stir. The dog moves in its sleep.

Quinn swallows, adrenaline zinging through them. They test the bindings systematically: hands, feet, torso, neck. Can't escape, can't get loose. A grunt of frustration tears at their throat.

The building creaks and moans around them, and the cold seeps in.

Has Bella abandoned Gracen, Quinn, and this dog to freeze?

Quinn draws their knees up and leans forward to conserve

body heat, but the rope tightens around their neck and they give up with a groan.

Minutes or hours drag by. Quinn tries to plan what to say to Bella when she returns but keeps losing the thread, head pounding and panic shooting through them as viscerally as lightning. Hot tears slip down their face.

Quinn's going to die. Like Viveca and Ms. Finch.

Like Douggy.

Maybe Sunny will care enough to report a random transient person not showing up for work, and Detective Boon will rescue them.

No, Bella will lie to Sunny. Bella will say Quinn left town, and no one will know any different, or care. Sheila will breathe a sigh of relief.

Gracen's family will miss him, at least. Maybe Boon will come for him.

Time stretches. Quinn sits with eyes closed, flexing every muscle to stop the numbness from spreading. The prickling reminds them again of moth feet, and they imagine transforming, free to fly—not as the well-loved butterfly, but the moth, ubiquitous and barely noticed.

If they could, they would fly to Kade in his cell, to see the adult he's become, to witness his pain and confusion and hope. To offer him the comfort of company, even if he would never know.

They would fly to Sheila and, with their wings, flutter

prayers of strength and hope toward her, so even if Quinn doesn't make it, Sheila might come through for Kade.

And Paz. She's probably out with someone else, holding someone else's hand. Considering someone else's words. With minuscule movements of their antennae, or with their prickly little feet, Quinn would tell her it's okay. And that they fucked up and they're sorry and if somehow Paz and Quinn are together again, Quinn will not let her go.

Quinn finds a kind of calm, and when Gracen eventually jerks upright, they call his name, low and deliberate.

He leans toward them in the gray light, eyes gleaming. "Oh, god, you're okay."

Ridiculously relieved, Quinn asks, "Are you?"

"Yeah." He makes a dry hacking sound—a laugh or a cough. "I mean, I've been better."

"Did Bella bring you here?"

"Bella? No. Celeste. My old girlfriend." He blinks rapidly. "Oh, god. This is my fault."

"Bella's my roommate. She's gone crazy, but it was something about—"

"It's about Douggy," he finishes. "Celeste wanted to get payback for Douggy's death because she thought she loved me. She killed those people, for me."

Quinn cuts him off. "It's not your fault. Whoever they are, they're a fucking psycho, okay? We're going to get out of here. The cops are looking for you, it's only a matter of time."

He gives a humorless snort of laughter. "It is my fault. It's all my fault. Those women—they're dead because of me. Because I opened my big mouth."

He's shaky and pale. Quinn wonders how long he's been without food and water. "It's going to be all right," they say, wishing they believed it.

Gracen straightens and looks entreatingly at Quinn. "No. Celeste is going to kill me when she comes back. Her whole thing was getting justice for Douggy, and now she knows she killed the wrong people."

Quinn doesn't like the hysterical edge in his voice. "What do you mean?"

"I killed Douggy. We were playing, after school. I dared her to drink a nasty concoction with Death Caps in it. I was so sick of her, so sick of the special treatment and the attention and the way everything went wrong because of her stupid face—and I was sick of hurting for her, knowing how she felt so bad about the things people said, the way they looked at her. But I didn't mean for her to drink it, not really. I didn't think she did…"

Gracen's sobs increase so that Quinn can't catch all the words. "Gracen. Calm down."

"I told her it would kill her, and I yanked it away. I meant to pour it down the sink. My best friend called—I must have left it sitting there. But when I went back to the kitchen, the clean blender was back on the counter, and Douggy was shut in her room and wouldn't talk to me. I thought she was pissed off with me for being a jerk."

Quinn had bullied Kade into drinking mustard once, as part of a game. He'd upchucked everything. "She got sick?"

"Puking and diarrhea and tiredness. Like my flu."

"Only you got better."

"And Douggy died. It wasn't until later, when my parents explained why the police asked all those questions, that I realized what must have happened. I made the poison smoothie. I left it in the sink. It was an accident, but it was my accident. I killed her."

Quinn stares at him, wishing they could make out his face better. "The podcast though—why tell everyone it was suicide?" Then Quinn gets it. "You started wondering why she drank it, when she knew it was poisonous."

Gracen nods. "If she wanted to die, maybe it's not all my fault. But you know what? It's still on me. Because I taunted that dog. I caused the bite. I broke our family."

Could this be what Douggy wanted to tell Kathy that long-ago night, that Gracen wanted to kill her? Had Douggy realized she'd really die? At eleven, she couldn't have truly understood the risks or the consequences. But Gracen hadn't either.

It's Sheila all over again. The awful things people do, out of pettiness, or loneliness, or pain. The unbearably permanent, disproportionate consequences.

Quinn wants to tell him it's okay. That it was an accident. But Douggy is dead, and Gracen moved forward, with a wife and a daughter, money and success. It's not fair.

Gracen reads Quinn's face. "I killed her. And now I've killed these women. Viveca. Alicia. My mother."

Quinn frowns, about to ask about his mother, when an engine cuts through the constant white noise of rain and wind.

"It's Celeste," Gracen says. He dips his head to wipe his face against the shoulders of his jacket, then sucks in a deep breath. "Listen. I think she'll let you go. She knows you loved Douggy. That's why you're here. You impressed her, so now that she realizes I'm the evil one, she's dedicating this sick revenge to you. I'm pretty sure you'll get out of this alive if you don't piss her off. Tell my wife what I said, okay? Tell her I always knew I didn't deserve her, and I'm grateful for every second we had. Tell her to make sure Aurie knows I would have given anything to see her grow up, and even though I'm not there, I love her so much, forever and ever."

He looks at Quinn, tears pouring down his face. With an ache in their throat, Quinn says, "You're not going to die!" but he won't unlock his gaze, and finally they nod in acceptance. Outside, the vehicle stops, the engine turns off, and a door slams.

"Mommy's back!" comes Bella's voice. The dog dances as a door in the side of the structure opens. Bella is silhouetted against the light of day, and then the door closes behind her. Fluorescent lights flood the space from above, and Quinn blinks in the glare as Bella hurries toward the dog. She looks clean and brisk and warm, a messenger from an outside world of central heating and hot showers and accessible food.

"Good boy, Totes," Bella says, crouching to scratch the dog and pull him close. "Look at you, you didn't get tangled up this time! Good boy." She surveys Quinn and Gracen. "You're both awake, wonderful! Sorry it's so cold." She nods to Quinn. "I was telling Gracen, I keep meaning to buy a space heater, but it wouldn't do anything anyway. The ceiling is too high."

"Bella," Quinn says. "What are you doing?"

Bella makes a rueful face. Her hair is shining, twisted on top of her head, and her lipstick is a bright pink that brings out the healthy color in her cheeks. "I'm sure you have tons of questions, but just a sec. I've got to feed Totesy, okay? Animals first, those are the rules!"

"Let us go, Bella. This is crazy."

Bella walks to a large sink on the far wall, carrying two dog bowls. "Uh-uh-uh," she says. "This is not crazy. That guy—" She turns and points to Gracen with her elbow. "He's the crazy one. He killed his own sister. I mean, yeah, my aunt died in a fire I started, but it was mostly an accident, and she deserved it. His sister—your best friend, right?—she was just a little kid." She rinses out the bowls, then fills one with water and dumps a can of food in the other.

Quinn waits for Gracen to explain Douggy's death had been an accident, but he doesn't. His eyes are closed, his mouth moving almost imperceptibly. "I'm sorry about your aunt," Quinn says carefully as Bella sets the dog's bowls down and stands between Quinn and Gracen with her hands on her hips.

"I'm not sorry," Bella says. "Oh my god," she adds, brightening. "You should have heard Sunny when I called us in sick this morning. She is not a happy camper. She says we better be back tomorrow first thing, and if Denise quits, we're both fired. Which is clearly BS, since then where would she be?"

Quinn blinks. "Right."

Bella turns. "I hate standing over you guys, I feel like I'm lecturing to little kids. Hang on, I'll get my chair." She triangulates a spot and plops down a plastic chair. "So. Did Mr. Hot Mess over there bring you up to speed?"

Quinn glances at Gracen. He's reciting a mantra or casting a spell. Quinn should play dumb, play for time, pray for the cavalry to arrive. "He didn't make much sense. But, Bella, can we have some water? My mouth tastes like dog shit, and whatever you gave me left me parched. I'm guessing Gracen needs some too. Or food? Do you have any food?"

"That guy has the bladder of a squirrel," Bella says. "We start with the water bottles, next thing you know, everyone has to pee and it's a whole thing." She addresses Quinn. "So, you might not remember because of the drugs, but I started telling you last night. Gracen's the guy I fell in love with, and he broke my heart when he turned out to be such a mama's boy, and then I thought he must be a good, kind man."

Quinn nods.

"By the time I realized that, my life had gone to shit in a million ways. Abusive boyfriend, dropped out of college, a series of shitty jobs, a little flirtation with addiction… I was going nowhere fast. Long story short, I clawed myself up to clean and sober, started earning enough money to have choices. But I was lonely. And then I heard Gracen on a podcast, talking about how his sister killed herself because of being mistreated. I realized he and I were meant to be together. No one in the world is better than I am at punishing the wrongdoers.

"Oh my god, you should see your face right now. Don't worry, I'm not power-mad. Trust me. Can you imagine the kind of people who would be mean to a little girl who was shy because her face was bitten by a dog? These are legitimately awful people! And Gracen's mom, she was a piece of work, right? I mean, I thought she was, although now that I know she was right to blame him… Well, maybe I shouldn't have killed her. But she was a real bitch."

"I thought Gracen's mother died in a fire," Quinn says and adds, "Oh."

Bella nods. "Here's the thing though. Since Gracen's a piece of shit and I never should have loved him or believed him to be a good person or done anything for him, I have to find a way to make what I've already done meaningful. I mean, it's meaningful in the big picture—Douggy's death is somewhat balanced by these other deaths, right? But I want it to mean something to the living. And when I learned you used to be Douggy's best friend, that made all the difference. You loved her and you still miss her, and you're actually a good person who cares about your brother and stuff—so, I'm finishing this with you in mind.

"Gracen's got to die, and you'll be my witness."

Bella turns to Gracen, and tears gather and threaten to spill over her mascaraed lashes. "I would've accepted you, you know. We all make mistakes. You didn't have to pretend to be better than you are."

Gracen doesn't respond. After a moment, Bella delicately wipes below each eye with the tip of a forefinger, then rises and addresses Quinn. "I need to prepare the poison. I had to go with dried mushrooms this time of year, but I'm almost positive this will work. I spent two hours googling this morning. It's going to be hard to watch, so brace yourself."

Quinn looks to Gracen in disbelief, waiting for him to fight back. His face is blank, eyes down. Quinn says, "Don't do this. Bella, you don't get to *kill* people." Bella is walking away with a bounce in her step, but she smiles back at Quinn.

"Sorry," she says. "Bella was just made up. And this? This is what I'm good at."

34

KIRSTEN

The second my phone buzzes, I snatch it up, still keeping an eye on the Tarbells' house across the street. "Any luck on the warrant?"

Eb says, "We've got it, but don't you dare go in. I'll be right there. We've got more info on Bella Carton too."

I'm praying no one's inside but bracing myself for the possibility that Quinn and/or Bella are dead in there. No matter how loudly I pounded or called through the front door, the only result has been a greyhound sticking its nose around the end of the drapes to gaze at me before withdrawing.

Through the phone, I hear a door slam, the engine start. He's literally leaving now. I relax a little. "Tell me."

"First of all, Sunny's been paying Bella under the table. Bella told her she was a domestic abuse victim on the run from a cop boyfriend. She didn't want her Social Security number in the system, and Sunny was sympathetic."

"Is Bella Carton her real name?"

"Only if she's a sixty-year-old Black woman who lives in Kansas City or a thirty-eight-year-old Caucasian in West Virginia."

"How about this house? Sunny told me Bella was house-sitting. Is she registered with an online service? Were you able to get in touch with the owners?"

"She told another server she was pet-sitting through Rover, but Rover won't release information without a warrant. Riley's going to follow up. The owners are the Tarbells. They took possession in September, then left around Thanksgiving for an extended vacation. The neighbors have only seen the pet sitter since then."

"Great." Must be nice to take off like that, although I have to wonder why bother moving only to leave for months.

"I got a fingerprint off Bella's name badge from her locker at the diner. When we ran it, we found Bella's real name is Celeste Carter. She was adopted by an aunt after the death of her mother, and the aunt and one of her cousins died in a fire when she was thirteen. She's got a sealed juvenile record. Her adult sheet includes drug distribution, prostitution, arson, and assault."

"Just who you want staying in your house while you're away. Did you find a connection to Quinn or to Gracen Ridpath?"

"Nothing on Quinn prior to working at the same place and moving in together. Gracen though—the drug distribution charges took place in Corvallis in 2015 and '16, while she was a student at OSU. Gracen was a freshman there, fall of 2016."

"Shit. We need to find them."

"We've got to hope there's a clue in that house."

Eb arrives. He tries the front door with his mechanical lockpick, but it's persnickety. I smash the narrow window that runs along one side of the doorframe with a brick. He gives me a look but reaches through to turn the deadbolt and doorknob lock.

Inside, we yell out our presence and quickly confirm the house is deserted with no signs of a struggle. Then we split up to see what we can find—especially anything that might give a sense of another location Bella/Celeste might have taken Gracen and possibly Quinn.

In the bedroom with the wig on top of the vanity and the gift wrap leaning up against one window, I check a nightstand drawer with gloved hands, surprised to find prescription pill bottles belonging to the owners. Who leaves prescriptions behind for the house sitter? Then Eb yells, "Docker!" and I follow his voice to the living room but don't see him.

He pops into view in a doorway next to the entryway, through which I see a slice of brightly lit garage. Eb's face is grim. "I know why the owners didn't respond to our calls."

"Oh, shit," I say.

"Smelled a trace of it as soon as I came in here, and when I opened the driver's side door, I knew…"

He leads me to the trunk, where bundles of opaque plastic secured with silver duct tape give off the unmistakable odor of human decomposition.

I turn back toward the home's interior with a renewed sense of urgency. Celeste Carter has zero qualms about killing. We need to find her fast.

35

GRACEN

Celeste has been humming to herself by the sink for ages, chopping and measuring and, finally, plugging a high-speed blender into an outlet that protrudes from the wall. Gracen tries not to watch. He tries to make his peace mentally and, although he doesn't believe it's possible, to send his love to Mac and Aurie, hoping they'll feel a sense of him before he dies. Hoping in the end they'll value who he tried to be, separate from the reality that will come out when Celeste's crimes come to light.

Whatever Celeste is about to feed him is going to be nasty. Not the slow-but-fatal Death Caps he accidentally-on-purpose killed his sister with, but something quicker. Considering the way she so effectively drugged him to get him here, he has no doubt she's capable.

He strains to see what she adds to the blender, but it's too far away. There's gingerroot and a dark-brown container that might be cocoa, a handful of something dry and crumbly and, he thinks, a bag of sugar—wouldn't want death to taste bitter! She pries open capsules too small to see and tips the contents in, then blends for a good five minutes before pouring her concoction into a container.

She approaches him as ceremoniously as if bringing hemlock to Socrates, except Gracen's death comes in an off-brand stainless-steel water bottle with chipped paint and a unicorn sticker. He marvels at his mind, grabbing at little sprigs of amusement rather than soberly contemplating death. He'd always thought most people's last act must be hoping desperately for an afterlife. If it takes concentration to get there, Gracen will fail.

"Don't drink it," Quinn says. He tears his eyes from the approaching flask and sees how pale Quinn is, how they're jerking rhythmically against their bonds as if they might work free. "Spit it out. Don't go along with this!" He wants to comfort them, to tell them not to worry, not to fight. Everything will come out right in the end.

Celeste wears a calm smile. She knows he'll cooperate. Even if he didn't deserve this fate, what's the point of resisting? She'd replace one kind of death with another. Or worse, hurt Quinn until he complies. He shudders, imagining his mother's last moments, and feels, for a moment, close to her, the way he vaguely remembers in the long ago, before Douggy died. He and Mom both seeing the same last face. That's something.

Celeste kneels beside him. "Drink," she says softly. It's more of an offering than a command. He lowers his mouth to the straw.

"Gracen, don't," begs Quinn.

The beverage is thick and smooth, sweet and chocolatey. He detects the cloying taste of stevia, and something nutty—hazelnut?—but then a moldy, earthy flavor overwhelms the other notes. His mouth is full of mud.

He gags, pulling back. Celeste watches patiently, unmoving. He can see each eyelash, the jewel-like striations in her iris. He lowers his head and gulps, propelling the liquid to the back of his mouth to avoid the foul flavor.

"Not too tasty, is it?" she asks, false sympathy in her voice.

He shakes his head but sucks until the straw catches air and gurgles against the bottom of the cup.

Celeste sets it on the floor. The dog readjusts itself with a sigh. Celeste stands and removes Gracen's blankets, and he wonders if she'll free him, if he'll be able to stretch and get his blood flowing before he dies, but she only shakes them out and settles them over his legs more smoothly, then tucks them around his waist. One, she reserves for herself and sits cross-legged on it next to his mat.

"Now, we wait," she says.

"How long?"

"I don't know. It could be ten minutes or an hour. I planned to test it on Totes here, but I couldn't bring myself to do it.

Poor guy has had such a raw deal. I adopted him as a test subject, but now he's my best friend. After all this is over, I've promised him doggy utopia, nothing but cuddles and treats twenty-four seven."

Gracen leans back against the pole, shifting his shoulders uncomfortably. He closes his eyes, tuning her out. Whatever was in the smoothie is already worming its way inside him. He imagines the diagram of the flayed man, veins and arteries highlighted from head to toe, the amazing network of branches servicing every millimeter of flesh and bone. A sparkling chimera of chemical magic galloping through him, leaving chaos in its wake.

Dimly, he hears Quinn's voice, pleading with Celeste. "You can make this right. Call 9-1-1! You don't have to go through with this."

He's glad in the end someone cares—even if he doesn't.

So much discomfort has built up in his body...tingling and numbness, swelling and chafing, the ache of cold. Irritation from the fabric of his clothing bunched up and pressing around his armpits, his groin, the waistband of his pants. The pressure of his bladder. The burden of ignoring all of that lightens, and then the aches and pains are gone. His whole body is gone.

Is he dead already? Was it that easy?

But he can hear his breath sawing in and out as insistent as waves on the beach, as loud as an echo chamber. And he's not free. An ember planted in his belly emanates heat, a fuse burning toward his brain, out to his extremities. He anticipates explosion. Any second—boom—he'll be one with the universe. Untethered, once and for all.

Instead, he lands in the tree house.

He blinks, confused by the shift. He must have been dreaming before, and of course he's dreaming now—Celeste nothing but a figment his brain dug up from the past to administer the punishment he deserves.

He's gone insane, or perhaps sane, and everything seems so clear.

The floor beneath him is cheap plywood, patterned with amoebic water stains and mildew. The walls—barely worthy of the name—are gray planks salvaged from pallets left outside the lumber yard. Another sheet of plywood wedged crookedly above keeps some of the rain off on a wet day, but not enough to stash snacks or blankets. Everything must be packed in and packed out.

Douggy—dead Douggy—is still here. Half-rotted leggings reveal the bones of her calves, but the arms she clasps around her knees as she huddles in one corner are mostly fleshed. He remembers that fuzzy purple sweater she'd borrowed from Mom on a cold morning and refused, giggling, to give back. He doesn't want to see her eyes, her face, but looks despite himself, soul seeking soul.

Is she really here? Is he? Is a dream just a dream or another layer of reality?

As if in answer, he hears Celeste's voice in the distance. It's okay, she says. You're going home. Her cool fingers press against his hot forehead and then his swollen, numb hands, as she frees them from their bonds and rubs them between her own.

Douggy's eyes are the same dark brown as ever—dancing with brightness, lively, giving and seeking humor and warmth. But the sag of her yellowing skin, the way her teeth show through a rotted place in her cheek—he cannot forget she is dead. That warmth, that humor, is not for him.

"Douggy!" a voice calls. It's a boy's voice, and Gracen turns his head curiously. Who else can exist here? This is their place, their home, the work of their father's hands. But there, below on the ground, is an older boy, a teenager.

It's the asshole who won't leave Gracen alone, who teases him on the bus, who terrifies him if he catches him on the street. Brett Armstrong.

"Leave!" Gracen tries to say. He's in charge. This is his dream, his brain, his home. His sister.

But Douggy jumps up, smiling and whole. "Brett! I found a salamander!"

"Hey, cool. Want to hang out by the creek?"

"Yeah. Did you skip school?"

Gracen yells again. "Leave! You're not welcome, douchenozzle!"

Douggy doesn't seem to hear him and clambers down the ladder.

"Your brother still being a dickwad? I can make him behave," Brett says to Douggy.

"Yeah...but leave him alone. I don't care," she says.

Gracen remembers. Douggy and the douchewad became friends that last summer and fall. He saw them in the tree house, watched from afar in disbelief as his sister confided in the jerk—and Brett confided back, talking about his father and how he could never please him. Gracen had been jealous, but wasn't he glad she didn't follow him around as much? Shouldn't he be glad she had a little extra friendship before she died?

His mouth fills with saliva, and he's at the railing, spitting, hoping he won't barf. Why is his stomach so messed up?

Douggy's back in the corner, rotting. "I'm not a dick," he tells her. "I love you. Why did you even hang out with that kid?"

Swiftly, she leans toward him, snarling, and he jerks back. "You hated me. You wanted me to go away. You wanted to kill me."

"No," he says helplessly. "I only meant to teach you a lesson. I needed space. I needed you to know how invisible I felt, like our parents thought I didn't need anything and you needed everything."

"Did you feel sick? Did you feel poisoned? Did you feel like your body was turning inside out, torturing you?"

"No. I'm sorry..."

"Do you remember what you called me? Do you remember the things you said?"

He does remember, so many moments of petty anger. He told her she was hideous. He told her no one could ever love her. He told her it looked like someone carved her face off and put it back inside out and backward. He said she was grotesque and should never go out in public and he wished she had died when the dog attacked. He told her she didn't deserve anything: not parents, not her cozy bedroom, not ice cream or cuddles or birthday presents or friends. He told her with words, with sighs, with looks of disgust. He told her once or five times or every second of every day. It didn't matter, because he was her big brother and whatever he said was etched into her soul.

"Why would you say those things?"

"I was...lonely. Hurt. Angry. Ashamed. Always. Because I destroyed everything."

Douggy turns toward him. He shrinks back against the railing, wanting to pull out of the dream and into death, only one delusion away.

"I forgive you," she says, and she's whole, and well, scarred and unscarred, here and vibrant and gone and echoing through the universe. Her eyes dance with warmth. "I love you. You are always my brother. I forgave you even then."

His eyes widen, and he remembers her—the reality of her, her joy and her strength, the way even in the wreckage of their family, she was strong and steady and loving. She would hug their reeking, hungover father. She would tickle their overworked, short-tempered mother. She would play with Gracen when he was sick or bored or irritable and put up with his endless sniping, letting it roll off because she was happy to be around him.

"I...can't—" he says. He can't forgive himself. He didn't mean to kill her, but he introduced the possibility into the world and left it there, a temptation. He planted the seeds of self-hatred in her and watered them with resentment and jealousy. Viveca's cruel words would have rolled off her back. Alicia Finch's undermining of her return to school would have faded into the past. But Gracen gave her both a reason to leave and a way out.

"I loved you, Douggy," he says. "I still do." She's not real, he knows that, but he tells it to the void. He tells it to death, and to the stars, and to Celeste and Quinn. He loves his baby sister, and he doesn't so much see the photo Mom kept on the fridge as feel it—the weight of baby Melissa in his arms, her fuzzy hair and her clean baby smell. Her gummy smile that inspired him to win another and then another.

On another plane, Celeste's fingers have been massaging his throbbing hands. Her voice has been nattering in the background, as pointless as the chittering of a squirrel. Tiny threads of connection to his body, about to give way as that which was once Gracen Ridpath dissolves into—

Something thuds, and Celeste yells, "Fuck!" She releases him, and he gasps, aware suddenly that he's not dead. He's still here, hearing, seeing, hurting. He blinks rapidly, trying to focus. Celeste scrambles toward Quinn, who's torn an arm free, and they're both yelling.

The noise multiplies, as if he were in a cauldron of chaos. His body burns with pain, his vision blurring, doubling, tripling.

Celeste is back, and he screams at the jerk of the rope. Her hands yank him upright, clutch his shoulders. He forces his eyes open and is pulled toward the void of her pupils. When he loved her in college, they'd stare from pillow to pillow and murmur about how it had never been like this with anyone else. How they were soul mates.

"Die!" she cries and thrusts him back. His head slams into the pillar. The crack in his skull echoes backward through time, as if the dog just toppled the fence again. As if Douggy's about to run to save him. All that was and all that will be echo around him, muffled like the dream of sound after a gunshot. The void is so close he can feel it, a black hole, the comfort of the end. He launches a steady beam of love toward Mac and Aurie and holds the belief in his heart that it will be infinite and eternal, cradling them.

But Celeste won't let him go. She's smacking his cheeks. "Tell them what you did!" she screams. "Say it!" Slap! "Say it!"

Obediently, he opens his mouth and forces words out, becoming aware of a foul, bilious taste, a wretched odor, even as he does. "I killed her. I killed Douggy," he manages.

"He did not!" The words are loud and clear and project through the chaos and the void, echoing with power. Echoing with truth. "His father did. Warren Ridpath confessed earlier today."

Gracen is thirteen, holding the heavy glass pitcher of the blender, full of brownish green gunk—spinach and mushrooms and blueberries, sugar and cocoa and yogurt—smelling both delicious and gross, like sour chocolate milk. His fingernails are packed with black dirt he'll have to scrub before Mom sees. "Get lost! You're a dickwad!" Douggy yells, and the TV blares in the other room with annoying SpongeBob voices and the landline in the kitchen is ringing off the hook. He grabs the phone and stretches it toward the sink. "Hey, Blake," he says, phone tucked under his chin. And in his hand, the blender tilts, and gunk puddles around the stainless-steel drain. He turns on the tap. "Yeah, I can play. When?"

The gunk washes through the little black holes, and he sticks the blender under the stream of water, shakes it, then dumps it out and repeats.

It all goes down the drain.

Something yanks his scalp, then he feels a sting at his throat. An insect bite? It's that knife, the keen edge of her knife.

She's going to cut his throat. He's really going, right now, and tears pour down his face.

Dad, why?

The universe has no more answers.

Forever in my Heart, he thinks to Douggy, and in the tree house of his mind, she leaps. She'll throw herself across planes of nonexistence to get between him and the blade, and he smiles sadly. It's too late. They're both already dead. Just like Dad wanted.

36

KIRSTEN

"This better be it," Eb says, fingers tapping an uneasy rhythm on his knees in the passenger seat. It's mid-afternoon, and we're on our way to a property owned by the Tarbells in nearby Horace, which Celeste rented earlier this year. We discovered a lease in their file cabinet and a copy of a receipt: cash up front for six months. It looks like they skipped the background check and paid a high price.

Tension makes my muscles hum with suppressed energy, and my foot is heavy on the gas. "Carrie will let us know if they find another lead. We have to check. Gracen and Quinn could already be dead."

"Or Quinn could be in on it."

"My hunch—neither of them are. They're both semi-alibied. But I'm ready for anything." I realize it's true. The trail's so hot, I haven't been second-guessing every move. There's nothing as heady as that urgent anticipation, that sense of rightness.

My stomach turns over.

"The nice thing about thinking one of them is involved is one fewer victim."

"True." We both know we may already be too late. The killer didn't spend a lot of time with Viveca or Alicia. At every step I did my best, and just like in the Sanchez case, it might not be good enough.

I glance at the GPS map and swing off the rural highway onto a back road. "This feels pretty remote."

Eb says, "It's more secluded than I imagined." The woods are dense all around us, making the gray afternoon even gloomier.

We pass a few houses, and then I turn into the driveway of an unlit single-wide trailer landscaped with railroad ties and meager shrubs. Thick trees loom above a thin strip of back lawn. Eb says, "Sure looks like no one is home."

"Maybe there's a basement or a back room. This has to be it." My fingernails cut into my palms.

The carport is empty. If Celeste is here, she dumped or concealed her minivan elsewhere. We approach the front door and pause to listen—nothing—then make our way around the outside of the house. No lights, no sound. Eb pauses on the back patio. There are homes twenty yards away in either direction, but I don't see light through the trees. Eb looks up at the overcast sky.

"Look," he says and points into the trees.

"Um…a forest?"

"No. Higher."

I do. The forest rises into a hill. On top, a structure is visible, somewhat askew and with a sagging roof. Four windows glow with light that looks harsh and blue from this distance. Now that I'm looking for it, I can make out a line of shadow running through the dense trees. "There must be a way up. Before that broken-down house. Wasn't there a gravel road?"

We hurry back to the car.

The gravel crunching under the wheels sounds louder than sirens. Near the top, I pull over into long grasses along the side of the road.

Eb and I ease the doors shut and walk toward the building, visible through the trees, probably a couple hundred yards away. As we approach, a vehicle comes into sight in the small gravel lot.

Celeste's minivan.

I tap Eb's arm, and we pause, taking stock before leaving the shelter of the forest. The pole barn is maybe two and half stories high, walled with rusting corrugated metal that rattles in the stiff breeze. The windows are far too high to see through. There's one industrial garage door, big enough to dock a tractor trailer, and one steel entry door.

Cautiously, we circle away from the doors and approach

from the side. Yelling voices become audible, and as we draw closer, a calmer voice sounds in counterpoint.

I find a wallet-sized gap in the metal sheeting, about three feet above the ground, and peer through. Celeste is visible, crouching near a post where someone—Gracen?—is tied facing away from me. Beyond the two of them, I recognize Quinn, also on the floor. A dog barks, and a quiver of satisfaction moves through me.

"It's Celeste," I hiss. "Gracen's tied up. So is Quinn."

Eb retreats to call for backup, then returns to whisper, "They're on the way. I'll test the door."

I'm glued to the gap, shifting from eye to ear every few seconds, straining for words.

Then Quinn roars, and one of their arms flies out in a wild gesture before they start jerking wildly at what must be further bindings.

Celeste lunges toward Quinn, momentarily separate from both hostages. Something glints in her hand, and I know we can't wait.

"Go!" I scream to Eb.

He shoots me a startled look as I lurch into a sprint, so full of adrenaline I barely feel my hand rip open on the rusted seam as I push off.

I'm at the door, flinging it open. For a split second I think he's not coming. Then he's with me, shouting, "Police! Weapons down!" as we burst through.

Harsh fluorescent light glares into my eyes. The dog barks with incessant panic. Quinn is shouting and straining toward Gracen. Celeste is already there. She glances at us. I have an impression of huge dark eyes, a slash of a mouth, before her hands close on his shoulders and she slams him back against the post with a scream.

"Stop! Police!" Eb and I close in. I don't see a weapon.

"She poisoned him!" Quinn yells. "He's dying! Hurry!"

"Step away," Eb tells Celeste, projecting over the dog's barking. "Back off with your hands up."

She doesn't seem to hear. She slaps Gracen, shakes him by the shoulders. "Tell them what you did. Say it!" she insists.

Gracen moans, and Celeste slaps him again. "Say it!"

He seems to rally. I see the shine of his eyes as he looks at her, and his voice comes out loud and strong. "I killed her. I killed Douggy."

I step closer. "He did not. His father did. Warren Ridpath confessed earlier today."

Celeste turns toward me, face darkening. "You lie." One hand darts to her boot, and before Eb or I have any chance to react, she's holding the knife at Gracen's throat. Eb and I edge closer.

"Drop it, Celeste," I say, utter calm in my voice. My grip on the pistol is steady and cool. "Gracen didn't kill anyone. You can still get out of this."

Outside, vehicles grind up the gravel road. Red-and-blue lights strobe through the windows.

Quinn calls, "Bella! He's innocent! You can still save him!"

While she ignored my words, she stirs at Quinn's. She shifts her weight and looks over her shoulder at me. "He's innocent?" she asks in the voice of a child.

"Gracen and Douggy were just playing. The father tried to kill them and their mom."

Celeste holds the knife out and drops it. It rings against the concrete floor.

"Back away, slowly," Eb says. "Hands up. That's right."

She's in a semicrouch, hands in the air, facing Gracen with her back to us. Eb's at my side, reaching for his handcuffs. I see Viveca's temple, bone exposed to rain. I see Alicia Finch's fuzzy yellow socks. I see two bodies curled in plastic cocoons, and my finger twitches, just enough.

One last wolf, I think.

Eb stiff-arms me, and my bullet hits the rafters as the door flies open. Cops rush in and bring Celeste Carter down.

37

QUINN

As soon as the nurse pulls the privacy curtain shut, Quinn struggles back into their clothes, ignoring the rope burn around their neck, the bruises around their wrists and ankles, and the strain of their wrenched shoulders. The sorest spot is their right thumb, dislocated when Quinn tore it free from the duct tape, and the most serious is the concussion.

None of it matters to Quinn. They survived, and for now, gratitude is fountaining like an oil strike. Despite the terror of being drugged and tied like a dog, a helpless witness in Celeste's mad enactment of love or justice, they'd held on to hope.

The hospital wants to keep Quinn overnight. If they had anywhere else to go, they'd argue, but Celeste's insanity has lost them another home.

Quinn lowers themself back to the parked gurney, feeling

better in last night's sweats despite their ripeness. Worming back into their clothes and tugging them into place was exhausting. Their mind keeps up the joyous cartwheels. The chance to keep trying with Kade, to keep going with their art, to approach Paz and see if she's still interested… At some point last night, Quinn let go of all those things, and to have them back is an amazing gift.

Before they let the thought go, they grab their phone and compose a text to Paz. Sorry I didn't tell you I was leaving. Shit was going down—family stuff. Do you hate me? Can we meet when I get back?

The text goes through, and only then do they realize it's around three a.m. Paz probably—hopefully?—has notifications turned off. They hold their breath anyway, in case she responds right away with a "Screw you" or a "See you at school"—the former pissed off, the latter dismissive but better than nothing. The least likely outcome is "Yes, let's meet, it's okay." But it could happen. Sometimes, amazing things happen. Beautiful things. Like Detectives Boon and Simonson bursting through that pole barn door in the nick of time.

No notifications, and Quinn tucks the phone away as a knock sounds on the glass beyond the curtains. They say, "Come in."

The door slides open, and a nurse with long cornrows pokes her head in.

"We have a room for you. I'll be right back with a chair—uh-uh, don't bother saying it. You can walk once you're up there, but you're riding up."

Quinn closes their mouth and shrugs agreement, and the nurse transports them to a small single room. "Did you have any other belongings, dear?"

"I'm wearing everything I came in with," Quinn says, wondering when they'll be able to get their phone, laptop, and extra clothes from the Tarbells' house. Starting again from nearly zero. *This is, again, a trust fund–worthy emergency. I'll have to swear to Gramps I'm not making a habit of it.*

"The doctor will check in with you later. Try to get some rest."

"Thanks. How can I find out where my friend is? Gracen Ridpath. We came in together."

The nurse raises her eyebrows. "I heard about that. My understanding is he's in the ICU, but stable. You'll have to wait to visit until they move him."

Quinn doesn't want to know, but at the same time, they need to. "And the other one? The woman who attacked us?"

The nurse shakes her head. "I don't know about that. But you're going to have a visitor soon who might. There's a detective who wanted to be notified once we got you settled in." She gives Quinn an assessing look. "Are you up for that? I can tell him to wait. Doctor wants you to rest."

Quinn wants to know everything, now, but the idea of

seeing Simonson makes them tremble. Clearly, they're still a little shaky. "I'm okay. Could you get me some water, please?"

"You bet."

When the detective knocks and enters, Quinn is sitting back against their pillows, fingers itching for their sketchbook as images from yesterday continue to cartwheel in and out of their mind. Their eyes widen at the sight of the familiar duffel bag he carries.

"Quinn DeCelles? Not sure if you remember me. Detective Simonson. I brought some of your things from the Tarbells' house."

At this evidence of simple kindness, Quinn's throat thickens. Their voice cracks as they say, "Thank you."

Simonson asks, "May I sit down?" and settles himself in the flimsy-looking bedside chair without waiting for an answer. "How are you doing?"

Quinn shrugs with an awkward smile. What can they say? Weirdly, wonderfully grateful and happy? Resisting sleep because I'm savoring my aliveness? Terrified because someone I trusted rationalized killing without blinking an eye? "Kind of freaked out."

He gives a wry smile, like he can read the subtext. "You have every right to be."

Quinn nods. "Thank you. You came just in time." They seem to remember saying that a dozen times last night, to anyone who would listen.

He smiles warmly. "It would have been nice to figure it out a little sooner, but…we got there."

He clears his throat. "I actually came to get a more detailed statement from you, and then, if you have any questions, you can ask me. Let's start with how you met the woman you knew as Bella Carton, and how you came to live with her."

Quinn blushes as they admit how easily Bella won them over, going from bitchy detractor to trusted friend with barely any effort. When they describe how Bella knocked them out Monday night with CBD drops, the detective interrupts.

"We found flunitrazepam in her things—commonly known as 'roofies.' The effects you experienced seem closer to that than the few drops of CBD she claimed."

"I should have realized—"

"She's pretty good at covering up. Did she ever warn you not to go in the garage?"

Quinn frowns. "No. I don't have a car or anything. I don't think we even talked about the garage."

"The homeowners—the Tarbells—had been killed and stored in the trunk of their car."

Quinn shudders. "After they hired her to house-sit?"

"She'd rented another property from them, near the pole barn where she brought you and Gracen. We think once she identified the barn as a good place to hold Gracen, she took steps to get the Tarbells out of the way. Then it was a matter of preserving her false identity and living in the nicer of the two houses—and taking care of the dogs, of course."

Quinn blanches. "I thought we were becoming friends."

Detective Simonson leans forward. "We think she realized your past identity early on, from gossip at the diner. Gracen had described you as Douggy's best friend in the podcast, so she had no beef with you. Until the point when Gracen confessed, I suspect she thought of you as a potential alibi or hostage.

"Don't feel bad for being taken in. That woman has been killing almost without consequence since she was a kid. If you'd discovered who she was before she was ready for you to know, you'd probably be dead now."

"Where is she? I saw Detective Boon shoot, but no one would tell me if she was hit. It got so chaotic."

He inhales deeply. "Celeste Carter is fine. She's in jail right now, and I have no doubt she'll go to prison for the rest of her life."

Quinn's hands are cold, twined in their lap. The moth looks the same as ever, but the desperate fantasies of last night are right below the surface. Articulating what they wished for most had brought them strength. They'd been as fierce as Douggy. They rub their injured thumb and smile, remembering pulling free of the duct tape. Just a desperate effort to buy time, but Douggy would have been proud.

"What about Detective Boon?"

"Boon's okay," Simonson says, studying Quinn.

"Why did—" Quinn stops, worried they'll sound ungrateful. But they finish anyway. "Why did she shoot? Wasn't Bella—I mean, Celeste—wasn't she surrendering?"

His voice becomes more formal. "Detective Boon is on suspension pending an inquiry. It's policy in officer-involved shootings. You'll be asked to describe your viewpoint. Can you tell me what you saw, while it's fresh in your mind?"

Quinn closes their eyes and pictures it. Celeste flew toward Quinn when they tore their hand free, but when the door slammed open and the detectives came through, she'd rushed back to Gracen.

Everything after that is a blur. The fiery pain in Quinn's hand, the sudden chaos of shouting. "I remember Detective Boon screamed at Celeste to get away from Gracen, and she yelled back, saying he deserved it, everyone she'd killed had deserved it, for Douggy's sake. And then Detective Boon said no, their dad had tried to kill both of them, kill the whole family. You could tell Celeste didn't want to hear it. I was yelling too, trying to get through to her, and finally it seemed to sink in. She looked like she'd been hit, physically hit, and when you told her to move away, she started doing it."

Quinn sees it in their mind's eye. "She was putting her hands up when the gun went off."

"Could you see both hands?"

"I...think so."

"And they were empty?"

"Yes. She'd dropped her knife."

Simonson nods, looking somber. "More questions will probably come up, but I'll let you rest for now. The doctor expects to release you tomorrow. Do you know where you'll be?"

Quinn winces. "I guess the Best Bet Motel in Meander."

When he lets himself out, there's an interchange of voices in the hall outside, and before the door swings shut, Sheila enters. A camel-colored wool coat is folded over her arm, and her lipstick is fresh and red. She sits with Quinn for a long while.

By mid-morning, Quinn's had a few hours of sleep and a shower, and they've changed into fresh clothes from the duffel. The police still have their jacket and boots and better hoodie. Gracen's on the same floor, and one of the nurses gives Quinn his room number after breakfast.

Quinn's bruises have darkened, and a heavy fatigue aches through their joints and underlies their thoughts. They can't wait to sleep somewhere other than a hospital, but the buoyancy remains. Carrying their bag, they pause at Gracen's door, hearing a child's excited voice inside. Quinn knocks.

The door opens six inches, and a woman's face appears. She's wearing red-framed glasses, and her long dark hair is pulled into a messy twist. Dark eyes scan up and down, and she smiles warmly. "Quinn, right?" Without waiting for an answer, she announces over her shoulder, "It's Quinn!" and ushers them in.

Gracen's propped up with pillows, his little girl burrowed close to his side. She peeps at Quinn with a shy smile, then hides her face against his chest.

Gracen looks good, considering. It's the person next to the bed whose appearance startles Quinn. "Detective Boon!"

"Call me Kirsten," the detective says. "I'm not on duty here." Her blond hair straggles from an unwashed ponytail, and her face is puffy with exhaustion.

"Am I interrupting?"

The woman who let Quinn in thrusts out a hand. "Absolutely not. I'm Mac, Gracen's wife. Gracen told me how brave you were. I'm so glad you're okay."

Quinn takes the hand with both a surge of pride and an urge to protest. Before Quinn figures out what to say, the little girl interrupts.

"Daddy, look! A tattoo!"

"Shh, honey."

"It's a butterfly! Can I look?"

"It's a moth. A hawk moth," Quinn corrects automatically, as the girl crawls toward them. One arm is encased in a purple cast, and she struggles to stay balanced as she reaches for Quinn.

"Aurie, no!" Mac says, with a laugh. "Let Quinn talk to Daddy. They didn't come to show you their tattoos!"

"It's okay," Quinn says. Aurie touches the moth with a cautious forefinger.

"Hawk moth," she says. She holds up a small stuffed animal. "This is Zee-ba. I want a Zee-ba 'too. Right here." She points to her shoulder, hidden under a bright-purple fleece pullover. "Or here." She points to the web of her thumb.

"Come talk to me when your Mom and Dad say yes." Quinn can't help grinning.

Mac grabs the child under her arms and hefts her off the bed. "You and me, lady, are not getting any tattoos today. But we'll get a yummy snack. Nice to meet you in person," she adds to Quinn. "You'll have to come to dinner soon. I'll get your number from Gracen."

The door shuts behind them. Quinn looks from Kirsten to Gracen. "I don't want to interrupt. I just wanted to see that Gracen was okay."

"Sit down," Gracen says. "They pumped my stomach, and my internal organs aren't exactly happy...but I'm going to recover. Celeste gave me a cocktail of psilocybin, MDMA, and dried morels. It was pretty trippy, and not in a good way."

"If her concoction didn't work quickly enough, she would have stabbed you or slammed your head against the post a few more times," Kirsten says.

The smile fades from Gracen's face. "I know."

Quinn perches on the edge of a visitor's chair opposite Kirsten, who scooches forward and looks at them both.

"I'm no longer involved in the case." She huffs a laugh. "But I wanted to tell you Warren Ridpath is going to be charged with Douggy's murder. He'd like to see you," she says to Gracen. "When you're up for it. He says he knows he doesn't deserve to, considering he tried to kill you."

Quinn cringes. Douggy and Gracen's dad. Until Sheila admitted to the affair, Quinn had barely spared him a thought. He'd been a nearly faceless adult, unimportant in the landscape of their friendship with Douggy. And yet, he was the crack in the foundation that collapsed multiple lives. They find an iota of pity for Sheila, who had loved him and who was the unwitting excuse for his monstrosity.

Gracen must be gutted. He shrinks into his pillows, and his voice sounds weaker. "I'll have to think about it. How would I go about that? Is he in prison?"

"Not yet. He's in the county jail prior to sentencing."

Gracen nods.

Quinn's not certain he knows the whole story. "My mom said they were having an affair. They were going to run away together."

Gracen's eyes widen. "I found a letter that mentioned an affair in my mom's things, but I didn't realize it was your mother." He pauses, looking into space. "They must have gotten together while we were at school."

"During the summer too." Quinn watches his face, seeing him conjure up all those summer mornings when Marjorie rushed out to work, leaving the kids in the care of the still-sleeping Warren until Sheila brought Kathy and Kade over to play. "I suspect that's what Douggy figured out. What she wanted to tell me that night, when I didn't sneak over."

Gracen's eyes widen. "That...makes sense. It would be something that would make you mad, but she'd want to tell you in person. And if you snuck over, it meant leaving your mom behind. She'd have wanted to keep Dad and your mom apart."

Quinn dips their chin. "That's what I was thinking." They add, to Kirsten, "But I still don't get it. If they were planning to run away together, why try to kill everyone? Was he just... insane?"

Kirsten shrugs. "I'm not a psychologist. All I know is, he told us he screwed up with Douggy and Gracen and they were 'broken.' He was obsessed with wiping the slate clean. Then the reality of Douggy's death horrified him. He tried to blot it out with even more alcohol, and when he got sober, he tried to redeem himself with volunteer work. Nothing worked. By the time we tracked him down to see if he'd killed Viveca or Alicia, he was desperate to confess.

"It must be difficult to hear this about a parent," she says to Gracen. "But I had to make sure you know the truth and know you have the option to speak with him. Anyway, I'm glad you're both okay. I wish you the best." She stands to leave.

"Wait," Quinn says impulsively. "Can I ask you—The whole thing keeps playing in my head. You shot your gun. I heard it. Why? Wasn't she giving up?"

Kirsten presses her lips together, then shakes her head and shrugs. "She killed so many people," she says. "And sometimes the system doesn't work." Suddenly, she looks a decade older. "I couldn't handle it."

From down the hall, Aurie's voice rises in song. A moment later, she and Mac enter. Seeing the worn look on Gracen's face, Quinn joins a round of goodbyes, then follows Kirsten out of the room and down the hall.

"Wait, Detective—thank you. You and your partner saved us. You came just in time."

"We were just doing our job." Kirsten gives a hollow laugh. "If you hadn't managed a distraction just then, things would have gone down differently. You're the hero. I'm just a cop with issues. And I'm about to get all the time I need to figure them out." She glances sideways at Quinn. "I've decided to quit."

Quinn's not sure what to say to that. "You saved us," they repeat. "I'll always be grateful. Good luck, wherever you end up."

"Thanks for saying that. I appreciate it." Head down, Kirsten quickens her steps and walks away.

Quinn continues outside. Earlier, Sheila hadn't offered them a place to stay—but she did offer them a ride to the Best Bet and lunch along the way. The two of them need to discuss their new plan to travel back east together, to visit Kade and Gramps. If possible, if Kade agrees, both Quinn and Sheila may attend the sentencing hearing.

Quinn waits on the bench under the overhang outside the sliding doors, letting the winter sun hit their face, letting their thoughts quiet—but images from last night are still foremost in their mind. They dig for the sketchbook in their duffel. It's not going to be a tattoo, obviously, but something is germinating in their mind, a series of images that wants to peel out and onto the page.

Their phone buzzes, and absently they reach for it. Paz's name is on screen, and Quinn's heart does a dip. They'd almost forgotten they'd texted her at three in the morning. They're afraid to tap it open, but they do.

You are so goofy! No sorries needed. Micah told me re: emergency. Can't wait to see you, my heart is with you🫂🩶

The grin is still on Quinn's face when Sheila pulls up with two little girls in the back. She leans to push open the passenger door.

"Quinn, meet your sisters. This is Sarah and this is Geena."

Quinn shoots Sheila a bemused smile. They buckle in and turn to the back seat with some trepidation. The little girls are about five and six years old, and they look a lot like Sheila.

"I'm Quinn. Nice to meet you."

"Do you like pancakes? Mom said we could get pancakes for lunch," says the one Quinn thinks is Edie, although already they're not sure.

The other one says, "Everyone likes pancakes," and rolls her eyes at Quinn.

Quinn laughs, reeling from Sheila bringing them along—and introducing the girls as their sisters.

Their phone buzzes again. More from Paz? They say, "One sec, I have to check this. But I'll think about the pancake thing, I promise."

It's Kade's name on screen. Their heart skips two beats. They swallow hard and tap the message.

Heard you're in hospital. Get well. Will send email.

Tears rise to Quinn's eyes.

Sheila reaches to touch their knee. "Everything okay?"

Quinn blinks and takes a deep breath. "Kade just texted me for the first time in years. Everything is, well—as good as it gets."

38

GRACEN

On the table in her pediatrician's office, Aurie sniffs her wrist, freshly free of the cast, and makes a face. It's only been six weeks since her fall, but the skin is fish-belly white in contrast to Aurie's other arm—and it's stinky too. Doctor Maria laughs. "You probably want to take a bath! How does it feel?"

"Umm…cold? And skinny." Aurie pokes it dubiously, as if it might belong to someone else.

"Maybe it needs exercise. What do you think, Dad?" the doctor asks.

"We could put the cast back on," Gracen teases.

"No!" Aurie says and yanks her sleeve down.

The doctor pats her shoulder. "No worries, Aurie. No more casts unless you break another bone. Let's have you hop down on the step. Don't forget your horse! Next time I see you that arm will be big and strong again."

Aurie clutches Zee-ba to her chest, and Gracen reaches for her hand. "Tell Doctor Maria thank you."

"Thank you!" Aurie says.

As they walk back toward the car, Aurie alternately skipping and staring down at her arm, he asks, "How should we celebrate? Ice cream? Cupcake? Or do you want to go straight home and pump iron?"

"Daddy, what's pump iron?"

"Lifting weights up and down to get stronger. Like in the exercise room with the barbells."

"I want to pump iron!" She thrusts her arms up high.

Gracen buckles her car seat and tousles her hair, then gets in the driver's seat. He can't wait to tell Mac, currently out of town at Simone's, how Aurie picked weight lifting over cupcakes.

The February day is cold and sunny, the world basking in unaccustomed light and the soothing sight of blue sky after so much gray. "I have a better idea, pumpkin. Barbells are mostly for grown-ups because they're so heavy. How about we go to the playground for some exercise instead, and then we can still get a treat on the way home?"

Aurie's quiet. He glances into the rearview mirror and sees her face has become serious. "I don't know if my arm wants to go on the monkey bars."

Gracen pulls out of the parking lot. "Oh yeah? Why not?"

"It doesn't want to be broke again."

"Ah." Gracen's about to point out she went to the

playground many times with her cast on, but Mac waves a red flag in his mind and he tries another direction. "Your arm is a little bit scared you might fall on it again?"

She nods.

"You remember how you climbed on the bars a hundred thousand times without getting hurt and you even fell down a lot, and you only broke your arm once?"

"Daddy, it's only one hundred!" She giggles.

"You only climbed on the bars a hundred times?"

"That's only the biggest number."

"Okay, hon. But you see what I'm saying?" It's what Mac has told him over and over. The same thing his parents probably told themselves every day and night after Douggy was bitten—the odds of the chain breaking *and* the fence giving way *and* the dog reacting aggressively right at that moment were a million to one against. Statistics offer no comfort, but they can make you braver.

"No," Aurie says.

"It's okay to feel scared. It's smart to take extra good care of your arm. But if you're too careful, your arm won't get strong and do all the fun things again, right? Didn't Doctor Maria say you should exercise?"

Aurie nodded.

"Tell you what, pumpkin. If you go up on the bars, I'll go with you and catch you if you fall."

Her eyes widen in the mirror. Gracen has always been a

downer at the playground, trying to be a calm, safety-conscious role model with two feet on the ground, flinching when Mac and Aurie get exuberant.

"Let's go!" she yells jubilantly.

His pep talk worked too well. Aurie has no interest in the swings, the slides, or the big wooden pirate ship full of ramps and stairs and tunnels to clamber through. She only wants the monkey bars, which she'd fallen from almost two months ago while balancing on top and shouting, "Take a picture!" In making his offer, Gracen had forgotten how high they are. A full six feet tall, so a four-foot kid can hang freely. It's not that high when you're five-eleven—unless you're on top instead of underneath, where you belong.

"You sure you want to do this, honey?" he asks, despite his intention to support her and keep his mouth shut.

She nods. "You said."

"We could start with an easier thing. Get your wrist warmed up a little and work our way up next time. I could hold onto you while you go across on the bottom of the bars."

She narrows her eyes and sets her jaw. Gracen's stomach flips looking at the long stretch between the top rung of the ladder and the first monkey bar. "How do you even get up by yourself?"

Huffing a sigh that's so Douggy, it takes his breath away, Aurie removes her jacket and nests Zee-ba in its folds. She pushes up the sleeves of her sweatshirt, rubs her hands together, and climbs the four rungs. There's no way she can reach the bar, and surely, that's reason enough to go back on his word. He'll climb with her—but not until she's big enough to get up by herself.

She sets one hand—her strong hand—on the right vertical bar, and her weak hand on the left, and swings back and forth like a little pendulum to inch her way up. Then she gets both legs wrapped around one side, and her rubber soles give her a tiny bit of traction. She lunges for the first monkey bar on top and catches it, barely, with her right hand.

Grinning like his little girl just won Olympic gold, he startles when a mom hangs a nearly bald toddler upside down by its knees at the other end of the bars. She steps back to take a video as the kid giggles and drools, hanging by its knees. A second woman is spotting, ready to catch if there's trouble, but Gracen's heart is still in his throat.

The bars shake suddenly, and Aurie yells, "It's my Daddy's turn! Get off!"

He turns to see she's not only gained the top—but she's holding on with both hands and using her legs to stamp.

"Aurie, stop that!"

The women rush to their toddler, whose face crumples in fear.

"I'm so sorry!" Gracen tells them. "Aurie, we share!"

Sullen, she scrambles back to a sitting position. "It's our turn, Daddy."

The mom with the video camera swings the toddler onto her hip and shoots him a small smile. "It's okay. We're working on sharing too." They retreat, and Gracen's left alone with his daughter, heart pounding.

Aurie rubs her freshly healed wrist, not meeting his eyes. Gracen mind-loops what could've happened—the toddler falling, the spotter moving an instant too late. The head-first impact, the angle of the neck. The attempt at resuscitation. The eternity waiting for medics, the toddler paralyzed—or dead. And Aurie—his Aurie—

Tears fill his eyes. He turns his back on the monkey bars, breathes. Breathes.

"Daddy?" Her voice is very small.

He blinks, hard, then turns. She's holding on with one hand and rubbing the freshly healed wrist with the other.

"Are you coming up?"

"Aurie," he says. Then starts again. Nothing happened.

Does the world really almost end a hundred times a day?

He tries to smile. "You got pretty mad when you thought that kid wasn't waiting his turn, didn't you?"

She looks down, lip trembling.

"I'm not mad at you, hon," he says gently. "But it was

dangerous to shake the monkey bars. You both could have gotten hurt. Next time, say it with words, okay?"

She nods. Once.

He smiles a little. If only it were that easy. If only he could tell eight-year-old Gracen to drop his stick, to leave the dog alone. That everything would work out so much better if he just...stuck to words.

But Warren, Celeste...words may not have been enough. Maybe the right words, at the right time? His heart aches.

"You want a hug?" he asks. Aurie shakes her head.

"Hey—you know, you got all the way up when I wasn't looking! You did it!"

"Of course I doo-d it," she says with a grouchy frown. "I always do that part."

"Well. It must be my turn. Let's get one quick picture for your mom. She'll be so proud of you," Gracen says. *And of me...unless Aurie falls and breaks the other arm.* He snaps it, then trots to the other end of the bars and propels himself to the top. Getting his legs up is awkward but only takes a few seconds, and Aurie's giggling by the time Gracen breathlessly achieves a sitting position on top of the bars facing her.

"You did it!" she says.

"'Course I did. I couldn't let you have all the fun!" His heart is beating a little too fast, and the ground looks weirdly far away, but he can't get the smile off his face. He leans close and gives her a raspberry on the cheek.

"Daddy! Stop it! We need a picture of bofe of us."

Gracen leans back dangerously to take a selfie that makes it look as if he and Aurie were suspended in space. When he puts the phone away, he looks around. Yep, it's a long way down. "Okay, pumpkin. We got up here. Now how do we get off?"

She glances down as if looking for inspiration. Abruptly, the light goes out of her face. "I can't do it!"

"Wait, wait. You're my little monkey. Of course you can!"

"But, Daddy. My arm is hurting."

"Oh. Well. I'm glad you told me. Maybe I can go down first? And then, if your arm isn't ready for climbing down yet, I'll catch you."

She gives a tiny nod. Gracen has a mad urge to stand up and leap off but imagines breaking his ankle and Aurie never daring to climb again. He scoots his butt to the edge, dangles his legs, and drops to the ground.

Aurie's tears magically disappear, and she launches herself at him. "Catch me, Daddy!"

Later, after pinky-swearing he won't disappear while she's gone, a new ritual that hopefully will fade as the terror of Celeste's actions recedes into the past, he drops her at Jane's. All his anxiety now is for himself. Weeks ago, disliking the way his father's invitation to visit kept weighing on his mind, he'd applied to visit him in the state prison. Yesterday he received an emailed approval, complete with instructions: what he can and can't bring or wear or discuss, where to park, what to expect while he's there.

Gracen is carefully turned out in tan tech pants and a favorite gray sweater. His beard is trimmed, his hair clean, his teeth brushed and flossed, as if he were going out to dinner rather than visiting a killer. He doesn't know what he expects to get out of the meeting. He's been numb, stuck in the eye of a hurricane, since Detective Boon announced his father's guilt and the past kaleidoscoped into a pattern he's still trying to understand.

The highway is dense with tractor trailers heading north, and distracted by his thoughts, he finds himself stuck behind a timber truck that puts its hazards on as the highway slopes upward. Blinker on, Gracen snags an opening and moves into the left lane to pass. He's boxed between the eighteen-wheeler and a concrete median divider, his foot heavy on the gas and an SUV coming up fast behind him, when the big rig's cab swerves over the line toward him. Gracen's palm hits the horn automatically as he veers to the left, tires juddering against the rumble strip. The concrete median rips away the driver's side mirror, and his stomach flips as he wrenches the car back into the left lane. Instinctively, he flashes his blinker and, with a glance behind, pulls into the right lane in front of the guy who almost smashed him dead.

He's shaking, his face hot and cold at once. In the rearview, the tractor trailer travels smoothly between the lines as if it had never strayed. The trucker lifts a finger from the wheel in laconic apology, but Gracen's heart is pounding so hard he thinks he might pass out, and he shunts off the highway at the next exit.

There's no *there* there—just a rural route extending into farmland. He pulls to the side of the road with a self-conscious grimace, watching the car that had exited behind him speed past and away.

In the mirror he meets his own eyes as his heart slows. *I almost died*, he tells himself, as if saying the words will make sense of it. It's too ridiculous. He survived Celeste, only to be sideswiped off the face of the earth by a log truck? All these years, part of him believed he deserved death for killing Douggy. *Forever in Hell*, carrying his own doom.

Apparently, clearing up that little misconception doesn't give him a pass on traffic accidents.

His heart still pumps too quickly, but it's steady. The strange calm inside him has shattered. He blinks at the clock on the dash. That whole near-death experience probably took less than a minute, but he can't be late. He starts the car and approaches the on-ramp, then slows.

North, toward the prison, or south, toward home?

Part of him longs for solitude. He feels raw. But he turns north. He needs to see the man who killed Douggy and who as good as killed Gracen's mother. Who nearly took out Gracen too, in childhood and again on that lonely pandemic night when doom coiled so tightly around him, he swallowed all the pills in his apartment with a vodka chaser.

Gracen needs to look at the bastard. To see on his face what time and alcohol and monstrous guilt have done to him. Then hang that picture of his dad up on the wall of memory and walk away.

THE END

READING GROUP GUIDE

1. Have you ever visited an old home, like Gracen and Quinn, to find it changed? What was that like? How did it make you feel?

2. Kirsten has trouble trusting her instincts in the aftermath of the Sanchez case. Have you ever had a moment where you doubted your gut? How did you learn to trust it again?

3. Discuss the significance of dogs in the novel. When do they show up? What consequences do they have?

4. Gracen often finds himself comparing Aurie and Douggy. Why do you think Gracen does that? Did you notice any similarities between the two girls?

5. Compare and contrast the two main marriages in the novel, Mac/Gracen and Kirsten/Trav. How are they similar? Different?

6. What did you make of Kirsten's obsession with finding "wolves"? Where do you think that comes from?

7. Both Gracen and Quinn have tattoos that affect them in one way or another. How do they each perceive their tattoos? How are their perceptions similar or different?

8. Compare the main sibling relationships in the novel, Gracen/Douggy and Quinn/Kade. Are there elements in these relationships that you see in your own relationship with a sibling?

9. Even though Douggy died over a decade ago, she still has a powerful influence on Quinn's life. Do you have any childhood friends you're still close with? How do they impact your life now?

10. What did you make of Kirsten's reasoning for pulling the trigger? Did you agree with her justification?

A CONVERSATION WITH THE AUTHOR

Where did you get the idea to write *Who Knew the Ridpath Girl*?

Around Halloween, I noticed jack-o'-lanterns lined up on a neighbor's porch, two large and two small, as if they were a family posing for a picture. At the same time, I was starting to see smashed pumpkins around town. The ideas collided and created the image of a disturbed stalker interfering with the family of jack-o'-lanterns as a sort of secret message, a threat to the family itself. The image lodged in my head like a grain of sand in an oyster, and like a grain of sand, it became unrecognizable over time. In the final manuscript, the jack-o'-lanterns make a brief cameo appearance in Gracen's photo album—and the stalker has bloomed into something different.

This novel deals with a lot of heavy topics: addiction, abuse, eating disorders, guilt, murder. What is your process like while writing? How do you take care of yourself while diving into darker themes?

For me, writing—and reading—fiction that recognizes life can be complex and difficult *is* self-care of a kind. As a young adult, I often felt very alone, keeping up a pretense of being okay amid people who seemed to have skills and knowledge and resources and safety nets that outstripped my own. Books reminded me that the world was much wider than my tiny life and limited perspective could show and let me feel less alone.

The difficult stuff is likely to touch everyone's life at some point and to some degree—if not directly, then through loved ones or community members. I enjoy real human characters who deal with real human suffering, so I can learn from them and feel for them and know that, usually, we come out the other side—sometimes even stronger than before—and I try to stay true to that in my writing.

Why end the book with a moment of Gracen's near death?

In the aftermath of the kidnapping, Gracen is giddy with gratitude for his life with Mac and Aurie, and this new idea that he's not as terrible or as deserving of doom as he's always believed. But a lifetime of guilt and self-hate doesn't magically disappear—mental habits become entrenched, and Gracen has been knocking himself down since childhood.

It seemed unlikely that he could turn his mindset around in six months, but I wanted the reader to understand he was on an upward trajectory and had the strength and insight to succeed in truly changing. His desire to say yes to Warren's request for him to visit was key to that—and that impulse felt very true to the character.

But when he heads out to visit the prison, he's not ready. He's glorying in his ability to be a less fearful parent. The semitruck (a logging truck full of Douggy's namesake tree) brings home the reality that he's not living in some happily-ever-after fantasyland. Random events can still snatch him prematurely from his family. Gracen recognizes that he desperately wants to claw some understanding of his life and Warren's effect on him before that happens.

Kirsten and Trav's relationship is a difficult one. Do you think they work it out now that Kirsten is off the police force?

Even though they're my characters, I'm not altogether sure. At the end of the book, Kirsten is in crisis, so recovering a base level of mental health needs to come first. So much of her identity has been wrapped up in her work, and she has to figure out who she is without that. After, it could go either way. She and Trav both handled the situation poorly. For them to let go of blaming each other and figure out how to move forward is a lot to ask, and I suspect they'd need marriage counseling and a deep dive into what their marriage means to each of them.

Did the novel ever evolve or change while you were writing it?

Definitely. A novel—especially one with multiple points of view and storylines—is a huge beast that my brain can't really pin down until it's all on the page. At the conception of an idea, I often have a sense of where I'd like the plot to go, only to realize that it doesn't quite make sense. I initially thought Quinn and Gracen would be held prisoner for much longer, for example, over a course of weeks, but even given absolute power over their fictional universe, I couldn't quite buy that Celeste was the kind of mastermind who'd be able to cover her tracks that well. She was clever, but the police had numbers and expertise on their side.

Is there anything that you hope readers take away from this novel?

My intention was to create an immersive, multidimensional world with haunting characters who feel real, and I hope that although the events are dark, something positive will stay with readers—Quinn's perseverance and bravery, Gracen's creativity and love for his daughter, Kirsten's dogged struggle with her own biases. And for anyone who struggles and feels alone, I hope you'll reach out and keep reaching out until you get the kind of help you need.

ACKNOWLEDGMENTS

This book has been a labor of love, and I'm grateful for the wonderful humans who contributed in so many ways:

My readers, whose appreciation gives me the courage to continue!

The writing community, especially Pacific Northwest Writers Association, Willamette Writers, Sisters in Crime, the Authors Guild, and the Writers' Police Academy. These organizations provide priceless and varied support. Writing would be a much lonelier and more difficult road without them.

Critique group members Scott Bigger, Lou Maenz, JS James, and Adam Miller, whose feedback was generous and invaluable.

The AG: Anne Ettel, Kathy Haynes, Dale Ivory, and Susan Stecker Jones. Your unfailing good-humored support and practical encouragement helped me through all the months of ups and downs.

The remarkable team at Sourcebooks, especially my editor, MJ Johnston, for insight and guidance in elevating the story; Hartley Christensen for patience and a plan; Manu for considerate and compassionate recommendations; Annabelle Harsch for an eagle eye; and Anna-Lisa Sandstrum and Jordan Standridge for getting my books into stores. And to those who remain behind the scenes—I appreciate you too!

My literary agents from Corvisiero Literary Agency, Lizz Nagle and Alisha West, for their ongoing offerings of wisdom, perspective, and championship.

My parents for their enthusiasm and for spreading the word to hapless strangers up and down the Eastern Seaboard.

And finally, to my husband for being the chief cook and provider of faux bacon, in addition to floor washer, sounding board, and canine entertainer—extra love and thanks.

ABOUT THE AUTHOR

Stacy Johns lives and writes in Oregon's beautiful Willamette Valley. As she was once a librarian, she can't seem to get enough of the world of books. Three times per day, rain or shine, she is dragged away from horrifying yet lyrical thoughts of murder and walked by Riley the dog.